AMONG
THIEVES

AMONG THIEVES

M. J. KUHN

SAGA PRESS

LONDON SYDNEY **NEW YORK** TORONTO NEW DELHI

SAGA PRESS

AN IMPRINT OF SIMON & SCHUSTER, INC.

1230 AVENUE OF THE AMERICAS, NEW YORK, NEW YORK 10020

First Saga Press hardcover edition September 2021

SAGA PRESS and colophon are trademarks of Simon & Schuster, Inc.

For information about special discounts for bulk purchases, please contact Simon & Schuster Special Sales at 1-866-506-1949 or business@simonandschuster.com

The Simon & Schuster Speakers Bureau can bring authors to your live event. For more information or to book an event contact the Simon & Schuster Speakers Bureau at 1-866-248-3049 or visit our website at www.simonspeakers.com.

Interior design by Michelle Marchese

Manufactured in the United States of America

1   3   5   7   9   10   8   6   4   2

Library of Congress Cataloging-in-Publication Data is available.

ISBN 978-1-9821-4214-8
ISBN 978-1-9821-4216-2 (ebook)

For my husband, Ryan,
for never doubting that this day would come

I

RYIA

There were guards nearby. Ryia could smell them—and not just because they stank of wine. She ducked into an archway, pressing her back against the stone and holding her breath. They clanked past in neat rows, long, thin swords dangling from their belts, purple tunics swaying in the foul summer breeze. Members of the Needle Guard, the king's private army. They turned south, no doubt heading toward the slums where the Festival of Felice raged on.

North of the trade docks, the city was quiet. The nobles of Carrowwick didn't worship the goddess of luck. For them, the festival was more of an inconvenience than a celebration. A nuisance—a distraction. In other words, it was exactly what Ryia had been waiting for. After all, it wasn't as though she could just stroll in through the Bobbin Fort's front gate.

The southern wall of the fortress was less than a stone's throw away. A thirty-foot vertical with only the tiniest of handholds. She looked sternly at her fingers, dark eyes flashing.

"You lot up for this today?"

Her fingers didn't answer, but she didn't need them to. This wasn't the first time she'd made this climb. If Callum Clem had his way, she doubted it would be the last time either, and if there was one thing she had learned in the past year, it was that Callum Clem always had his way.

Black fabric billowed out behind her like a silken shadow as she pulled herself up stone by stone with unnatural speed. The muted strains of off-key fiddle music from the celebrations to the south were punctuated by the slight scraping of sharpened steel knocking against the wall.

"Patience, loves," she murmured to the half dozen axes lining her belt. "You'll get your chance, don't you worry."

Guards fidgeted on the top of the wall, some six inches above her. She paused, lightly sniffing the air. Two of them. Sniffed again. One five paces to her left, the other twenty or more to her right, if she wasn't mistaken. She chuckled silently to herself. Ryia was never mistaken. If she was, she would be rotting in one of the Guildmaster's cells by now.

A colorful burst of light illuminated the sky, and Ryia was on the move again. The firework faded to ashes. In the seconds before the next burst of color, she vaulted over the wall, sprinted across the ramparts, and dropped over the opposite side, scurrying like a spider down into the courtyard below. The guards fidgeted with their armor, hiding their yawns behind gauntleted hands as the light show went on. Blind as desert moles.

Though that might be an insult to the moles.

Ryia pulled a bundle of leaves from the pocket of her cloak. They looked dull in the silvery light of the moon, but she knew in daylight they were vivid green. Outside the Bobbin Fort, there was only the Needle Guard to contend with. Inside, things got a little more complicated. The cloying taste of lemon burst on her tongue as she popped the leaves into her mouth. She wrinkled her nose.

Disgusting, yes, but if it were any weaker, it would be more useless than a long sword in a tavern brawl. Anything less overpowering than lemon balm would be hard-pressed to throw off the nose of a lapdog, let alone a proper Adept Senser.

Hopefully she wouldn't run into either.

She slunk forward a few steps, pausing behind a statue of Declan Day. Her fingers danced over her throwing axes as she studied the castle, bathed in the light of the fireworks. One . . . two . . . three windows over . . . one floor up. She gave a feral smile. The southern-facing window swung open, no doubt flooding the room inside with the scents of piss and fish. Carrowwick perfume, as the foreign sailors liked to call it.

This was going to be even easier than she'd hoped.

But just then the scent of stale urine vanished, replaced by a violently different odor. Mulched earth. Decay. A horribly familiar, creeping rot that sent her nostrils itching and tingling. Ryia froze and sank into a crouch, her right hand drifting up to grasp one of the long-handled hatchets strapped across her back. It was coming from the east.

She dropped her hand, melting back into the shadow of the statue. Not two seconds later came the sound of hushed voices, echoing from the east end of the courtyard.

". . . sending me along with the party going to the auction. You know what that means . . . ," one voice was saying. Male. He sounded like a weasel . . . or maybe a snake? Either way, the fact that he sounded like anything at all meant that the people entering the courtyard were not Adept servants. A good sign.

She could see them now: one tall and thick, one short and slight. The short one whipped around to face the other. Female. A shock of braided red hair caught the moonlight. "I know drinking wine before your shift is against protocol," the woman answered coolly.

"Oh come on, Evelyn, I've heard the stories. All bets are off, Garol said . . . ," Weasel-mouth continued. He sidled closer to Red, reaching for her waist.

Ryia slid around the statue. Just a few steps to the castle wall. Then she'd be out of sight for good and those idiot guards would never even be aware of her existence.

The distinctive ping of metal on metal rang out as Red poked a needle-thin blade into the man's left shoulder plate.

"Have you forgotten who you're talking to, Maxwell?" she asked. "You could always check with my old bunkmates from the South Barracks if you need a bloody refresher."

Ryia stifled a laugh as Red rammed her elbow into Maxwell the Weasel-mouth's gut. She reluctantly turned away from the show. Twice the entertainment factor of those half-assed productions the Harpies put on in the Carrowwick Fair. Maybe these nobles and their hired swords were good for something after all.

She latched on to the stone wall, skittering up the side of the castle. She paused just beneath the open second-story window, listening. Nothing but deep, even breathing punctuated by snores so loud she was surprised she hadn't been able to hear them outside the fort wall.

Another burst of color and light lit up the sky as she slipped into the room, casting her shadow over carpeting that probably cost more than half the slats in the Lottery. A few sputtering candles burned in their spun-glass wall sconces, dimly lighting the massive, four-poster bed along the back wall. On top of the bed lay what looked like a lumpy net full of dead fish. The lumpy net, of course, was Efrain Althea. Son of the queen of Dresdell's sister, and a lesser prince of the far southern kingdom of Briel.

Ryia didn't really give two shits who he was. Clem's orders were always stunningly clear, and they didn't tend to include titles and honors.

She stalked across the room, sliding one of the hatchets from her back and twirling it expertly between her fingers. Thin, leather-wrapped handle. Slender, razor-sharp bit. Was it normal to be attracted to a weapon? She was only kidding, of course . . .

Mostly.

Faster than Efrain could blink his wine-bleary eyes, Ryia was upon him. The bit of her hatchet tickled the rolls beneath his cleft chin.

"You'd have to be even dumber than you look to scream," she said. "You see, you might startle me. And when I'm startled . . ." She dragged the sharp edge lightly across his throat. Not enough to draw blood. Just possibly enough to draw urine.

Efrain nodded hurriedly, and Ryia pulled back with a smile. She strode calmly toward the spindly table on the far side of the room, then sniffed a flagon of blood-red wine. Undoubtedly Brillish—didn't smell rank enough to be Gildesh. She wrinkled her nose and reached for a chunk of bread instead, tearing into it as she turned back to Efrain.

"You've been in this city a few weeks now. I take it you know who I am?" She gave another lupine smile, flashing her hatchet toward his watery eyes.

Her face was completely hidden by the shadows of her hood, but her weapons had a reputation of their own. After all, the Butcher of Carrowwick hadn't earned her title by handing out bundles of daisies and kisses on the cheek. He sputtered as he caught sight of the markings on the blade in the low light. Ryia tutted softly, pacing back toward him.

"Looks like Felice's luck is not smiling down on your pampered ass tonight, eh?"

She tucked her hatchet away, then leaned against the bedpost, ripping back into the bread.

"I—I don't know what I'm supposed to have done," Efrain finally stammered, pulling himself to his feet. His voice was just as obnoxious as she remembered it. Nasally. Whiny. A thick Brillish accent pulling at his vowels.

"My dear prince. Lying isn't going to make this go any easier for you." Ryia's eyes grew hard, obsidian chips glinting deep in her skull. "You took something from Callum Clem. I think even you're smart enough to know that was a bad move."

Ryia watched, amused, as his jowls started to tremble. Prince or no, anyone who set foot inside the city walls of Carrowwick had heard stories about Callum Clem. Heard how he had joined his first syndicate at the age of seven, killed his first man before the age of ten. How over the past three decades he had duped and double-crossed almost every son of a bitch in the Lottery while still managing to keep his head. He was as cold as he was calculating. As slippery as he was ruthless. Just looking at Callum Clem the wrong way could earn you a beating. Stealing from the man? Well, that was as good as a death sentence.

Efrain reached for the bedside table with wine-swollen fingers, throwing shaky shadows on the walls.

"I have money. I have it right here." He pulled a bag of coins toward him, counted out ten silver halves and five golden crescents, and held them toward Ryia. She scooped up the coins, pocketing them as Efrain looked on, hopeful.

"I'll consider that a gift," she said. "Because we both know that's nowhere near enough to cover your entire debt."

"M-my entire debt?"

Ryia took another bite of bread, speaking around it as she chewed. "Thousan' crescents, by Clem's coun'."

His face reddened in outrage. Or maybe that was panic. "A thousand gold crescents? How in Adalina's deepest hell do you figure that?"

Adalina. Ryia had always found it ironic that the do-nothing nobles worshipped the goddess of toil.

"Cost of the Foxhole. I think he's being generous, personally, but then I've always thought Clem was a bit of a softheart." Her grin widened as Efrain's dark cheeks paled three shades in the muted candlelight. She wasn't sure if anyone had called Clem that before. Or if anyone had ever suggested the Snake of the Southern Dock had a heart at all.

"The Foxhole?"

It had been one of the most popular gambling houses in the Lottery. One of the best scams Clem had ever run . . . until the raid. The Needle Guard had torn the place to pieces—and the Saints with it. The gang had been the most powerful force in the Lottery for years, and now they were the laughingstock of everyone south of the trade docks. Clem had never been a laughingstock before, and, unsurprisingly, he was not taking it well. His rage made him even more dangerous than usual: a king cobra where he had once been only a viper.

"I hope for your sake this stupidity is just an act, because if not, I'm not sure how you manage to wipe your own ass."

She dusted the bread crumbs from her hands. Then she pulled the hatchet from her back again and dived across the room, pinning Efrain to the wall, one hand at his throat.

His whole body bobbed as he sucked in a shocked breath. Ryia leaned toward him, hissing in his ear. "A whole company of Needle Guard suddenly growing the stones to take on the Saints? Now where in the hells would they get the motivation to do something like that?" Efrain swallowed. Ryia went on: "Did you really think you were still one step ahead of us?"

Efrain sank to his knees as she released her grip. There on the floor, he drew one trembling breath after another. Ryia paced beside him, watching, head cocked like some lethal bird of prey.

"Please. I have more coin. You can take it. Take it and you will never see my face in the Lottery again, I swear it . . . I swear it by the goddesses Adalina and Felice—by the spirits of my ancestors."

His eyes were wet as he peered up at her from the floor, pulling his Brillish namestone from the neck of his nightshirt. Pathetic. "You're looking for mercy? From me?" She shook her head. "Efrain, you half-wit. I thought you said you knew who I was." She watched his eyes grow wide as she spun her hatchet playfully around her nimble fingers.

"What are you going to do?"

"I would think someone whose lips are wrapped so tightly around the Needle Guard's teat would know the Dresdellan punishment for theft." She leaned over, separating out the index finger of his right hand.

"Theft?"

"Yes, Efrain, theft," she said in the mock-patient tone of a frustrated schoolteacher. "We've been through this. You stole from the Saints of the Wharf. And don't misunderstand me—we will have our repayment." Her lip curled as she looked at the finery in the room. "Goddesses know you should be good for it. I'm just here to deliver a message. A reminder of what happens when you think you're smarter than Callum-fucking-Clem."

She slammed her weapon down, slicing through his finger at the second knuckle. She pulled her other hatchet free of its sheath, clocking him in the back of the head with its butt before his scream had a chance to leave his lips.

Ryia pocketed the finger with one hand, letting Efrain's unconscious body flop to the floor. She turned to leave, then paused as a roughly hammered iron coin fell from his breast pocket. It rolled a few unsteady inches before Ryia stopped it with her boot and picked it up, examining it in the light of the fireworks still bursting in the sky outside. She rubbed a thoughtful thumb over the blank front side, turning it over and examining the back. There, stamped into the shoddily wrought coin, was the faint imprint of a kestrel skull.

Ryia looked back down at Efrain, nudging his senseless form with a toe. "Well, that explains it." She shook her head. "What in the hells have you gotten yourself into?"

Her question hung unanswered in the night air when she caught another whiff of it. That grisly smell of blood, old cellars, mildew, and decay. That terrible weight in her nostrils. Danger. And not just any danger. Her nose tingled painfully. This was the particular aura of danger that accompanied only the most deadly fighters in Thamorr—a scent she was horribly familiar with.

An Adept was nearby.

She froze, ears pricked as the door beside the bed creaked open. A tall shadow drifted into the room on silent feet. Like every Adept raised on the Guildmaster's island, he was completely bald, clad in a long black robe trimmed in the brightest blue. His right cheek was marred by a brand of the Brillish royal seal. This was Efrain's personal servant, then. The Adept's nostrils flared as he turned his head slightly. There, inked on the side of his hairless skull, was a swirling letter *S*. A Senser—a watchdog used by the merchants and nobles of Thamorr to sniff out threats of violence.

Thanks to her speed and her use of lemon balm, this one was a little late to the party.

Ryia eyed the hatchets still clutched in her hands. Of the two types of Adept magic-wielders, Sensers were the weaker fighters by a long shot. Kinetics were the tricky, speedy bastards. Sensers were usually good at sounding the alarm and not much else. If she moved quickly, she could kill this one before he got the chance. . . .

The Senser turned his head again, his eyes resting on her at last. They were as blank and lifeless as every other branded Adept servant Ryia had ever encountered, so unlike the cruel and cunning eyes of the Guildmaster and his own personal army, called the Disciples. If she slit this slack-faced Senser's throat, the Brillish crown would see it as a loss of gold and nothing more. After all, they had paid the Guildmaster good money for a mindless servant . . . not for a human being. But Ryia knew better than anyone just how human the Adept truly were.

Still, he had seen her. If she didn't kill him, he would trot off and sound the alarm. She flexed her fingers, tightening her grip on her hatchets. The Butcher of Carrowwick didn't show mercy, right? She had killed dozens of people in this city: guards and mercenaries and freebooters. But this Senser was none of those things. He was a slave, trapped in a life he might never have chosen, if he had been given the chance to choose at all. It was a fate Ryia could relate to.

In her moment's hesitation, the Senser turned from the room in a whirl of his cloak, off to fetch someone who would ruin her fucking night, no doubt.

"Shit," she said under her breath. She then patted the still-senseless Efrain on the shoulder. "It's been fun, Efrain. Let's do this again sometime, shall we?" She hurriedly tucked the coin into her pocket. Then she slipped out the window and into the night.

Less than a minute passed before Ryia was on the far side of the fort's high walls again. The alarms chased her down the alleys, but she was already gone, nothing more than a shadow on the wind. The guards would know who had come to visit Efrain Althea tonight. But she had faced worse than the Needle Guard before. Much worse.

The salt breeze tugged at her hood as she wound her way back toward the dying party on the southern docks. She tossed Efrain Althea's severed finger up and down, whistling an old Gildesh sea shanty as she went.

2

NASH

Claudia Nash watched the mud drip slowly from her boot to the delicate wooden table beneath her heel as the clock ticked past the quarter-hour mark. To be fair, she wasn't actually sure the soupy brown liquid pooling on Bardley's table was mud. After sloshing around the docks of Carrowwick Harbor, it could be anything, really.

Well, she thought, tapping one dark finger against her kneecap, *if Bardley didn't want his sitting room tea table ruined, he shouldn't have kept me waiting so long.*

Honestly, after ten years of running with Clem's crew, she expected a little more respect than this. But the lace merchants in this pisshole were way more arrogant than the fish traders she had grown up with down on the Gildesh border. They always thought they were better than her, and they wanted her to know it.

She didn't even bother to turn her head when she finally heard the prissy click of footsteps entering the room.

"Glad to see you've made it, Miss Nash," Bardley said, extending a hand as he swept through the door surrounded by a flurry of fine silk. "I know it's a bit late, but with the chaos from the heretics' festival, you understand."

Nash raised an eyebrow, looking down at the merchant's hand before tilting her neck sideways, releasing a series of loud cracks. Bardley rubbed his fingers together in apparent irritation, withdrawing his hand and taking a seat on the pristine sofa.

He eyed the destroyed table, curling his lip in irritation, but all he said was, "I trust Callum has sent you with good news?"

There was no way this prig was on first-name terms with Cal Clem. Nash pulled a jingling bag from the pocket of her salt-stiffened coat and tossed it onto the table.

"That's right," she said, her voice raspier than a stack of decade-old ledgers.

Bardley leaned forward, plucking the linen bag from the table before the waves of the Shit Sea streaming from Nash's boots could reach it. He poked around the contents with his little birdlike fingers before tutting deeply and shaking his head.

"I thought we had agreed on five crescents per unit."

Nash ran a fingernail between her two front teeth. "That's right."

"Miss Nash—"

"It's just Nash." It was actually just Claudia, but if anyone was dumb enough to call her that, she was likely to rip out his throat and show it to him.

"Nash, then," Bardley said, clearly irritated. "I know all about the little games your kind like to run. Allow me to make myself clear. If you cheat me, it will not end well for you."

He snapped his fingers, then looked meaningfully toward the open doorway in the corner. Nash followed his gaze, swallowing as a hulking shadow lumbered into the room.

Its black linen cloak rippled as it took a step forward into the candlelight. Her stomach squirmed. Its eyes were focused squarely on Bardley, as though awaiting an order. But of course it was. That was all the Adept servants did 99 percent of their miserable lives: Stand still, wait for the master to clap.

There was no pattern to how the Adept babies were born. Or possibly it was just a puzzle nobody but the Guildmaster had managed to crack. No one knew how he and his loyal Disciples could tell which babies would grow up to have powers—how he tracked them down from every nook and cranny of Thamorr before they could even sit up—but the Guildmaster was always right. And they always grew up to become . . . that.

Nash could still remember Ma's sobs the day the Guildmaster's blue-sailed ships came to take her baby sister, Jolie. It had been stupid of them to name the child before her first birthday, everyone knew that, utter lunacy to get attached, but Ma had taken the risk. And it had not paid off. Nash's father was away at sea; he didn't even know he had a second daughter yet . . . but somehow the Guildmaster did. But that was irrelevant. This Adept couldn't be Jolie. This one was male—not to mention white as a Borean winter, ten shades paler than Nash at least.

It turned its head, and she squinted. In the light of the candelabra sitting beside the window she could just barely make out the letter inked onto the side of its pale, bald head.

K

A Kinetic. She eyed the creature's left cheek. Just as she'd thought. Rebranded—more than once. That told her two things: This twat Bardley wasn't important enough to get an invite to the proper Guildmaster's auction, and he was slimy enough to buy an Adept illegally.

Lovely. Cal always managed to find the most charming business partners.

She chewed the inside of her cheek absently as she ran her eyes over the Adept. This one probably wasn't very powerful. In Dresdell, the only real Kinetics—the ones capable of stopping swords and splintering walls with their minds—were tucked away inside the Bobbin Fort. They were all dangerous nonetheless. Unnaturally strong and faster than a damned dragonfly. But Cal didn't keep Nash around because she was easily intimidated. In fact, she was pretty sure the only reason he had taken her on all those years ago was because she had been bold enough to use her last two silvers to track him down and ask to join the Saints. If she hadn't backed off from the most fearsome syndicate lord in Carrowwick at the tender age of fourteen, she sure as shit wasn't about to do so with a spoiled little prat like Bardley now.

Nash leaned back in her velvet chair.

"Impressive, but it doesn't change our deal."

"And what deal is that?"

"Five crescents a unit . . . and a ten percent cut to the Saints."

"Ten percent?" Bardley's lips curved into a smile so smug Nash had to forcibly resist the urge to pop him in the jaw. "No, no. I'm certain I would not have agreed to such an outlandish figure. Especially not with such a . . . low-ranking syndicate. I seem to recall it was seven percent."

Merchants. If there was anything Nash had learned in her twenty-four years, it was that they were even dirtier than the gutter rats of the Lottery. If Bardley thought he could leverage the Saints' recent downfall into a deal here, he was sorely mistaken.

Nash leaned forward, resting her elbows on her knees and splitting her lips into a wide smile. It grew even wider when she saw Bardley flinch. Her carefully sharpened canines tended to have that effect on people.

"You can bring all the Kinetics and all the little jokes you want, Bardley, but if you try to short the Saints"—she pawed through the bowl of nuts on the mud-covered table—"at the very least, you're going to be stuck going through the bullshit taxes of Briel's legal trade. At worst?" She popped an almond into her mouth with another grin. "You might just find yourself face-to-face with Cal's most famous friend."

Bardley scoffed, but Nash saw that beneath that fine doublet he was sweating like a sailor in his first storm. Mention of the Butcher did that to a man.

"I could work through the Harpies."

Nash's chest rumbled with a gravelly laugh. The Harpies—good for nothing but licking boots, as Cal liked to say. They had enough smugglers to run the best black market south of Volkfier, the Carrowwick Fair, sure . . . but mostly they dealt in dice halls and brothels.

"Good luck finding one of those Harpy bastards who can talk the shopkeeps in Sandport into buying your shit-poor lace at five crescents a bolt."

"Shit-poor—" Bardley opened his little pink mouth like a babe about to cry for milk, then shut it again. He repeated the motion twice more. No more words came out. Nash's smile widened again as she pushed herself to her feet, leaning over to pat him amiably on the shoulder.

"There's a good man," she said. "I'm heading back south again at the end of Juli. I'll send my men to pick up your next shipment then, if you're ready."

Neither Bardley nor his precious Kinetic moved an inch as Nash gave a wink and sauntered from the room, leaving a trail of filthy boot prints in her wake.

THE MERCHANTS' quarter was eerily silent. Nash pulled a battered old pocket watch from her coat, catching the moonlight on its face. Just past two in the morning. Most of her crew had run off to the Mermaid's Tail the second the *Seasnake's Revenge* had butted up against the southern dock. The brothel was close—just along the northern edge of the Harpies' territory—but that wasn't really Nash's style. The dice hall beside it, however . . . She ran her tongue over her teeth. The night was still young enough to turn a pocketful of coppers into silvers.

The streets grew louder and busier the farther south she moved. A hundred faces swam past in the dimly lit alleys, all blotchy red with drink. Halfway to the Tail she paused, wrinkling her nose as she watched a familiar silhouette stumbling through the slowly dispersing crowds. Harlow Finn.

The leader of the Harpies was an impossible man to forget. His spine was so twisted that Nash had to imagine every lurching step must be agony. Then there were the boils. They covered his pale flesh from head to toe. His claim to fame—proof he'd survived his bout with the Borean Death during the plague years. Nash always felt like she could still smell the sickness on him. She bit back a shudder.

Beside Finn, obviously struggling to match his painfully slow pace, was a short, slight figure in a deep purple coat. A woman. How much wine would someone need to guzzle to find herself eager to climb into Harlow Finn's bed? Nash wondered. Well, she supposed, there was no accounting for taste.

Then the woman turned her head, a finger of lantern light brushing along her cheekbone. Nash slowed to a stop, hiding her face in her collar as the pair picked their way toward the skeletal tangle of naked masts crowding the Harpies' docks. Nash spent enough time at sea that there weren't many faces she recognized in this city, but that was definitely one of them. Round and cherubic, but somehow also deadly and sharp. Pale gray eyes cut deep into paler cheeks.

Tana Rafferty. A Kestrel Crown. Not just any Crown—Wyatt Asher's second-in-command.

Now what in the hell would she be doing skulking around with Harlow Finn at two in the damned morning?

Trying to make her six-foot-tall frame as small as possible, Nash nudged her way past a man emptying his guts into the gutter. There was no way Rafferty was walking out on the Crowns, was there? Asher's syndicate brought in twice the coin the Harpies did with their fighting pits alone. Besides, as far as Nash knew, the only person to betray Wyatt Asher and survive was Callum Clem.

Rafferty was sharp, but she was no Cal Clem. Asher had to know she was here . . . but why?

Nash kept her distance, walking a parallel path through the twisting alleys. She paused as the unlikely duo slowed to a stop beside the Undertow, the dice hall just beside the Tail. She leaned one arm against the moldering siding beside her, peering through the misty shadows across the dock.

Finn and Rafferty were clearly in deep conversation. What were they saying? Maybe she could slip down the next dock, come up on the Undertow from the back alley . . . ?

But the moment had already passed.

Rafferty drew a small, weighted pouch from her pocket. Coins. Bigger than coppers, from the looks of it. Nash could almost feel the weight of the small bundle as Rafferty slipped it into Harlow Finn's waiting claws. It vanished into the ragged folds of the man's jacket. He limped into the Undertow, leaving Rafferty to slip away with the wind.

Wyatt Asher was paying the Harpies? For what? Since when had anyone but Harlow Finn himself given half a shit about the third syndicate of the Lottery? Unless . . .

Nash ground her teeth. Dammit. She had hoped not to see that pompous son of a bitch tonight. This was supposed to be a short stopover, a quick detour on her way to bring a fresh shipment of dormire's blood to the Borean port town of Volkfier.

Maybe it was nothing. She stopped, hovering at the corner of Threader's Lane. Four alleys left would take her back to the *Revenge*. She could pretend she hadn't seen a damned thing, collect her coin from those drugged-up northerners, and get on with her life. . . .

"Damn it all," she said, turning right instead. Her Borean friends would have to suffer the weight of a clear mind a little longer.

Smuggling Brillish drugs and third-rate lace might bring in enough coin to keep her out of the gutters, but if the Kestrel Crowns and the Harpies were working together, that had to mean there was a big job in the works. Big jobs meant big money.

And big money was something Cal Clem was going to want to know about.

3

TRISTAN

Drunken shouts echoed all the way from the docks to the edge of Braider's Corner as colorful sparks rained down from the sky. Soon, the fireworks would end, and the inns along the southern trade docks would be bursting at the seams with drunken fools in ridiculous costumes. For many, the Festival of Felice was over. For Tristan Beckett, it was just beginning. "Th' game's Nobleman's Luck . . ." Tristan pushed his voice into a drunken drawl as he collected the cards on the table with deliberate clumsiness. He winked at no one in particular. "Since you lot can hold your wine, I know there ain't a nobleman among us. We'll call't Sailor's Luck."

The four men seated around his table chortled appreciatively. Tristan picked up the last four cards, stacking them on top of the deck with carefully crafted indifference. He split the deck lazily in half. "How many've you lot are in?"

"Me," grunted a ruddy-cheeked man wearing a wooden crown. The woman seated on his lap cheered as the other three men agreed.

"A full-table game! That's what Felice likes t' see," Tristan said, making sure to let his voice carry. He reached into his pocket, flicking a dingy silver half onto the table. A bold first wager. The other men hesitated.

"Do I see real coins on this table? Finally," said a voice with a thick Borean accent.

A tall, slender man sauntered toward their table, parting the smoke like bed curtains. He smiled at the woman on King Drunk's lap. "Where I come from, a man is not so afraid of risk as these little mice-men from Dresdell, playing with their coppers."

The woman smiled at the newcomer, eyes running from his messy blond curls to the lean muscles of his chest, peeking out from a half-unbuttoned shirt.

"Mice-men?" King Drunk asked, shooting a concerned look at his companion as she started to toy with her long, dark hair. He reached for his purse so quickly Tristan thought he might throw a shoulder out. No one in the Lottery could say the newcomer, Ivan Rezkoye, wasn't a professional. In the past few months, Tristan had seen him run this little game a hundred times. Almost often enough to forget the time he'd been the drunken idiot diving for his coins.

Almost.

Tristan shuffled the cards, stacking them in his favor with practiced speed. His hands slipped, crimping the bottom card of the newly stacked deck ever so slightly. He cut the deck, burying the crumpled card in the middle.

"Care t' cut your luck?" he asked King Drunk.

The man cut without looking, his fingers naturally finding the crimp.

"What are the rules to this game of yours, mouse-man?" Ivan asked, flashing a dazzling grin at the brunette, now halfway off King Drunk's lap.

King Drunk gave a derisive snort. "What kinda idiot puts down good silver on a game he doesn't even know?"

"Idiot? Perhaps I am just hoping to get lucky." Ivan slung the woman another smile. She blushed.

"Ye want a total've twelve," King Drunk said, almost shouting as he tried to keep his companion's attention. "A king and a dyad is a perfect hand, but a nine and a three'll work if no one's got better."

Ivan tapped his chin, as if in deep thought. "And if no one has twelve?"

"Then you'll want close to twelve as you can get," said the brunette. "But no higher."

Tristan scooped up his cards. Two aces, just as he'd planned.

"Who's lookin' for another card?" he asked, holding the deck out, waggling his eyebrows. "C'mon now, the cards'nt gonna take themselves."

At least one of them had to draw one or his carefully stacked deck wouldn't be able to save him. But that was what Ivan was there for. Well, partly anyway . . .

Across the table, Ivan was whispering conspiratorially with the slender brunette, who had now completely removed herself from King Drunk's lap. Her former comrade ground his teeth in irritation, snatching up another card. Tristan smiled, plucking his planted card from the deck. A Valier stared up at him, the card version of one of the somber guards of the Dresdellan throne, clad all in fading purple ink.

"Last round for bets, yes?" Ivan said. "Come now, do not be shy. I want to buy the lady a cup of *stervod*." He swept a golden crescent from his purse and dropped it on the table, looking at the drunk. "The bet is to you, mouse-man."

"Call me a mouse one more time, blondie," King Drunk said, slamming a dingy crescent onto the table. Tristan tossed his coin in next, and the last man followed.

Ivan flipped his cards first. Two dyads. Four. A dismal hand.

"That's what ya bet on?" King Drunk cackled. He flipped his own cards. Eleven.

"*Schwachschiss*," Ivan swore in Borean. "You Dresdellans and your pitiful card games." He pushed himself up from the table. The woman hurried to follow.

"Can't win 'em all, m' northern friend," Tristan called after him.

The third man flipped his cards. An eight and a three.

Tristan tutted. "So close, so close."

He flipped his winning hand over, watching Ivan finally shake the brunette and stalk away. The Borean pulled a button at the back of his collar. His own invention. A cascade of black fabric flooded over his bloodred shirt. He swept his shoulder-length curls into a bun as he melted away into the crowd, his hawklike eyes already searching for his next table of victims.

"Sorry, fellows," Tristan said, "looks like Felice was looking out for me that hand." His voice caught as King Drunk's hand slammed down on the table.

"Felice, my ass. You're a fucking cheat."

Tristan shared a bemused look with the man beside him. "A cheat? How do you figure? You saw me shuffle th' cards right on the table. You cut th' deck yourself!"

The third man pointed a wobbly, accusatory finger at the drunk. "Yer just mad you started this game with a crescent and a woman an' ended with neither."

Tristan gave an apologetic smile. "That's just th' way the cards fell. I'm sorry, my friend. I'll tell you what—you call the next game. How's that for fair?" Tristan wiggled the cards in front of the drunk's face. "What'll it be? Gildesh Wine Merchant? Maybe a li'l Bobbin Draw?" Before getting stuck here in Carrowwick, Tristan hadn't known a single one of these card games. After all, *cards were the swindler's pastime*, as his father said. But Tristan had always been a quick study. Now he could stack the deck for a hundred games or more.

King Drunk ripped the wooden crown from his head and pushed himself to his feet, his pipe threatening to fall from his cracked lips. "How 'bout we play gut the cheat?"

Tristan laughed, but his heart rate tripled as he caught sight of the steel at the man's belt. Not a run-of-the-mill sailor. A freebooter. Despite the fact that he was probably moments away from being eviscerated, Tristan couldn't help but note that it was a little galling to be called a cheat by someone who held up lace merchants for a living. The other men at the table scattered away into the bar, finding new homes at less contentious tables.

"If you find a cheat to gut, let me know," Tristan said, voice hardening. "Now come on then, fair's fair." He looked at the crescent as it disappeared into King Drunk's fingers again. "Pay up—you can play me for it next game."

"So you can have another chance t' cheat me?"

Tristan's palms were slick with sweat. It wasn't often he wasn't able to talk his way out of things. He looked the man up and down. Suddenly he wished he'd picked on a much smaller drunk.

But just then, the man froze. His face paled as his eyes flicked between Tristan and the space just over his left shoulder. He cast the crescent back onto the table.

"I see wha' this is," he grumbled. "Take your damned gold."

Tristan let out a breath as the man ambled away. "Well, you certainly took your sweet time getting here."

Ryia leaned against the rotted wooden pillar behind him, picking nonexistent dirt from her fingernails with the blade of one of her hatchets. The distinctive weapon announced her reputation to anyone too foolish to know who they were dealing with. The Butcher of Carrowwick.

"Oh, fuck off. Sometimes I have better things to do than beat up little boys for you." Her voice was raspy and melodic, like a summer wind sweeping through tall grasses. She stalked across the room, stopping just in front of him.

"Let me guess . . . drinking your weight in Edalish ale?" he asked.

"I'll have you know I was on *very* important business for our dear friend tonight," she said, stroking a finger along Tristan's jawline. He jumped. Not one of her fingers.

He ducked away from the severed digit. "You're disgusting, did you know that?" She just gave her usual wicked grin. Tristan looked warily toward the finger, now bouncing back and forth between Ryia's hands. "Whose is that, anyway?"

"Someone who was a *royal* pain in Clem's ass," she said cheekily.

Tristan rolled his eyes, scooping the mound of coins into the purse tied on his belt. "It's a good thing your axes are sharper than your jokes."

Ryia raised her left hand, crossing the first two fingers. She was strangely familiar with the vulgar gestures of the middle kingdoms for a Brillish girl . . . then again, Ryia was familiar with vulgarity of every sort.

Her eyes flicked to his purse. "How much you bring in tonight? Enough to keep Clem's dogs at bay?"

"You tell me," he said, trying and failing to hide his bitterness. "You're his prized pup, aren't you?"

Ryia just smirked, clearly unfazed by the accusation. But of course she wouldn't be upset. She might even be proud. After all, she had *chosen* this life. She hadn't been roped in and scarred with the Saints' brand against her will like Tristan had—she'd volunteered to be Clem's strongman. To spend the rest of her days shaking down and carving up anyone who got on the Snake's bad side. Sure, there were plenty of gutter rats in this city who gladly signed right up, but Ryia, whatever she was, wherever she had come from, was no gutter rat. Tristan would never understand how she had come to decide the Saints' life was the one for her.

He picked up the cards and gave them a lazy shuffle, peering around the bar. "Now that my muscle has decided to show herself, I can take enough risks to make more than a few crescents."

Ryia shook her head, picking her teeth with her tongue. "No deal. I've got to see Clem."

"I'm sure he can wait a few hours to see that horrific trophy of yours," Tristan protested, glancing toward the pocket the severed finger had disappeared into.

She pursed her lips, the scar along her left jawbone puckering as she pulled something small and iron from her cloak. "That's not all I need to show him." She tossed the thing to Tristan.

A coin, about the size of a copper. He flipped it over in his hand, running a thumb over the poorly engraved mark before looking grimly back to Ryia. "Oh, for Adalina's sake . . . Clem's not going to like this."

4

RYIA

Agust of wind buffeted Ryia's face as she stepped outside the Miscreants' Temple. It was moist. Warm. Like breathing air directly from a street dog's mouth.

"I wish autumn would hurry its ass up already," she griped, slogging through the gutter.

"Summer just started." Tristan looked at her sideways, sweeping his dark hair out of his eyes. "Maybe if you didn't insist on wearing long sleeves, you wouldn't hate it so much. Or smell so bad." He gave an overdramatic wince as Ryia punched him in the arm. "Besides, I thought you folks from Briel were tough in the heat. Isn't it like this year round down there?"

Ryia fiddled with the intricately carved namestone around her neck. The mark of any citizen of the kingdom of Briel, some two thousand miles to the south. "Maybe down in Safrona. It was drier than Rolf's breakfast bread where I grew up."

Not completely false. Also not strictly true. Just like most things she said.

Tristan chortled as they wove their way toward the slipshod

row houses lining the southernmost wall of the city. "That bread really is awful."

"So are Dresdellan summers."

Tristan shot her a crooked grin. "I'm not the one who told you to come here—I'm sure there's plenty of need for a butcher up in Boreas."

"Oh, there was. You should hear what they call me up there."

Tristan laughed. Ryia didn't. The three months she had spent in Brünhavert had been the most miserably cold, windy months of her life. She had honestly been relieved when the Guildmaster's smirking Disciples had tracked her down that time.

"Wait, are you ser—" Tristan started.

"Shh." Ryia flung out an arm, catching him in the chest.

"Ow—what was that f—"

"I heard something," Ryia said, shrinking back a step, nostrils flaring.

"So what? There's a party going on. Did no one tell you?" Tristan teased. But all the color drained from his skinny face at the hiss of voices on the adjacent street.

"I'm afraid I don't understand the problem, Mr. Griffith," said the first voice. Calm, measured, and cold. A scalpel slicing through flesh.

Callum Clem.

Ryia glanced at Tristan, now pressing his back into the building behind him like he was hoping to fall through to the other side. Given his penchant for corporal punishment and his unpredictable nature, there probably wasn't anyone alive who really *liked* Clem . . . but Tristan hated him.

Not surprising, since Clem had nearly gutted him the night they met. Only someone very young or green as a clover field would have been stupid enough to try to cheat Clem so brazenly. Tristan had obviously been both. It honestly begged the question how he'd survived the past sixteen years at all.

As for Ryia? Well, she had worked with some pretty nasty sons of bitches in her years on the run. Highwaymen, assassins, and thieves, the lot of them. Clem was probably the slyest, most calculating man she'd ever worked for, but there was a strange sort of comfort in that. After all, she would need to run some calculations herself to stay hidden from the Guildmaster. It had been almost a year since his Disciples had last sent her running, but they would track her down eventually. Sometimes they showed up in her newest city before she had so much as taken off her coat, metaphorically speaking. Sometimes she was able to eke out a life for a few years before they came to break down her door, but no matter how well she hid or how far she ran, they always found her.

It was maddening the way that asshole could follow a trail that wasn't there. Someday she would learn his secret and be free of him forever . . . or she'd just lop his hairless head from his shoulders and be done with it. Either way was fine with her.

Pushing daydreams of a gloriously headless Guildmaster from her mind, Ryia edged forward. She peered around the corner. Four shadows split the street beyond. Clem stood on the right, alone on the cobblestones. He was not a tall man, nor was he particularly large, but his ego made up for all that. His hollowed cheekbones and hooked nose stood out sharply in profile, his short blond hair almost silver in the moonlight. As always, he looked like he had dressed for a dinner party. Fancy clothes, impractical shoes. Probably just another show of confidence—unable to run, but unconcerned. After all, Callum Clem would never run from anything.

"Of course you don't understand the problem," sniped the ratlike man on the left, presumably Mr. Griffith. He was flanked by two beefy-looking bodyguards. "I know the way your *kind* operate. It's why your little operation is circling the drain at the moment. Your Saints have been asking for a comeuppance for years, and now you've gotten it."

A smile crept up Clem's face. It was cold, laced with a hunger that had always been there but had grown more and more pronounced every day since the fall of the Foxhole.

"Is that so, Mr. Griffith?" He scratched his chin with one immaculate finger. "If you have such a poor opinion of my . . . associates, it begs the question why you agreed to do business with us in the first place. You signed the contract, yes?"

Griffith clenched his fists. "Well, yes, I signed the—"

"Then I'm afraid I can't help you. We've done our part. I expect five hundred crescents added to the Saints' coffers by the end of the week, or I'll have to arrange a little meeting for you with my Butcher."

"Looks like I'll have to check my schedule, eh?" Ryia whispered, nudging Tristan.

Misbehaving Saints, business partners gone wrong, rival gang members caught in the wrong alley . . . it was Ryia's job to deal with them all. It didn't make her very popular . . . unless infamy counted. Ryia liked to think it did. Tristan just looked vaguely ill.

Ryia's nostrils exploded with the raw scent of danger as Griffith snapped once and four silhouettes became six.

The new shadows in the alley were dark robed and solemn. Adept Kinetics. Tristan flinched as they grabbed Clem by the arms, hauling him off the ground with inhuman strength and speed. Their faces remained completely expressionless as they reared back, slamming him against the darkened shop window behind him. There was a reason Adept Kinetics were so expensive. A reason why the men who owned them reigned supreme in their respective corners of the world. Ryia curled her lip as she silently weighed the word. *Owned.*

The Kinetics' arms held steady, unyielding as stone as they ground Clem into the glass pane behind him. The Guildmaster's Kinetic Disciples were by far the strongest Kinetics in Thamorr, but even the weaker, brainwashed ones, like these two, were pretty damned unbeatable. They moved faster than the human eye and were stronger than a dozen oxen. They had appeared in the alley, seemingly out of thin air. Had lifted Clem like he weighed no more than a single leaf of parchment. It was almost impossible for anyone untouched by the mysterious magic of the Adept to face one and live. In the days before they had been broken and enslaved, Adept had ruled the world. It wasn't hard to see why.

"You shouldn't have come alone, *Callum*," said Griffith, tightening his fist. The Kinetics mimicked the motion obediently, grabbing Clem by the throat and squeezing. One face was female, the other male. Both were blank and passionless. "Your cockiness has always been your undoing. I'm sure Asher in particular will appreciate the irony."

Ryia reached for her hatchets, cracking her neck. Why *did* Clem insist on walking these streets by himself? Until recently, his reputation had been his armor. But now? Clearly things had changed with how far the Saints had fallen.

Words and bluster couldn't save him from the death blow of a Kinetic.

"Wait," Tristan whispered, grabbing her forearm. His face was white.

Ryia nudged him. "I know you hate the man, but my gold comes from his pockets."

"No," Tristan said. "Look. He's smiling."

Ryia could see the serpentine curl of Clem's lips from here, even as a trickle of blood spilled from between them, his face reddening. Clem nodded toward the Kinetics holding him.

"Yours?"

Griffith blinked. "They belong to the company."

Clem's smile widened. "Do you have the blood?"

"Do I . . . what?"

"I wasn't talking to you, Mr. Griffith."

Griffith's bodyguards suddenly stepped forward. One struck a match, lighting a fast-burning torch, while the other drew a short metal rod from his coat sleeve. A branding iron.

Ryia froze, teeth clenched as she watched. One guard heated the iron while the other pulled a small container from his pocket.

"What are you doing?" Griffith's voice grew half an octave higher with each word as he lunged for his guards—about as effective as a puppy nipping at a horse's hooves.

"You see, Mr. Griffith, I did not come alone. *You* did. These are not your men, as you just noted—they are the company's men."

"My company."

"Not anymore."

The branding iron hissed as one guard dipped it into the liquid filling the container. Blood—Clem's blood. The guard stepped forward. He hesitated . . . then pressed the brand into the first Kinetic's cheek. The Adept fighter blinked as Clem's blood ran down her face, working itself into the new burn on her cheek, then immediately released her grip.

The other Adept followed suit as soon as he was marked, lowering Clem to the ground and falling, dead-eyed, to attention, now ready to obey Clem instead of this Mr. Griffith.

"Hayworth does not seem to share your low opinion of me, Mr. Griffith. We have made an arrangement. As of this morning, the majority stake in Hackle Holdings belongs to me. As a responsible investor, I can't possibly allow you to continue to head the company." Clem shook out his long, thin arms and took a step forward. "You know . . . I heard a rumor you signed a deal with the Saints of the Wharf, is that correct?" He tutted in mock disapproval. "Common street gangs . . . I think Hackle is better than that, don't you?"

"But I . . . but you . . . ," Griffith sputtered, looking around the empty street for help and finding none.

"Goodbye, Mr. Griffith." A mad breed of joy danced in Clem's silver-blue eyes as he snapped his fingers.

Tristan hid his face in his hands as the Kinetics sprang to action, but Ryia didn't look away. They moved with quick, efficient brutality, motions blurred like those of a dragonfly's wings as they went about their bloody business. They were unarmed, but they didn't need weapons to get the job done. Bones cracked like twigs under their hands. Their unnaturally sharp nails cut through flesh like hot piss cut through fresh snow. In an instant, poor Mr. Griffith lay on the ground in pieces.

"Get someone to clean that up," Clem said, dismissing the Hackle Holdings guards and his new Kinetics. He stepped neatly over a pile of tangled intestines as Ryia rounded the corner. "Did you enjoy the show, Butcher?"

He greeted her without looking up. Sometimes Ryia swore he was a Senser, somehow escaped from the Guildmaster's mysterious spell. But she knew that was bullshit. There was only one free Adept in all of Thamorr. She should know.

Not that living her entire life with one eye over her shoulder really counted as "freedom." No matter where she ran, she always felt like she was a fly caught in the Guildmaster's infinite web, just waiting for him to finally scuttle across the map to devour her.

"It didn't look like you needed my help."

Clem inspected the hem of his emerald coat for blood. "I do hope you've come with good news."

"Not exactly."

His thin lips curved, forming either a grimace or a smile. Of the two expressions, the grimace was far less dangerous. "Don't tell me my Butcher has been bested by that odious creature."

"Hardly. You'll be getting your payments from that prick, don't worry." She tossed the finger to him. "And I've left him with a nice reminder of our time together. Should send a pretty clear message."

Clem examined the severed finger with mild interest, pocketing it as though it were as ordinary as a pen. "Good." He dusted off his trousers, carefully shined shoes reflecting the moonlight. "But that's not why you're here."

Ryia drew back her hood, letting her inky ponytail fall over one shoulder. "No, it's not." She pulled the Crowns' coin from her pocket, turning the stamped side toward Clem.

A muscle in his jaw twitched. "We should speak in private. Feel free to bring your shadow with you," he said, indicating the corner where Tristan was still lurking out of sight.

The Snake of the Southern Dock didn't wait to see if Tristan and Ryia were in tow as he turned, making his way toward the Saints' row house.

THE GROUP of Saints drinking in the foyer of the row house cleared out the instant Clem opened the door. He didn't seem to notice or care, walking past the Saints' cook, Rolf, as he grabbed the cups off the table and disappeared into the kitchen. "Wait upstairs," Clem said, vanishing down the long front hall without another word.

Tristan shot Ryia a horrified look, and she grinned, mounting the rickety wooden stairs and winding her way up to Clem's apartment.

Ryia reached out to open the door, but someone inside beat her to the punch.

"Well, if it isn't the infamous Butcher of Carrowwick," grumbled a familiar voice. Ryia raised her eyes several inches to meet Nash's gaze. "Shouldn't you be out dismembering someone?"

"Shouldn't you be out stealing someone's hard-earned gold?"

"Excuse me, I don't steal gold," Nash said.

"No, just ships."

"I haven't stolen a ship in months," she replied. "Although there is this beautiful little cog on the southeastern dock. Right next to the textile quarter . . ."

"There it is." Ryia mounted the last step, patting Nash on the shoulder.

Nash shrugged out of reach. "Don't get familiar. Get too close and I might have to show you what these can do." She bared her teeth, showing off her razor-sharp canines.

"Don't tease me like that. You know you're just my type."

Nash rolled her eyes. Her brow furrowed as her gaze fell on Tristan. "And who the hell are you?"

"That's a damned good question," Ryia said, chuckling. "What's it going to be today? An ex-pirate? Maybe a Gildesh merchant's bastard son?"

Color returned to Tristan's face for the first time since the alley. "Today I think I'll be a runaway Borean *medev* guard," he said, naming the mysterious fighting force of the northernmost kingdom in Thamorr. "What can I say? The celibate life just wasn't for me."

"That's not what I've heard," Ryia joked.

Nash chortled, and Tristan gave her a sarcastic glare.

The truth was, no one really knew where Tristan had come from. Maybe one of his increasingly elaborate lies had been the real story, maybe not. It didn't really matter anymore. He wore Clem's brand now. It might not be quite as effective as the Adept's blood-brands . . . but it would still give anyone who came across the boy a good idea of who they could sell him back to. He wouldn't be leaving Carrowwick for a long, long time, that was certain.

"What are you doing here, anyways?" Nash asked, looking her up and down suspiciously.

Ryia scoffed. "Don't worry, the Snake's all yours." She pulled the battered iron coin from her pocket, flashing its kestrel skull at her in the dim light of the stairwell.

"Didn't realize you were looking to hire out your dirty work," Nash teased.

Ryia shot Nash a glare. She wasn't exactly afraid of Clem, but it was just asking for trouble to joke about working for Wyatt Asher under this roof. The Kestrel Crowns were the Saints' biggest rivals in the Lottery, after all.

"Where'd you find it?"

"On Efrain Althea."

Nash let out a low whistle. "Well, that explains a hell of a lot."

"Don't know about a lot, but it explains the Foxhole for sure," Ryia said.

As shoddy as the iron coins looked, the Kestrel Crowns didn't hand them out lightly. Each coin won its holder a favor—usually the convenient, untimely death of some rival or enemy. And each one had to be earned by doing the Crowns a favor in return . . . such as orchestrating the downfall of the Saints' most profitable gambling hall.

"Looks like Asher's going in for the kill," Tristan said. "Why now?"

"Don't ask me," Ryia said.

"I don't have to ask you," said Nash.

"How could I forget? Nash the infamous smuggler knows all."

"Of course I do. Why do you think I'm here?"

Ryia gave her a wink. "The usual reason?"

"Oh fuck off," said Nash.

The smuggler had survived Clem longer than most—almost a decade, last Ryia had heard. Rumor had it there was a reason for that. Of course, there were worse ways to buy protection in the Lottery than sleeping with a syndicate lord, but still, the idea of being in the same room as a naked Callum Clem made her skin crawl. Then again, she had never really seen the appeal of naked men at all.

Ryia sauntered past Nash into the apartment. She had seen Clem's personal chambers dozens of times over the past year, but they never failed to simultaneously awe and repulse her. However run-down the rest of the row house might look, this room left no doubt that the man who lived here was someone of importance.

Or at least thought he was.

Plush rugs nearly as fine as the ones she'd seen inside Prince Efrain Althea's room covered the floor, and the walls were lined with cherry-wood bookshelves that had to be of Gildesh make. A disgustingly gaudy gold-and-crystal chandelier hung over the center of the room, casting its yellowish light over the otherwise dim chamber. Ryia peered up at it, wondering briefly who lit all those candles every day. And why? One of these days, the whole south row was going to go up in flames because of Clem's obsession with his fucking chandelier.

But trying to understand anything Callum Clem did was a recipe for madness. He read like an old poem; everything could be expected to have three meanings or none at all.

The Snake swept into the room like a frigid wave. The smell of chamomile flooded Ryia's nostrils as Ivan Rezkoye strode in behind him, his shirt half-unbuttoned, blond hair spilling onto his lithe shoulders. If he was surprised to find a whole host of people in Clem's sitting room, he gave no sign of it. Of course, when Ivan wasn't working, his face rarely gave a sign of anything at all.

"Let me see that coin," said Clem.

Ryia flicked it to him with her thumb. He caught it mid-step without flinching, flipping it over twice in his palm before handing it to Ivan.

The Saints' chief forger held the coin up to the light of the chandelier, spinning it back and forth, running his fingers over the rough-hammered edges. He held it close to one vivid green eye, inspecting the symbol stamped onto the back.

"It is genuine."

"Are you sure?" Clem asked.

Ivan bristled slightly. "It is my job to be sure. Besides, exactly what kind of *dummklav* would forge one of these coins? It would be suicide."

"It would seem that with the Harpies in his back pocket, my dear old friend has decided to make a play for the Lottery," Clem said.

Nash's jaw dropped before she could catch herself. "You already knew?"

For as long as Ryia had been in Carrowwick, the Harpies had been pretty harmless, dealing mostly in whores and keeping to themselves. But now they'd chosen sides . . . just in time for the Saints' downfall. That was no coincidence. What had Wyatt Asher promised them?

Clem traded his emerald coat for a burgundy dressing gown and settled into one of his chairs, his manicured fingers steepled in thought. His eyes pulsed with intensity—a thinly veiled madness that had caught flame alongside the Foxhole and had only grown steadily clearer in the days since. "It appears we have cause to remind everyone who rules these docks."

Nash stepped past Ryia, snagging one of the apples sitting in the bowl on the spindly table beside Clem. She then slouched into the chair across from him, biting into the fruit. "I'd bet my left tit this means there's a big job in the works."

Not many people would be bold enough to invite themselves into Clem's apartment and help themselves to his food without asking, but that was Nash.

"How astute," Clem said thinly. He crossed to the fire, setting a kettle and staring pensively into the flames. He was silent for so long that Ryia assumed they were dismissed, but just as she turned to leave, he spoke again. "Everyone get some rest. I'm going to need you all ready at sunrise."

Ivan peered out the window, surveying the already brightening sky. "Ready for what, exactly?"

Clem removed the kettle from its hook as it started to whistle and poured a mouthful of steaming water into a comically tiny teacup. "To find out what that rat Asher is cooking up with Harlow Finn."

Ryia nodded. "And once we do?"

"Simple." Clem's lips curved into a smile that might have been handsome if it wasn't for the insanity lurking at its edges. He pulled Efrain Althea's severed finger from his pocket and set it delicately on the table before lifting the teacup to his lips. "We ruin them all."

5

TRISTAN

"Excuse me, sir. Sorry, apologies, excuse me."

Tristan pushed through the late-morning crowds on the docks, hands brushing the pockets of anyone unfortunate enough to come within arm's reach. He had fourteen coppers in a matter of seconds. Fourteen coppers to lay down against his debt to Clem. That meant only . . . eighty-five thousand to go. Or was it ninety by now? It was hard to keep track when Clem kept adding the cost of keeping him alive to his total.

As though a flea-bitten cot in the crowded attic of the Miscreants' Temple was that expensive. Really.

He scratched his false beard as he slipped toward the trade docks. He had to be careful, even in disguise—it was somewhere just shy of suicidal for a Saint to hover this close to the Crowns' territory these days. But Clem's orders had been loud and clear—figure out what Wyatt Asher and the Harpies were up to. It would be pretty hard to accomplish that without leaving the southern dock.

A blast of salt air washed over him as he slogged north along the docks. He let out a soft breath. The Saints' docks were positioned inland, along the sludgy mouth of the Arden River, but the trade docks overlooked the sparkling waters of the Yawning Sea. So beautiful, so open, so . . . free.

"Gonna stare at the water all day, dumbass?"

Tristan blinked, stumbling back into the building behind him as a stocky man shoved past.

"Some of us have places to be," the man grumbled.

"Sorry, sir," Tristan said, but the man was already gone. He felt his pockets. And so were his fourteen coppers.

Curses.

He pushed himself back to his feet, then frowned as his hand caught on a slip of parchment nailed to the wood behind him. A notice. There were dozens of them—maybe hundreds—fluttering in the wind all along the trade docks, every few steps, each adorned with the image of a delicate ship pressed into deep purple wax. The Baelbrandt crest. A notice from the king?

Tristan tugged the paper from its rusting nail, teeth clenched. There it was. A sketch of a dripping axe blade. Someone had spotted Ryia the last time she had broken into the Bobbin Fort. The Butcher's crimes were finally catching up with her. All because Clem wanted to prove a point. Efrain Althea might be useless, but he was still Thamorri royalty. Baelbrandt would send the Needle Guard after her for this—or worse. Tristan shuddered at the thought of the king's Adept servants streaming through the streets, hunting for the Butcher of Carrowwick.

But he knew what Ryia would say. *You should have seen the notices they put up when I was in Fairvine*, or something of the sort.

He peered over his shoulder to make sure no one was watching before crumpling the notice into a ball and tossing it into the water. No sketch of her face, at least. But still, he would have to warn Ryia to be more careful. Not that she would listen. It was exhausting, honestly, caring so much for someone who seemed not to care for herself at all.

A bead of sweat wound a disgustingly slow path down the center of Tristan's spine as he settled into a shady corner. From there he had a clear view of Stitcher's Street, the invisible border between the Crowns' territory to the east and the Harpies' docks to the south. He leaned back against the building, pulling an empty crate in front of him like a table. Next, he pulled three battered, empty walnut shells and a small stone from his pocket, setting them on the crate.

"All right, step on over! Who's brave enough to test his sight against the speed of the infamous Falcon? How about you, sir?" He looked a tattered merchant up and down. "I think I can best you. I'll give you two-to-one on me, that's how confident I am. No? Well, how about you, ma'am?"

It might seem foolish to draw attention to himself when he was supposed to be spying on the Crowns, but in a place like the Lottery, the only way to blend in was to stand out. A quiet man was suspicious. A bustling man an easy target. But a loud, obnoxious fellow running an obvious scam? That was as good as invisibility.

The temperature rose in tandem with the blazing sun as he sat behind his makeshift table. Half a dozen sailors fell into his trap. He would let them win a game or two—just enough to convince them to bet more than a few coppers. Then he went in for the kill. And all the while, he was watching the length of Stitcher's Street, the constant thrum of bodies winding back and forth through the docks and alleys, waiting for some sign, some useful hint of what Asher and Finn might be up to. Or at least that was what he was supposed to be doing.

If Tristan was being honest with himself, he would have to admit that he was mostly eyeing the ships. They came into the harbor from all directions, waving flags of every merchant fellowship and kingdom. From the south came vessels bearing wine from Gildemar and spices from the far, vast kingdom of Briel. From the far north came furs and coal courtesy of the icy, mountainous Boreas, and ships bearing weapons for the Needle Guard sailed in from the neighboring Edale. He even thought he saw the sapphire sails of the Guildmaster's island tacking against the wind. Off to collect some Adept infant from one of the northern kingdoms, no doubt.

Tristan coughed, eyes flicking back down as he shuffled his shells around with deliberate slowness, allowing his latest mark to pick the correct one.

"Ah, you've got me this time. Care for another go?" Tristan slid a silver half onto the crate beside the shells.

The sailor puffed his sunburned chest. "I'm not sure you can afford it," he said. He tossed his own half onto the table, leaning forward on his knees to closely watch the shells.

Tristan smiled, showing him the stone before covering it with the centermost shell and mixing them around the table. Midshuffle, he lifted the back edge of the shell, stowing the stone in the palm of his hand before continuing. One of the other Saints, Roland, had showed him this scam and said Tristan had mastered it faster than anyone he'd ever seen. Now Tristan was easily the quickest hand at Shells in the whole syndicate. The sailor's eyes almost blurred as they struggled to follow the speed of it, but when the shells finally came to rest, his face split into a smile.

"That one," he said, pointing to the shell on his own right.

Tristan's eyes darted up as he saw a tall shadow slipping down Stitcher's Street. One of the Crowns, off to meet with the Harpies? No, just a Needle Guard making his rounds. He looked back to his mark. "Are you sure about that? I'm a fair and honest man. I'll give you one chance to change your bet."

"No, that one on the right."

Tristan sighed. "All right then," he said, pulling back the left two shells. In the same motion, he slipped the stone from his palm beneath the center shell. Of course, when he turned over the right shell there was nothing there.

He scooped up the pair of silver halves. The sailor gaped at the shells on the table, grabbing the other two and flipping them over himself, finding the stone underneath the center cover.

"Twice-damned dodger," he swore.

"You're more than welcome to try your luck again. Double or nothing? Tell you what, I'll even allow you to pick two shells for the price of one." The sailor lifted his hand in Ryia's favorite vile gesture, stalking away from the table. Tristan grinned at a nearby Needle Guard. "I guess not, then."

The guard didn't smile back.

Tristan shrugged, his gaze wandering up to the sky as a bird swooped overhead. A magpie, to be exact, winging its way toward a tall, stone-walled building on the edge of the trade docks. The one hung with the banner of the Messengers' Fellowship; a black-and-white pennant of a bird in flight.

The steadiest business there is, Father always used to say. Long after gold had lost its charm and men no longer had a taste for bread and wine, words would still hold their value. Messages would always need a way to span the five kingdoms of Thamorr.

The magpies swarmed the tower, black feathers on top, but where the white should have shone through on their stomachs were feathers the color of lilac. The color of Carrowwick, capital city of Dresdell, smallest of the five kingdoms. Leaving from the uppermost windows of the building were more birds, these far more interesting and varied in their color. Some had bellies of blue, others orange or yellow, each bird trained to fly home to one of the great cities of Thamorr.

Red-feathered birds had the farthest to fly, returning to Oryol, capital city of the snowy kingdom of Boreas, some four thousand miles to the north. The vivid yellow would be heading to Fairvine, along the southwestern coast of Gildemar, Dresdell's neighbor to the south. The birds arrived in great wooden crates, living in the tower of the Messengers' Fellowship until it was time for them to wing their way home with a letter tied to their leg.

Tristan looked bitterly at his wrist—the place where Callum Clem's brand lay, scorched into his flesh. Burned there the day he bartered his service for his life. Two snakes encircling a Saint's head like a halo. Just like those painted birds, no matter how far he managed to fly, that mark would make sure he would always end up right back here, in Callum Clem's pocket. After all his trouble, he'd escaped one prison just to end up in another.

"Who's next, who's next? You've got to have eyes like a hawk to beat the Falcon. I'm not sure you lot are up to it," Tristan mocked with a wink, juggling the shells and returning his attention to his assignment.

At the end of Stitcher's Street was the alley leading to the Upper Roost, the Crowns' massive apartment hall. Tristan could see some of the lesser Crowns flitting in and out of the alley . . . and not a single Harpy in sight.

The Harpies' sprawling stretch of dock lay to the south. It was just barely visible through the tight-knit structures of the Saints' territory, and from what Tristan could see, it was empty. Quiet as a temple to Felice. He pursed his lips, flicking a shell into the air and catching it on the back of his hand. Whatever agreement Asher and Finn might have, they certainly didn't seem to be advertising it. Maybe the rest of the Crowns didn't even know. Or maybe that Nash woman hadn't seen what she'd thought?

Another hour passed. Seven more marks. Two dollops of bird excrement dripped onto his shoulders from the sky. All he did was watch. Watch and listen.

"Two ships lost to the damned pirates on the Luminous," one shabby-looking man said to another.

"No fights in the Catacombs tonight?" a rough-voiced sailor griped. "Where'm I supposed to meet a lady?"

"Have you not heard've the Tail?" the scraggly man beside him remarked.

Hundreds of conversations bounced over his eardrums, but still no sign of Harlow Finn. Or of Wyatt Asher. Or of anything at all, really.

He sighed, pocketing his earnings. A generous amount of sweat had pooled along the waistband of his trousers. He had earned a total of six halves and twelve coppers and he had seen absolutely nothing. The information that Asher was keeping his new alliance a secret would have to be good enough.

Tristan pushed himself to his feet, casting one last look around the busy corner. Masts peeked from between the toppling structures to the north; Needle Guard roamed the streets, their boredom palpable. He wiped the perspiration from his forehead, careful not to remove his false eyebrows in the process. But he swore he felt the moisture freeze into a thousand tiny icicles on his skin at the sight of a familiar cloak slipping through the crowd.

A cloak he hadn't seen in a long time. The ones he had checked for over his shoulder every day for the past few months. The storm-gray cloak of a Shadow Warden. His stomach lurched. There was only one reason a man like that would ever wind up in a place like the Lottery.

They'd found him.

Tristan ducked his head into his collar. His wrists weren't clapped in irons, so they clearly hadn't seen him yet. He just had to keep clear of them. And keep Clem from finding out. If he knew who was looking for him . . . goddesses.

Forget his ninety thousand coppers of gambling debt. The bounty on him had to be ten times that figure.

Tristan darted down a side alley, quickly walking through brackish puddles without breaking into a full-out run. He knew he was heading deeper into the Kestrel Crowns' territory, but Wyatt Asher and his cronies were the least of his worries now.

His hands clenched into fists in his pockets, ears pricked, listening for the whisper of fabric on stone. How could they have found him? Had someone recognized him in this goddess-forsaken corner of this wretched city? It was all Clem's fault. If it wasn't for that son of a snake, he could be halfway across the Völgnich Mountains by now, two kingdoms away, holed up with some Borean fur traders.

He jumped half out of his skin at the sound of footsteps behind him. *Calm down.* Just a passing Needle Guard. He'd lost them. Surely they could never navigate these filthy alleys with his own ease. He kept one eye over his shoulder as he slunk around another corner. He just needed to find somewhere to lie low. Figure out exactly how much they knew about where he was hiding.

Then he crashed headfirst into a wall of hard muscle and charcoal-gray fabric. He paled, looking up into the face of a tall, sallow man.

To the average Dresdellan, he appeared to be a rather dour, rather wealthy traveler. A nondescript sword hung from his belt; a simple cloth doublet peeked out from beneath his sweeping cloak. But Tristan's eyes were not Dresdellan. He had seen these men in action before. The Shadow Wardens were the best of the best. Almost quick enough to rival the unnatural magic of an Adept Kinetic in a fight. Elite armed forces from the powerful kingdom of Edale, Dresdell's neighbor to the north.

Tristan braced himself as the man combed him over, waiting for the flicker of recognition to light those hawkish eyes. But there was none. Could Ivan's disguise really be enough to save him?

"Blimey, I'm sorry about that," Tristan said, sending a violently strong Dresdellan accent shrieking through his tone.

The Shadow Warden grunted, eyeing Tristan's mud-spattered clothing with distaste. Tristan's breath snagged in his throat as an iron-clad hand snapped onto his arm.

"You look like Asher's type. Where are the Catacombs?"

The Catacombs?

Tristan felt like he'd just been clunked on the head with something very heavy. Was it possible that these men weren't here to haul him away?

All he wanted was to escape from this conversation, but in this part of town giving away information for free was suspicious. Even the Shadow Wardens were bound to know that.

He forced a yellow-toothed smile. "You sods planning to make it worth my while?" he asked. "You look like you've got some gold tucked away there."

The man pulled his cloak aside, flashing the hilt of his sword. "How about steel?"

Tristan held up his filthy hands, backing away, eyes still averted. "All right, no need for that. Catacombs are that way, over on Flaxen Row." He pointed west with his chin. "Don't think there's a fight there tonight, though."

The Shadow Warden studied him carefully. Could he feel the veins in Tristan's arm, throbbing with the force of his fear-maddened heart?

At least a century passed before the big man finally released him. He turned in a violent sweep of his cloak, stalking silently out of the shadowed alley.

"Flaxen Row," Tristan heard the man's muffled voice say from around the corner. "But I doubt Asher'll be there if there's no fight. Tomorrow, maybe."

"Tomorrow?" another voice grumbled. "So we've got to stay the night in this filthy pit?"

Tristan held his breath, peeking around the corner.

"Unless you want to trust a message rat with this?" said the Warden Tristan had crashed into, waving a small roll of parchment in the other man's face.

Their voices faded as they both turned west, moving through the close-knit buildings toward the Catacombs.

Tristan sucked in a sharp breath of relief, smashing himself against the rotting walls of the building behind him and sinking to the ground. So they hadn't come for him. This time, at least. They'd just come to deliver some message. . . .

One too important for a bird to be trusted with, apparently—or a local scroll runner. A message for Wyatt Asher, of all people.

Tristan rose, dusting his grimy jacket distractedly as his brain struggled to stitch the threads together. Clem's newest game had just gotten very, very interesting. The Shadow Wardens were headed to the Catacombs tomorrow night. He ducked into the stoop of an old shop at the northern edge of the Saints' territory, pulling the false beard from his face and shedding his patchy coat. He ran his fingers nervously through his dark hair, trying to calm some of the tangles with still-shaking hands.

They needed to get someone into the Catacombs, which wouldn't be easy . . . but Tristan had a feeling Clem would risk it.

After all, if a dock rat like Wyatt Asher was in direct communication with the king of Edale, Clem was going to want to know why.

6

NASH

"Are you almost done?"

Nash had been sitting in this chair so long it was starting to feel like the seat was made of a thousand tiny needles. She knew their disguises would need to be good to get them into the Catacombs . . . but this felt like a bit much.

Ivan leaned forward, dabbing dark red paint onto her forehead. "I would have finished half an hour ago if you did not keep fidgeting like a *kindt*."

"A what?"

He leaned back to examine his handiwork. "A child."

Finally, Ivan was satisfied. He pulled a stained jacket from the back of the chair, tossing it to her. It reeked of stale whiskey and body odor. Nash held it out at arm's length.

"Felice, this smells even worse than my own jacket."

"Are you sure about that?"

Nash gave him a side-eyed glare, inspecting the jacket closer. It was dark gray and structured, made of old, beaten cloth that looked like it had been tied to a mainmast through a year's worth of summer storms. The left lapel sported a roughly stitched patch bearing a symbol anyone who sailed the coast of Gildemar was bound to recognize: a bearded skull with crystal eyes. The symbol of the Gildesh pirate, Salt Beard, and his crew.

"Have you gone mad?"

"What?" Ivan turned away, facing the gilded mirror and sweeping his hair into a tangled knot at his neck. The usual blond was gone, replaced by a reddish-brown hue that glowed in the light of Cal's chandelier.

"You think just anyone can get away with wearing this patch?" Nash had heard stories of lesser pirates who tried to fly Salt Beard's flag in order to intimidate their way into some easy scores. None of those stories had happy endings for anyone but Salt Beard.

"Anyone? No," Ivan said, smearing violent streaks of color over his own face with deft, practiced motions. "But I think I can. And by extension, so can you. You *do* want to get into the Catacombs tonight, yes?" He strolled past her, disappearing into the closet.

"You're awfully cocky."

"I prefer to think I am 'confident.'"

"What's the difference?"

"Trust me, Nash," Ivan said from the closet. "This is not my first day in this *verdammte* city. And look." He re-entered the room, dressed in worn boots, patched trousers, and a linen shirt ripped halfway to his navel. Nash averted her eyes from the cut lines of his pectorals. "All of my limbs are still attached, are they not?"

"Fine." Nash pulled on the jacket, throwing out her arms. If it would help get them the information they needed, she would wear the damn thing. "Happy?"

He looked her over one last time, sharp eyes flitting from the patchwork of scars he'd drawn on her face to the tattered clothes and empty scabbard at her belt. He turned away with a curt nod. "Very good. Time to go."

IVAN MOVED through the Lottery like a spooked cat. Bobbing, weaving, turning without warning. Nash sighed, lunging forward to catch up as he darted east, skirting the bustling Carrowwick Fair.

"The Catacombs are that way, you know that, right?" she asked, stiffening as they passed a stall selling illicit Adept with more brands on their cheeks than Wyatt Asher had fingers.

Ivan rounded another corner. "Are you going to question me all evening? That will become tiresome."

His eyes flashed, looking almost hazel now against his faux-bronzed skin. Just a few hours ago he'd been unmistakably Borean; now he passed easily for Gildesh. A lot of the Saints thought Ivan's only value was his ability to charm women out of their gold with his handsome face. Nash disagreed—Ivan was valuable because he had a thousand faces.

It wasn't exactly his fault every last one of them happened to be fucking flawless.

"Fine." She slung him a grin. "You're the expert in this shithole, I guess."

"That is not really news to anyone else."

"Maybe not. But if we're ever at sea, you'd better listen to—" Nash broke off, cursing and leaping backward as a shadow scrabbled along the gutter beside them, a half-molded morsel of bread clamped in its filthy teeth.

Ivan's stony face made its best attempt at a frown as he followed her gaze. Amusement flitted behind his eyes as he looked between the tiny rat and Nash's towering frame.

"What is this? The most fearsome smuggler on the Yawning Sea, afraid of vermin?"

"First off, I'm the most fearsome smuggler on *all* three seas," Nash replied, wiping her sweaty palms on her jacket. They came away dirtier than they started. "And I'm not scared. I just don't like the disgusting little shits."

"I see," Ivan said, lips twitching in concealed humor. "You are on a ship some ten months of the year—I would think you would be more than familiar with rats."

"The only things living on my ship are what I allow to live on my ship. And that doesn't include rats." Nash peered down at the gutter, but the creature had already scurried back to whatever disease-riddled hellhole it had crawled out of.

"Are you ready?" Ivan asked.

"Am I ready?" Nash gave Ivan a mock-pitying look. "This is hardly my first—"

"Just follow my lead."

Then, right before her eyes, Ivan transformed into an entirely different person. His usually somber face lit with a cocky grin, his hips sinking into a confident swagger.

"I am not here to lose tonight, Simone," he said in a lilting, Gildesh accent as he approached the pair of Crowns guarding the door. "So keep your bad luck to yourself, eh?"

Nash's hand twitched habitually to the knife at her hip before she remembered it wasn't there. No one without a Kestrel Crown tattoo made it within spitting distance of the Catacombs with a blade. Nash had never been much of a fighter in the traditional sense, but she still felt naked without an ounce of steel on her. Especially knowing Ryia was too busy tailing Tana Rafferty right now to swoop out of the shadows if they got in too deep.

How in the hells did Ivan look so calm? She bit the inside of her cheek. The information they obtained here had better be worth the years the stress was taking off her life.

The Crown at the doorway held up a hand as they approached. Marcus, was it? Or Matthieu? Either way, the man didn't appear to recognize her. Ivan's mask of scars had clearly done the trick. The patchy-bearded man distractedly patted them both down.

"Any open seat. They'll come round to take your wagers each fight," he said. He paused, eye catching on the patch on Nash's lapel, the matching symbol on the cloth tied around Ivan's wrist. "Don't start any bullshit."

"Us?" Ivan asked, drawing a hand to his chest. "Never."

The Crown rolled his eyes, waving them through the door. Nash followed Ivan into the smoky darkness.

She had never been inside the Catacombs before, but there were a dozen places just like it dotting the coast from Fairvine to Volkfier. The faces might be different, but the smells? Those were always exactly the same. The sharp tang of dried blood and rat piss washed over her as Ivan steered them toward a stained booth.

"We will have a good view of Asher from here."

"Where is he?" Nash breathed, craning her neck to peer over the cushioned benches set for the fighters' masters. There was no sign of the Kestrel Crowns' leader.

Ivan shot a meaningful look toward the back corner. There, shrouded in the smoke of half a hundred pipes, was an empty table.

"There's no one there," she said.

Ivan stared flatly at her. "Why should there be?"

"The first fight's about to start," Nash said, still carefully averting her eyes from the pit in the center of the room. "He's going to miss it."

Ivan's gaze turned to the pit as a whistle rang out. "He does not care if he sees the fights. As long as someone is losing, he is winning. Do not worry. He will be here. Once we see who he is meeting with, perhaps we will be able to figure out why."

Nash's stomach twisted as she finally looked at the pit herself.

Two Kinetics stood on opposite sides of the blood-spattered ring, clad in black-and-blue robes in moldering disrepair. Their clean-shaven heads were both marked clearly with thick, black *K*s, and mottled brands marred their left cheeks. The Kinetic closer to Nash looked like its face had been rebranded about five or six times. Unsanctioned trade of Adept servants was illegal in all five kingdoms . . . but then again, so was dormire's blood, and it looked like half the bastards in this place were high on the stuff. Even the Guildmaster had trouble extending his rule of law to places like the shadowy corners of the Lottery.

Kinetic fighting, on the other hand, was perfectly legal. And openly encouraged. The Second Guildmaster had outlawed wars between the kingdoms of Thamorr some three hundred years ago, so squabbles between kings were now solved in single combat, Kinetic versus Kinetic. No need to spill human blood that way. Though Nash was still on the fence about the idea that Adept didn't count as "human."

Any king to defy the Guildmaster's decree of peace and start a war—or, really, any king to piss off the Guildmaster in any way— would find himself cut off. No more trips to the auction. No more Kinetics. No more Sensers. It had happened to the last king of Boreas, Leonid Avendroth, some fifty years ago. Some said Avendroth had threatened war with Edale, others said he had threatened war with the Guildmaster himself. The truth was, no one knew exactly what the old king had done to attract the Guildmaster's wrath, but . . . well, a family called the Tovolkovs now ruled Boreas. The local rulers might like to play around like they had real power, but everyone knew the Guildmaster ran Thamorr.

Nash's heart surged halfway up her throat as she studied the second Kinetic in the pit. A female. Shit. Its complexion was dark as Nash's. But this one was so small. It couldn't possibly be Jolie . . . could it? Her sister would be six feet tall by now, no? Both Ma and Dad had been near giants.

Breathe, Nash.

"Tonight's first fight, straight from the Brambles, the backyard of King Descartes Devereaux himself, servant of Abel Chrysoux!" the Crowns' charismatic fight caller boomed from the center of the pit, gesturing toward the bulky male, dead-eyed at his left. A reedy-looking man—Abel Chrysoux, Nash assumed—waved from the crowd.

"And our challenger, belonging to Aedin *fija di* Sarwell of Briel, the terror of the western coast!" A bulky Brillish woman fidgeted in her seat a few rows down, eyes locked on her Adept fighter. The announcer flung his arms up. "Odds are four to one against the challenger!"

Half a dozen Crowns picked their way through the crowd, taking bets. The nearest one swaggered up to their table, jingling his pouch of coins. "What'll it be?"

Nash instantly recognized him. Owen . . . something. Vaguely handsome, if a little weasely. One of Tana Rafferty's favorite toys.

Ivan counted out a small pile of coppers, picking his teeth with his tongue. "Seventeen coppers on the mountain."

Owen chuckled. "Smart man. How about you?"

"Not as smart, I guess," Nash said. She pulled a silver half from her pocket. "One half on the little one." If she had to watch this bullshit, at least she could root for the underdog.

"A risk taker." Owen ran his eyes over her. "I like that."

"Keep on moving, *mincehom*," Ivan said, dropping the Gildesh insult as fluently as if it really were his home tongue.

The Crown's grin faltered at the sight of the symbol on Ivan's wristband. He gave Nash a final wink, walking away as the announcer's voice filled the tavern again.

"Last bets, folks! Don't be shy—you fuckers came to win some gold tonight, didn't you?"

The crowd cheered. Nash joined in, but her guts still swirled and clenched uncomfortably beneath her filthy jacket. Asher's booth remained empty. Damn it. She looked back to the pit. The fight caller blew his whistle again, and the two Kinetics sprang to life like a pair of hunting dogs. It was mesmerizing, the way they moved. Fluid. Unnatural. Almost too quick for the eyes to follow. The female dove forward, punching toward the male's chin. It ducked aside, reaching out with hands the size of cooked hams. The smaller evaded, leaping up to strike again before being pushed back.

The violent dance went on, and would continue until one of them lay dead on the floor. Kinetics were expensive, and fighting was risky. A loss could cost a trader hundreds or even thousands of crescents. But a win? A string of wins spanning the length of the coast? That could be lucrative. More than a few honest merchants had been known to turn once they got a taste for the pits.

"There he is."

Nash jumped as Ivan whispered in her ear. She noticed for the first time that his leg was resting against hers.

"Where?" she breathed back. Even with her head spinning at Ivan's sudden closeness, she wasn't dumb enough to look around.

He didn't answer, but Nash didn't need him to when she felt the shift in the room. The chill wind any good captain carried with him. From the corner of her eye, Nash could see him. Tall, thin as a rapier, dust-colored hair cropped neatly around his narrow face. And, of course, the kestrel that sat on his forearm. The bird's beady eyes darted around the room, looking like a bloodhound sniffing out a runaway.

The wind blew past as Asher stalked to the empty table in the back corner. He pulled a dead mouse from inside his coat and slipped it to the kestrel, who snapped it up eagerly, head bobbing as it forced the meat down its gullet. Disgusting? Yes. Surprising? No. If there was anyone in Thamorr who Nash would expect to walk around with dead rodents in his pockets, it was Wyatt Asher. Now they just had to wait until his mysterious new business partners arrived. Hopefully they would be able to sneak close enough to figure out what he was up to. . . .

"I am not sure I have ever seen you so uncomfortable before," Ivan whispered, so close his breath tickled her ear. His eyes continued to scan the room, no doubt looking for the gray-cloaked Shadow Wardens Tristan had encountered.

"Who said I'm uncomfortable?" Nash asked, pulling her leg away from his to clear her head. What was the matter with her? Ivan's tricks worked like a charm on giggling dock whores and simpering fools . . . Nash was neither.

"Your eyes," Ivan said. "Would you feel safer if your dear Callum was here?"

Nash couldn't stop herself from snorting at that. "Only an idiot would feel safer in that case."

"Probably true," Ivan mused, still scanning the crowd. "Though I have heard he has a soft spot for you."

"'*Soft* spot.' Not sure he'd like your choice of words, there," Nash remarked.

"So it is true, then."

It wasn't. "I didn't say that. You're smart. You know rumors are bullshit ninety-nine percent of the time."

"Yet you have never challenged those rumors before."

Nash flushed a shade as his eyes locked on hers. "Look, this city is infested with rats—most of them human." She eyed the room surrounding them in distaste. "What better to keep them off my back than a snake?"

Ivan's calculating stare flickered for a second, but before he had the chance to respond, the room sent up a loud roar.

Nash whipped around to look at the pit. The male Kinetic lay limp on the floor, blood surging from a vicious wound in its throat. A shiver went through Nash as she looked at the female. It had returned to its starting position, eyes flat and emotionless as the blood dripped thickly from its fingernails.

That definitely wasn't Jolie. Even if it was the same body that had been born as her sister. Now it was just a beast. A monster, even. What in the hells did the Guildmaster do to those infants once he carted them off to that island of his?

"And the risk pays off!"

Owen was back, dropping a small pile of halves onto the table. Nash scooped them up, pocketing them.

"That it does. Says something when the only one at the table with no balls has the most balls, eh?"

She turned to Ivan, but he wasn't paying attention. His eyes were locked over her shoulder, on Wyatt Asher's shadowed booth. As she turned her head to follow his gaze, Ivan suddenly kicked out with his foot, catching a passing freebooter neatly in the shin. The massive man stumbled, then spun to glare at them.

"Watch your fucking feet."

"Perhaps if you were not so . . . round, you could watch your own feet," Ivan said, exaggerating his fake Gildesh accent with every consonant.

Nash's eyes widened, and she turned slowly, shooting Ivan an incredulous look. Spying on Wyatt Asher required some serious blending in. Starting a fight with this walking brick wall helped them to do that . . . how, exactly?

"Say that again, peacock," the man challenged, uttering the slur for a Gildeshman. It had been as good as a death wish to use that word in the slum where Nash had grown up. Even now, all these years later, it made a chill creep down her spine.

Ivan was on his feet. And about half a head shorter than their new friend. Nash blinked as he poked the freebooter in the sternum with one finger, holding up his inked wristband and spouting a string of Gildesh curse words so foul even Nash's father would have blushed to hear them. The mountain of a man eyed Salt Beard's symbol. Three more men materialized behind him. Oh, this was not going to end well. She knew it was a bad idea to wear this fucking jacket.

"Marcel," Nash said, spitting out the first Gildesh name she could think of as she leapt to her feet, grabbing Ivan's arm. "We're going to miss the next fight." She widened her eyes meaningfully, hoping he got the hint.

Clearly, he didn't.

Ivan wrenched his arm away from her, lunging toward the first freebooter. He caught the man by surprise, shoving him back a step, toward the rear door.

"Looks like we're all gonna miss this fight," the massive freebooter rumbled. "Boys?" Suddenly Nash found her arms snared behind her back.

The Catacombs transformed into a multicolored blur as the four freebooters dragged her and Ivan past Asher's corner booth. There was another man sitting across from the Crowns' leader now. Dressed all in charcoal gray . . . If she could just get a look at Asher's new business partner's face, see who exactly he was meeting with . . . maybe they could salvage a tiny scrap of the job.

But it was too late. The wall of muscle behind her shoved her forward, pushing her out the back door and into the filth-strewn alley beyond.

"This ain't Golden Port—Salt Beard's name don't mean shit this far north," the giant man growled.

As someone who sailed all three seas, Nash begged to differ. There were Boreans north of Volkfier pissing themselves at the mention of the brutal pirate of the Yawning Sea.

"What's so funny, longneck?"

Longneck. Because she was tall. How original. Nash was about to tell him so when a flash of light burst on the ground at their feet. Firecrackers. All four freebooters leapt back, but Ivan dove forward. He grabbed Nash's wrists, and they both started to run.

"Time to go."

"You don't say."

"Follow me," Ivan said, looking back nervously as the sound of the freebooters' shouts drew closer.

"What in the hells does it look like I'm doing?"

"No, I mean . . ." Ivan pulled on his collar, then his sleeves. Buttons popped free, releasing a layer of carefully coiled fabric. Midnight blue. The exact same shade as the shadows on the docks. It flooded over his coat, rolling all the way until it hit the ground at his feet. He gestured at her, pulling a matching cap over his dyed hair.

Nash clumsily followed suit, nearly tripping over the new cloak as it spilled from the collar of her foul-smelling coat. Her heart hiccupped as Ivan grabbed her hand mid-trip, yanking her sideways down the street behind the Carrowwick Fair. A dead end. Everyone knew that.

Still eyeing the adjoining alley, Ivan pressed them into the shadows lining the walls of the long-derelict bakery at the end of the street. Nash's breaths flitted unevenly between her lips as she felt his body come to rest against her own. This was the closest she had ever stood to the disguise master. She could feel the heat of his skin, feel his heartbeat through his shirt. It was steady and calm where hers felt wild as the hoofbeats of a charging cavalry. The cavalry only charged faster as he pressed closer to her still, crushing them both against the wall.

They stood motionless in the darkness until one, two, three, four enormous, stupid pirates streaked past on the next street, barely giving their hiding spot a passing glance. When the alley was clear, Nash swallowed the fireflies flitting around inside her chest, shoving Ivan away.

"What the fuck was that about?" She pretended to peer around the corner while really hiding the flush that had come to her face. What was the matter with her?

Ivan faced her, his eyes cold and calculating as always. "I got it."

"Got what?"

"What we came for." Ivan peered around the corner, checking for angry freebooters, then set off at a smart pace, heading back toward the southern dock.

"What exactly would that be?" Nash asked, tumbling along in his wake. What could he have possibly seen or heard over all that chaos?

"An address."

Nash blinked. "That's it?"

"You clearly do not know the Butcher. It will be more than enough."

7

RYIA

Ryia had never thought of her line of work as "boring" before, but if that wasn't the right word to describe tailing Tana Rafferty, she didn't know what was.

She followed Tana from the merchants' quarter to the Carrowwick Fair, watching her whisper in the ears of merchants and laborers looking to earn one of the Kestrel Crowns' infamous coins. The nights were spent camped in the shadows outside the Upper Roost while Rafferty enjoyed some . . . quality time with a few of the other Crowns. Only one each night. And only men, Ryia noticed with disappointment. How dull.

She was just starting to tune out the rhythmic squeaking of the bedframe for what felt like the dozenth time when a man passed her. He bumped into Ryia with a wiry shoulder, muttering an apology before lurching into a nearby tavern. Ryia squinted after him, then looked down at the tiny square of parchment now clutched in her gloved fingers. Cameron—one of Clem's newer recruits. Someone needed to teach the bastard the fine art of subtlety.

Sinking into the shadows beside the Roost, Ryia unfolded the paper. Three words in Ivan's angular scrawl.

15 Second Spool

She popped the paper into her mouth, mulling over the words as she chewed. Second Spool was a street—northern tip of the merchants' quarter, up by the Needle Guard's barracks. Nice part of town. Not the kind of place Lottery rats usually met. Finally, something interesting to do.

First, she had to make it to number fifteen Second Spool before Wyatt Asher did, see who in the hells he was meeting with, and why. Next . . . well, that was where things got a little fuzzy. Quiet observation? Torture and intimidation? Every day was a dice roll with this job.

At this hour, the streets north of the Lottery were wrapped in sleep. Sprawling, elaborate houses lined a street that was dimmer than Nash's wits . . . with the exception of a single, winking window at the far end of Second Spool.

If that wasn't the place she was here to stake out, then she was King Duncan Baelbrandt.

She scaled one of the massive houses, careful to avoid the decorative spires she could only assume were there to impale birds in flight. Using the rooftops as her road, Ryia skittered down the dark street. She was less than halfway there when she paused, gritting her teeth. The house with the lighted windows was definitely 15 Second Spool. Because it reeked.

Not the usual stench of this disgusting city that the everyday nose could detect. It was an almost painful twinge in her nostrils, pulling her attention toward the stooped inn at the end of the road.

She crouched behind a black-shingled dormer, peering toward the inn. A shadow stood just beside the wrought-iron gate. A Kinetic. She swore under her breath as the Kinetic lifted his arms. The second-story window unlatched and opened, seemingly of its own accord. Not just any old Kinetic, then. No Disciple, either, but still, this Kinetic was a rare one—and powerful. Probably worth a small fortune.

Shit. Tristan was right. The Shadowwoods really must be involved here. The only question now was . . . what exactly were they involved in? With any luck, she was about to find out.

Leaning back against the dormer, Ryia combed through the pockets of her cloak. *Lemon balm, lemon balm . . . there.* Her fingers closed around the bundle of dried leaves. She put a few on her tongue, then rubbed the rest over her forehead, her arms, her chest. The leaves were generally enough to throw the average Senser's nose off, but her target had Kinetics that could open windows with their damn minds—his Sensers were probably strong enough to match.

Shit.

Ryia reached down, running her fingers gently over her various axes. Finally, she unbuckled the belt of throwing axes, shrugging out of the shoulder sheaths holding her long-handled hatchets. She solemnly stowed all her weaponry in the shadow of the rooftop.

"Sorry, loves. I really am. You'll have to sit this one out," she said. "I'll be back for you. Now, don't you give me that look."

She didn't like the idea of going anywhere without her hatchets. More times than she cared to count, they were the only thing that had stood between life and death for her. Or life and one of the filthy Guildmaster's Disciples. But if she kept her weapons on her, she might as well just waltz in the front door singing at the top of her lungs. Even the strongest Sensers had a weakness—one she knew all too well. Despite the rumors swirling around them, they couldn't read minds, or sniff out a cheat at a gambling table. The only thing a Senser could smell was physical danger. The intent to harm. Somewhere else, she might be able to trust in the chaos of a crowd to mask her own dangerous scent, but here on this lonely street she would have to be a bit more careful. Without her hatchets, she was less deadly. Hopefully that would be enough to let her slip past them.

Ryia looked at the inn, then to the street below. It was a long way down. And a long way across. But entering the inn from the ground wasn't an option—the skills she'd stolen from those Sensers all those years ago made that plenty clear. She'd have to hit the inn from above. Impossible . . . or it would be if she were an average person. But the Sensers weren't the only Adept she'd borrowed abilities from.

She leapt across the street, flying twenty-some feet through the air before landing on the roof of the inn. Pressing herself firmly against the rooftop, she crawled toward the edge, laying a practiced ear against the wooden slats. Nothing. No sounds of fighting or fucking or anything in between. That meant this mysterious target of hers had rented out the entire inn. And hopefully it meant she had beaten Wyatt Asher here. She still had time to get settled in for eavesdropping before the meeting began.

Shimmying to the edge of the roof, Ryia swung her legs over the side, dangling from the gutter like an icicle. She let go, landing gracefully on the narrow sill of the window the Kinetic had opened moments ago. She paused to make sure no one came running, swords drawn . . . then sank into a crouch, daring to peek into the room.

It was empty. A small bed was in the corner, its blankets rumpled. A decanter of wine sat on the bedside table, a lip-stained goblet beside it. A writing desk was positioned beside the window, papers littered haphazardly on its surface, all bearing the same looping signature. She couldn't quite make out the name from here. . . .

A familiar sound cracked the shell of silence shielding the quarter, and Ryia whipped her head back toward the street. The screech of a bird of prey. A kestrel, to be specific.

Ryia grabbed on to the peaked roof and pulled herself back up into the shadows of the gable. Asher. She braced herself beneath the roof just over the window as voices wormed their way through the inn toward her ears. Garbled and soft, like they were speaking underwater.

Then came the rusty creak of an old hinge, and the voices were clear as day.

". . . appreciate your discretion, Mr. Asher." Sniveling. Whiny. Ryia knew that voice—it had just been pleading with her for mercy a few days before. Efrain Althea. So that was who was staying here. Or at least hiding out when he wasn't inside the fort walls.

"I just hope this is worth my time, *Prince*," said a second voice. Raspy, yet somehow distinctly mucoid. Asher.

If there had been any doubt before, there wasn't any now. Efrain Althea was the only prince in the entire city, as far as she knew, since the Dresdellan queen didn't have any sons.

"You will want to watch how you address me, Mr. Asher."

Asher snorted. His beast flapped its wings, the ruffling of feathers wafting through the room. "In Safrona or Duskhaven, maybe. But you're in my city, Prince. You can bring as many fancy Kinetics as your dear brother-in-law lets you. It doesn't change the fact that these are my streets."

Only the oldest daughter of the queen of Briel had claim to the Brillish throne, but everyone knew Efrain was the only Althea child without claim to *any* throne. His younger sister was married to mad old Tolliver Shadowwood, king of Edale. Ryia poked her head down, sneaking a peek into the room. The men stood a pace apart, Asher tall and bony, Efrain distinctly round. Efrain stepped back, pouring himself a glass of wine so dark it looked almost black. He took a seat, waving the wine at Asher.

"Care for a glass? Finest from Doreur. Rich, cut with the sweetest plums of the spring harvest."

Asher gave Efrain a pitying look as he settled into the chair beside him. "I'm afraid I don't partake."

"Shame," Efrain said, swishing the glass from side to side the way only the most pompous of shits ever did.

"I'm surprised dear Tolliver approves of you supporting Doreur's vineyards," Asher said lightly. "I suppose it's the Gildesh in you that makes you partial?"

Efrain's head snapped up, looking like a child caught stealing sweets. He cleared his throat, pointedly setting his wineglass down. "On to business. You've ensured the cooperation of the Harpies as instructed, I hope?"

Asher's lips twitched. He reached his left hand into his pocket. Or rather, what remained of his left hand. Two lonely fingers and a thumb. The rest belonged to the Needle Guard now. A perfect illustration of the difference between Asher and Clem. Asher was a bold, reckless man. Clem . . . well, he still had all ten fingers.

Asher pulled a wriggling green shape from the pocket. A grasshopper. He held it out to the bird.

"Here, Sybaris."

Efrain wrinkled his nose as the bird ripped into the insect, tearing it in two with a sudden peck. Asher gave a haunting smile, rubbing his palms together.

"I have taken the Harpies under my wing. As *requested.* Though I don't see why it was necessary."

"We'll be needing their ships."

What?

Asher seemed similarly confused. He let out a braying laugh that was surely as deadly as Clem's smile.

"Ships? Are we going after the Ophidian?"

Ryia almost laughed herself. The Ophidian: mythical sea creature, sinker of ships, devourer of souls, all that bullshit. An old legend like the one about the gigantic ice bears the Boreans believed used to haunt the northern reaches of the Völgnich Mountains. Stories left over from the days before the Adept servants were servants at all, when magic was something to be feared, not bought and chained. Those days were long gone now.

"Oh, no, Mr. Asher," Efrain said, stone-faced. "Did my brother-in-law's men not tell you? Our target is a good deal more dangerous than that. But a lot easier to find."

Asher scratched his bird's chin. "Is that so? Where exactly might that be?"

"The Guildmaster's island."

Ryia nearly lost her grip on the splintery old wood. A shock of rage flooded through her at the mention of the bastard who had made her life a living hell for nearly a decade. The man who had witnessed her second birth, figuratively speaking . . . and who seemed pretty fucking determined to witness her death as well. For a moment she was drowning in memories of smothering darkness, surrounded by suffocating smoke and blistering flame, head spinning as the scent of danger seared her nostrils for the first time. . . .

Asher's derisive chuckle pulled her back to the present. "I beg your pardon?"

"The Guildmaster's island, Mr. Asher. The Guildmaster has something my dear brother-in-law is very interested in." Efrain leaned back in his chair. "You understand the political sensitivity of the matter. This agreement cannot be traced back to Edale, which is why he is offering you such generous paym—"

"To risk ending up in a cell beneath the Guildmaster's manor? Or losing my head? My entire operation? Two hundred thousand crescents is far from generous," Asher said flatly. "Tell Shadowwood I refuse. And tell him to lay off the dormire's blood while he's at it. Clearly the rumors are right—it's addling his brain." He moved to stand.

"Do not forget, Mr. Asher, you and your Crowns owe me."

"Yes, well, an iron coin can only buy you so much."

Efrain swirled the wine in his glass again. "Have it your own way. My brother-in-law is a generous man. I'm sure with some negotiating, I can get him to agree to raise that figure. Perhaps . . . double it."

Four hundred thousand crescents. That could buy an estate, a fleet of ships, an island off the coast of Boreas.

But Asher just laughed. "Have him triple it. He could promise me every crescent in the Shadow Keep's treasury, for all I care. A dead man has no use for gold."

Across the room, Efrain began to sweat. He pulled out a roll of parchment with near-dripping hands.

"Now, let's not be hasty, Mr. Asher." He unrolled it, flinching as the bird shrieked again. "This is all my king requires. An artifact of Declan Day."

"And what does your dear Tolliver want with some dusty old relic from him of all people?"

Declan Day, the world's most famous traitor. The man who ended the Seven Decades' War—the drawn-out fighting between those with Adept powers and those without—that had rocked Thamorr three centuries ago. He was a born Adept. The most powerful Senser in history. And instead of fighting with his fellows, he had joined with the ungifted, used his power to hunt down his own kind, and fit them for shackles and collars. Named himself the first Guildmaster of Thamorr. The Adept had been servants to the ungifted ever since.

"It's not my job to know what he wants with it, Mr. Asher. It's my job to procure it for him. Are your Crowns up to the task, or are they not?"

Asher moistened his lips thoughtfully as he stared down at the parchment. In the light, Ryia just barely made out a sketch of something on the other side of the paper. She could almost feel the gears turning in his head as he weighed his options: his life against a fortune and a madman's errand.

After a long silence, Asher set the scroll down on the desk just beside the window. Ryia pressed herself farther still into the shadows. "I'll have no use for a crown if I have no head to wear it on, Prince of Nothing," he said, storming across the room and wrenching the door open.

Efrain winced at the mocking title and chased after him. "I'd beg you to reconsider. I will be in the city until the end of Juna. If you would . . ."

The rest of the sentence was lost as the door snapped shut.

The lock clicked, and Ryia swung her legs down, landing on the sill. She was irritated with her hands for shaking as they grabbed hold of the scroll Asher had so carelessly tossed aside. An artifact of Declan Day, something to be stolen from the Guildmaster's island. Something King Tolliver Shadowwood wanted . . .

Her breath caught as she unrolled the scroll. A sketch, scrawled in charcoal. Not the original, just a copy, from the looks of it. Traced from some older document. There were at least two more copies of the sketch strewn on the desktop beside Efrain Althea's other belongings, now that she looked closer. The drawing featured a small device, about the size and shape of a writing stick. It stood on its point, hovering over a rough outline that was unmistakably the continent of Thamorr . . . a map. All around the drawing of the strange, ancient device were captions and notes in a looping language Ryia couldn't read. Old Dresdellan, if this really was Declan Day's work.

Efrain may not have told Asher what this device was for . . . not that Asher would have cared beyond what the thing was worth, but Ryia had a sickening feeling she knew what it did. For centuries, it had been a mystery how Declan Day had managed to root out all the Adept during the war. How he had captured them all.

How, even now, the Guildmaster and his Disciples managed to find every Adept infant in the kingdoms long before any sign of power showed itself in them . . . but there had always been rumors.

Rumors that the Guildmaster could sniff out every magically gifted human in all of Thamorr. Rumors that made no sense, given the actual nature of a Senser's powers . . . not to mention the fact that the current Guildmaster was a Kinetic. But they were rumors that Ryia had known for a long time must be true. How else would he have tracked her down in that goddess-forsaken corner of Boreas? Or that tiny village in the deserts of Briel? She had lived as a mercenary, a highwayman, a fucking *weaver*, for Felice's sake . . . but it had never seemed to matter how quiet she stayed or how far she ran. He always found her.

An artifact of Declan Day.

What if this ability was not a power of the Guildmaster's, but of this device? She studied the drawing again. A magical writing stick, filling the map beneath it with the location of every Adept in Thamorr? This was what he had used to locate her again and again. Ryia flushed with anger. She had been kept on the run for almost a decade by a *pen*? But that had to be it—what else would the king be willing to shell out four hundred thousand crescents to a piece of shit like Wyatt Asher for? He didn't just want this crumbling old relic—he wanted the Guildmaster's power. Not his magic, but his reach. After all, whoever controlled the Adept controlled Thamorr, that much had been true for over three hundred years.

Ryia didn't give two shits about controlling Thamorr. She wanted only one thing. *Freedom.* It was the only thing she had wanted for as long as she could remember. She had done a thousand terrible things to win it temporarily over the past nine years. She had stolen, lied, and killed more times than she cared to count. But now here it was, real freedom. A permanent escape from her life on the run from the Guildmaster and his Disciples—and the chance to completely fuck over the man who had destroyed her life for all these years—but she would have to go right into the viper's nest to get it.

She weighed the risks, then tucked the scroll down the front of her shirt. Her mind raced as she shuffled the papers around on the desk to disguise the missing copy. Clem would be interested in this job. She had no doubt he would be just as interested in showing up Wyatt Asher as he would be in the chance to earn four hundred thousand crescents. If the king of Edale wanted this device—this *Quill*—she didn't think he'd be overly picky about which criminal syndicate managed to steal it for him. Besides, Efrain Althea owed them a favor. If the Saints got the job done, the payout would be theirs to claim . . .

Or, at least, that was what she would tell Clem.

But there would be no payout. Not for the Crowns. Not for the Saints. Not for Tolliver Shadowwood.

She pulled herself back onto the roof before Efrain could return to his chamber, then paused, staring up at the night sky. She would have to run again when this was over, but this would be the last time. Her eyes glinted in the starlight as fear and vigor rushed through her veins in equal parts. It was settled, then. She would help the Saints find this Quill. She would help them steal it.

But then she was going to destroy it.

8

IVAN

I van had spent the past three years in Carrowwick. All this time
and he still could not understand why the air felt like it was
sweating. Smothering him like a knitted blanket, coating him until
his long hair felt soaked enough to wring out. He resisted the urge
to try as he cut east along Threader's Lane, making his way back to
the Saints' row house.

He had given Cameron the note for the Butcher nearly an
hour ago and had finally managed to shake the smuggler not long
after that. He liked Nash just fine, but he could not have shown
up to the Carrowwick Fair with a shadow. After dark was the only
time the best supplies were offered—and only to those proven not
to be Needle Guard in disguise. Sealing wax in the colors of every
noble house in Thamorr, rare poisons crafted from flowers that
only grew in the vast deserts of Briel, every type of illegal weapon
from slender pirate swords to Gildesh throwing stars.

His forgery kit had been running low for weeks now. But not
anymore. His trip to the Fair had been particularly fruitful tonight.
He patted the front of his coat, feeling the lumps of wax tucked

there. Cornflower blue—the color of the Darcrewe family. Clem's favorite to impersonate in writing. Wealthy enough to carry some weight with the merchants, not important enough to raise any unwanted questions. Now all that was left to do was head back home to the row house.

Scuff.

Ivan paused as the sound slipped past the lull of waves sloshing against the seawall beside Threader's Lane. Feet on stone. The Saints of the Wharf knew better than to lurk around in the shadows like cockroaches. Could one of the Crowns have grown bold enough to follow him here? The Saints had fallen far in recent weeks, but surely not so much that their own front doorstep was no longer safe. . . .

The lane was a dead end, but still . . .

He pursed his lips, eyes darting up and down the narrow street. Eleven.

Eleven possible escape routes. Twelve, if he felt like tossing himself into the river. Hopefully it would not come to that. The foot scuffed again, and Ivan turned on his heel, whirling around to challenge his less-than-stealthy visitor . . . but there was no one there.

Cough.

Just below his line of sight. He looked down. A *lochranz*. An urchin, no older than ten. He sighed. Scared of a child. Kasimir would have laughed himself into a fit. He winced at the thought.

"What is it?" The question came out harsher than intended, perhaps. But he already knew the answer when he saw the scroll tucked in the child's fingers. Of course. One of the Messengers' Fellowship's human magpies.

"I'm looking for Ivan Rezkoye?" the child said, his voice hardly louder than a whisper. He held the scroll as though he expected it to burn him.

"I will take it to him," Ivan said flatly, reaching out for the tightly rolled parchment.

The child drew back. "I'm supposed to deliver it directly to—"

"I do not care what you are supposed to do. You will give the scroll to me. Now."

The child flinched as Ivan grabbed the scroll from him. He turned the parchment over in his fingers. Who would be sending him a message by magpie? A foolish question.

Ivan's fingers trembled as he ran them over the scroll. It felt like charred flesh beneath his fingertips. Charred flesh and iron bars. The message runner was gone by the time he turned the scroll over in his hand, fingers gently brushing over the dark blue seal, the shape stamped into the wax. A shark's tooth. The mark of *Haisefven*. The Shark of the North and his resistance. His dear brother, Kasimir.

He had waited so long to see that seal. Sent his meager payments winging their way north in secret month after month, waiting to hear back from the *Fvene*, those still carrying on Kasimir's movement while he was imprisoned for the crime of challenging Boreas's tyrant king. Shooting a cautious look over each shoulder, Ivan pried the seal apart, squinting to read in the light of the half-hidden stars.

Ivan,

> *Sav den cilver. Den psen es veseln.*
> *Den Keunich sajt Haisefven necht friyleben.*
> *Haisefven echt tuerden am 7 Novebir.*
> *Gott weich nim; Gott gevt nach.*

▲

His heart battered against his rib cage as he read the words again and again, anticipation melting into dread.

Den Keunich sajt Haisefven nécht friyleben . . . What did the *Fvene* mean? The king said Kasimir was not eligible for release? The price of release had been set four years ago, based on the sum of his offenses. Did the throne of Boreas expect them to believe Kasimir had somehow committed another crime while under guard by the *medev*? There had to be a mistake. He cradled his neck in his left hand.

Haisefven echt tuerden am 7 Novebir. The line scorched into his vision, searing and smoking until the words were branded there. *Tuerden.* Dead. Kasimir was set to be executed the seventh of Novebir. Less than six months away.

So it had all been for nothing. All his work with Kasimir, and everything he had done since. Dissolved like snowflakes in the sea. Ivan may have saved his own neck by hiding out in this *pizhlache* of a city, but if Kasimir was to die anyhow, then what was the point?

He stuffed the letter into his sleeve, breezing into the row house. But no. The members of Kasimir's resistance, his *Fvene*, did not give in. Not until their last breath joined the cold Borean winds. He would not leave his brother to rot in the cells beneath Oryol. He just had to find something the vile *Keunich* wanted more than gold . . .

Preferably something besides his own body strung up on that mountaintop.

The house foyer was nearly empty, just Nolan and a few others playing dice in the corner. Ivan pulled his dyed hair from its tangled ponytail. It was a good thing there were few people to sense this frantic energy seeping from his skin. He would need to get that under control before Clem arrived. For the leader of the Saints was a shark too, in his own way. Just one ounce of weakness served as a drop of blood in the water. Since the incident with the Foxhole there was no telling how Clem would react to that weakness. Ivan did not have any intention of finding out.

He stalked to his chambers in the back of the house, pulling up a loose floorboard beneath his bed and stowing the scroll inside.

There. He eased the board back into place. Perhaps now that it was shut away, his thoughts would stop flitting around his skull like flies in a glass jar.

He traded his dirty pirate coat for a handwoven robe. As he walked to the bathing chamber to fill a bowl with fresh water, he felt a shift in the air.

The entire row house grew silent, the air taut as an Edalish bowstring. He moved to the sitting room and slouched against the windowsill, dipping his hair into the bowl of water. That could only mean one thing. After all, in the symphony of the Saints, Callum Clem was always an unexpected change in key.

Ivan watched the streaks of reddish brown swirl around the bowl like liquid rust, working his fingers through the rest of his long hair, pulling the color free. Already the blond began to show through. The dye was his own special mixture. Perfect for quick disguise changes . . . absolute hell when it rained.

"Good to see you've made it back in one piece," Clem said, striding into the room. "I trust you've caused no damage to my dear smuggler?"

Ivan shook the last bits of tawny brown from his hair and turned toward the window. "Nash is fine. Or she was, last I saw." He opened the glass pane, dumping the ruddy water into the alley beyond.

He wondered if what Nash had said was true: that the rumors about Callum Clem and his beloved smuggler were truly no more than just that. Where Harlow Finn and Wyatt Asher frequented the Lottery's brothels, Clem had always been a bit more . . . particular. Nash was the only woman he had allowed into his bed in all the years Ivan had been in this city. And if they were not involved . . . perhaps the Snake of the Southern Dock simply had no interest in such things.

Clem nodded, making his way across the room toward the desk in the far corner. It was covered in an assortment of papers the Needle

Guard would find most interesting. A carefully organized collection of ledgers, agreements, and contracts. A sum of Clem's business dealings, more illegal than not. He placed a crisp slip of parchment on the leftmost pile, straightening it until its edges were perfectly flush.

Ivan threw his sopping hair behind his shoulders. He settled into a decaying armchair in the corner, pulling his latest project toward him. The disguise was a new challenge. A structured piece, swaths of purple and gray fabric stitched together, a panel of fine Carrowwick lace just over the heart. When he was done, it would be indistinguishable from a true Needle Guard uniform. Getting caught wearing it would be as good as suicide, but Clem did not seem to care for things like caution any longer. Only time would tell if that would be the Saints' salvation or their destruction.

No matter how calm the Snake appeared on the outside, Ivan could see through the illusion. The man was becoming unhinged. It was only a matter of time before his desperation to regain his status caused him to do something truly terrible.

Clem turned from the desk, fixing him with his piercing gaze. "The job?"

A dangerous question. A dare. Ivan pulled a stitch of gold threading tight. "The Butcher is tracking down Asher's contact as we speak."

"Good. When should I expect her?"

Before he could respond, another energy shift rocked the house. Nolan's braying laugh echoed through the walls. Strained. Oversold. Like he believed if he did not laugh hard enough, he might be punished. With the Butcher, that was not impossible.

Ivan pointed toward the doorway with his chin, pulling another stitch through. "Now, it would seem."

If Callum Clem was a change in key, the Butcher of Carrowwick was a dissonant chord. Out of place. Alarming. Powerful. Ivan did not miss the disgust with which Clem looked at the mysterious mercenary from Briel. And lately, the fear. Ryia was on borrowed time. She was useful for now, but the moment her threat exceeded her usefulness she would be gone, just like all the others before her. Clem never had a second-in-command. Anyone who came close was as likely to find themselves at the bottom of the Arden as they were to get a pat on the back.

It seemed he had not forgotten how having a second had worked out for Wyatt Asher all those years ago.

Clem turned back to the desk, filtering lazily through the neatly stacked scrolls as the sound of footsteps echoed down the hall.

"Come to bring me more fingers?"

Ryia paused at the foot of the stairs leading to Clem's apartment, changing directions to enter the sitting room instead. Her face twisted into the wolfish grin that gave the poor Beckett boy heart palpitations. "Sadly, no. Just information. But I think you'll find it nearly as satisfying."

Clem looked up. "Dare I hope your confidence actually matches your worth, for once?"

"I know what the Crowns were up to."

The Snake turned to the cold fireplace, struck a match, and coaxed a fire to life despite the already sweltering temperature of the room. "Allow me to guess. The assassination of one of Shadowwood's rivals?"

Ryia shook her head, lowering herself into the lumpy chair across from Ivan. She seemed . . . frantic. Ivan could not put his finger on why. Her posture was as relaxed as ever, but she was vibrating with an unexplained energy. "Theft."

Clem was silent for a long moment, staring into the fledgling flames. "Theft? Do you mean to tell me there are no thieves in Duskhaven?"

Ivan considered the question. It was a good point. Why would the king of Edale send his envoys all the way to Dresdell to hire a thief?

"It's a matter of . . . political sensitivity," Ryia said, propping her feet up on the rotting table in the center of the room.

Clem eyed her filthy boots with distaste. "Isn't it always?" He returned to his desk, lifting a ledger, seemingly at random, and looking it over with glazed eyes. "Who is this sensitive mark?"

"The seventh Guildmaster of Thamorr."

"The seventh . . ." Clem blinked. It was the first time Ivan had ever seen him struck speechless. He cleared his throat, cracking his most dangerous smile. "Then it looks as though Felice has smiled upon me. The Crowns are finished. My dear old friend will be dead before the summer is through."

"There's the bad news."

"How so?"

"Asher didn't bite."

Clem blinked again. "So the Kestrel Crowns are up to . . ."

"Nothing, anymore." Ryia leaned back. "Which leaves one job wide open for the taking."

"Tell me, Butcher"—Clem's fingers tapped the edges of the ledger, a musician keeping time—"why did Wyatt turn down this job?"

"I seem to recall him saying something about it being awfully difficult for dead men to spend their crescents."

"For once, I must agree with the man."

"Your call. But I think a dead man might find a way to spend this many crescents."

Clem was silent for so long that most would have assumed he had not heard, but Ivan saw the slight twitch in his nostrils, the madness sparking in his eyes. He knew it was only a matter of time before he asked the question.

"How many crescents?"

Ryia slid a fingernail between her front teeth. "Four hundred thousand."

Inconceivable. What in *Yavol's* realm could be worth a sum that massive? Ivan's eyes flicked to his chamber door. Toward the floorboard where he had stowed the scroll. If King Tolliver wanted something badly enough to pay nearly half a million crescents, what might the *Keunich* of Boreas be willing to trade?

The life of one traitor, perhaps?

"For what?" Clem asked, his face guarded, his eyes bursting with renewed interest.

Ryia pulled a crumpled piece of parchment from her cloak. Tongue pressed between her lips in apparent concentration, she smoothed it out on her leg.

"Some dusty old relic." She leaned forward in her seat, stretching to hand the paper to Clem without standing. "Asher's contact is our mutual friend Efrain Althea."

"A dusty old relic . . ."

Ivan could not see much from his chair, just a few lines of notes scrawled hastily with far too much ink, but he did not miss the look that crossed Clem's face. He was too distant to hear it, but he was quite certain the Snake's heart rate had just tripled, sending the hints of a flush creeping out of the neckline of his impeccably starched shirt.

It was gone an instant later as he lifted a hand to his immaculate beard. "What kind of relic?"

"He didn't say, but what the hell do we care? Four hundred thousand crescents. You could buy the Bobbin Fort from the damned Baelbrandts with that kind of coin."

Even more so, Clem could build his own *verdammte* fort with that kind of coin. Buy every disorderly house from here to Golden Port. Bribe every last member of the Needle Guard to look the other way when the Saints came to call. All he needed to do was leverage Efrain Althea into hiring them for the job . . . a simple enough task.

Clem tapped one finger on his desktop. The Snake of the Southern Dock was always calculating. Profits, people . . . here he was calculating risk.

Secretly, bent over his stitching, Ivan was doing the same.

Stealing from the seventh Guildmaster of Thamorr was suicidal. As was stealing from Callum Clem. He bit the inside of his cheek. Was he bold enough to do both? If he had to cheat death this time, Kasimir would not be there to pull him from the fire . . . but if he did nothing, his brother would never be there to pull him from the fire again.

"And how would you suggest we go about stealing this prize from the most secure fortress in Thamorr?" Clem drawled. "Without finding ourselves locked in the Guildmaster's dungeon or sinking to the bottom of the Luminous Sea, I mean?"

Ryia flipped a throwing axe around her fingers with frightening dexterity. "I'm not the mastermind here. I just gather the information—you can do whatever the hell you want with it."

Clem turned back to his desk, pulling a map toward him. Smuggling and trade routes were traced onto its surface in dizzying loops of colored ink, spiraling through the three seas, and up and down the length of the Arden. He traced a finger along the eastern coast, to the Luminous Sea beyond, to the Guildmaster's island, nestled just off the eastern coast of Edale.

"Our problems begin with our arrival," Clem said. "Thamorri ships are not permitted to make port there. And we can hardly pass a mainland ship off as one of their own."

He was right. The island was a stronghold. The only vessels permitted to dock belonged to the Disciples of the Guildmaster, narrow sloops used to fetch Adept infants from the kingdoms of Thamorr.

Ivan still remembered the fear in the eyes of every new mother in Nordham each time those vivid blue sails appeared on the horizon. Those ships were unmistakable. Unmatched. Trying to imitate one would not get them far.

But what other option did they have? The island was impenetrable. Giant cliffs, jutting hundreds of feet above the crashing waves, according to the stories. The only landing was the harbor, guarded day and night by Disciples—the Sensers and Kinetics the Guildmaster deemed too powerful to sell off to the mainlanders. The ones who stayed back on the island to train the young wards. The ones who would someday be up for the job of Guildmaster themselves, when this one died. They could never sneak past forces such as those. Unless . . .

Ivan looked up. "What about the auction?"

The Guildmaster's auction. The sale of the oldest of the Guildmaster's wards to their new masters. The ships docking at the island would undoubtedly be searched, scoured by Sensers. The nobles in attendance would be walled in by Kinetics. There would be thousands of prying eyes to see them, instead of just a few hundred Disciples and students. In short, stealing something would be nigh impossible . . . but at the auction, they would at least have a chance at getting their feet on dry land.

Ryia scoffed. "Because it's not like the nobles on this shit continent all know each other or anything."

Clem's eyes were no more than slits. "We wouldn't need to be nobles. Just merchants wealthy enough to garner an invitation."

"You expect gutter rats from Carrowwick to blend in in a place like that? We'd stick out worse than Asher's ring finger. And how will we ever find that tiny relic on an island none of us has ever been to?"

Clem's lips curled into a lethal smile. "You said it yourself. You just gather the information. It's my job to make use of it." He turned back to the desk. After a long silence, he looked up. "You may leave."

Ryia disappeared down the hallway, no doubt heading for the Miscreants' Temple.

Clem snaked out of the room without another word, mounting the stairs to his apartment. In the instant before he disappeared into the shadows, Ivan caught his expression. It was one of a fox that had hunted for one mouse and instead caught two. He was already plotting, then. A dangerous thing, to be sure. But so was Ivan.

His blood alternated violently between boiling hot and icy cold as he stitched in silence, sewing the Baelbrandt crest into the right breast of the uniform.

Gott weich nim; Gott gevt nach. The last line of the letter.

Gott takes away; Gott gives again. It was an old northern saying, one Kasimir had adopted for his resistance. Ivan had said the words over and over again, spoken them by way of greeting and parting, lived and breathed them . . . but in all this time he had not really believed them. For his entire life, he had only witnessed the first half of that saying, had only seen all the things Gott took away. Now he understood why.

Gott gevt nach. Boreans were a hard people. Their deity was the same. Gott would not hand him the things he wanted most—such as his ticket home. His brother's freedom. Victory for the *Fvene* and the people of Boreas over *Keunich* Andrei Tovolkov's regime of terror.

If Ivan wanted it, he would have to take it.

He tightened his grip on his sewing needle, squeezing so hard he nearly bent it in half. He just had to find the nerve. . . .

The tattoo hidden on his scalp seemed to burn with the thought. The one that matched the symbol on the wax seal of that horrible scroll.

One more job. One more job, and Kasimir could be free.

9

EVELYN

Of all the disgusting things a body could produce, vomit had always been Evelyn Linley's least favorite. Not that she was fond of the others, but after years of training and living in close quarters with twenty-odd men at a time, she'd become numb to the rest. For some reason vomit had never lost its . . . charm. Which was bloody unfortunate, considering her nose was only inches from it.

The acidic smell filled Evelyn's aching skull, dragging her from bleak dreams. Before she was even fully alert, her stomach turned again. She rolled across the splintery floor, spewing another vile mouthful to her left. It burned her throat, leaving behind the taste of regret and misery. She wiped her lips on the back of her hand, blinking as she sat up, her head spinning like a top.

The shutters were tightly drawn, the lamps extinguished, but she could sense the sun blazing brightly outside, could feel its heat baking the room. In just a few hours' time, it would be as hot as the fort kitchens in this tiny room. But what did she care? Evelyn ran her hands over her long face, pushing the tangle of unkempt red hair behind her ears. She grabbed a half-empty bottle of *stervod* from the floor. Hopefully, she would be piss drunk again by then.

She hesitated as the sound of raised voices echoed dimly from the alley below her window. The bottle hovered an inch from her lips. In a pisshole like this, shouting was nearly always followed by shoving, maybe a few punches. If no one stopped the gits, blades would be drawn, and the gutters of Leech Alley would run red.

She looked at her sword, crooked on the floorboards where she had tossed it two days before. Her fingers twitched, unconsciously reaching for the familiar, well-worn hilt. . . . Then she ground her teeth, tilting the bottle upward instead, letting the Borean liquor numb her from the inside out. Let the gutters run red, then. A few days ago it would have been her problem. Now? Her only problem was finding the bottom of this bottle. Then the next. Then the next.

Funny how simple life became once it fell completely to shit.

And all because of the Prince of Nothing. Efrain bloody Althea. Because the queen's idiot nephew couldn't keep himself out of trouble for a two-month visit to the fort. Because of one measly finger.

Evelyn cast the bottle aside, the aggressive burn of *stervod* mixing with the already delightful smells of vomit and filth. Twelve years of training. Nineteen years of Father's meticulous planning, bled dry in a blink. She'd gone from the youngest Needle Guard captain in a century to retching in some Lottery hovel in the span of one night.

The king had stripped her of her title. Her armor. Her bars and honors. Dismissed her from the Guard the moment the Butcher slipped their nets. Not a slap on the wrist. Not a demotion. A full dismissal, after years of perfect service. She scrubbed a hand over her face again. If the Brillish prince's Senser hadn't sounded the alarm quickly enough to catch that fiend, how in the hells was she supposed to?

The other guards had been waiting to see her fail for a long time now. Their sneers had been nothing but predictable, but her trip home to the Linley estate? That was where she had started to crumble like day-old toast. Father had turned her away at the door. *Only those contributing to the future of the Linley name shall be allowed into the estate, and that no longer includes you, Evelyn,* he'd decreed.

He was right, of course. Father had spent hundreds of his hard-earned crescents on her training, so she could rise through the ranks of the Guard. To ensure she would be named Valier, join the king's personal guard, pull the Linley name into the ranks of nobility.

She thumbed the ring circling her middle finger, bearing the Linley family crest, the image of a crossed crescent and quill. She knew she wasn't fit to wear it any longer, but she couldn't abide taking it off. *Shite.* She punched the wall beside her. Evelyn had singlehandedly taken her family's ambitions and sent them rushing down the Arden with the daily refuse. She would do anything to take it back. But there was nothing she could do. Nothing but drink and wait to die.

Evelyn felt around for the bottle of *stervod*, now dripping its contents onto the floor a few steps away. Just as she tilted the bottle upward, the sharp rap of knuckles echoed on her door. She pushed herself to her feet with a groan. The floor swayed beneath her. When Evelyn reached the door, she paused, one hand resting against the rotting wood. In this part of the city, it was as good as suicide to fling a door open unarmed and half-pissed.

She opened the door, and there, in the dingy inn hallway, stood a man a few inches shorter than her, blond hair cropped neatly against his skull, vivid blue eyes crashing like sunlit waves in their sockets. He was dressed entirely too well for the Lottery, that was for sure. Fine leather shoes, well-fitted trousers, and a thin black doublet. He could have passed for a merchant. Maybe even a minor lord. The stranger extended a hand, giving a smile that sucked every last speck of warmth from the room.

"Captain Linley?"

"If you thought that title still belonged to me, you would never have come looking for me here."

His smile widened. A street dog baring its teeth for a fight. "A fair point."

Without waiting for an invitation, he prowled into the room. The man sniffed the air, obviously unoffended by the odor. He seemed to revel in it, if anything, eyeing the puddles of sick and empty bottles with satisfaction.

"How did you know I was here?" she asked. Evelyn hadn't told anyone where she planned to go. Hadn't known herself until she'd stumbled down Leech Alley a few days ago, drunk and bleeding from a tavern fight she could hardly remember.

"The same way I knew you had been dismissed from the guard. Turned away from your family's estate?" He tutted softly. "To cast out their own flesh and blood . . ."

She narrowed her eyes. "Answer the question."

The man spread his arms. "This is my city, Captain. As her ruler, it is my job to know everything that happens within her walls."

A seed of deeply planted loyalty bloomed in Evelyn's chest. "Duncan Baelbrandt the Second is the ruler of this city."

"But of course he is."

Evelyn pushed her hair back again, trying to convince it to stay behind her shoulders. It didn't listen. "Are you going to tell me what you want, or should I be reaching for my sword?"

"What I want?" The man lifted a hand to his breast as though shocked. "It hardly matters what I want, Captain. Not to you, at least. No, I've come here to discuss what you want."

"That's none of your business."

He reached into his pocket, removing a small scroll. "I'd like to make it my business."

Evelyn's eyes widened to the size of dinner plates as she unrolled the parchment, catching sight of the seal at the bottom of the page. Purple wax. A Dresdellan galleon, fitted with sails of lace. The Baelbrandt family crest. And the writing above . . . unmistakably the hand of King Duncan's scribe. She had grown up surrounded by his whorls of ink, the way his letters leaned slightly to the right, the tiny loops on the *G*s and *Y*s. Sparing a suspicious glare for her visitor, she began to read:

> *By order of the King of Dresdell, Duncan Baelbrandt the Second, His Majesty and Lord of the Bobbin Fort, the criminal known as the Butcher of Carrowwick is called for arrest. Any Guard or citizen who manages to succeed in his capture will be rewarded with a Valiership. In the name of Felice and Adalina, and the Duality of the Heavens.*

"It would seem our beloved king wants the Butcher quite badly. Something I think you and he have in common."

Evelyn glared at the man through red-rimmed eyes. She rolled the parchment, wagging it in the man's face.

"Where did you get this?"

"The voices of kings carry all the way down to the gutter, Captain," he said. His pleasant smile plagued her spine with a thousand spiders. "I've brought it here to show you that you can still get what you want. So you believe me when I tell you I can give it to you."

Her heart stuttered. "And why would you do that?" She studied him carefully with her chestnut eyes. "I know all about you."

"Hardly."

"The Butcher is your barking dog, *Clem.*" She watched his angular face for signs of surprise. There were none. But he did nothing to deny it.

"Dog? No. I prefer to think of the Butcher as my sharpest sword. Undoubtedly useful . . . but even the best blades can be sold. Traded for something better when the time comes."

"Traded?" she repeated slowly. "What do you want?"

Clem lifted a hand, scratching his thin beard. "Your assistance, Captain. In return, the Butcher is yours."

"Explain."

"Guidance," Clem said, crossing the room and examining a cracked vase in the corner with apparent interest. He waved his fingers with a flourish. "Information."

Evelyn's freckled fingers tightened, crushing the scroll. She might be beaten, she might be an outcast, a failure, a burgeoning gutter rat, but she was no traitor. She would never sell Dresdell's secrets—especially not to a weasel like Callum Clem.

"I'm not giving you shit on the Needle Guard. Or the fort. Or the royal family. I might be disgraced, but I still have some sense of honor." She thrust the ruined scroll back into his face. "You'll have to find another drunken mess to play turncoat, I'm afraid."

Clem laughed, the sound of ice scraping against the hull of a ship. "You misunderstand, Captain. I have no interest in such things." He strode back to the door.

"What exactly is it you're looking for, then?"

His hand on the doorframe, Clem looked over his shoulder. "Just an invitation to a rather exclusive party."

Evelyn blinked, confused.

Clem turned the knob. "I must be going, Captain, really—as I'm sure you know, I'm a busy man." He cast a final look around the dingy room. "But if you tire of . . . this . . . I trust you know where the Miscreants' Temple is? Nine in the morning. Tomorrow."

Without another word he was gone, leaving Evelyn alone in the fetid darkness, the king's scroll clutched in one hand, a half-empty bottle of *stervod* in the other.

IO

TRISTAN

Tristan woke to find a small pool of sweat in the hollow of his chest. He sat up, pushing his lank curls out of his eyes and stretching his stiff joints. He winced as his knee painfully popped. The straw mats on the attic floor of the Miscreants' Temple were not exactly Edalish featherbeds, but he supposed it was better than sleeping in the gutter.

Across the attic, a few other Saints too lowly to have a room at the row house were already chattering, undressing after a long night's work.

"You know what would go with this ale?" Roland said wistfully, sloshing a half-full mug. "A nice bowl of tuna and mint stew." He sighed, pulling his tattered begging costume off over a belly that Tristan's mother would have said looked like it didn't need any more stew.

"If you're so homesick for Linway, why don'tcha just go back?" mocked Cameron. He was a twitchy boy, maybe two or three years younger than Tristan, his face perpetually smeared with dirt.

"Fuck off, Cam." Roland pulled a half-soiled shirt over his

shaggy head, eyes falling on Tristan. "Ah, the Saint of Soaps is finally awake." He thudded across the room, thrusting the lukewarm mug into his hands. "Morning pickup?"

Tristan looked down at the cup with a curled lip. Ale. No doubt already sour with the heat. Not to mention that it was no later than nine o'clock in the blessed morning.

Only vagrants and Gildeshmen find their cups before noon, Father's voice sneered in his head.

Tristan upended the cup, pouring a large gulp of ale down his throat. Definitely sour. It was an effort not to retch.

Cameron frowned. "Saint of Soaps?"

Roland flopped a beefy arm across Tristan's shoulders. "That's right—you weren't around when this one washed up on our docks. Showed up on a ship of freebooters out of Stornburg. Filthy sons of bitches. Stank up the Temple for a week, but not this one. This one was clean as the day he popped out of his mam's hole."

Tristan thought about pointing out that babies were actually pretty disgusting when they came out of their mothers but decided against it.

Roland dropped his voice to a stage whisper. "Tried to cheat Clem outta near two hundred crescents."

Cameron's mouth opened into a perfect O. "And he's still alive?" He stared at Tristan as though he was expecting him to topple over dead at any moment. But of course, Cameron had been raised on these streets. Grown up hearing of the terrors of the ruthless Callum Clem and his Saints of the Wharf. If Tristan had as well, he wouldn't have tried to cheat the man.

Or at least he would have been more careful about it.

Tristan forced a smile, ducking out from Roland's arm. "I'm still alive."

"But how? Why?" Cameron still looked like someone had just told him Boreas was a made-up land filled with mythical creatures.

"Isn't it obvious?" Tristan said. "Because I'm the best there is."

Roland scoffed. "If you was the best there was, you wouldn'ta been caught."

"What does that make you, Roland?" Tristan teased, wagging his hands in front of the man's face, flaunting all ten fingers. Roland only had seven left. Made him awful slow with the cards.

"Now *you* fuck off," he grumbled with a laugh, settling on the nearest cot. "I—"

But he stopped short as a tawny head poked itself into the rafters. Nolan. "Clem's pulling together a meeting in the back room," he said, his voice a wheedling rasp.

Tristan blankly stared at him. "So what, you want us to clear out?"

He had only seen the back room of the Temple once—the time he had nearly lost his head. That was more than enough for him. When it wasn't being used to interrogate cheats or shake down crooked merchants, it was reserved for Clem's inner circle, the highest ranking Saints.

"No dumbass, you're supposed to go to it." When Tristan didn't respond, Nolan rolled his eyes. "Go ahead, take your time. Clem's a patient man." He disappeared back down the creaking ladder.

"See how many fingers you've got after this," grunted the Roland-shaped lump of blankets beside him.

THE DOOR to the back room was simple. A slab of unadorned wood, stained flat black and set with a tiny brass knob. Most wouldn't even give it a second glance—Tristan certainly hadn't on his first trip to the gambling house. Not until he was being hauled through it, at least. Dragged inside and thrown to the floor in a bloody mess at Callum Clem's feet.

What did Clem want this time? His head spun as he recalled his close call with the Shadow Wardens the day before. Tristan had been so careful when he told Clem about them . . . about how they were looking for Asher. So careful not to show his hand, not to give away the original suspicion that they may have been there for Tristan. This had to be about something else . . . but what?

Before he had the chance to second-guess himself, Tristan reached out, knocking twice. He winced as the door creaked open, steeling himself to meet the gaze of Callum Clem . . . but for the second time in near as many days, he found himself greeted by the towering form of Nash the smuggler.

"You're just in time," she said.

Tristan edged past her into the room. The door shut behind him. "In time for what?"

"Who the fuck knows."

Enlightening.

"Do not be such an *arsch*, Nash," said another familiar voice. Tristan looked across the low-lit room to see Ivan lounging on a stuffed chair.

Nash flashed him a hollow grin, her unnaturally sharp canines standing out against the dark golden hue of her cheeks. "Not all of us take a death sentence as well as you, Mr. Rezkoye."

"It is not a death sentence," Ivan said flatly. "It is a job."

A job. Tristan rubbed his palms together nervously. "Who's the mark?"

The silence that followed was so tense Tristan could feel the dead air vibrating against his eardrums.

Then: "The seventh Guildmaster of Thamorr."

Tristan's eyes grew wide. So that was what the Crowns were after. It had to be.

"Good luck with that," he said, taking a seat diagonal from Ivan.

The Borean fixed him with a stare. "You had better hope we have good luck. You are coming with us, *yunger*."

"I'm—what?" he stammered.

Nash leaned against the wall, seemingly determined to stay as far away from Ivan as possible. "What did you think you were called here for?"

Tristan's nerves gave way to a smile. "You expect me to believe Clem thinks the Guildmaster will be fooled by my card tricks?"

Nash shrugged. "Maybe he just thinks your prissy ass will help us blend in at the auction."

Tristan's forced smile slid from his cheeks, his mouth running dry.

This *was* a death sentence. The Guildmaster's island was a breeding ground of Adept, crawling with wards and the dangerous, sharp-minded Disciples who taught them—and that was just on a regular day. For the auction, they also had to worry about the brainwashed, branded Adept servants that would be brought from the mainland, accompanying their masters. And if those unnatural beasts weren't enough, there were always the guests themselves. . . .

To sum up, he'd be trapped on a two-square-mile island with a few hundred of the deadliest creatures in existence, and all the men who had spent the last few months scouring Thamorr for him.

"How does Clem expect to get into the auction?" He chose his next words carefully. "I've heard that island is teeming with Sensers."

In his memories, Tristan could see them. Standing beside every king and queen. Roaming up and down the smooth steps, slipping between neatly placed chairs. Their shaven heads glowing in the southern sunlight . . .

"And Kinetics," Ivan added. "There are bound to be. But when have you ever seen Clem reveal his plans?"

"Not even to you?" Tristan asked, looking at Nash.

Before she had a chance to respond, the door banged open. One of Clem's bruisers, a massive Saint by the name of Brendan, shouldered his way inside. His stringy black hair hung into his eyes as he dragged a shadowed form in by the wrist.

Ivan rose fluidly to his feet. "For Gott's sake, let her go, Brendan." He pulled a measuring tape seemingly out of nowhere. "She is not some ship rat you caught cheating dice. She was invited here."

The shadow shook free of Brendan's grip, stalking into the room like a wary cat. Tristan could practically see the woman's hackles rising as she turned in a circle, taking in each of their faces. She was tall and wiry, muscles built for speed rather than power, a controlled braid of bright red hair piled on top of her head. Her face was dotted with freckles. *Spots of Adalina*, Father would have said, voice dripping with disdain. The marks of hard work done outside.

She spied Tristan, her nose scrunching up in vague recognition. Like she had seen his face before but couldn't quite place it. He looked away.

"Lift your arms, Captain," Ivan said.

"It's not 'Captain' anymore," the woman said. Her voice was rough, as though she either used it far too much or not at all.

"Evelyn, then," Ivan amended, winding the measuring tape around her waist, then her hips.

"What are you measuring for? A bloody casket?"

Nash grinned. "I like this one already."

Evelyn turned, studying Nash like the smuggler was something unpleasant she had just stepped in. The door flew open again.

"All right," griped a voice Tristan would recognize anywhere.

Ryia looked more disheveled than he had ever seen her, her hair a wispy black cloud around her narrow face, cloak hanging haphazardly off one shoulder, Brillish namestone dangling loose on its leather strap.

She wagged a hatchet at them, the razor-sharp bit flashing in the lamplight as she spun it lazily around her thumb. "Who wants to tell me what dear Clem found important enough to interrupt my leisure time?"

"What does a scut like you do for *leisure*, I wonder," spat Evelyn. Her lips were drawn back in distaste, her spine so rigid it looked likely to snap as her eyes darted from Ryia to her hatchet and back again.

Ryia cocked her head to one side, running her tongue over her teeth as she looked Evelyn up and down. "I can show you if you'd like," she said with a wink. She shot an appreciative look at Nash, pointing at Evelyn with her chin. "Who in the hells is this?"

Nash picked absently at her fingernails. "How should I know?"

"She is our ticket into the auction."

Tristan stiffened at the new voice. As always, it reminded him of leather-soled boots treading on the soil of a graveyard. Quieter than a breath of wind, more threatening than steel being drawn. Everyone present turned as Callum Clem swept into the room.

"What?" Evelyn burst out.

Ryia snorted. "That instills confidence."

"You never said anything about going to the auction," Evelyn said.

"No one is going anywhere just yet." Clem settled on the hard wooden chair beside Tristan, lacing his fingers together and draping them over his knee. "I have just spoken with our dear friend Efrain Althea and made the appropriate arrangements."

Evelyn's face scrunched up in evident surprise. "Such as?"

"The kind that get us paid," Clem said.

"By whom?" Evelyn asked.

Clem paused, and for a moment Tristan was certain he was going to lie. But then he replied, "Tolliver Shadowwood."

"The Mad King of Edale—how did you lot get involved with that filthy warmonger?" Evelyn said.

Tristan suppressed a wince. King Tolliver had a bit of a reputation in Thamorr these days. Perhaps that was because he insisted King Descartes Devereaux had kidnapped and murdered his eldest son, Dennison Shadowwood . . . despite there being less than a single shred of evidence. Aside from the missing son, of course.

Rumor had it Tolliver had killed his own son in order to ignite a war with Devereaux's kingdom, Gildemar. Take over their gold mines. But rumors were rarely truth.

"That is not your concern," Clem said smoothly, his calm demeanor a thin veil hiding the brimming impatience and energy beneath.

"If it affects the kingdom of Dresdell, it is my concern."

Clem smiled, his hidden madness threatening to peek through. "If that is the case, then it truly is not your concern. This matter is between Tolliver Shadowwood and the Guildmaster. Are you satisfied?" He waited a moment. Evelyn said nothing. "All right then. Now, before we can begin our plans, I need to confirm some suspicions I have, and for that I need some information. Maps, to be specific. Blueprints. You know what I am referring to, I'm sure. And where they're kept?" Clem's grin widened as Evelyn stubbornly buttoned her lips. "I thought so."

"What makes you think I'll tell you?"

"Because you're here, Captain," he said. "And because if I don't get my prize, you don't get yours."

Tristan looked between them, but of course Clem did not elaborate. He fixed Evelyn with his most paralyzing stare. A snake about to strike.

She hesitated for a long moment, evidently wrestling with herself, then set her jaw. "Fine."

Clem leaned back, dusting an imaginary flake of dirt from his trousers. "Excellent."

Across the room, Nash gave a cough of irritation. "The redhead might know what you're talking about, but the rest of us sure as hell don't. Where are we going?"

"Needle Guard barracks," Clem said, his eyes never leaving Evelyn's souring face. "Captain—or, excuse me, *Miss* Linley can get inside, I am sure."

"I'll get your ruddy maps. As long as you use them to commit your crimes *outside* Dresdell."

Tristan noticed Clem made no such promise. The Snake simply said, "Once those are in hand, we can truly begin. But you are all here because I will need your skills for what I have in mind."

"Can't you tell us now?" Tristan blurted out. His stomach dropped to his knees as Clem's eyes bored into his. *What plan could possibly include me?* was the real question he wanted to ask.

"All in good time, Beckett. But I daresay we will have use for those quick fingers of yours. And before you ask, if you are not willing to use them for this job . . . Well, perhaps you will need to say goodbye to them altogether. That goes for all of you."

"Yeah, yeah, we hear you. Help or be maimed," Ryia interjected. "We should really look into formalizing that as our motto."

There was a tense silence where Clem and the Butcher glared at each other Finally, the Snake broke eye contact and said, "Nash, if you wouldn't mind? A few details."

Tristan let out a long breath as Clem's shadow disappeared from the room, Nash close behind him. The meeting was over, then. And Tristan felt as though he had learned . . . nearly nothing. Except that Clem was getting more insane by the minute. He had survived the Lottery for so long by being smart—cautious. That was his reputation. How in Adalina's name was gallivanting off to the auction to steal from the most powerful man in Thamorr either of those things? Clem had finally cracked.

Ryia suddenly clapped her hands, and Tristan jumped half a foot in the air.

"All right then." She looked innocently to Evelyn. "When are we going?"

Tristan half expected the entire Temple to burst into flames from the force of Evelyn's glare.

"*We?*"

Tristan didn't recall ever meeting this Evelyn woman before, but as straitlaced as she seemed, she certainly carried that sword like she knew how to use it. And Ryia . . . he'd seen her in action plenty of times. If blades were about to be drawn, he wanted no part of it. He closed the door behind him, leaning against it as Ryia's rasping laugh echoed from the far side of the splintered wood. Maybe it was finally time to run. Steal one of Ivan's costumes and make for the southern border, lose himself in the forests of Gildemar.

As Clem had hinted earlier, Tristan had initially stayed in Carrowwick because he felt strongly about keeping all his limbs attached. Since then, he may have found another reason to remain with the Saints . . . a sharp-tongued, hopelessly beautiful reason.

Leaving Carrowwick would mean leaving Ryia.

He clenched his fists, shoving his way through the Temple. Even putting his feelings aside, as much as he hated to admit it, he needed Clem. Needed the Saints' reputation. Otherwise a scrawny thing like him wouldn't have lasted a fortnight in a place like this. And without so much as a handful of coppers to his name, places like the Lottery were all he was likely to find. His vision flickered, his breaths rapid. He just needed some air.

The back door to the Miscreants' Temple snapped shut behind him as the thick, humid air of the alley washed over him. His step off the stoop was cut short as a bulky, hooded man crashed into him, knocking him into the gutter.

Tristan sputtered, but before he could push himself to his feet, he felt a hand on his shoulder. A silent threat. *Stay down*. Tristan shivered despite the heat as he felt the tickle of breath on his ear.

"Tired of working for the Snake yet?" the man asked, his voice a buzzing fly in the wind.

Tristan opened his mouth, then shut it again stupidly.

The man gave a knowing laugh, then slipped a folded letter

into Tristan's muddied fingers. "A better offer for someone with your background."

In the instant before the man pulled his hand away, Tristan caught sight of the small tattoo marking his left thumb. A kestrel skull. The *Crowns* had a better offer? Why?

Then his eyes fell on the letter itself, and the world faded into a senseless blur. There, inked neatly onto the crisp parchment, was a name Tristan hadn't seen in months—had tried his best not to even *think* since slipping aboard that pirate skiff on the Rowan River.

His head spun like he'd had one too many cups of wine. By the time he looked up, the hooded man was already gone. Tristan's mouth grew steadily drier as he flipped through the possibilities, each one flashing before his eyes like the pages of a book.

The Crowns knew who he *really* was. Which meant they knew who was after him. He unfolded the letter with shaking hands. There it was, spelled out in fresh ink. They knew his secret—and they wouldn't keep it quiet for free. Tristan owed the Crowns a favor. He crumpled the letter, shoving it into his breast pocket.

Tristan didn't know what they would ask him for, or when they would ask for it, but he did know one thing—there was nothing he wouldn't do to keep Wyatt Asher from spilling his secret.

II

RYIA

"Is that really necessary?"

Ryia peered over her shoulder at the disgruntled former captain as the pair stalked through streets filled with the gray, hazy light that came just before dawn. "Is what really necessary?"

"That strut?" Evelyn tossed back her fiery hair, thrusting her chest up and stepping in a terrible imitation. "For Adalina's sake, you look like a Gildesh show horse."

Ryia waggled her eyebrows suggestively. "Might ride like one too—care to find out?"

"Ugh" was all Evelyn managed to articulate. A vein in her long, pale neck twitched as she balled her fists.

Ryia grinned. It was too easy to rile this one—almost no sport in it at all. She cracked a knuckle. "So, are you going to tell me where I can find these maps, or am I just making this up as I go along?"

The captain's jaw twitched, but she still kept herself in check. "I'm not letting you within a block of the Guard's base if I can bloody help it."

"Well, you can't bloody help it," Ryia said, mimicking her

strong Dresdellan accent. "Not if you want whatever Clem promised you." She laughed as Evelyn ground her teeth to stubs. "If you want something from the Snake of the Southern Dock, you have to play by his rules. Ask Tristan what happens if you don't."

Ryia pulled one of her throwing axes from her belt, miming a quick slice across her own throat. Evelyn's hand twitched toward the needle-thin sword at her waist.

"Bit jumpy for a guard, aren't you?"

Evelyn pursed her lips. "From what I've heard, relaxing around you means losing a finger or two. You're very dangerous to defenseless, sleeping sods, aren't you?"

"If my marks happen to be sleeping when I stop by, that's their problem, not mine."

"Spoken like a true, honorless thug."

Ryia's eyes suddenly lit with recognition as she looked the ex-captain over. She threaded the axe back into its leather sheath midstep. The crabby, redheaded guard from the fort—the one she'd easily given the slip in the courtyard. "Were you sweet on him, Evelyn? Old Efrain Althea? Pay him a few nighttime visits on your rounds?" She winked, indicating the elaborate ring circling Evelyn's middle finger, bearing a crest of a crescent and quill. "Did he give you that, there?"

"Even if I had an ounce of attraction to the Prince of Nothing, I would never sully the integrity of my station like that." The captain glowered at her, stuffing her ringed finger into her pocket and picking up her pace. "If you had even a shred of morality, you would understand that."

"Oh come on, don't you ever have any fun, Captain?"

"Don't *you* ever shut up?"

The exasperated look on Evelyn's face when Ryia said nothing in response was priceless.

The silence between them stretched until they could see the

Needle Guard barracks silhouetted against the thick clouds to the east, just outside the southwestern wall of the Bobbin Fort. Ryia appraised the sprawling structure. Crawling with guards and guards-in-training, but not a single Adept within an axe throw, from the smell of it. Why did Clem think they needed the captain? Ryia could have pilfered these maps single-handedly, even if she had no idea where they were.

Though already she had to admit Evelyn's advice on the timing had been helpful. The hour just before dawn—the overnight watch was tired, some drunk. As long as they could get in and out before the bells rang and the morning watch took over, there would be no need to silence anyone. She snuck a look at Evelyn out of the corner of her eye. She didn't know what Clem had offered the captain to make her turn her cloak, but Ryia doubted she'd turned far enough to run a sword through her fellow guardsmen just yet.

"All right, Captain," Ryia said, "which way in?"

Evelyn rolled her eyes, looking pointedly toward the open archway to the training yard. "Exactly how many options do you see?"

Ryia eyed the flat stone wall rising like a crashing wave in front of them. "Thousands."

"You expect me to believe you can climb that?" the captain said stiffly. "How?"

"Maybe I'm half-squirrel," Ryia said mysteriously.

"Slow the jokes, Butcher."

"For all I know, I'm not joking."

Evelyn glared at her. "What is that supposed to mean?"

Ryia lifted her namestone, letting it spin on its leather strap. One side was blank, the other engraved with a series of complex symbols. In Briel, everyone wore a stone like this; one side carved with the names of the mother's lineage, the other side with the father's, written in Old Brillish. If Ryia's namestone were real, the blank side would mark her a bastard.

"Well, I'm all human," Evelyn said. "So we'll be using the doorway. They won't expect it. Your everyday idiots aren't thick enough to try to waltz into the building that houses every armed guard in the city."

"But we're not your everyday idiots, are we, Captain?"

"No. We're worse."

Evelyn ducked through the open gate, snaking through the barracks and training yards. Ryia kept one eye on the captain and the other on the paling sky as they darted from shadow to shadow, cutting across a courtyard toward a turretlike structure. Two purple-clad guards roamed around the tower in listless circles. Ryia couldn't see the rings under their eyes from this distance, but she could tell from their posture that they were there—the poor bastards were exhausted. The whiff of danger wafting off them was almost weaker than the smell of stale piss on the wind.

They bolted toward the door to the tower as the guards passed, griping quietly about how their comrades had gotten leave to go to the Satin House.

Blackness clawed at Ryia's eyes as the door whispered shut behind them, only the barest hints of the pale, predawn light streaking in from narrow windows that may have been archer slits in the days before the Guildmaster banned all war. Evelyn struck a flint, holding it to a long, thin candle. As the light filled the room, Ryia had to admit that Clem had a point in recruiting Evelyn's help after all.

The inside of the tower was one large, spiraling staircase. One end wound straight up and out of sight above them. The other snaked down below the ground. And every inch of the curved walls was covered with books. Some were leather-bound tomes thick enough to knock a man senseless. Others were skinny things, bound in the thin paper of Briel. Shelves were piled high with scrolls, either dusty and yellowed with age, or looking so new the ink might still be wet. No apparent rhyme or reason to any of it.

But Evelyn seemed to know exactly where she was going. She slipped down the staircase, eyes darting from side to side, like she expected the books to come alive and ambush them. Ryia hid a deep breath, eyeing the descent into darkness with distaste. Of course it had to be under the fucking ground.

"What is all this shit?" Ryia asked, flicking a scroll with calculated flippancy as she forced herself to follow.

"Show a little respect. This *shit* is the records of the throne of Dresdell."

Ryia cleared her throat, trying to ignore the weight of the dust and mildew creeping into her skin. "What are they doing here? Shouldn't they be inside the fort?"

Evelyn lifted her nose another inch into the air. "This is the most secure place in all of Carrowwick."

Ryia blankly stared at her. "Clearly."

"There are more guards inside these barracks than anywhere else in Dresdell. You'd never have gotten two steps inside that archway without my help."

"I've been giving your Needle Guard pals the slip for over a year. Now, if there were some Adept here . . ."

"A well-trained guard is worth ten of those dead-eyed beasts." Evelyn held out her left hand as they rounded the final curve of the staircase, spilling into the basement below. A vicious, knotted scar cut across her palm. "Assassination attempt on Princess Bellamy last Januar. Dozen bloody Sensers in that throne room, but I was the one who stopped the blade." She bristled. "Something you'd think the king would rank higher than his worthless nephew's finger."

Evelyn walked her own fingers along a row of scrolls, pulling a few loose.

"The harbor . . . the island . . . arena . . . manor . . . there they are. That should keep that snake of yours happy," she said, moving to stow them inside her coat.

Ryia snared her wrist. "Not so fast, Captain. I need to make sure Clem's getting what he asked for."

"You think I'd lie to you?" The captain sounded indignant.

"In this line of work, it's safest to assume everyone is always lying," Ryia said, unrolling one of the scrolls. "Something you might want to remember now that you're one of us."

"I am not one of you," Evelyn said. "I will never be one of you."

"If you say so." Ryia pompously shook the paper out, studying it at arm's length.

She was getting claustrophobic just looking at the damned thing. Of course, that might be the basement pressing in on her, forming moist shackles of darkness around her ankles and wrists. . . . *No.* She pushed the thought away, focusing instead on the inked lines on the parchment. She had heard that the island was small, but this was minuscule. Just over a mile and a half from end to end, according to the markings.

The only passable waters were to the south, the heavily guarded harbor the sole place port could be made. But that didn't matter anymore. They'd be going in as merchants, whether that was suicidal or not. Ivan was already working on their disguises, Nash and her crew already cleaning the smell of piss and dormire's blood from her precious ship. What mattered now was finding the Guildmaster's Quill once their feet hit dry land . . . and then ending the reign of that bald-headed son of a bitch once and for all.

Her eyes flicked over the buildings sketched on the parchment in fading ink, taking in the layout of the Guildmaster's infamous island for the first time. There were five in total. Two sets of barracks along the eastern cliffs, one for Kinetics, one for Sensers. The Guildmaster's manor and its infamous dungeon tucked along the northern peninsula. The auction and tournament arena to the west. The massive bell tower in the thick-walled courtyard just off the arena's southern edge.

"Were you planning on memorizing the blasted thing?"

Ryia arranged her face into a grin before raising her head. "I—" she started. Then she froze, nose pointed toward the stairs like a hunting hound on the trail.

Danger. The tower was suddenly rank with it.

"Get down!" she hissed, diving behind a bookshelf so old it looked like it might collapse at any second.

"What?"

"Get down! And put that candle out. Now! Unless you're no longer interested in keeping that head of yours."

"Are you threatening me, scum . . . ?"

Evelyn trailed off as the door to the tower creaked open above their heads. She dove to the ground beside Ryia, snuffing the candle out against the filth-encrusted floor. Phantom images swam before Ryia's eyes as the stagnant air faded to near blackness. She could almost hear the rattling of chains . . . could almost feel the metal biting into her flesh . . . taste the thick, warm salt of blood as the cup tilted toward her mouth . . .

Pull it together.

"Watch change?" she asked Evelyn.

"You'd better hope not. Because if it is . . . *shite*." Evelyn's sentence dissolved into a gasp as the distant sound of a bell clanging echoed down the stairs.

"What?" Fresh guards might be a little bit of a challenge, but nothing unmanageable.

"Remember those Adept you were missing before?"

"Oh, terrific," Ryia whispered. "How many?"

"It'll be two of them, if the schedules are still the same. Sensers. They sweep the whole barracks every watch change."

"And you didn't tell me this before . . . why?" Ryia asked, rummaging through her cloak pockets.

She could feel Evelyn's glare in the pitch-darkness even though she couldn't see it. "If you hadn't taken a bloody decade down here, it wouldn't have been an iss— What the hell is this?"

Evelyn broke off, obviously confused as Ryia thrust a bundle of lemon balm into her hands. Ryia crushed a few leaves between her teeth, cringing at the taste. "Chew them."

"How is munching a handful of leaves going to help anything?"

"Just do it." Ryia edged around the bookshelf, holding her breath as light seeped into the basement chamber from the stairwell.

Evelyn's lips curled in disgust at the flavor of the lemon balm. She raised one eyebrow in a silent question as the light filled the basement. Ryia shook her head, putting up one finger. One Senser, lantern in hand. No sign of the second. Yet.

The Senser drifted, almost dreamlike, into the basement. His eyes were blank, his face slack, nostrils flaring with every step. It was always unnerving to Ryia just how brain dead the real, island-broken Adept were. His robes were spotless, shining silk . . . but he wouldn't care if they were made of burlap. Or poison ivy, for that matter. Once an Adept was fully trained, they would stand blankly at attention as their master slit their throat if he wanted to. She had seen it firsthand. But now was not the time to dwell on such memories.

Ryia waved Evelyn furiously forward as the Senser disappeared behind one of the shelves to the right. Outside, the bells were still tolling. They had less than a minute before every guard in this twice-damned city was awake and milling around the courtyard outside. Ryia had faced worse odds, sure . . . but still, that was an awful lot of trouble to go through before breakfast.

Evelyn crept past her, chomping on the leaves like a cow chewing its cud as she mounted the stairs. The Senser's lantern light bobbed between the bookshelves below as they tiptoed up the dusty staircase. Still holding her breath, Ryia eased the tower door open, waving Evelyn through. Moving as swiftly as freshly loosed arrows, they bolted through the shadows, slipping out the arched doorway and back into the city.

Ryia savored the scents of seaweed and raw sewage as they flooded over her. The too-moist breeze. The tang of sea salt. Anything but the suffocating stench of mildew and cobwebs. She spat her half-chewed lemon balm on the ground. Beside her, Evelyn did the same.

"So, that's your trick, then?" she asked, looking toward the mashed leaves. "Where'd you learn that?"

Ryia forced a smile, pushing away the image of the Senser's lifeless eyes and listless stride. "Secret of the trade."

"Have it your own damned way. I have no interest in learning any trade of yours anyways." Evelyn patted the scrolls nestled in her pocket to make sure they were still there. Or maybe like she couldn't believe they were there—like she couldn't believe what she had just done. "Robbing the records . . . robbing the damned Guildmaster. You lot are bloody insane. And stupid."

"Insane I will gladly give you, but stupid . . ."

"Risking your lives for, what? A few crescents? Yes, I'd say that's stupid."

"You haven't been in the Lottery that long, Captain. The Saints are already last in the pecking order these days. With the Crowns and Harpies all snuggled up, it's only a matter of time before we start washing up dead on the shores of Golden Port."

"So you're all just trying to get yourselves killed instead of waiting for Asher to do it, then?"

"Maybe."

"Fine by me. Anything that gets a few more Lottery scum off the . . ." Evelyn trailed off mid-sentence, gaze locked over Ryia's left shoulder.

"What's the problem, Captain?" Ryia grinned, turning to find a ragged piece of parchment tacked to the doorframe beside her.

A notice, written in grandiose script, set with the seal of the king. An arrest notice—the same one Ryia had seen fluttering from every corner of the docks since the night she had visited Efrain Althea.

"By order of the King of Dresdell, Duncan Baelbrandt the Second, the criminal known as the Butcher of Carrowwick is called for arrest . . . blah, blah."

So, the king of Dresdell knew her name now, or at least her title—so what? *The Butcher* was only one of her names, anyway. She had many. Evelyn squirmed, obviously nervous to be spotted in the company of such a horrible criminal as the Butcher of Carrowwick, but Ryia truly could not care less. King Duncan was about as threatening as a kitten compared to what else was hunting her.

She turned to the captain, gesturing toward the image of her signature axe blade drawn just above the notice. "The king's sketch artist is absolute shit. Doesn't look a thing like me."

Evelyn wasn't amused. "You don't take anything seriously, do you?"

"This is practically a love note compared to the flyers I got in Gildemar."

They skirted a carriage with the shutters drawn tight. "You don't understand anything. Do you realize your little stunt has soured relations between Dresdell and Briel? Because of this—because of *you*—we're on the brink of war for the first time in three centuries."

"And?"

"Seriously?" Evelyn rounded on her. "Goddesses, you're impossible. Duncan Baelbrandt would tear these docks apart to find you. And he should. After what you've done, you should be rotting in a cell under the Bobbin Fort right now. Even Callum Clem won't be able to save you from the whole Needle Guard."

There was a long silence. Finally, the disgraced captain snapped, "What?"

"Oh, nothing, Captain."

But it was not nothing. Ryia folded the arrest notice, tucking it neatly into the pocket of her cloak. Evelyn had just unwittingly handed her a way to make sure Clem did not accompany them on their voyage to the Guildmaster's island.

A wicked smile spread across her face as they slunk back to the Southern Dock. Perhaps it was time to see just how far Duncan Baelbrandt would go to avenge his dear nephew's finger.

12

NASH

If there was one thing Nash hated, it was waiting. It made her skin crawl, kept her glancing over her shoulder, though she was never really sure what she was worried she'd find back there. But here she was, stuck in the row house, waiting for nightfall.

It had taken only two days to prepare the ship for the journey to the island. Tonight they were set to leave for the auction—and not a moment too soon. The auction was to start in less than three weeks. In perfect weather, it took a little over two weeks to sail that far south, and this time of year the weather on the Yawning Sea was far from perfect. If they left tonight, they would make it with a day or less to spare, by Nash's estimate—and Nash's estimates were rarely wrong.

Cal had packed a bag and set it beside the door before heading out to check on some side business or another a few hours ago. Evelyn had been off the hook ever since she and the Butcher returned with those maps early this morning; Nash doubted they would ever see the ex-captain's uptight ass again. Ivan had left moments later to stock up on supplies at the Carrowwick Fair. Nash's crew was loading provisions onto the *Seasnake's Revenge*; the Butcher was off doing whatever the hell she did, probably with the Beckett boy mooning after her. Someone should really stop that poor, lovesick fool before he got hurt. Literally.

The door to the row house flew open, banging against the wall with a shudder. Nolan, coming back from the tavern again, no doubt. *Damned drunk.* Nash made to stand, but froze when she found half a dozen Needle Guard charging through the open doorway instead.

"What in—" She stopped short as a slender rapier blade tickled her throat. She eyed the Needle Guard calmly. "How can I help you . . . gentlemen?"

She counted. Seven Needle Guard crammed into this ragged pile of driftwood. Nash might be able to hold her own in a tavern brawl, but against trained soldiers? She wasn't too proud to admit when the odds were shit.

"We are here by order of the king," answered the nearest guard. He was tall and lanky, with a face that reminded Nash powerfully of a weasel. "Here to arrest the mercenary known as the Butcher of Carrowwick."

"Ah," Nash said, mind racing. If the Needle Guard had made it all the way to the row house, they had to have marched through the whole damned Lottery. That wasn't good. "Well, I'm afraid I can't help you there."

"You sure about that?" Weasel-face said, pressing his sword point against the soft skin of Nash's throat. "How do I know he isn't hiding out in one of those rooms back there?"

Nash carefully schooled her expression. *He.* The Guard still thought the Butcher was a man?

"Look, I don't know where he is," Nash said. Thinking quickly, she flicked her eyes toward the ceiling. "He comes and goes—I haven't seen him in days."

The guard watched her closely. "Check the second floor," he said to the men behind him, never taking his eyes off Nash.

Four of the men streamed up the stairwell, leaving three guards downstairs. Still terrible odds, but she liked them a damn sight better than the ones she'd had a second ago.

"You gutter rats are worthless," Weasel-face taunted. "If it was up to me, I'd torch everything south of the trade docks. Start fresh."

The sound of splintering wood echoed from upstairs. The door to Cal's apartment. Those fuckers had better not so much as breathe on that man's chandelier. Weasel-face glanced up at the sound, his sword point drifting an inch to the left.

Nash lunged right, ducking under the sword and ramming her head into the guard's chest plate. She heard the air whoosh out of his lungs, replaced by frail gasping. She stepped over the wheezing man, grabbing a rickety old chair from beside the sitting room table. The remaining two guards' swords sang shrilly as they wrenched them from their sheaths.

She lifted the chair above her head. The first sword struck the seat. The soft, rotting timbers swallowed the blade, yanking it from the guard's fingers. Nash shoved the chair forward. The wooden seat slammed into the third guard's chest. She kicked the fork between his legs for good measure. She had just enough sense left in her adrenaline-drenched brain to grab the bag she'd seen Cal pack from beside the door before bolting out into the afternoon sunlight.

The alley outside was empty, but it wouldn't stay that way for long. Shattering glass and shouts of alarm swam through the thick summer air, coming from the docks.

The docks. Shit.

If the Needle Guard had learned where the Saints slept, could they have also discovered where they docked? She needed to get to the *Seasnake's Revenge* before the king's men did or they would never make it out of the harbor. First the Foxhole . . . now this. Clem would have a fit. This couldn't be Asher's doing again . . .

could it? But why else would the Needle Guard suddenly know where to find the Butcher? Why now?

It was pointless to ask questions when there was no chance of getting an answer. She tucked the thought away and stopped at the corner of Threader's Lane. She looked right, over the dilapidated row of shops crowding the street leading to the southern dock where the *Revenge* was anchored, all dressed up in her pretty new sails. Then left toward the sounds of chaos coming from the Carrowwick Fair.

The job came first. That was the first law of the Lottery. *Fill your own pockets and let everyone else fill theirs if they have the stones for it.* Surely Cal was already on his way to the ship. Nash knew she was a damned fool if she thought the Snake of the Southern Dock would wait for her. . . .

She swore, turning left and dashing north toward the Carrowwick Fair.

The job came first, but without their crew, the job was dead from the start, right? She had no clue where the Butcher was, or the Beckett kid, but she knew where Ivan was. The black market. The beating heart of the Lottery. Ivan was something of a genius, but even he couldn't talk himself out of a pair of manacles.

Clutching Cal's bag tightly under one arm, Nash flew over the cobblestones. She had hardly made it two alleys when she saw the first company of Needle Guard. Hand brushing the knife in her belt, Nash slipped through the battered door of a long-abandoned shop. She crouched in the shadows as they thundered past.

She then dodged and weaved through the Lottery, hiding from the sounds of footsteps and breaking glass. She darted into the gloom as another row of polished helmets streaked by, glinting in the orange sunlight. How many Needle Guard did it take to raid a few square miles?

Dread coursed through Nash as she reached the black market.

Just as she had expected. The Fair was an absolute wreck. Stalls lay upended, smashed remnants of about a thousand crescents' worth of illegal goods scattered all over the filthy street. Nash leaned over, picked up a shattered vial, and sniffed it. *Vitalité*. Probably from the same shipment of the drug she'd smuggled in from Gildemar this week. What a waste. At least she'd gotten paid up front.

Footsteps approached her from behind. A straggling Needle Guard? Maybe a cocky Crown, come to gloat, if this really was Asher's doing. She spun around, lunging for her knife. Her intestines performed a series of complicated acrobatics when instead she found herself face-to-face with Ivan Rezkoye.

He looked at the knife. "You came charging into a raid armed with . . . that?"

She flipped the blade end over end with a grin. "Heroic, I know."

He bent over, scooping an unbroken vial of dormire's blood from the ground. He shook it gently, then slipped it into his pocket. "I was going to go with 'foolish.'"

"Foolishly heroic, maybe."

That had to get a smile out of him . . . but no. "I assume our timeline has changed?"

"Nothing gets by you."

He grabbed another vial from the ground. "Is Clem already on the ship?"

Before Nash could answer, they were interrupted by a gravelly voice. "What have we here?"

Four men slunk from the brothel across Leech Alley from the Fair. Three of their chests were bare, one peeking out from the neckline of a filthy shirt. All marked with the Harpies' tattoo, a winged woman with breasts the size of potato sacks.

"If it isn't Clem's favorite sea rat," the man on the far left chortled. His eyes flicked to Ivan. "And his favorite bear stroker! We're in luck, gents."

Ivan stiffened at the middle-kingdoms slur for someone from Boreas, his fingers now threatening to break the vial of dormire's blood.

Nash lifted her knife. "You might want to rethink your wording."

All four men pulled swords from their belts in response. Their builds were all lopsided, three right-handed, one left. Probably some of the freebooters Finn paid to stick around and defend his shipments. Nash tightened her grip on the tiny knife in her sweat-slick fingers. "Foolish" was sounding more and more accurate all the time.

Nash looked around for a better weapon as the Harpies backed them into the brick wall. Nothing in sight. How was that even possible? This was the Carrowwick Fair, for Felice's sake; it was usually dripping with illegally traded swords and daggers. She looked at Ivan and—was that boredom she saw?

He wasn't even looking at the Harpies—his bright green eyes were focused slightly higher, on something just behind them.

Nash followed his gaze, eyes widening at the figure perched on the second-floor window of the inn beside the brothel, bathed in late afternoon sunlight. None other than Evelyn Linley. What were the chances that their little scuff had ended up right outside her front door? She stood on tiptoes, red hair tucked into a braid down her back, freckled fingers of her right hand wrapped comfortably around the hilt of a long, needle-thin sword.

Then Evelyn leapt, soaring through the air. Her boots slammed into the back of the front-most Harpy with bone-breaking force. He sprawled to the cobblestones with a whoof.

Evelyn turned in a circle, sword pointed at each Harpy's chest one after the other, her feet dancing over the ground like salt spray on a ship's deck.

"Lay down your weapons and I might let you walk."

One of them cackled. "What was that, girly? Why don't you run along home?" He looked back at the brothel. "Or is *this* home?"

He nudged the man beside him. "Few cups deep and I wouldn't turn 'er away."

Evelyn straightened. "Go ahead and give it a try. Wouldn't be my first castration."

Nash had a feeling the captain wasn't kidding.

The first freebooter swung. Evelyn ducked beneath the whistling blade, delivering a devastating uppercut to his bare stomach and clocking him around the temple with the bulky hilt of her sword.

"All right then—who's next?"

She got the answer as the remaining two men both went for her. She stooped low, whipping her thin blade sideways to score a deep gash in one Harpy's thigh. He screamed and collapsed, blood streaming down his calf as she kicked the other in the groin, forcing him to his knees. A well-placed boot then struck him in the chest. Nash thought she could hear the crunching of his clavicle as he fell backward, Evelyn's sword point tickling his patchy throat.

"I will give you one more chance," she said, her accent growing steadily stronger as her cheeks flushed a brighter red. "Set that blade down and I'll let you walk away."

"Evelyn!" Ivan shouted.

Nash snapped her head around to see the first of the fallen, the one Evelyn had kicked harder than a spooked horse, back on his feet. His sword flashed in the burnt-orange light of the sun as he cut toward her middle.

Evelyn had no time to turn and parry. But something small and silver flitted through the air from one of the rooftops, turning in an impossibly sharp arc to embed itself in her attacker's throat. A throwing axe. Evelyn leapt back, startled, as the corpse crashed to the ground, his blade clattering to a stop at her feet.

"Mercy's a curse, Captain," jeered an unmistakable voice.

Nash looked up as the Butcher plunged from the sky like a raindrop. Tristan sprinted into the Fair next, doubled over, clearly out of breath. After all these months of chasing after the Butcher, you'd think he would be used to her breakneck pace by now. Ryia bent low, picking up her axe and wiping it clean on the dead man's shirt as the other three Harpies scattered.

She stuffed the weapon back into her belt, looking from Nash and her pitiful knife to Ivan, and finally to Evelyn, who was still flustered and flushed.

"What are we standing around for?" she asked. "Don't we have a ship to catch?"

13

RYIA

ell, that was a mistake. Ryia shook herself as she sprinted through the city, Nash and the others close behind. She should have stayed out of it, let Captain Honor clean up her own damned mess. Of course, maybe it was just a coincidence the way Nash's eyes had followed the path of that axe, the way Evelyn had squinted at her like she'd shown up dressed as a Borean *medev* guard. Maybe no one had seen the weapon curve. . . .

She unconsciously tapped her belt. Ryia had practiced with these weapons more hours in her life than most people had slept in theirs, but that wasn't the only reason she never missed her mark. She was connected to these blades in a way few could understand.

She slid on the cobblestones, skidding to a stop as half a company of guards sprinted past them one alley over. They were heading for the docks. Ryia shared an anxious look with Nash and Tristan, then drew her largest hatchets from the sheaths across her back. Whose idea had it been to leak her location to the Needle Guard?

Oh, right.

It had better be worth it. If Clem somehow made it onto that ship . . .

"Go on. I'll take care of these assholes," she said, turning to chase down the guards.

Tristan nodded obediently, but Evelyn stepped forward. "You will not draw the blood of a single member of the Needle Guard. Not while I'm around." She pulled her sword free of its sheath, leveling the blade at Ryia's heart.

"You sure you want to do this, Captain? I've seen you in action. Not impressed." Ryia whirled her hatchets around her wrists. "Here's a tip—the fighting goes a lot easier when you don't waste time trying to purge everyone of their sins."

"It sounds like you're telling me that having a conscience is a crime."

Ryia laughed. "South of the trade docks it is." She tapped her breast pocket, feeling the stolen scrolls rustle beneath the heavy black fabric. "Look, you've got us our maps, so your job is done. Run along now."

"You heard your master, *pup*. If he doesn't get his prize, I don't get mine. Besides, the sooner your honorless arse is out of Dresdell, the better in my book. I'm getting you onto your bloody ship."

"You sure you're not just getting sweet on me, Captain?"

Evelyn didn't respond, but she looked roughly like someone had just told her to swallow a dock rat whole.

Ryia patted her shoulder, pushing past her. "It's all right. It happens all the time—just ask Ivan—"

Ryia broke off as the familiar smells of brackish water and rotting fish were suddenly replaced by the crushing scent of mildew. Blood and earth and decay. The strongest she had smelled in years. Now? Of all the fucking times—

"Are you all right?" Tristan asked. She didn't answer, and he leaned forward. "Ryia, are you okay?"

She turned left, then right, trying to get a lock on the scent. "Get to the ship," she said. Then she grabbed hold of the nearest windowsill and clambered up the wall and out of sight.

Ryia skittered across the rooftops, stopping to crouch behind a gable and sneak a peek toward the trade docks to the north. Maybe she was wrong. Maybe the Needle Guard were just more dangerous than she had thought, or maybe her nose was extra sensitive today. . . .

Her stomach turned to lead as her eyes found the sloops docked there. Disciples.

It had been nineteen months since she had seen ships like those. The ships that had dogged her, haunting her steps for the past nine years. If they were already docked, the Disciples were already in the city. Combing the streets. Looking for her.

Well, that settled it—she had officially overstayed her welcome in this city. She knew what would happen next . . . a fate she had narrowly escaped a dozen times before. The cunning Disciples would come for her with every ounce of strength they had in those miserable bones of theirs. If she was caught, she wouldn't be leaving Carrowwick alive. She was dangerous, not just for her skills, but for how she'd obtained them.

The Guildmaster could hardly let the secret get out that Adept gifts could be stolen, could he?

They would open her throat and leave her to bleed into the gutter. Then throw her into the Arden, or let her be found by the Saints so she could be buried under a headstone with a name that wasn't her own. Have her bullshit namestone hung in some tree outside the city. Right—no thanks.

She poked her head over the edge of the rooftop, peering down at the docks. One thing at a time. Disciples aside, her plan was going perfectly. The Lottery was currently in turmoil, the maps in her pocket, Callum Clem still nowhere to be found. Now all that was left was to get the crew out of Carrowwick, preferably before those Disciple bastards removed her head from her neck.

She looked down at her crew. Tristan took the rear while Evelyn prowled up front, fluid as a jungle cat. Between them were Nash and Ivan, the respective brawn and brains of the team. They tumbled to a clumsy stop a stone's throw from the *Seasnake's Revenge*, halted by two burly guards.

"Is that Evelyn fuckin' Linley? Hangin' around with this dock scum?" the guard on the left chortled. "Oh, Patrick'll love this."

His companion added, "Didn't take you long to find your proper place, did it?"

Evelyn's jaw set firmly, but her hand didn't even twitch toward her sword. She looked from side to side instead, searching for an escape route.

Ryia rolled her eyes, pulling two smaller throwing axes from her belt. "We have to do everything, don't we?" she remarked to the weapons, flying them toward the guards.

Reaching out with her stolen Kinetic power, Ryia guided one toward the front man's spine, and pulled the second around to lodge itself in the other man's face. She grimaced as it drove home. Retrieving an axe from a skull was always disgusting work.

Tristan jumped back as both men flopped, lifeless, to the dock. Ryia forced a cocky grin, waving down at them. Evelyn glared up at her, then turned in a huff as Nash dragged the group toward her ship, casting its imposing shadow over the docks a few steps away.

Ryia hopped off the edge of the roof, hooking her fingers around the gutters and dropping to the ground some fifteen feet below. "Don't worry about it—I'll get them," she called after her teammates, wiping the gory bits clean and returning the axes to her belt.

Her comrades sprinted up the gangplanks and onto the *Seasnake's Revenge*. Still not a Disciple in sight. If her luck could hold just a few minutes longer . . .

Then her nose caught fire. The vile stench of danger was so immediate, so potent that her knees almost gave out. Ryia pulled the two long-handled hatchets from her back again, spinning and raising them in an X above her head just in time to catch the scimitar as it whistled toward her skull. The force of the blow was inhuman. Her arms shook but didn't buckle. Without her Adept abilities she would never have been strong enough to hold it or fast enough to block it in the first place. There was a reason everyone in Thamorr bowed to the Guildmaster and his Disciples; because it was certain death to face one.

At least, it was supposed to be.

"Grayson, we meet at last," the Disciple said softly.

Ryia stared up at the man holding the blade. At the swirling robes of vivid blue, the cruel eyes, the shaven head tattooed with a tangle of elaborate symbols.

"That's not my name," she said. "Not anymore."

Something curdled in her stomach as the Disciple studied her. Something she hadn't felt since the last time she'd been face-to-face with one of these bald motherfuckers. Fear. All the Adept were tough in a fight, but the Disciples were all stronger than any mindless branded servant on the mainland. She gritted her teeth as the man smirked down at her. At least she would have no qualms about killing him, if she got the chance. The brainwashed Adept hadn't chosen their lives, but this asshole had certainly chosen his. Chosen to help the Guildmaster find and enslave the other Adept. Chosen to help the Guildmaster hunt her down.

Fear spiked in her again as her nose seared once more, this time the stench coming from her left. Shit. She ducked into a ball, rolling out from underneath the Disciple's blade, frantically leaping back. A second Disciple appeared on the docks beside her, his own blade moving so fast that it was nothing but a blur of polished steel. She stumbled back, falling solidly on her tailbone as the sword swung down. It missed her by less than an inch, connecting firmly with the splintering dock.

Ryia struggled to her feet again, eyes flicking toward the *Revenge*. She spun her hatchets, the steel bits singing as they cut through the thick summer air. She had an important decision to make. Fight or run . . .

To get to the ship, and to salvage the mission, she needed to fight. . . . Her stomach clenched as both Disciples took a dream-like step forward. Their tattoos seemed to swim in the humid air as they took another step, blades at the ready.

She had to fight.

On second thought . . . fuck that.

The Disciples swung in unison, blades reflecting the light of the setting sun as they moved to cut her to pieces. But it was too late—Ryia was already gone. She was nothing more than a jet-black blur against the horizon as she turned from the *Seasnake's Revenge* and ran for her life.

14

EVELYN

"Turn here!" Nash shouted.

Evelyn veered right, sprinting onto the rickety dock that held the smuggler's beloved caravel. The gleaming ship looked out of place on the southern dock, adorned with three blisteringly white sails, furled tightly against their masts.

Nash blew past, bounding up the gangplank far more nimbly than Evelyn would have expected from someone of her size. A sweat-soaked Ivan came next, followed by the cocky boy named Tristan. He looked so bloody familiar. She must have arrested him before.

Evelyn pulled herself onto the deck just in time to see Nash clap the shoulder of an unidentified greasy man. One of Nash's crewmen, probably. He had a hooked nose and great furry pep-pered moths for eyebrows.

"Clem on board?"

The man's throat bobbed like a pelican trying to swallow too large a fish. "Over 'ere," he said.

Nash wiped a fingerful of sweat from her forehead, leading the rest of them down toward the belly of the ship. Tristan kept peeking over his shoulder, no doubt searching the rooflines for his precious Butcher. He had to realize he was out of his depth there, right? That mercenary would gut him sooner than bed him, no doubt.

Evelyn jumped at the unmistakable scrape of a sword leaving its scabbard.

"What the hell, Luc?" Nash said, hands raised as the man pressed a rusty sword against her neck.

A few of the crew reached for their own belts but froze as half a dozen more men and women popped from the ship's woodwork, blades already drawn. Who were these people? They definitely weren't Needle Guard. . . .

Tristan's head snapped back and forth in panic and confusion while Ivan's nose wrinkled with evident distaste, his hooded eyes registering dim recognition as they slid slowly from face to face. Was this Nash's crew? Oh. That couldn't be good.

"This ship doesn't just belong to me—it belongs to Callum Clem," Nash said. "Think about that long and hard before you do anything too stupid."

"But what if they do not care about Callum Clem any longer?" asked a new voice. Soft and wheezy, like it was whistling through a hole in the side of a lung.

Nash started laughing, her neck scraping uncomfortably close to that criminally neglected blade.

"Really, Luc? Harlow Finn? You fancy yourselves Harpies now? I know you like your trips to the Tail, but for Felice's sake . . ."

"This isn't about some whorehouse," Luc grunted.

"If you say so." Nash peered around the hold. "What have you done with Clem? He's not even here, is he?"

"He did not make it aboard, sadly," said the whistle-voiced leader of the Harpies. Evelyn's eyes widened as he lurched into view, his boil-covered face passing inches from her. The mark of the Borean Death. She'd seen it before, but not on many survivors. No wonder he wore the blemishes like medals of honor. "He was . . . delayed. By a few Needle Guard. As soon as I saw that, well, I knew my chance had finally come."

"Fucking hells, Finn, did the Death addle your brain that much?" Nash asked. "This is Callum Clem we're talking about. He won't be penned up for good. And if you go through with this, then as soon as he's back on these streets, anyone sporting a Harpy tattoo is a dead man."

Finn patted Nash's cheek with a gnarled hand. "The Foxhole is gone, my dear sweet Nash. With Clem safely locked in one of Baelbrandt's cells . . . I think the Saints are finished. Especially now that I am in possession of all Clem's favorite pets as well." He cast his eyes around the hold, lingering on Tristan. "Although we seem to be missing one, by my count. Where is that rabid little dog of his?"

Evelyn frowned. Where *was* the Butcher? Beside her, Ivan cleared his throat. He gave her a meaningful look, then wriggled the fingers of his right hand, pinned behind his back.

"No matter," Finn said when it was clear the Butcher would not be making an appearance. "Tie them up."

Evelyn peered closer at Ivan's hand as Finn snapped his fingers. There, clutched in Ivan's grip was a small vial filled with a deep purple liquid. *Dormire's blood.*

Ivan mimed taking a deep breath and holding it. Evelyn gave a minute nod before turning back to face Harlow Finn as his men closed in, rope in hand.

"Perhaps you are right, Finn," Ivan interjected. "Perhaps the Saints are finished. Will you not even give us the chance to join your Harpies?"

Finn's haggard face lit. He cocked his head to one side, then held up a hand. The rope-wielding Harpies paused. Finn's sunken eyes appraised Ivan from head to toe.

"I don't have too many men working my . . . establishments. But I daresay you might be able to earn me some crescents."

"I can make you a very rich man," Ivan said, flashing a calculated, dazzling smile.

Finn took another step closer. The idiot.

Ivan opened his hand behind his back, letting the vial tumble through the air. It shattered on the splintered wood at his feet.

In small measures the illegal Brillish drug had a mild calming effect. The no-good layabouts who breathed it from their cheese-cloth sacks were always recognizable by their red-rimmed eyes and drooping jaws. In larger doses, the drug was a bit more potent.

Finn gasped as a cloud of noxious, purple gas mushroomed through the hold. Then he dropped like a stone, senseless.

Holding her breath, Evelyn drew her sword. She slashed out blindly, warding off any Harpies who may have managed to escape the noxious cloud as she yanked Tristan away by his collar. Through the haze, she saw Nash duck out of Luc's hold, treating him to a quick rabbit punch to the nose before allowing Ivan to drag her out behind him. They exploded from the hatch, vaulting over the rail and landing with near ankle-breaking force on the dock.

"This way," Nash said, pushing herself to the front of the pack.

"We're just going to leave the ship behind?" Evelyn asked, perplexed.

"In case ye didn't notice it, it's got a bit've a Harpy infestation," said the man next to her—one of the few members of Nash's crew who had not joined Luc's mutiny.

"So . . . the mission is scrapped?" Evelyn tripped over her own feet, struggling to keep up as they tore over the docks, knocking passersby out of the way, desperate to get out of sight of the *Revenge* before Finn's men could shake off the effects of the dormire's blood and give chase.

"I didn't say that. . . ." Nash's signature sharpened canines flashed as the smuggler shot her a massive grin. It didn't quite reach her eyes.

"Then where are we going?" Evelyn asked, peering over her shoulder at the rooftops behind them. She half expected to see the telltale swirl of the Butcher's black cloak catching the wind. Nothing. Where had that maniac run off to, anyway?

"Best not to tell you, Captain," Nash said. "I have a feeling you're not going to like it. . . ." She turned to her four remaining crewmen mid-step. "Let's head toward Buttoner's Road."

They chuckled appreciatively. Clearly they knew what Nash meant to do, even if Evelyn didn't. One of them said, "About time."

Nash cut through the alleys running parallel to the docks. She held out a hand to stop them in the shadows of a street sign reading BUTTONER'S ROAD. They paused, looking back out at the docks as a few scattered Needle Guard rushed past. As soon as they were out of sight, Nash waved them forward, sprinting toward a tiny cog bobbing by itself on a lonely dock at the mouth of the Arden River.

"You have another ship?" Tristan asked through panting breaths.

" . . . Not exactly."

"Not *yet*," corrected the crewman who had spoken before.

"You're going to steal a ship?" Evelyn exclaimed.

The crewman gave a toothless grin. "'Ow d'you think she got the las' one?"

Evelyn replied, "There is no way I'm letting you sods steal a ship. Besides, these docks are crawling with the king's men, in case you hadn't—"

"What about Ryia?" Tristan asked.

Nash swung herself onto the ship, pulling at the ropes and gesturing for her limited crew to do the same. "If she hasn't already been poked full of holes by the Needle Guard, she'll track us down. Hopefully before we shove off. Like a damned bloodhound, that one. Now take this line, would you? We can't exactly hang around here all day. . . ."

"I'm not helping you commit a class-one crime," Evelyn said, folding her arms.

"I think we'll manage without you," Nash called down from the deck. "You coming, Beckett?"

Tristan hesitated, then trudged reluctantly on board, grabbing the line that Nash offered him. But there was no need for the poor, lovesick boy to worry.

There, silhouetted against the tangle of salt-blasted buildings a few docks away, was the Butcher. Evelyn looked to the others. No one else seemed to have noticed her yet. She pelted toward them, terror etched across her scarred face. *Not so fearless confronting the Needle Guard after all, eh?* Evelyn smirked. But the smug expression withered and died as she caught sight of what was actually chasing the Butcher.

A *Disciple*. A real Disciple.

The Guildmaster's personal army of Adept was small but powerful. All the Adept were dangerous, but the Disciples were far more unnerving than the servants on the mainland. For one, they were stronger than the Adept the Guildmaster sold to the mainland lords and merchants. And then there was the matter of their . . . personalities. Unlike the gentled Adept the Guildmaster auctioned off every year, the Disciples' minds were sound. Adept walking around with thoughts of their own—Evelyn had been floored the first time she had seen it for herself. Thankfully, most of the time they kept to themselves, holed up on the Guildmaster's island.

Father always used to say Disciples only came to the mainland on two occasions: when an Adept baby had been born or when someone had royally mucked something up. Despite her infantile sense of humor, the Butcher of Carrowwick was no baby, so it had to be the second one this time.

Had the Guildmaster somehow found out about Clem's plans to infiltrate the auction? If so, they were all as good as dead.

"Wait!" Evelyn said, leaping up onto the deck of the cog. "The But—"

"Not you, too," Nash said, not even pausing to look. "We have about ten minutes to get clear of the harbor before we're hemmed in by Harpies or worse. You don't know Ryia. She'll find us before we take off."

"That's not—" Evelyn started as Nash blew past. "She's right there!"

Evelyn threw her hands up, gesturing back toward the docks, but no one was paying any attention. The Disciple rapidly approached. Faster than a beat of a hummingbird's wings, it pulled a massive scimitar from beneath its robes.

The Butcher's beady eyes were locked on the ship. She was trying to outrun the thing . . . and she was undoubtedly going to get sliced in half. Would the king still award a Valiership if Evelyn only brought him the mercenary's head?

At the last second, the Butcher dove to the ground, dodging the Disciple's scimitar. Another blue-robed figure burst from the next alley, raising a slender sword. The tattooed beast brought the gleaming blade down in a vicious stab, skewering the Butcher like an Adalina's Day pig on the spit. . . .

Or not. The blade didn't touch her at all.

The Butcher now stood a few feet away from the Disciples, baring her teeth like a cornered animal, fingers twitching on the handles of her hatchets.

The Butcher said something that was lost to the wind. Then, before Evelyn's eyes could even make sense of what was happening, it was all over. Both Disciples lay dead on the docks, blood pooling beneath them, dripping between the slats and into the sloshing waters below. The Butcher kneeled over one, freeing a hatchet from its neck.

The Butcher's eyes were as dark as shadows as she cast them back to the ship. When her gaze found Evelyn, she thought she saw a twinge of fear there, buried somewhere in the crushing blackness.

"Hold up, assholes!" she shouted, darting down the dock and up the gangplank just as Nash's crew started to pull it in. The Butcher smiled her bone-chilling smile, sliding onto the deck beside Evelyn.

"What does a person have to do to get a Disciple sent after them?"

"Hmm?" The Butcher looked up, as though just noticing her. "Those? Oh, just some old friends of mine." She gave her usual grin, but the fire behind it was stolen by the fact that her hands were shaking. "You do me a few favors, and I might just teach you some of those moves."

She reached out, wiping her blood-soaked axe blade on Evelyn's shoulder before sticking it back into the sheath across her back.

"What the hell happened?" she called to Nash, sauntering across the deck.

"You made it," Nash said, giving a relieved grin. "I'll be sure to thank Felice for giving us that much, at least. She's been a bit of a bitch today, as you can see."

"The *Revenge*?"

Nash's smile grew sour. "Long story. The highlights are Luc is an ass, and now Harlow Finn owns the *Seasnake's Revenge*."

"I see . . . Well, you didn't waste time finding a replacement." The Butcher knocked on the mast. "You know how to sail one of these?"

"If there's a ship I can't sail, I haven't found her yet," Nash replied, shaking out another line.

"That a euphemism?" Ryia asked. Nash just stared intently at the small red flag at the top of the mast. The Butcher moved to slink away, and Evelyn lunged forward.

"No you don't!" she hissed, ducking as a stray line snapped overhead.

"I don't what?" the Butcher asked absently, arrogance threatening to float her head right off her bloody shoulders.

Evelyn snared the mercenary's sleeved wrist in one hand. "You can't just—"

Ryia whirled, pulling her arm out of Evelyn's grasp. Evelyn gritted her teeth as the Butcher leveled a hatchet at her throat. A second later she seemed to get ahold of herself, slipping the weapon back into its sheath and tugging at her sleeves.

"I can't what, Captain?"

"Can't get out of this without explaining yourself. You might have gotten lucky that no one else was looking, but I know what I saw. A brace of Disciples in Carrowwick Harbor."

". . . Your point?"

"My point is that this mission is already belly up if the Guildmaster knows what we're doing."

Ryia laughed in a way that flushed Evelyn from the neck up. "Don't flatter yourself. The Guildmaster doesn't give half a shit about all of you," she said, gesturing around at the rest of their crew.

"That so? What's he after you for, then?"

"What does it matter to you?" Ryia stepped sideways to let one of Nash's men by. "You worried about me, Captain? I knew you'd come around."

Evelyn gave chase. "It matters because you're risking this whole damn mission."

"How's that, love?"

"He's the most powerful man in the world," Evelyn said, nearly shouting now as Nash yelled something about a dock line across the deck. "If he recognizes you—"

Her words jumped back down her throat as the sail above them fluttered free, sending the cog lurching away from the dock at last. Evelyn stumbled, falling into the rail as Nash steered them toward the rushing tendrils of brackish water where the Arden met the Yawning Sea.

As the ship jerkily nosed its way into the open water of the harbor, Evelyn felt the Butcher's hand trail over her shoulders, her fingers leaving prickling embers of what must be rage in their wake.

"Then I guess you lot will have one hell of a distraction, won't you?" Her gravelly voice rumbled over Evelyn's ears like cartwheels on cobblestones.

"Help Collick with the brace, would you?" Nash shouted across the deck. "Unless you want to wait here to see whether the Harpies or the Needle Guard catch us first!"

The Butcher gave Evelyn one last look, fingers walking over her throwing axes in a silent threat. "Sure thing, Nash, since I'm such a fucking expert sailor. What in Felice's name is a brace?"

Nash rolled her eyes. "Do I have to do everything?"

"Was that a proposition?"

The smuggler seemed to ignore her. Then said, "Heads up." The yard swung freely, trailing a line that nearly took off Tristan's head. Nash laughed. "Sorry, kid—gotta pay attention!"

"So do you," said another voice. Ivan. He stood at the bow, his startling eyes locked on the horizon to the west, where the setting sun was blocked by the sails of half a dozen ships.

Each of those vessels was flying the purple sails of the king's navy. The Needle Guard were onto them. If they were caught now, Evelyn could forget the Valiership—she would be lucky to avoid a cell.

Nash swore violently, steering the ship sharply to the left. "That's all right," she grunted. "They don't call me the empress of the Three Seas for nothing."

"Who calls you that, exactly?" asked the Butcher.

Nash didn't answer. There was a long moment of silence as she cranked the wheel farther to the left, guiding them straight across the Arden.

"You do realize there's a cliff there?" Ryia remarked.

Nash laughed again. This time it was echoed by her crew, all of them apparently unfazed by the massive wall of jagged rock on the opposite bank of the Arden. "Let's hope Baelbrandt's men are as blind as you are."

Nash wove through the other ships departing into the sunset, bringing the cog closer to the raging currents swirling around the cliffs.

The king's ships were on the move, heading for the mouth of the river, jockeying for position, trying to keep an eye on all the vessels in the crowded harbor at once. As the last rays of sunlight fell on the cliff, Evelyn's mouth dropped open.

There was a gap.

Not large, maybe fifty feet wide—barely enough for them to fit. She could feel everyone on board holding their breath as they slipped between the massive rock walls and into the stillness beyond.

"Furl that sail," Nash said, her golden eyes on the cliffs that had swallowed them.

Nash began spinning the wheel to the right. The ship groaned, the rudder protesting as it clumsily made the sharp turn.

Nash gritted her teeth, muscles threatening to snap as she cranked the wheel back to the left.

"Do you actually know what you're doing?" Evelyn asked, voice taut as her fingers threatened to dent the rail beside her.

The smile Nash gave her could have charmed the quartermaster at the Linley estate. "At the helm of a ship, I always know what I'm doing." She shot Ryia a wink. "Feel free to take that as a euphemism too."

Ryia gave a rasping chuckle as they rounded another spire of rock. Then the salt breeze of the Yawning Sea hit Evelyn in the face harder than one of Mother's slaps. The broad expanse of the sea rolled out before them, spitting them into the ocean some two miles down the coast from Carrowwick Harbor.

"It's almost like it's my job to know every route to open water along the western coastline," Nash said.

Tristan whooped in relief. Evelyn sagged forward, letting out a breath she had been holding for at least a minute. Even Ivan looked pleased in a flat sort of way.

"Great, so we've made it through literally the easiest part of this entire shitshow." A muscle in Evelyn's jaw twitched as Ryia cut through the celebrations. "Congratulations. Now, does someone want to grab Clem from below so he can tell us what the hell we're doing next?"

Clem.

The name sucked the excitement from the air.

The Butcher looked around the deck. "Is there a problem?"

Silence. Then Nash cleared her throat. "Cal may have been arrested by the Needle Guard."

The Butcher's monstrous face twisted into an emotion halfway between amusement and horror. "You can't be serious."

"We should go back for him," said Ivan.

"Go back? And do what, break into the Carrowwick dungeon?" Evelyn asked, incredulous.

"Ryia could do it," Ivan said.

"Not if I have anything to say about it," Evelyn said. She had helped break into the archives, and she had helped steal a bloody ship, but she wouldn't help break a criminal out of the cells under the Bobbin Fort. She had crossed more than a few of her personal, moral lines in the past few days, but there was a limit to what she would do. There had to be—otherwise she was no better than the guttersnipes all around her.

"You wouldn't be able to stop me," Ryia said. The picture of bloody arrogance, this one.

There was a long silence. Then Tristan said, "The whole harbor is on lockdown. We barely got out—could we even get back in?"

Nash hesitated. "It would be tricky . . . but if we wait until after dark . . ." She looked at the remaining members of her crew. "I think I could do it."

Another period of silence as everyone's minds tried to untangle the same knot. The Butcher finally broke it. "Think this through carefully. This would mean scrapping the whole mission. No payout. And we have no guarantee Clem's even still alive. . . ."

The air aboard the stolen cog grew tight as the words sunk in. *No guarantee Clem's even still alive.* No doubt the rest of them were thinking about what would happen to the Saints without the protection of the infamous Snake of the Southern Dock. Their enemies were already closing in around them . . . without Clem, they were probably all screwed. Dead Saints would be washing up on the shores of Golden Port in no time, as the Butcher had said the night they broke into the Needle Guard barracks. But Evelyn had her own problems.

The bargain she had made, the whole reason she was even here, was with Clem and Clem alone. The Snake had made it clear she would receive no payout if he didn't get his bloody prize, so if they killed the mission, she could say goodbye to her chances at earning her Valiership . . . but if they didn't turn back now, he might not even be alive by the time they returned to the city. The kingdom of Dresdell did not take death penalties lightly, but this was Callum Clem they were talking about. One of the most dangerous, infamous criminals in Carrowwick. If anyone's misdeeds earned them a trip to the gallows, it would be him.

The Butcher finally cleared her throat. "It looks like we have a decision to make."

"What are our options?" asked Tristan.

"Try to rob the most powerful man in all of fucking Thamorr, without any plan or help from the one man who could have pulled off this suicidal job," Nash said.

Tristan's eyes widened. "What's another option?"

"Give up the only payout that could save the Saints from complete destruction to go back and try to save a man who might already be dead," said the Butcher. "And also probably die."

"And . . . the third option?" Tristan asked hopefully.

"Throw yourself into the Yawning Sea right now and drown."

"That is not helpful, Ryia," Ivan replied.

"Helpful? No. But it's accurate. Without the payout from this job, the Harpies and Crowns will eat the Saints alive."

"Without *Clem* the Harpies and Crowns will eat the Saints alive," Ivan countered.

"Well, that ship has already sailed. No pun intended," the Butcher said.

"I say we go to the island," Evelyn announced.

Certainly, if Clem was executed before they got back she wouldn't have a prayer of collecting her prize . . . but the Snake of the Southern Dock was a slippery bastard. There was a chance he'd get himself out of the mess he was in, and if that was the case, Evelyn's only hope of getting what she had been promised was completing this mission. It was a small chance, but if they went back to Carrowwick now she was guaranteed to get nothing.

"Well, well, well, look at the balls on this one—metaphorically speaking only, of course," the Butcher said, chortling.

"Without Clem's plan, we will never make it off of that island," Ivan said stiffly.

"Without the payout from this job, we won't make it until the end of the summer in this city," the Butcher said. "If Clem's already dead, then the Crowns and the Harpies will have no reason to hold back—they'll pick us off one by one until there's not a Saint left in Carrowwick. You know Finn and Asher would love the opportunity to disembowel Clem's organization—and all its members. This job could give us enough coin to rebuild and keep them off our backs."

"And if he is still alive?" asked Ivan.

Ryia grinned darkly. "If he's alive . . . failing this job is probably as good as handing in our resignation, isn't it?"

"You can't just *resign* from the Saints," Tristan said. Something in his tone told Evelyn if that were an option he would have taken it already.

"Exactly," said the Butcher. Tristan paled as he caught her meaning. "Now, call me crazy, but I'd rather be mostly fucked than entirely fucked. Or do you disagree?"

Silence stretched among them as each member of the crew weighed the odds. Evelyn's calculations were already made. It didn't take long for the others to reach the same conclusion. Both options were shite, but only one had even the slightest chance of success.

Finally, Nash took the helm. She steered the ship south, setting a course for the Guildmaster's island. "Felice help us all."

15

NASH

For Nash, setting off into the ocean always felt like coming home. This time, it would have felt more like home if the deck beneath her feet had belonged to her ship. If half of her oh-so-loyal crew hadn't sold her out for a few free trips to the Tail. If the only man capable of pulling off this goddess-forsaken job wasn't trapped in a Bobbin Fort cell fifty miles up the coast . . . but Nash had never had much use for complaining.

Complaining about a bad hand did nothing. A good gambler always played her cards as best she could. A good cheat just stole a new set of cards . . . or, in this case, a new ship.

A gust of southern wind washed over the deck, causing the sail to luff. Nash peered at the tell-tale, bearing off a bit farther starboard. The sail sprang taut again. These summer winds would be murder on their schedule. It was always hell to get to Briel when the wind wanted to push her the wrong way the entire journey. At this pace, they were likely to miss the whole damned auction.

They'd have to make up some time once they cut east into the Luminous Sea.

She turned at the sound of splintering wood on the stern. The Butcher stood over an odd pile of crates, pawing through them like an ice bear through a fur trader's campsite.

"Is there anything edible on this ship?" Ryia asked, lifting a piece of salted beef with two fingers. Obviously the dregs of the supplies from whatever voyage this tiny ship had last taken.

Nash pointed at the beef with her chin. "Looks like you're holding it."

Ryia gagged, thrusting it from her and wiping her fingers on her cloak.

"Scared of a little mold?" Nash laughed.

Tristan skipped across the deck, ducking beneath the lines. He had come alive the moment they'd hit open water, though he clearly knew nothing about sailing. Maybe he really was a merchant's brat after all.

"Ryia doesn't eat meat," he said.

"Excuse me?" Evelyn leaned back from the sword she'd been sharpening.

"What's the problem, Captain?" Ryia asked.

"The famed Butcher of Carrowwick doesn't eat meat."

Ryia looked nonplussed. "I don't see your point."

"You maim people for a living."

"Allegedly." Ryia winked, flicking an axe into the air and catching it behind her back.

Evelyn shook her head. "You're impossible."

"One of my best traits, I think. Don't you, Tristan?"

Tristan nodded like a damned fool, and Ryia waved a hand toward him.

"See? Tristan agrees. But really, are we going to stop for supplies? Even if I was willing to munch on dead cows with you animals, I don't think there's enough here to last us a month. You'd think we didn't plan this at all."

Nash chewed on her lip as she tacked south across the eye of the wind. "We're already moving at the speed of a Duskhaven snail in this wind. If we want to make it to the auction in time, you're going to have to make do with whatever food is left on this bucket."

"Then I hope you won't need me for whatever plan you manage to cook up, because I'm going to starve to death."

Evelyn rolled her eyes. "Is she always this dramatic?"

"Sometimes even more so," Tristan said. He leapt back as Ryia aimed a lazy slap at his arm.

At that moment, the hatch swung open, landing with a bang on the deck.

"What is this?" Ivan asked, poking his head out of the hold. The bag Cal had packed and left by the door of the row house dangled from his hand.

"Hell if I know," Nash said. "I'd say ask Cal, but . . ."

Ivan pursed his lips, pulling a firework from the bag. "Where are my supplies?" No one answered, and he surged onto the deck. "My wax? My tools? My fabrics?"

Nash scrubbed the back of her neck with one callused hand. "Do we really need all that?"

"Only if you plan to survive this job."

After a long moment of silence, Nash sighed. "Fine. Rest up a bit, folks. We'll be there by sunup."

"'There'? Where is 'there'?" Evelyn scratched an eyebrow, visibly agitated. "Has everyone forgotten we're on a stolen ship? We don't have the papers to dock anywhere."

"That's not going to matter," said Santi, Nash's longest-standing crewman.

"How in Adalina's name is that not going to matter?"

Nash just shook her head, tacking port toward the coastline. "Clearly you've never been to Golden Port."

NASH WAS no stranger to the city of Golden Port. Just the opposite, actually. Her stomach turned as the sun peeked over the horizon. They had sailed through the night, and she could now see the city's harbor in the distance, cast in shadow. She had been born and bred in this festering pit, the slum-riddled town that straddled the border between Dresdell and Gildemar. There were too many memories tied up in those streets. Too much Claudia, not enough Nash.

She counted out five coppers, slapping them into the dock agent's palm. The mousey little man squinted from the coppers to the ship and raked his eyes over the crew. Nash stood tall at the lead, Ryia cracking her knuckles just behind her. Both Evelyn and Tristan looked as though they might be sick. Ivan looked handsome but bored.

"Your papers?"

"Taken by the wind." Nash slipped the man an extra coin.

"Tragic. Happens all the time," the man said, pocketing the coppers and stepping aside.

Evelyn looked beyond appalled. She opened her mouth, seemingly to tell the docking agent off for letting them in illegally, but Nash grabbed her arm, pulling her away from the man. "Come on, you lot. Let's get this over with."

"Which way's food?" Ryia asked, a hand roaming absently over her stomach. Now that Nash thought about it, this was by far the longest she had seen the Butcher go without eating.

She pointed toward Shepherd Street with her chin. The Butcher took off without another word. Evelyn bolted after her, muttering, "Someone's got to make sure she doesn't kill anyone."

Tristan wasn't far behind, clinging to Ryia like a shadow.

After they disappeared into the throng, Ivan cleared his throat. "I take it you know where to find what I need?"

Of course she did. The one part of this damned city she had managed to avoid for the past ten years. Skuller's Lane.

They walked in silence through the crowded streets. Within three blocks Nash had broken the wrists of three pickpockets, and Ivan had neatly sidestepped two puddles that looked suspiciously like blood. Nash looked over at him as they passed a tavern that was far too rowdy for this time of the morning.

"You all right?"

"No," Ivan said flatly, surprising her. "With Callum in prison . . ."

"That silver tongue of his has gotten him out of tighter binds than this," she said, trying to convince herself as much as him. "He'll be okay."

"What does *that* matter if he is a thousand miles away?" Ivan asked. "He was the one with the plan, Nash. Have you forgotten?"

"No, I haven't forgotten," Nash said. That was the whole reason they were in this damned city at all.

"If we arrive on that island without a plan, we will be dead before we reach the shadow of the Guildmaster's bell tower."

"I don't think anyone's arguing with that," Nash said.

"What exactly are you arguing, then?"

"We might not have Cal Clem, but we still have some serious brains on this crew. And some strong fighters. Not to mention a badass ship captain and, er, whatever Tristan is good for." Nash grinned as Ivan suppressed a smile. "Don't get me wrong—there is at least an eighty percent chance that we are totally fucked. But a twenty percent chance of success? That's a hell of a lot better than most card games, and thousands of bastards still play those."

"Yes, and they lose."

"Only the ones who play fair."

Ivan stared at her for a few steps. Then: "Do you actually know where we are going?"

"Of course I do."

And there it was. Skuller's Lane. Ten years and not a damned thing had changed. How was that even possible? It was almost as though the street was her own personal nightmare, kept in pristine condition.

Nash pointed Ivan toward the seedy shops and stalls lining the street, averting her eyes from the second-floor apartment halfway down the lane. "Knock yourself out."

She leaned against a half wall of crumbling brick as Ivan chatted amiably with a pair of vendors a few yards away, undoubtedly charming them into selling sealing wax for half price or less. Hopefully, he would get what he needed quickly so they could all get the hell out of this place. Even at the best of times, dry land felt like a prison. But this alley was a hundred times worse. She couldn't feel the wind or smell the salt of the sea. It felt like she was locked in a coffin being lowered into the ground.

Her fingers found the leather strap around her neck and tugged it from beneath her shirt. She fidgeted with the small disc of granite, running her eyes over the elaborate carven whorls. They were starting to fade after years spent at sea.

"Is that a namestone?"

"What?" Nash jumped, tucking the necklace back into her shirt. "No, it's nothing." She turned to face Ivan, reaching for one of the bags in his arms, eager to change the subject. It was small, full of what looked like tiny black beads. "What's all this?" She read the label. "*Trän vun Yavol.* Some kind of Borean sweet?"

Ivan pulled the bag away with delicate fingers. "You will not want to eat those."

"Why not?"

"They are worth more than your ship."

He tucked the sealing wax and face paints into his satchel along with the pouch of mysterious capsules. Nash's stomach leapt at Ivan's closeness as he reached out, pulling the necklace back out by its strap.

"What do they mean? The carvings?" he asked, examining the circular, looping scrawl.

Nash cleared her throat. "They're names."

"Your gods, yes?"

"They don't worship gods in Briel. They follow the ghosts of their ancestors. Which are kept"—she tapped the stone gently, pulling it from Ivan's hands—"in here."

"I did not know you were Brillish."

"I'm not," she said quickly, stuffing her hands into her pockets. "My ma is. Was."

Was. Nash still remembered how she'd found her mother, sprawled on the floor of the bedroom. The Gildesh Whisper. Such a nice name for such a horrible sickness. A brutally quick, bloody death. It spread through Golden Port like wildfire every few years, carried on the filthy backs of rats and pigeons. She suddenly felt like her skin was crawling, a hundred rats skittering over her flesh. . . .

She shook her head, looking at the packages peeking out from the top of Ivan's satchel. Fabric. Sealing wax. His mysterious little capsules. "Got everything? We should find the Butcher before she starts a riot. Or worse."

Nash turned, heading back the way they had come. After several steps, she could still feel the weight of Ivan's gaze. She looked over her shoulder at him. "What?"

"Nothing," he said. Was that a blush she saw as he turned away? He was silent for a few steps as they wove through the crowds back toward the harbor. Then: "I heard they hung namestones. After . . ."

He wasn't wrong. The forests in Briel were full of the stones, dangling from the branches of the trees, clattering together in the wind. The traders called them the whispers of the dead. She had always meant to hang Ma's stone, she had just never managed to find the right place.

Nash was saved the trouble of answering the question by a familiar drawl.

"Can we get moving, already?" The Butcher leaned against a tailor shop stoop, munching on a golden apple. "Whose idea was it to stop in this pisshole anyways?"

The look Evelyn gave her could have poisoned a scorpion.

Dread settled over Nash like a heavy blanket as she led the group back to their stolen ship. It would be fourteen days before their feet hit solid ground again, and that would be on the Guildmaster's island. They had only two weeks to come up with a plan that would keep them alive. A plan as good as Callum Clem's. Nash's guts turned to stone. If they didn't think of something spectacular . . . they were all going to die.

16

RYIA

Ryia's belly dropped and twisted alongside the crashing waves as the cog bobbed through the Yawning Sea. She had booked passage on her fair share of vessels in the past nine years, but those had been skiffs and small boats sailing up and down the rivers of Edale and across the ice lakes of Boreas. The open ocean? That was an entirely new beast.

And, if that wasn't enough, there was also the heat. Dresdellan summers might be miserable, but they were nothing compared to the suffocating air of the southern sea. She supposed she should be grateful they had managed to make it this far south at all. It had been dicey for several days. So dicey that Ryia had almost started to regret her decision to leave Clem behind. Almost.

They had been chased out of Golden Port by Captain Brodeur's flagship pirate vessel. Nash had to take a detour around the archipelago off the coast of Gildemar to give them the slip. Then came the storms. Three solid days of surging waves, whipping winds, and driving rains that had soaked them all to the core. Nash said they should be thankful for the change in the wind. They may be wet and bedraggled and heading for certain death, but at least now they would make it to the auction in time.

All in all, it had been a terrible journey so far. So terrible that Ryia joked they should name their ship *The Hardship*. No one seemed to appreciate her humor.

"And just like that, the hand is mine," said Tristan, tossing a pair of tens onto the pile of cards on the overturned crate in front of him with one hand and taking a bite of the carrot held in the other. "Pay up."

A round of grumblings greeted him as the rest of the crew dug into their pockets, tossing random odds and ends onto the crate. They'd spent all their coin back in Golden Port, but a win was a win, so each gave what they had. Nash threw down a pair of wine corks. Ivan added a broken pencil. Ryia tossed a rusty lockpick onto the pile. Tristan might be the most junior member of their crew, but he was a lucky son of a bitch when it came to Bobbin Draw.

Maybe it was foolish to waste time with card games when they didn't have more than the ghost of a plan, but there was only so long a person could stare at a pile of maps and blueprints, waiting for inspiration to strike. They still had eight days. Eight days to figure out where the Guildmaster kept his magical Quill hidden, how to steal it, and how to escape the island with their lives intact.

"So," Evelyn said as she clumsily shuffled the worn playing cards, dealing another hand. "What's so bloody special about this Quill anyways?"

"It's worth a damned fortune, that's what's so special about it," Nash said, scooping up her cards and examining them.

"I know that," Evelyn said. "But aren't any of you curious as to *why*?"

Ryia picked up her own cards, steeling her expression. Maybe she should have let the Harpies snuff the captain out back at the Carrowwick Fair. The rest of the team was made up of thieves and con men—people used to thinking in terms of gold and nothing else. But if Linley kept calling their attention to the mystery of the Quill, they were bound to figure it out eventually. And if they discovered what it did . . . who knew what they would want to do with the thing then.

"Not really," Tristan said, examining his cards again, then sliding a wine-soaked cork into the pot at the center of their crate-table.

"Perhaps we should care," Ivan said thoughtfully, placing a broken paintbrush next to Tristan's cork. "Perhaps if we knew what was important about this relic, it would help us figure out where the Guildmaster has hidden it."

"Exactly," Evelyn said, pointing at the disguise master. "We should take a break from staring at the same three ruddy maps all day and try to puzzle out why anyone would want to steal it."

Even Nash looked interested now. Shit. This conversation was getting out of control fast.

"Maybe it's made of something really rare," the smuggler mused.

"Something so rare that a few ounces of it would be worth four hundred thousand crescents?" Ivan said, sounding unconvinced.

"Could be," Nash said defensively, tapping one finger on the edge of her cards. "What's rarer than gold?"

"I doubt this Quill is important just because it's worth a lot of gold," Evelyn said. "Tolliver Shadowwood is a bloody king—he already has enough wealth to last three lifetimes at least." She chewed on her lip, putting her cards facedown on the crate and steepling her slender fingers. "It has to be worth more than crescents. It has to be worth . . ."

"Power?" Tristan unexpectedly piped up. He flushed immediately, busying himself with his cards.

"Exactly," Evelyn said, picking her cards back up and slamming a bet of a broken button onto the makeshift table.

"And what's a bigger power move than cheeking the fucking Guildmaster of Thamorr?" Ryia asked, forcing her tone to stay casual. "He'd be a legend for pulling the wool over the eyes of a man like that."

"Except that he does not want credit for the theft," Ivan pointed out. "He came all the way to Dresdell to hire his thieves and be sure his tracks were covered."

"And for good reason," Evelyn said. "The Guildmaster will use his Disciples to beat into a pulp whoever steals this ruddy thing."

It was a good point, as much as Ryia hated to admit it. If whoever stole the Quill intended to use it to locate all the new, unbranded Adept, they would have to wait, what, at least ten years before the first babies started showing real signs of magic? Until then, they would just be running a very dangerous nursery. Something prickled in the back of her skull at the thought—was she wrong about what the Quill was used for? Or was Tolliver Shadowwood just a fucking idiot?

Across the makeshift table, the others were still bickering back and forth about the value of the Quill. Ryia let out a bark of laughter to cut through the chatter.

"You want to know what's so important about that Quill?" she said. "The fact that it's important to the Guildmaster. That's it. Maybe it's made of ophidian bone, maybe it's the pen Declan Day used to sign the treaty to end the Seven Decades' War—who gives half a shit?" She looked at her own cards again, then folded without betting. "Shadowwood's planning on using that Quill as a hostage—I'd bet my boots on it. Looking to trade it back to the Guildmaster for something he wants. Some extra Adept or something, or—"

"Gildemar," Tristan said. "To destroy them for kidnapping his son, I mean."

Ryia threw a hand out toward him. "Or Gildemar. Look, if we

get too distracted trying to understand how these fucking nobles think, we're never going to figure out where the damn thing is."

There was a long pause, then Nash said, "The Butcher's right. We know it's important, and we know we can make a shipload of gold off the thing. What else is there to know?"

"Well, there is one more thing to know," Tristan said. Dread crept up Ryia's chest . . . but the boy just dropped a pair of sevens on the crate. "That I am the champion of Bobbin Draw."

The energy around the table lightened as the rest of them threw down their cards in defeat.

Ryia always knew she liked that little con man.

"Wait—" Evelyn said, throwing out a hand as Tristan moved to gather his paltry winnings. She fanned the pile of cards out on the table. "Why are there five sevens in this deck?" She pointed an accusatory finger at Tristan. "You've been cheating!"

There was a long pause, and everyone but Evelyn burst out laughing, the conversation about the Quill seemingly already forgotten.

The ex-captain's face reddened. "You've all been cheating this whole ruddy time." She unfolded her legs, pushing herself away from the makeshift table. "That's why I haven't won a single game this entire trip, isn't it?"

"Maybe you're just bad at cards," Ryia said, grabbing a handful of almonds and popping them into her mouth.

"And dice," added Nash.

"Right, and bad at dice," Ryia agreed.

In response, Evelyn raised her right hand, crossing her first two fingers and turning her palm in.

"What's this? Vulgarity from the honorable captain?" Ryia asked, holding a hand to her chest as though aghast.

"Oh, let it rest, Butcher," Ivan said. "She is—"

"*She* is capable of standing up for herself, Rezkoye," Evelyn said. "Stow the pity."

Ivan shrugged. "Fine, then I will tell you . . . You are terrible at dice."

"How can anyone be *good* at dice?" Evelyn asked, exasperated.

"Come prepared," Tristan said, pulling a pair of dice from inside his coat.

"Loaded dice? Really?" Evelyn asked. "Who just walks around with loaded dice in their pockets?"

The ex-captain's eyes grew wide in exasperation as every other person sitting around the overturned crate sheepishly pulled dice from their pockets.

"You lot are unbelievable."

"Here, I have an extra set," Nash said through a mouthful of potato. She shifted her weight, pulling another pair of dice from her pants pocket and holding them out to Evelyn.

"That's not—that defeats the entire point of playing," Evelyn said, folding her arms.

"Suit yourself," Nash said, setting the dice down on the deck beside the captain and pushing herself to her feet. "Now if you layabouts will excuse me, I'm off to check our course."

The rest of the group scattered from there, but Ryia saw Evelyn's freckled fingers dart out, grab the loaded dice Nash had left, and stuff them into the pocket of her coat.

UNSURPRISINGLY, the loaded dice did not help Evelyn's chances over the next few days of games. Cheating might seem easy, but it was still a skill that had to be perfected. Ryia was confident they'd make a crook out of the captain yet, though—she was already well on her way. An accessory to the theft of a ship, on the run with four of the most infamous criminals in Carrowwick. Well, three of the most infamous criminals in Carrowwick and Tristan.

The sun sank below the waves yet again. At this moment, Evelyn was down in the cargo hold with Ivan, going through yet another iteration of the forged auction invitation. An important step—and one where Evelyn's knowledge was vital. If they didn't have an accurate-looking invitation they would never make it past the Disciples at the dock, and Evelyn was the only one of them to have seen this year's invitation.

Across the deck, Nash and Tristan were working on their dance steps. According to Evelyn, the tournament the first day of the auction concluded with an after-party. Tristan picked up the steps so quickly he was now helping Evelyn teach the others. Nash, on the other hand . . . Ryia bit back a laugh as the smuggler trod on Tristan's toes for the thousandth time.

While everyone else was busy with their other odd tasks, Ryia was stuck on map duty. They had traded off for days now, one person at a time stuck shuffling through their stolen blueprints, trying to answer the half-million-crescent question: Where was the Quill hidden?

Clem had studied the maps for less than a minute before he had known. Less than a twice-damned minute. The whole crew had been staring at these maps until their eyes blurred, but they still had no clue. Fuck Clem and his paranoid genius; he had told not a single one of them any part of his scheme. If he had, they wouldn't be in this mess right now. Arguably, if Ryia hadn't gotten him arrested they also wouldn't be in this mess . . . but all that was a pointless line of thought. That arrow had left its bow a long time ago.

Where was the damned thing? She shuffled her papers, images of the barracks, arena, and bell tower blurring together as she pulled out the blueprint of the manor for the dozenth time. Would he keep it in his house with him? It made sense to keep it close. She looked over the faded lines. There were four floors to the manor. She was pretty sure it wouldn't be in the basement; all that was down there was the Guildmaster's infamous dungeon. Her eyes widened as she looked over the dungeon map. What was that label in the corner? *Body chute?* A slide, cut into the wall, for the purpose of dumping the dead directly into the ocean off the cliff side. That seemed unnecessarily efficient.

Focus.

They were running out of time. Five days. They had five days to figure out where the Quill was and how they were going to steal it. Then, of course, Ryia would have to figure out how she was going to escape after she betrayed them all and destroyed it instead. Fleeing an island with no ship, not to mention her whole crew and the Guildmaster on her tail . . . One step at a time.

Ryia pushed back her long, black sleeves and massaged her temples, closing her eyes. She could crack this. After all, she knew the Guildmaster better than most. True, she hadn't exactly sat down for tea with the man, but she knew him well enough to have kept herself out of his disgusting claws all these years. Well enough to salivate at the idea of ruining his entire life by destroying the root of his power. That had to count for something.

Eyes still closed, she pictured his face. Cold. Sallow. Eyes like chunks of frigid sapphire. She could still see him, tall and slight, silhouetted against the flames, staring after her as she turned and sprinted into the trees.

"What in Adalina's name are those?"

Ryia's eyes snapped open at the voice. Ringing, clear. Like a sword being drawn from its scabbard. Evelyn Linley.

Her skin prickled, the hairs on her arms rising despite the heat. The ex-captain made her nervous for obvious reasons. She was the one who had *seen* Ryia back on the dock, after all. Seen how the Disciples had come right for her—and seen how she had knocked them over like a pair of rag dolls.

Only a complete moron would believe a normal person could

win a fight like that. She had to suspect something . . . but the captain hadn't said a damned thing about it since leaving Carrow-wick. Not to her—or anyone else, as far as Ryia could tell. Maybe she had forgotten in all the distractions. But how long could that luck hold?

Ryia turned, following Evelyn's gaze. Her chestnut-brown eyes were locked on Ryia's bare wrists. On the puckered, inch-wide scars encircling each one, pale as a corpse at the bottom of the Arden. Ryia tumbled headfirst into a cesspit of memory.

Rusted chains snared her wrists and ankles, tethering her to the wall of the chamber. The air was rank with the scents of mildew and dust and the blood of long-forgotten wounds. For years she had been down there, listening to the old man muttering to the darkness.

An endless parade of shaved, tattooed heads. They were brought into the chamber, black robes limp at their bare ankles, brands burned into their left cheeks. Not a single shred of fear registered in their eyes as, one by one, the hatchet found their throats.

"Adept from birth," the old man whispered, pouring the crimson stream over her tongue until she coughed and spluttered. "Adept from birth, it's in the blood. It's got to be in the blood."

"Ahem," Evelyn said.

Ryia blinked dumbly, pushing her sleeves back down to hide her mangled wrists. "Whatever I have the ladies of the Satin House do to me is none of your business," she finally lied, looking Evelyn up and down. "Unless you'd like it to be."

A flush bloomed from the neck of Evelyn's shirt, but she didn't look away. "Fine, keep your bloody secrets, but if you're looking to hide those scars, the worst thing you can do is cover them up." Her eyes combed over the patchwork of cuts and marks on Ryia's face. "When's the last time anyone asked you about one of those?"

"Your point?"

"You flaunt those marks like trophies, and everyone keeps their traps shut about them." Evelyn shook her head. "Even I know the best place to hide something is in plain sight."

The best place to hide something is in plain sight.

A rush of excitement stole over Ryia. She dove back to the maps, shuffling through until she found the one showing the whole island. Of course. The answer had been right in front of her this entire time. The one building they had all discarded without a second thought. The bell tower in the courtyard next to the arena.

The Guildmaster was confident. Bold in the way only the most powerful Kinetic in a century could be. But was he really crazy enough to hide the heart of his power somewhere so exposed?

She flipped through the drawings next: artists' renderings of auctions past. But it wasn't crazy. Not really. The bell tower was exposed, but the courtyard was surrounded by thirty-foot stone walls on three sides, connected to the arena on the fourth. Both the courtyard and arena were bound to be crawling with Disciples, not to mention watched by hundreds of prying noble eyes. It was the perfect place. It had to be there. She turned back to Evelyn with a grin.

"What are you so happy about?" asked the captain.

"Call the team together."

"Why?"

Ryia cocked her head to one side.

"You know where it is," Evelyn guessed.

"I know where it is."

17

TRISTAN

Water spread from the ship in every direction like a great sapphire carpet, calm and dazzling as *The Hardship* curved around the southern coast of Briel. Before them lay the Luminous Sea, behind them the Yawning, though Tristan had never been able to tell the difference. The border between them was like the one between the Saints' and Crowns' docks back in the Lottery, or the one between Edale and Dresdell: imaginary. Just a line some dead men decided to draw on a map.

He watched the sun as it reached its long, fiery fingers out from beneath the horizon. This was what he'd had in mind when he had stowed away on that ship out of Duskhaven all those months ago. The open ocean at his front, the wind at his back . . .

Of course, the illusion came crashing down any time he bothered to remember that certain death lay on the far side of this ocean. And in the crumpled letter tucked in his breast pocket.

He slipped his hand into his pocket, stomach sinking as the worn parchment brushed his fingers. He kept hoping one of these days he would discover the Crowns' threat had been nothing but an elaborate dream. He felt like the name on the letter was imprinted on his forehead for everyone to see. The name Wyatt Asher knew. The one that would damn him if anyone else discovered it.

But there were no Crowns on this ship. No one knew his secret here. His worries about the Crowns could wait until he got back to Carrowwick. He had plenty of other things to worry about in the meantime.

Rapid footsteps approached him from behind, followed by the unmistakable sound of retching.

Tristan whirled around, hurriedly withdrawing his hand from his pocket. He couldn't help but smile as he caught sight of the poor soul heaving her guts into the Luminous. The fearsome Butcher of Carrowwick. He settled in beside her as she heaved another mouthful into the dark waters below.

"What do you know?" he said. "Callum Clem's deadliest merc, brought low by water." He leaned back against the rail, his heart performing a daring backflip as she looked up, wiping her mouth with one long sleeve. "You know, that's information I could sell for a good bit of coin back in the Lottery."

Ryia cracked a carnivorous smile. "You tell anyone about this and you'll get to see how well you do your little card tricks with one hand."

He backed up a pace, both hands out as a gesture of peace. "All right, all right." He grinned. "Bet I'd still be better than Roland."

She snorted. "I think Captain Honor would be better than Roland," she said, looking toward the hatch to indicate Evelyn, sleeping below.

Tristan's smile dripped away slowly as he thought of the ex–Needle Guard captain. She must have a memory like a court scribe the way she kept looking at him, trying to place where she'd seen him before. Hopefully, she would have trouble remembering his face just a little longer.

"You all right there?" Ryia asked, clapping him on the shoulder. She gathered a mouthful of saliva, spitting the last traces of vomit out into the churning wake of *The Hardship*.

Tristan shook his head to clear it. "Yeah, why?"

"You look like you do every time Corrigan tells one of his lame ghost stories." She made a big show of chewing her fingernails like a scared child.

"Just a little nervous, I guess."

"You should be," Ryia said. "I mean, it *is* your plan we're using, so if it goes to hell, it's going to be your head." Her eyes darkened. The expression was gone an instant later, replaced by her usual cheeky wink. "I'll ask Clem to go easy on you."

"Thanks, but no thanks. I've seen Clem's 'easy.' It's not much different from his harsh."

Ryia turned away, looking out over the water. "He could be dead by the time we get back."

"He won't be," Tristan said bitterly. "You know he won't be."

Ryia was silent for a long time. Tristan recognized her usual dismissal. He was just turning to walk away when she cleared her throat.

"If you really hate working for the son of a bitch so much, why haven't you made a run for it yet?"

"If you want me dead that badly, you should just kill yourself. Quicker that way," Tristan said with a hollow laugh. "Otherwise I'll keep working off my debt, thank you very mu—"

"You're not completely brainless, Beckett. You know that debt of yours won't be settled until Boreas is south of Briel." She locked him with a haunted stare. "Only an idiot tries to play fair when they know everyone else at the table is a cheat. You want your freedom, you're going to have to take it. Kneecaps don't break themselves."

Tristan narrowed his eyes suspiciously. He had never seen Ryia take anything seriously before, let alone give advice. Any second now she would crack her dangerous smile and make some obscene gesture. . . .

But she didn't.

Finally, Tristan shook his head. "Not all of us know how to break kneecaps, Ryia."

She studied him a second longer, then averted her gaze, looking out over the ocean. "Lucky for you, I'm an expert. If we make it out of this in one piece, I'll give you some pointers," she said, her voice oddly hoarse.

She was silent for another long moment, and by the time she turned back to him, her face showed only her usual smirk. "So, you sure we have to trust the nimrod and the Borean to find the entrance to the tower?"

"Would you rather I leave you alone with Captain Honor?"

"Fair enough." Ryia leaned back against the rail beside him. "But hey, maybe the Guildmaster won't even bother hiding the door to his treasure."

"Something that valuable?" Tristan asked, shaking his head and wondering for the dozenth time what made this thing so valuable in the first place. What could Tolliver Shadowwood want with some antique of the Guildmaster's? It must be like Ryia had said a few days before. The king probably meant to hold it hostage, use it to trade for something else. A foolish move, if that *was* his plan. The Guildmaster could just march his Disciples into Edale and take the Quill back without granting Tolliver Shadowwood a single thing in return. It made no sense. . . .

"Who knows?" Ryia said, cutting through his thoughts. "The Guildmaster *is* the craziest bastard in Thamorr."

"You say that like you know the man." Tristan chortled.

"We go way back," she said with a grin. "I've stolen from him before, you know."

Tristan rolled his eyes at the obvious lie. "Have you? Good, then you'll be ready for this."

"You'd both better be ready for this."

Tristan jumped at the voice. Nash stood on the deck, arms folded. She pointed toward the northeast horizon with her chin. As Tristan turned his head, his stomach clenched so violently he thought he might follow Ryia's lead and be sick.

A low shadow clung to the surface of the water like a toddler to his mother's leg, just off the coast of Briel. It was surrounded by sails. Some broad, some small, some approaching from far up the northern coastline, some looping up from the south. The Guild-master's island, in full preparation for the auction.

It was too late for doubts now. The job had officially begun.

18

RYIA

The sun grew like a weed above the horizon. Ryia stood in the cargo hold of *The Hardship*, surrounded by strangers. Or at least they looked like strangers.

There was a tall, well-dressed woman in the shadows. The dark-haired girl beside her dabbed powder over the freckles dotting her nose. A few steps away, a younger boy leaned casually against the ladder, his hair styled in the severe cut popular in southern Boreas, his cheekbones sticking out like cliffs below eyes so blue they almost seemed to glow.

The man in front of Ryia pored over her with sea-green eyes. It was Ivan, buried somewhere under those layers of fabric and face paint.

"I don't need to remind you how important it is not to fuck this up, right?" Ryia asked.

"No," Ivan said, his Borean accent coming out more clearly than usual in the short, clipped word. "Now stop *schwindlin*, unless you would like for this to end up buried in your throat by mistake."

The "this" he was referring to was a straight razor held right at Ryia's temple.

"I don't know if I've ever heard you make a threat before, Ivan," Ryia said. "Keep that up and I might just want to finally see what all the fuss is about with you. . . ."

"Just get on with it," Nash snapped. "We don't have all morning."

Fear seeped into Ryia's stomach like tea from a bag as Ivan drew the razor across her scalp. A fistful of glossy black locks fluttered to the deck. When every scrap of hair had been removed from her head, Ivan grabbed a tiny pot of black ink, dipping his utensil in and painstakingly marking the newly exposed skin.

Evelyn peered anxiously through the hatch at the masts now converging from every direction. "Remind me again why we didn't do this out at sea with only the gulls for company?"

Ivan turned Ryia's head to catch the light. "The Adept are given a serum as children so they cannot grow hair."

"I'm aware of that," Evelyn said.

"Well then, would it not look odd if she had hair sprouting like reeds? No. A fresh shave." He held up his brush. "Besides, you try painting this design while Nash hits every *verdammte* wave in the Luminous Sea."

"Sorry, Ivan, next time I'll make sure to dodge 'em," Nash said.

Ryia took a deep breath, trying to ignore the pressing walls of the tiny space. "Make sure the tail curves up. And the top part bends over backward."

Ivan raised an eyebrow, never lifting the brush from Ryia's skull. "Which one of us is the expert forger?"

Ryia's eyes widened as Ivan reached for the lit candle beside them. "If you singe off my eyebrow, I *will* castrate you."

"I would like to see you try."

Ryia's retort was lost in a hiss of pain as the first dollop of hot wax hit her skin. Ivan swirled the half-dried wax around Ryia's left cheek. He followed with the red ink. A drop here, a drop there . . . then stepped back to examine his handiwork.

"*Fahlerlos*," he said, eyes glimmering with the smile his lips never seemed to form naturally. *Flawless.*

"I think 'terrifying' is the word you're looking for," Tristan said, looking queasy.

Ryia examined her reflection as Ivan held up a small mirror. Both words fit just fine.

The freshly stitched robes. The sea serpent brand on her left cheek. Her shaven head, marked with a swirling black *K*.

She adjusted the robes to make sure the hatchets lashed to her back were well-concealed. *Hiding in plain sight.* That was a game two could play, Guildmaster.

"All right, next comes the docking inspection," Evelyn said, looking about as uncomfortable in her dress and pointed shoes as a horse would in the same outfit. "Time to see if your so-called forger is as good as he claims to be."

Ivan pulled an ornate envelope from the pocket of his cobalt-blue jacket. "The execution is perfect, this I guarantee. As long as your memory has not failed you . . ."

"My memory is fine," Evelyn shot back, raised voice ricocheting around the narrow hold.

"Then we've got nothing to worry about," Nash chimed in. "Ivan's been drawing up false letters for Clem since—ow!" The smuggler cut her sentence short as Ryia elbowed her in the ribs.

"Not in front of the snitch," she said, looking pointedly at Evelyn's family ring, still circling her middle finger, cool metal sparkling in the sunlight streaming down through the open hatch.

Evelyn pursed her lips at the jibe. "If you're wrong, you lot won't make it five steps off the dock without an arrow in your skull."

"I like how it's 'we' when everything's going all right and 'you lot' when it's about to go to shit," Ryia observed. "Anyone else no-tice that?"

Evelyn shot her a glare that could freeze hot wax. "Adept ser-vants aren't supposed to talk. Maybe you should practice."

"I'm at a disadvantage there, Captain," Ryia said smoothly, ig-noring the shiver running down her spine. "Pretty sure they cut out the tongues of the true Adept."

A lie. Across the hold, Nash winced, lifting a hand absently to her jaw.

"Maybe that can be arranged," Evelyn said.

"For Felice's sake, give it a rest," Nash said, climbing out of the hatch. The structured Borean jacket and leggings made her look at least ten years older than she was. The auburn-colored wig just made her look ridiculous. She gestured to her costume. "I didn't spend every crescent I got from that prick Bardley on this shit so we can fail this job before it even starts."

Evelyn shouldered past Ryia, pulling herself up the ladder. "Get away from the bloody helm, Nash. I've told you five times." She grabbed her by the shoulders. "Stand here. Ivan here . . ."

She positioned every member of the crew carefully. When she got to Ryia she grabbed her by the collar, dragging her into place beside Nash. Evelyn's vivid brown eyes burst with contempt as they bored into Ryia's.

"You don't move. Your face doesn't move. You don't scratch an itch. You don't make any of your little comments. You don't say a damned word."

"I've never seen an Adept before, so that's helpful, thanks."

Evelyn's eyes narrowed, and Ryia immediately regretted saying anything at all. She could tell the captain was thinking back to the docks in Carrowwick. Back to the Disciples that should have taken her down. Remembering that there was really only one answer to the question of how she was still drawing breath. No normal person could hope to best a single Kinetic, let alone two of them . . . let alone Disciples. . . .

But she said nothing, just turned away and took her place beside Tristan as *The Hardship* drew steadily closer to the Guildmaster's harbor.

"You wreck my ship and you're dead," Nash murmured to the crewman at the helm.

"It's not *your* ship," Tristan protested.

"What do you mean it's not my ship?"

"We all stole it together—it's *our* ship."

"On the list of suspicious behaviors that will out you as thieves, where do you think bragging about theft is?" Evelyn hissed.

A droplet of sweat rolled down the side of Ryia's naked skull as the ship slipped past the skeletal masts of those already tied to the docks. This was it. The first real hurdle.

The auction was two days long. One full day to case the island, to set up the last few metaphorical dominos, and one day to actually pull off the job itself. There would be plenty of chances for them to get caught, but this was the first. The first test of the ramshackle plan they had thrown together in the absence of the brilliant Callum Clem.

Any misstep and they'd be marched down to the infamous cells beneath the Guildmaster's manor, where they would be questioned, tortured, and eventually killed. That was a comforting thought. . . .

"What now?" she asked through the side of her mouth as Nash's crew secured *The Hardship*.

The only response she got was an anxious *shh* from Tristan and a glare from Evelyn. A moment later two near-identical Disciples boarded the ship.

Near identical. They were all near identical: all bald, tattooed, and wearing the same damned blue robes. Really, it was lucky none of them were given names; the Guildmaster would have had a bitch of a time keeping them straight.

Ryia gave her eyes a dull cast, staring straight ahead at nothing. Her heart was still racing. Stupid thing. She held her breath as the Disciples stopped just in front of her, not releasing it until their eyes slid over her with cold disinterest.

They didn't recognize her.

Of course they didn't recognize her. It was beyond paranoid to think they would have. Not counting the Guildmaster, there were only five Disciples who had gotten close enough to see Ryia's face in the past nine years. Five Disciples who were now just five rotting corpses scattered around Thamorr.

The Disciple on the left clapped twice. "Search the ship. Come on, hurry up, we have dozens of these to check."

"Sorry, master," came the somber, many-voiced reply.

A flurry of blue robes streamed from the docks onto the ship. Adept in training. Their heads were shaven but uninked, their faces still wary and expressive, not dead and emotionless like the purchased Adept living as slaves on the mainland. So these hadn't been fully brainwashed. Not yet.

When, she wondered, did they lose that last glowing ember of free will?

They flitted over the decks and beneath the hatch, searching for contraband. Ryia felt Evelyn tighten beside her, but there was no need to worry. The only incriminating materials on board were the black beads Ivan had bought back in Golden Port, and those were tucked safely inside his trousers. She seriously doubted they would think to check there.

The Adept-in-training emerged empty-handed from the cargo hold.

"Nothing?" asked the Disciple on the right.

"Nothing, master," answered one of the young ones.

The Disciple on the left nodded, then turned to Ivan. He held out a hand and coughed expectantly.

Ivan shared a confused look with Nash as the Disciple sighed in irritation, snapping his fingers impatiently. They had never been around Disciples before, clearly. Had never seen an Adept express a human emotion before. Did they think they were all born as mindless zombies? They had to know the Guildmaster had his own free will—how else would he rule? And who did they think took over as the next Guildmaster when the last one died? One of the Disciples—always. Ryia didn't know the process, exactly, but she could only assume it was some kind of fucked-up gladiator-style battle for the title. If the Disciples were just as brainwashed as the poor saps that got sold to mainland masters, how could any of them step up and take on the mantle of Guildmaster? No. Some of them had to stay clearheaded. And impatient, from the looks of these two.

Ivan pulled the invitation from his jacket pocket, and the Disciple grabbed it with gloved fingers. He turned his head, and Ryia saw the S tattooed amid the intricate swirls of ink covering his skull. A Senser. She'd have to keep her murderous thoughts at bay, then. Always a challenge.

The entire crew held its breath as the Disciple looked over the invitation. Anxiety melted into sagging relief as he handed the envelope back to Ivan.

"Welcome to the Guildmaster's island," the Disciple said. He didn't sound very welcoming. Then he turned abruptly, descending back onto the dock.

Ryia shared a look with the others as the Disciples and their young charges disappeared up the gangplank to the next ship on the docks. They had done the impossible. They had made it onto the island.

AFTER MORE than two weeks trapped on that bobbing cork, the cobblestone path felt unnaturally hard under Ryia's feet. She might have sighed with relief if she wasn't currently dressed as her worst fear, walking straight toward the man she had been running from for nine long years.

The paths leading across the island were lined with vendors. Old men watched painted young women, holding out strings of jewels Ryia imagined would be one hell of a nuisance while scaling a wall. Sniveling noble children surrounded carts full of cakes and tarts. Their party was pushed aside as a troupe of dancers streamed from a ship waving the Edalish flag, heading for the arena. The performers' dresses were made almost entirely of feathers. Evelyn eyed them with a wrinkled nose.

The clothing became more and more ridiculous the closer they drew to the arena. Massive lace skirts, tights and velvet pants, doublets even Callum Clem wouldn't be caught dead in. The crowds were so thick, Ryia felt like she couldn't breathe. What a way to go, smothered by silk and body odor.

Finally the archway to the arena came into view. The twin pillars were made to look like Adept servants—one a bulky Kinetic, the other a wiry Senser—kneeling with their eyes to the ground. Their carved stone backs supported a massive carving of Thamorr. The unified kingdoms, borne on the backs of the Adept. Subtle.

The arena was massive. Even larger than the ones built for those ridiculous prancing show horses in Gildemar. It looked like half of a giant fruit bowl, smooth stone steps leading down to a base tiled in an elaborate mosaic in the same pattern tattooed on the Disciples' heads. The seats on the steps were already nearly full despite the crowds still surging through the archway, and at the bottom of the pit, some very familiar faces were arranged haughtily in the first row beside the auction stage.

In the first set of thrones, sipping tall goblets of clear liquor beneath a black-and-red banner featuring a snarling bear, sat four Boreans: the Tovolkovs. King Andrei, far on the left, reminded Ryia powerfully of a potato, albeit a potato someone had obviously tried to carve into a man.

Thankfully the children seemed to have taken after their mother, Queen Isabeth. She was taller than her husband by far. Slender as an adder and about as friendly, if the rumors were true. Despite the heat, the lot of them were dressed head to toe in furs. A status symbol in Boreas, but the morons would drown in their sweat before midday this far south.

Beside that dreary lot was the pompous-looking egret of Gildemar, the golden sigil suspended on a vivid teal background. All the people seated beneath it were plump and ruddy cheeked, aside from the queen Irisa, sister to old Potato Face. No matter what chains she wore, Ryia thanked the goddesses she hadn't been born noble. Imagine having to use your genitals to form a political alliance. Worse than torture.

The lace-sailed ship of Dresdell was next, positioned over King Duncan Baelbrandt and his party. Evelyn fidgeted at the sight of the purple-clad guards beside them. If it weren't for Ryia—for what she had done to Efrain Althea—Evelyn would be dressed all in purple, standing there beside her king right now. Ryia's stomach dropped, cheeks heating as a pang of something shot through her. Guilt? Impossible. She was immune to the emotion.

Next came a foursome seated beneath a bright orange banner bearing a storm-gray scorpion. Ryia couldn't help but stare at the woman seated in the left-hand chair. She had never seen this woman before, but she knew who she was. Queen Calandra

Althea. Dark hair, dark eyes, dark skin, all radiating with quiet, calm power.

She and her Gildeshman husband were flanked on either side by the children they had not managed to marry off yet: the crown princess on the left, Ryia's old friend Efrain Althea seated on the right. She almost lost her composure when she saw the jeweled glove covering his right hand, hiding his missing finger.

The last party, seated beneath a banner of a silver willow tree on a grass-green backdrop, looked as though someone had just pissed in their wine. She wasn't surprised; it was the party from Edale, after all. Tolliver Shadowwood sat on the left. He reminded Ryia of Clem. Calm and collected, his eyes flitting over every inch of the arena, watching and calculating. It was hard to believe this was the man foolish enough to think he would be able to hide the stolen Quill from the Guildmaster and his Disciples long enough to grow his own army from literal infants. Once again, Ryia was struck by the odd feeling that she was missing something about the Quill. She pushed the thought aside.

The woman seated beside Shadowwood was at least fifteen years his junior. She looked oddly familiar, but maybe that was just because she was the spitting image of her mother, Queen Calandra of Briel. Skin the color of mahogany, dark hair coiled into a bun at the crown of her head. The only sign of her Gildesh father was in her eyes—so pale a blue they looked sharp, like glinting shards of glass.

The chair beside her was empty, the other two chairs filled with squirming children. The empty seat, of course, would be for Dennison Shadowwood. So dramatic. Did they think he was just going to turn up and take his chair? If no one had tried to ransom the missing crown prince yet, it was because he was already dead.

"Quit *schwindlin*," Ivan hissed a few steps away.

She turned her head slightly to see Tristan clench his fists at his sides, staring stubbornly at the ground. He was grinding his teeth. And sweating like a Borean in Sandport. What was his problem? Aside from the obvious.

A hush fell over the crowd. The thick air snared in Ryia's throat as she saw . . . him. He swept across the stage, his rotten eyes combing the crowd, and his worm lips curled into a superior sneer. She could almost feel the heat of the flames, hear the rattle and clank of brittle chains splintering. The raw memory of charred flesh and blood swirled in her nostrils. Her fingers twitched, longing to reach for the hatchets hidden beneath her robes. She fought to keep her face still, her eyes dead as hatred pulsed through every inch of her.

The seventh Guildmaster of Thamorr had arrived.

19

IVAN

Ivan knew the most dangerous part of the job had yet to begin, but he could not help but feel relieved as his feet finally left the deck of that *verdammte* ship. Nash always said a ship was the purest form of freedom. How was it freedom to be restricted to twenty paces each way for weeks on end?

Perhaps he was still sour from his first sea voyage. Three years ago, stowed away behind sacks of leeks and crates of *stervod* on the first ship he found sailing south from Boreas.

Ivan shook the thought from his head, holding his shoulders back as he cast a cool eye around the arena. Evelyn had warned there would be a number of Adept here, but Ivan had never imagined this many. Dozens of bald, tattooed Disciples encircled the pit, blue cloaks swirling in the wind. They seemed even more dangerous after what Ivan had seen back in the harbor . . . now that he knew the Guildmaster's soldiers all had thoughts and minds of their own. Every noble, merchant, and child seemed to be accompanied by his own Adept servants as well, brought from

the mainland. These Kinetics and Sensers were the more familiar breed—stone-faced and branded, padding obediently at their
masters' heels, all of them purchased at this very event in some
year past.

The Kinetics received most of the attention, but anyone with
a brain knew the Sensers were the greater threat. The old stories
said they could read minds and see into the future. The Butcher
had brayed like a donkey when Evelyn had said as much. She insisted the Sensers would take no notice of them as long as no one
decided to start lopping off heads. Ivan was not sure how Ryia would
know something like that, but she had snuck in and out of the
Bobbin Fort half a hundred times and come out with all her limbs
attached, so she could not be completely clueless.

So far, it appeared she was right. Dozens of Sensers within a
stone's throw of where they sat and not a single alarm had been
raised. Hopefully, Ivan's team was just as conveniently oblivious
to his machinations when the time came. His stomach clenched
with guilt at the thought, but the guilt was pointless. The choice
between Kasimir's life and the lives of a few of Clem's dock rats
should be an easy one. "Should" being the operative word there,
unfortunately. He tucked the thought away.

Tristan fidgeted to his left. The usually cocky young con man
pulled anxiously at his coat, shrinking backward, trying to hide his
face behind his steadily curling hair.

"Quit *schwindlin*," Ivan hissed, elbowing Tristan surreptitiously
in the kidney.

The first lesson Kasimir had taught him: an innocent man does
not look uncomfortable in his own clothing.

Tristan clenched his fists, his eyes locked on his toes. Ivan wondered what was wrong with the boy. Tristan always had a measure
of composure not usually found in sixteen-year-old ship rats. The

night Clem had nearly slit his throat for cheating at the Miscreants' Temple, he had not broken a sweat.

Perhaps he was merely too callow for a job of this caliber. A job with a thousand elements, where only one had to go wrong for them all to end up rotting at the bottom of the ocean. He had tried to warn Clem the boy was too young, but the Snake had insisted on bringing him along. Ivan still could not fathom why.

He turned back to the stage at the base of the arena as a hush fell over the crowd. He had never seen the man taking his place on the center throne before, but there was only one person who could command that kind of attention. The seventh Guildmaster of Thamorr.

The Guildmaster's blue robes were stitched through with elaborate swirls of silver threading that danced and shone in the sunlight like flakes of snow caught in the wind. An absurd comparison on so hot a day. His scalp was a mesmerizing maze of black tattoos on pale, bare flesh, and the face beneath reminded Ivan of a melting candle, scraps of prematurely aging skin drooping over one another in a race to reach his stubby neck.

He held up his hands as though to quiet the already silent masses. "Welcome, fine guests from the kingdoms of Thamorr," he said, sounding like a *katz* welcoming a group of mice to its dinner bowl. "The Guilds thank you for the long travels that have brought you here.

"Tomorrow night the auction will take place. We have sixty-seven wards available for purchase. But first comes a day of celebration. Today we honor the truce among the kingdoms of Thamorr that began with the noble Declan Day. A truce that has held strong for nearly three hundred years."

Onstage behind him, a few nobles shifted in their seats. The Guildmaster appeared not to notice. Or perhaps he simply did not care. He clapped sharply, and the arena was filled with the clattering sound of horse hooves. His eyes sparkled with what Ivan was certain was mischief.

"Let the tournament begin!"

BETWEEN THE blinding sun and the reckless heat, the day wore on achingly slowly. But unfortunately there was nothing that could be done but wait. This was the first day of the auction—a full day of tournaments and celebrations. Every guest on the island was inside this arena. The Saints would have to wait until the show had ended to begin their work. There would be a bell tower to case, some last-minute supplies to steal, details to work out . . . and they would have precious little time in which to do it. But everyone knew day one of the auction was the tournament, and if they did not play along, they would certainly be caught.

So there they sat, useless and baking in the sunlight, stomachs curdling with anxiety as the hours ticked away. Adept-in-training picked nervously through the crowds, serving expensive foods from all five kingdoms from massive platters while the crowd watched fools, acrobats, and contests between armored men on horseback.

Ryia nudged Evelyn as the group of feather-clad dancers spilled from a chamber along the back wall.

"There had better not be a ruddy feather in sight tomorrow," Evelyn whispered darkly.

The dancers finished their twirling, and out came the prancing show horses of Gildemar. There were shows and displays of every kind, but the bulk of the entertainment featured Adept duels.

Ivan had been to the Catacombs a dozen times, but these fights were nothing like the brutal, bloody shows in the Kestrel Crowns' pits. Many of these wards were far stronger, far more precise than the Adept Ivan had seen fight before. Like the youths who had come with the Disciples to inspect their ship, their eyes were still sharp and alert. They fought with frantic energy, full of fear and adrenaline, where the pit fighters on the mainland fought mechanically, blandly . . . as though they were in a dream.

The servitude of the Adept had always bothered Ivan in some ways, but he had assumed the creatures were simply mindless from birth. Now he could see that was clearly not the case. Something was done to them to make them so obedient. So . . . *stehlen*. Stonelike. To allow them to grow nearly to adulthood before wiping them blank and selling them to the highest bidder . . . that seemed a whole new breed of cruelty.

Ivan watched with growing unease as the fights wore on. One Kinetic's face twisted in fear as it was magically strangled by its own robes mid-fight. Another fell victim to an arrow summoned from one of the Shadowwood guards' quivers. In one fight, a single Kinetic fought ten heavily armed soldiers and won in a matter of moments.

There was no death in these contests. The Guildmaster used his Kinetic power to stop each match before real harm could be done—after all, many of these wards would be for sale tomorrow. The goal today was not death but a display of prowess. Ivan noted the greed in the eyes of the merchants surrounding him. These men were fools.

This was not just a sales pitch. This was a show of control. The strongest Adept were never offered at the auction, everyone knew this. They stayed on to become Disciples. To serve the Guildmaster for the rest of their days. This was a threat, and a thinly veiled one at that. *Play by my rules*, the Guildmaster was saying. *You exist only because I allow you to exist. I could crush you in an instant.*

One look at the stage told Ivan this message was not lost on everyone. Tolliver Shadowwood stared past the show directly at the Guildmaster, looking positively murderous. Ivan narrowed his eyes. What did this Quill do, again? And why did King Tolliver want it so badly? Exactly what was it that he would be handing over to the Borean *Keunich* if all went to plan?

Ivan bit the inside of his cheek, pushing the thought away. The Quill was Kasimir's ticket to freedom. That was the only thing Ivan would be using the *verdammte* thing for. What did it matter to him what anyone else cared to do with it?

Ivan patted his forehead gingerly with his kerchief, careful to avoid removing the paint coating his face.

"You all right there?" Nash asked.

"Just the heat, *harz*," he answered. The Borean pet name felt strange on his tongue, but they were supposed to be husband and wife for this little charade. With this many ears around, anyone could be listening. "Is it not getting to you?"

"Not all of us are as delicate as you, love."

He shot her a look. "We will go up to Nordham this Januar. Then we will see who is delicate."

At long last the sun began to set, and the Guildmaster rose from his seat, turning to face the sweat-soaked crowd.

"The Guilds thank you for joining in today's celebrations. We know many of you have traveled long and are eager to return to your ships, and the rest are eager to begin the festivities in the courtyard."

Cheers greeted his statement, and the Guildmaster smiled slyly.

"But first, we wish to present to you the honored few of this year's trainees who will remain on the island to train the future generations of Adept servants." The Guildmaster waved one arm pompously.

Ivan squinted, focusing on the wards who stepped forward from the line. As he had suspected, they were the strongest of the day. One Kinetic at the end of the line bit back a smile. Another patted the ward beside it on the back in apparent celebration. The wards who had not been selected looked petrified. But of course they were. They knew what would become of them. Perhaps that was why they had fought with such vigor. They knew they were competing for one of the coveted Disciple roles. Competing to keep their wits and their lives intact. A pang of emotion burned through Ivan's belly.

What would happen to make them so flat? So vacant? Here they were, one day from being sold to the mainland lords, and they were still filled with emotion. Undeniably human. Was it the branding process that somehow sapped the life from them? No matter what it was, something had to happen to the purchasable wards between now and tomorrow afternoon to make them as obedient as the servants he had seen on the mainland before. Some treatment from which these grinning, young Disciples-to-be would be spared.

"The auction will begin three hours past midday tomorrow," the Guildmaster went on. "It will continue until the last ward has been sold."

Ivan shook his head to clear it, exchanging a look with Nash. The crowd began to churn, heading toward the bell tower courtyard.

"Are you nervous?" Nash asked quietly.

Behind them, Evelyn hissed, "You? Nervous? You two have nothing to worry about. We're the ones about to risk our hides." She nudged Tristan. "You coming?"

The boy nodded, eyes darting around. He followed as the ex-captain began to wind her way back toward the docks. The Butcher fell in behind, eerily still and silent. Ivan would never have dreamed she was capable of not punching something for this long. Perhaps he would have to put her in costume more often when they returned to Carrowwick.

Returned to Carrowwick. He caught himself. He would not be returning to Carrowwick with the others. And with the way they had left things . . . they would be wise not to return either.

"Come, *harz*," Nash said, grabbing his arm. "We have a party to attend."

They did indeed. But more importantly, they had a bell tower to case. Finally, they could get back to work. Ivan linked his elbow with Nash's, looking toward the tower. It poked up above the stage like the mast of a sunken ship over the waves. A massive, perfect cylinder of smooth stone positioned in the center of a small courtyard. The courtyard was surrounded by high walls, and its only entrance—or exit—led through the arena. The dying rays of sunlight glinted off the bronze bell as it sent its mourning toll out over the island. Ivan repressed a sniff of amusement as he remembered the conversation the day Ryia had solved the Guildmaster's puzzle.

"Our problems are solved, you lazy shits," she had said.

"How exactly do you figure?" Evelyn had asked, looking incredulous. "If it's in the tower, that makes our problems worse. The courtyard is guarded by half a dozen Disciples at least. You'll never get in."

"I'll just climb it."

Ivan had seen the Butcher climb a fifty-foot vertical like she was climbing a set of stairs, so he had not understood Evelyn's derisive snort at the time. Seeing the tower now, however, he had to agree. Not only did it look utterly unscalable with its smooth, polished sides, but it was completely exposed, visible from the stage and the seats in the arena.

Evelyn was right. If they had any hope of reaching the top of that tower and stealing the Quill, they would need to get inside it first.

"I've spent some . . . quality time with my fair share of merchants who hate their wives, but I wasn't aware that was part of our cover," Nash whispered.

She was right, Ivan realized, taking note of his posture. He was stiff, awkward, his hip held a few inches from Nash's as though he could not bear the idea of touching her.

"Sorry." What in *Yavol*'s realm was wrong with him? Flirting was usually as easy as breathing. Now was certainly not the time to lose his nerve.

He pulled Nash close, pressing against her as they entered the courtyard. There were people everywhere. Nobles, merchants, and vendors, all somehow already looking deep in their cups though the night had hardly begun. Adept servants hovered behind their masters, and all around them was a dull buzz of conversation. Figures and speculations. Who married his daughter off to which minor nobility. What Brillish cinnamon was going for these days.

"Now there's a pair of unfamiliar faces."

Ivan hitched a smile onto his face, turning toward the voice. It belonged to a squat Gildesh man with dust-colored hair and a deep complexion.

He thrust a hand out. "Peter Au—"

"Is that Peter Aurelle?" asked another voice. Southern Edalish by the sound of it.

"Elton Smithe," said Peter. "I've just been introducing myself to . . ."

"Veber," Ivan said smoothly, shaking the man's hand. "Kristofer Veber. And this is my wife . . ."

"Sveta. Aus Soulvik," Nash said, naming the southernmost Borean city, just along the border to Edale. Even after all their work on the ship, her Borean accent was nothing short of atrocious.

"Soulvik, eh?" asked the Edalish man, who, thankfully, did not seem to notice. "What line of trade you in?"

"Lumber transport," said Ivan. "The forests in Boreas are not getting any thicker—"

"—and the people are not getting any warmer," Nash finished.

"This your first year here? I don't think I've seen you before," said Elton, his eyes narrowing.

"Yes, this is the first year we have made enough of an impact to earn an invitation. But with luck it will not be the last!" Ivan said.

Peter waved over a nearby ward carrying a tray through the crowd. He grabbed two goblets, thrusting them into their hands. "I'll drink to that!"

Elton took a sip of wine, nodding slowly, still looking suspicious. "Lumber's a good business, should do well enough to earn an invitation back next year if you count your coins right."

Ivan held up his goblet, nudging Nash with his foot as she glanced toward the bell tower for the dozenth time. "To the first year of many, then."

"Indeed!" cheered Peter. He wet his lips with a clumsy tongue. "Now, we knew someone else in lumber, didn't we, Elton? What ever happened to old Master Grayson? I've not seen him in four years or more."

"Four years? Try nine, Peter! Have you not heard?" Elton leaned forward with the air of someone who took great pride in being the first to know the gossip. "Abner Grayson is dead. His estate gone. Lost to a fire."

"Is that so?" Peter said. "Terrible, just terrible."

"That's not the worst of it," Elton said. "When the Shadow Wardens sorted through the rubble they found a dozen Adept inside, branded with a dozen different seals. All dead."

"Purchased illegally?" asked Peter, appalled.

"Rumor said they weren't purchased at all," said Elton. "Stolen."

Nash fidgeted uncomfortably with the sleeves of her blouse. Elton gave her a curious look, and Ivan nudged her again. This Edalish man was getting dangerously close to catching on to their game. And Nash's evident discomfort was not helping.

Peter shook his head in disbelief. "And they were lost to the fire? What a shame. I hope the rightful owners were compensated."

"They weren't lost to the fire," said Elton, finally looking back to Peter. He drew a finger across his neck. "Throats were slit."

"Slit?" asked Nash, openly aghast, her false accent almost completely falling away. "But why?"

"Old man must have gone insane. Can you imagine such a waste of gold?" Peter said.

"Gold? That's what you're worried about?" Nash burst out, clearly disgusted.

Ivan was surprised that Nash would care. Few of Callum Clem's Saints would value any life but their own over gold, and few people anywhere would value the life of an Adept servant above anything at all. A sense of warmth filled him at the thought. The more he learned about the smuggler, the more fascinating he found her.

But he and Nash were stuck in a small courtyard on a small island surrounded by people who had come here expressly to purchase Adept as slaves . . . this was hardly the time or place to speak of rights for the Adept.

If Elton Smithe was not suspicious before, he certainly was now. One of his thick eyebrows flicked upward. "Concerned about the lives of the Adept beasts, are you, *Missus Veber*?" he asked, putting far too much emphasis on the name for Ivan's liking.

Ivan gave the pair of merchants a charming smile, draining his goblet and setting it on the table beside them. "This has been lovely, gentlemen, but I do not want to waste this music." He looked meaningfully toward the swirling masses of skirts and doublets at the base of the bell tower. "*Harz?* Shall we?"

Nash swallowed, closing her fingers around his. Ivan could feel Elton Smithe's eyes boring into the back of his head until they slipped into the swaying crowd and out of sight.

There was rarely cause for formal dancing in the Lottery, and there had been even less cause for it in Boreas. Evelyn and Tristan had shown them the basic steps aboard the ship, and they had practiced for hours, much to Ryia's amusement. And with good reason—a single misstep would give them away as outsiders.

Frauds who did not belong. Although it may already be too late for that.

"I know you are not used to it, Nash, but you need to let me lead," he whispered, his hand cupping the small of her back, trying not to think about how close the smuggler's face now came to his own.

"Fine," said Nash. "As long as you don't muck it up."

But Ivan was mucking it up. He could not recall Tristan's lessons. His mind was too full of Elton Smithe's suspicious looks, and, if he was being honest with himself, a healthy dose of guilt as well. By this time tomorrow he would be on his way to Boreas, and Nash would be . . . It was probably best not to think about that right now.

Nash cracked her signature smile as Ivan trod on her foot for the third time. "If I didn't know any better, I'd say you were nervous."

He held his arm out, spinning her away until only their fingers remained clasped. His heart stuttered again as she spun back into him, his hand closing on her hip.

"I am never nervous." Back in the Lottery that was utter truth, but here the words had the bitter flavor of a lie. He leaned in. "I have been in greater danger than this before."

"In the Lottery?" Nash chuckled. "Wyatt Asher would be thrilled to learn you're more afraid of half a dozen Crowns than an island full of Adept."

"And what of a base full of *medev*?" He spun her out again, sending her skirts whirling.

Nash laughed as she collided with his chest again. "I think I would remember if Cal Clem had gone after a *medev* base."

Ivan's mind wandered back to snow-coated streets as he steered them closer to the bell tower. He thought back to his brother's elaborate plans. His schemes and tricks and treachery. His bruised skin, stretched tight over what shards of bone remained in his face in the cells beneath Oryol . . .

"How did you end up with Cal Clem, anyways?" Nash's voice cut through his thoughts like an axe through lumber.

"The same way most people end up with him."

Nash snorted. "I have a hard time believing you were dumb enough to gamble your way into a pit you couldn't climb out of."

Ivan pursed his lips, hiding his amusement. Not exactly, but she had no idea how close to the truth that was. He and Kasimir had rolled the dice one too many times in Boreas. It had gotten his brother captured and him nearly killed. And here he was, back at the table again. Just like a true gambler, he had no idea when to stop.

20

RYIA

"Remind me again why I have to do this?" Tristan asked, trailing half a step behind Ryia and Evelyn as they followed the small crowd heading back to the docks.

"What are you talking about? This was all your plan," Evelyn hissed. The crowd thinned as everyone flitted off toward their own ships.

"This wasn't part of my plan."

"No, but this is what keeps your plan from getting me killed," Ryia said out of the corner of her mouth, studying the Edalish galleon they were walking toward. The same ship they had seen the feather-clad dancers coming from this morning. "Which is why you have to do this."

Tristan peered curiously out at the Disciples guarding the docks. He frowned; then he shook his head. "All right, fine. I'll distract the dock guards so you can get on board the ship. But once you finish your little thievery, I don't know how you expect to get back off without being caught."

"I won't get caught."

"How can you be sure?" asked Evelyn, lowering her voice as they neared the harbor. "These docks are guarded more closely than the bloody Bobbin Fort."

"I hope so," Ryia started. She shot one quick glance over her shoulder as the threesome darted off the path, hiding in the shadow of an overgrown shrub. She grinned. "The Bobbin Fort's not even a challenge."

"You're unbelievable," Evelyn said.

"Give it a rest, you two," Tristan said wearily. He pulled his cloak off, flipping it inside out to change from an ostentatious burgundy to an unremarkable black before replacing it. "When you hear the fight break out, you're safe to come out. Not before." He wiggled his fingers, giving them a stretch. "Wish me luck." He slipped back onto the path, heading toward the dock holding the galleon.

But he wouldn't need luck—this was a maneuver Ryia had seen him do a thousand times before. He would pick the pocket of one man, plant whatever he stole on another man, accuse the second man of being a thief, and sit back and watch the fireworks. Sure, the stakes were a little higher here, but it was a song they'd sung before. Tristan would be fine.

Ryia pulled a cord at the back of her robes, unleashing a cascade of rich purple. She tied the sash tight around her waist and ducked her head into the hood, blending seamlessly into the twilight. She pulled her hatchets from where they hid beneath her robes, refastening the shoulder sheaths on top of the cloak where she could reach them, then peered anxiously around the shrub, waiting for the signal.

"Do you have a plan?"

Ryia looked back at Evelyn. "A plan for what?"

The ex-captain rolled her eyes, picking absently at the closest leaf. "For stealing these bloody things. For Adalina's sake, you're reckless."

"What's reckless about it? I slip in, find the goods, then slip out—no one's any the wiser."

"It's not going to be that simple."

"Sure it is. I'll be quiet. And if someone notices me, I'll make sure to keep them quiet."

"Like hell you will." Evelyn glared at her. "Petty theft is one thing, but I'm not going to stand by and let you murder some poor innocent sailor."

Ryia peered around the shrub toward the tangle of masts crowding the harbor. "You noble types are all the same. No sense of adventure."

"You really are a monster, aren't you?"

Monster. For some reason the word made Ryia flinch. She couldn't imagine why—it was something she already knew. She *was* a monster. A monster born of blood and shadow in the cellar of that estate just outside Duskhaven. Only a monster could have survived what she had endured.

"If *I'm* a monster, then what the fuck is Clem?" she hissed, rounding on Evelyn. "Don't forget, you signed on for this, *Captain.* No one forced you—"

But Evelyn was ready for her. "When Clem came to recruit me, I was lying facedown in some shithole inn, up to my bloody eyes in *stervod.* Do you know why?"

Ryia drew back half a pace despite herself, bumping into one of the bushes concealing them. She cleared her throat, peering off toward where Tristan had gone to start a fight. Still nothing. "No," she finally said, glaring back at Evelyn.

Evelyn poked her forcefully in the sternum. "Because of *you.* I was one year away from being named the youngest Valier in a century. One year away from achieving what I'd been training for since I was nine years old. One year away from being able to support my family and protect my kingdom for the rest of my ruddy days. And I lost it all because of *you.*"

There was that absurd feeling of guilt again, curling like a snake

in her stomach. Ryia forced a sneer. "So you can't play soldier anymore. Move on," she said. "It's not like your precious nobles ever
needed you anyways. You could train your whole life and still fall to
the weakest Kinetic in Thamorr." She cocked her head. "Why don't
you go back to your father and your manor? He'll marry you off to
some nice old man. You'll pop out a few of his noble brats and—"

"I can't go back to my father," Evelyn said stiffly, fiddling with
the ring on her left middle finger. She never took the damned thing
off, even in disguise. The moron. "I've failed the Linley name."

Ryia peered out toward the harbor, then back to the path.
Where was that signal? "Swallow your twice-damned pride," she
said. "You s—"

"It's not pride," Evelyn interrupted, redness showing through
the layers of powder concealing her freckles. She clenched her
fists, knuckles on either side of the ring turning bone white. "He
wouldn't have me back."

Ryia opened her mouth, then shut it again. Finally, she said,
"Good riddance. You shouldn't want anything to do with a shit
father like that."

"A shit father?" Evelyn burst out. She looked around hurriedly,
but no one was close enough to hear. "A shit father?" she repeated,
quieter this time. "He is not a shit father."

"He threw you out the second you stopped being useful. That's
a shit father."

"What could you possibly know about it?" she spat. "You don't
even know your bloody father."

A low blow if Ryia had actually been a bastard. An even lower
blow given the real story. The job momentarily forgotten, she lunged
forward, pulling up the sleeves of her disguise to reveal her scars.

"I knew my father," she said, her voice low and hoarse as she
held her wrists in front of Evelyn's face. "Where the hell do you
think these came from?"

Ryia's heart beat steadily up her throat as she held Evelyn's gaze, waiting for the ex-captain to make a cutting remark. The retort never came. Ryia shook her head, pulling her sleeves back down over her wrists and peering through the foliage toward the still-silent cobblestone path.

"Come on. Focus. We have a job to do."

Stupid, she thought, avoiding Evelyn's eye. The captain was already suspicious. No doubt already thinking far too deeply about where she might have come from . . . but it was too late to worry about that now.

Ryia's knees went weak as a memory consumed her, almost as real as it had been all those years ago.

She faced a bald man twice her size, the letter K inked onto his skull. An Adept. It felt strange not to have shackles biting her wrists.

"Defeat one and you'll be free of these chains forever," the old man— her father—said.

She had no hatred for this Kinetic, but the hatred for those chains was enough.

Her nose wrinkled as an odor, no, a sensation *crawled into her nostrils. An itchy sort of tingle, mixed with the smell of blood and mold and dead things. A combination that set every alarm bell in her skull ringing. She hesitated, and the Kinetic's fist slammed into her temple, sending her sprawling to the filthy cellar floor.*

Panic welled up inside her as her father shook his head, reaching for her shackles. She rolled to the side, dodging the Kinetic's next attack at the last moment. Her father froze, mad excitement sparking in his eyes.

She felt something shoot from her as the Adept charged forward again. An invisible rope snaked out from her fingers, wrapping around one of the axes sitting on her father's workbench. The ones he usually wore belted at his waist. When she thrust her hand forward, the axe responded. It flew from the belt, burying itself in the Adept servant's chest.

"I knew it," her father murmured. "I always knew it!"

At that moment, her nose caught fire. Danger-danger-danger . . . *the word pounded through her head on a constant loop as the scent of blood and ashes seared her nostrils. A loud crash sounded upstairs, and the night descended into chaos. Blue-robed figures streamed through the blackness, led by a tall, thin man with a bald head. The Guildmaster, she recognized him from the paintings. He looked right past her, gaze locked on her father.*

"Abner Grayson," he said, his voice low and carrying. "The rumors of your experiments have become too troublesome to ignore."

"Experiments?" her father asked. Difficult to play innocent when he was surrounded by dried blood spatters and the stale scent of death.

"No one believes you will succeed," the Guildmaster continued, still taking no notice of her. He waved his thin-fingered hand, and her rusty old chains moved of their own accord, winding around her father's neck. "But the theft of Adept servants is a crime of the highest order."

She froze, looking from her father to the Guildmaster . . . then to the belt of axes still sitting on the work bench.

"Rosalyn, please," her father gasped.

But she did nothing. Nothing but run.

She grabbed the axes and the long-handled hatchets beside them with a shaking hand as she sprinted from the room. The scent of danger clogged her nostrils as she wrenched the lantern from the wall beside the door, thrusting it to the floor. The fire caught quickly, chewing through the old man's notes and dry wooden walls, filling the cellar with choking smoke.

There were more blue robes upstairs. She burst through a multicolored windowpane and rolled onto the snow-covered ground as the fire raged and burned. She did not stop running, did not look back until she reached the edge of the woods. From there she saw the shroud of smoke curling from the manor on the Rowan River. The Grayson estate, her father's home—her home—reduced to ash and memory. And silhouetted against the flames . . .

The Guildmaster. She could see his eyes from here, deep blue and vile, pouring their hatred into her. But he was too late. She turned and disappeared into the trees. Just another wisp of smoke, fading on the wind.

"Where's Tristan with that damn signal?"

"What?" Ryia frowned, dragging herself out of the episode. She peered around the edge of the shrub, looking toward the docks. The guards were still in place, but there was no sign of Tristan. Something was wrong. "Where did that little bastard get to?"

"He's been jumpy all day. Do you think he bailed?"

"Maybe," Ryia said slowly. But that didn't sound like Tristan.

She spared a look toward the arena. The party by the bell tower was still raging on, but it wouldn't be for long. Before the guests dispersed, she had to get into that ship to lift the disguises they needed.

"I'll do it," Evelyn said, reading Ryia's mind.

"You'll do what, exactly?"

"Just wait for my signal."

"What fucking signal?"

"You'll know it."

Evelyn meandered out of the bushes with a drunken stagger. Ryia had to bite back a smile as the usually somber captain flung out her arms, warbling an off-key rendition of some Gildesh love song.

Before long a voice hollered at her to shut the hell up. Evelyn whirled around clumsily, fists raised.

"Tell me that t'my face, ya coward," she slurred.

"I just did, you drunken git," the voice challenged.

The Disciples guarding the docks were on the move before the first punch even landed.

"We might make a half-decent outlaw out of you after all, Captain," Ryia muttered to herself, swooping past the dregs of the crowd and onto the docks in the blink of an eye.

Ryia dropped to hang from the edge of the dock and pulled herself arm over arm into the shadow of the galleon. *The Silver Swan.* Only the Edalish would name a ship something so ridiculous.

It was part of Edale's royal fleet, so breaking in was risky but essential. Evelyn should know. She was the one who told her about the arena's back door. The one that led right out to the bell tower courtyard. Guests couldn't access it, but entertainers were a different story.

Ryia sniffed the air. Nothing but salt spray and seaweed. The ship was as quiet as a Borean graveyard. For now, at least. In and out, easy does it. She climbed up the side of the ship, rolling lightly onto the deck.

"If I were a set of horrible dancing costumes, where would I be?" she whispered, giving the crewmen at the mainmast a wide berth.

She opened the hatch, peering down into the stifling darkness. They would be down there. Of course they would. She took a deep breath, forcing back thoughts of chains and manacles, and slipped below deck.

To her left were rows and rows of hanging hammocks. Muffled voices and lantern light bled from around the corner. She turned the other way. Cargo hold. Jackpot.

Her fingers whispered over the latch, easing it open. She slipped into the darkness. Ryia could feel the bile rising in her throat as the ship's hull closed in around her, squeezing like the coils of a massive jungle snake.

No.

Now was not the time for that. She breathed in through her nose. Salt. Wood. Fish. Just like the docks at Carrowwick Harbor. *Just like home?* Nope. No time to unpack that idea either.

Costumes . . . costumes . . . She felt her way through the hold as her eyes adjusted to the darkness. *There.* Lined up neatly on the far side of the hold. She turned in a slow circle. The trickle of moonlight sneaking in through the open hatch set the shadowed garments on the far side of the hold sparkling and glittering. With the right tools, Ivan could have sewn any one of these monstrosities himself, but knowing *which* monstrosity to sew had been the obstacle there.

"Ah," she breathed, fingers coming to a stop over a row of hanging garments marked *Day 2* in a looping script she could barely read in the dim, silvery light. And farther to the right . . . she smiled. *Auxiliary.* Such a fancy word for "extra." Pompous bastards.

"Don't mind if I do." She held a costume up, squinting to examine the disturbing lack of fabric on it. "Oh, the captain is not going to like—"

She froze mid-sentence, head turned toward the door like a hunting hound. It was faint, but she could smell it. Mold and decay. Danger. The hairs on the nape of her neck prickled to attention; her eyes went wide in the darkness as she scanned the hold for an escape route.

That was the problem with being belowground—or below-decks. No fucking windows. There was nowhere to run. That meant she had only one option left.

She dropped the costume and pulled her hatchets from her back, dropping into a ready stance as the hatch creaked open.

21

NASH

During their planning aboard the cog, Evelyn had referred to this party as the "drunken-git ball." Looking around now, Nash couldn't say she disagreed. It would be a miracle if half these merchants made it back to their ships in one piece tonight. No wonder the auction proper didn't start until tomorrow afternoon.

Ivan wrinkled his nose as the man closest to them turned, spraying a wide arc of vomit across the ground. "Disgusting."

"I promise never to vomit in your presence," Nash said solemnly, hand raised in a mock vow.

"You have broken that promise already, if I am not mistaken."

"What? When?"

"Two years ago," Ivan said. "The Lacemakers' Festival."

Nash flushed. "I don't remember that."

"I wonder why."

She grinned sheepishly. "Well, I promise never to vomit *on* you, then."

Ivan's lips twisted like he was trying not to smile. "That one you had better keep unless you would like for me to send the Butcher after you."

"Please." Nash pivoted them another step closer to the bell tower in the center of the courtyard. Just a few yards closer and they would be able to hide in its shadow and find the entrance. "She would never hurt me. She likes me better than you."

"How do you figure?"

"What can I say? She's drawn to my winning personality."

"Is that what you call it?"

Nash let out a bark of laughter. "Is this how you make all the women in the Miscreants' Temple fall for you? Because I don't get it."

"Are you sure about that?"

Her breath betrayed her, hitching in her throat as Ivan pulled her closer, his hand on her lower back, hips pressed against hers, lips just inches away. How did he always manage to make her head spin like that?

Nash pulled back a step, whirling out to the end of his arm. "Sorry to say I am," she lied. "But don't feel bad—I'm sure those tricks are fine for seducing your usual tavern girls."

"And what are you, then?" Ivan steered them toward the tower again, eyes darting around to see if anyone had noticed them. Nash was pretty sure everyone would be too drunk to notice a stampeding elephant right now, let alone a pair of people slowly maneuvering toward a building.

"Me?" She raised a hand to her chest, as though offended he would even ask. "I'm the empress of the Three Seas, remember?"

Ivan let out a short huff of laughter. Their steps pulled them together, and he whispered, "And why would an empress be working for a man like Callum Clem, I wonder?"

"I don't work for Cal," she said.

"Is that so?" He eyed the Saint brand peeking out from the neckline of her blouse.

"I like to think of us as business partners," she said. "I have a ship, which he needs. He has the crescents I need."

If Cal Clem hadn't agreed to take Nash on all those years ago, she would have died like a rat in the gutters of Golden Port, but still . . . The namestone hidden beneath her clothes suddenly weighed a thousand pounds. Ma would slap her silly if she could see her now.

"Spoken like true royalty."

Nash cleared her throat, forcing a smile as their steps finally carried them into the shadow of the tower. "I may be going to the deepest of the hells, but as long as I'm the richest son of a bitch there, that's fine by me."

Her tone was just a bit too light for the words to ring true. Most people would never have noticed the shift. But Ivan Rezkoye was not most people. His brow creased. She could sense the question forming on his lips.

"Come on, we need to find the entrance," Nash said hurriedly, shrugging out of Ivan's grip to push aside the shrubbery at the base of the tower. The mysterious Quill was here, tucked away in that tower. They needed to find Ryia and Evelyn a way inside. Nash couldn't believe they had come all this way to steal a pen. The damned thing had better be encrusted with every gem in Thamorr, with all the trouble they were going through to lift it.

Suddenly Ivan said, "Nash, stop."

"What? Why? We've almost got it. Then we can head back to the—" Nash broke off as Ivan grabbed her by the collar, hauling her upright.

"We need to leave. Now."

"Why?" Nash asked, straightening her blouse in irritation.

The blood drained from her face as she followed Ivan's gaze. That asshole merchant, Elton what's-his-name. He was speaking urgently with a Disciple. It was still strange to see the Disciple respond like a normal person instead of staring blankly into space like the Adept servants of the mainland. A small part of her perked up strangely at the thought. If Jolie had stayed on as a Disciple, would she still have her mind? Would she still truly be her sister? Nash tucked the thought away.

"So what?" she finally said. "That ass of a merchant is bitching to the Disciple about something. Why do we care?"

The last word came out small and hesitant as Elton whatever-the-hells pointed directly toward them.

"Because that man, Smithe, was suspicious of us from the start," Ivan said. "I believe your impassioned speech about Adept rights sealed our fate."

"I wouldn't call it a *speech*," Nash protested, flushing as Ivan dragged her to the far side of the tower, getting them out of the merchant's sight.

"Well, it does not matter what you would call it. We have been made. But this is why Ivan Rezkoye does not ever begin a job without a backup plan." He yanked at the collar of his coat, releasing a tab of brownish fabric. Working quickly, he undid several clasps at the neck of his short, silver jacket. A moment later the garment was ankle-length and canvas brown.

"Did that feel good? Referring to yourself in the third person?" Nash asked. "Because you sounded like an idiot." Ivan ignored her.

Fear-addled fingers made Nash's quick-change clumsy and frantic, but the last button was buttoned and the last sash tied in less than thirty seconds. Gone was Missus Veber, Borean merchant woman. Now she wore a knee-length black coat. Her skirt had been hitched down the middle to form trousers. A pair of spectacles and a rumpled hat pulled from a hidden pocket in her coat completed the transformation.

They slipped from the shadow of the tower, trying to lose themselves amid the drunken masses filling the courtyard.

"Stagger," Ivan said.

Despite the seriousness of the situation, Nash had to bite back a laugh as the usually composed disguise master slid into a drunken limp. She followed suit, grabbing a half-empty wine cup from a nearby table at random and stumbling along, forcing a foolish laugh.

"Where are they?"

"They are—do not look," Ivan said, breaking off as Nash did just that.

Elton Smithe, the rudest merchant ever to walk the earth, stood a few steps south of the bell tower, his beady eyes scouring the merry crowd. Beside him stood a Disciple. A Senser. Shit. Its nostrils flared as it angled slowly from right to left . . . searching.

The Senser's powers won't do it any good, Nash reminded herself, snapping her head back around and willing herself to remain calm. The Butcher had said they could only sniff out a physical threat, and so far she seemed to be right. As long as Smithe didn't recognize them now, they would be able to get back to the ship unscathed. As long as the Disciple didn't give too much thought to why they had been standing in the shadow of the bell tower, the job could go on as planned. . . .

Nash's stomach dropped. Except they hadn't found the entrance to the tower. Ryia and Evelyn would have to go in blind. Fantastic.

She followed Ivan's lead as he fell in behind a group of Brillish guards making their way toward the exit. Just a few more steps . . . Nash didn't release her breath until the creepy arena archway was behind them, nothing but a short walk to the docks in front of them.

"Well, that went well," she said.

"It could have gone worse," Ivan said darkly.

"How? We didn't get what we came for. And now the Disciples are on alert for intruders. How could it have gone worse?"

Ivan pointed to the right. "We could have ended up like that poor soul."

Nash looked where he pointed, over the hills leading north. A blue-robed figure dragged a skinny shadow away from the docks and up the path leading to the Guildmaster's manor. Some sorry wretch headed for the infamous torture cells. Nash narrowed her eyes as that pair entered a pool of moonlight, the skinny shadow's features suddenly visible. Was that . . . ? She pulled off her false spectacles for a better look. Dark, curly hair. Long, lanky limbs. There was no mistaking it.

"Ivan . . . that's Tristan."

22

RYIA

Ryia curled her toes as the bulky silhouette lurched into the cargo hold. He held a lantern in one hand, throwing long arcs of golden light over the deck. The glittery costumes lining the hull burst into full color, reflecting the flickering light so brightly it felt like someone had devoured the sun and retched it up inside the hold.

"Inventory rations twice a day," he said in a mocking falsetto. "The fuck does she think is gonna happen to 'em between dinner and breakfast?"

Checking rations? So no alarm had been raised. Her hatchets sagged to her sides as she relaxed. Hopefully he was quick about it so she could get this business over with and find Tristan. The plan was still on track.

Then the man caught sight of the costume she had dropped on the floor and the still-wet boot print beside it. His free hand slipped to the scimitar at his belt.

"Who's there?"

Shit. She leapt from behind a mountain of garish shoes, spinning her right-hand hatchet in her palm, aiming for the man's throat. Quick and silent, just like always. The bit was a hairsbreadth from his flesh when the unthinkable happened.

She hesitated.

Her hand wavered uncertainly as a single word curled through her mind. A clawing, scratching rat trapped inside her skull.

Monster.

Ryia stepped backward, shaking her head to clear it. Of all the moments to grow a conscience, now was really not the time.

The man dropped his lantern. It landed with a clatter on the deck but didn't break. He clumsily yanked his blade free of its scabbard, severing his belt in two in the process. Oh, this would be too easy. He had no idea what he was doing with that thing. She rolled forward, ducking between his legs and springing to her feet behind him. She aimed her left-hand hatchet toward his neck, cutting toward some crucial veins. . . .

Monster.

"Are you fucking kidding me?" Ryia hissed to herself, breathless as she hesitated for a second time. She probably had only seconds before this idiot thought to shout for help. Then it would all be over. No costumes. No Quill. No freedom.

The voice taunted her again as she swung under the man's sloppy guard, but this time she was ready for it. She pulled back at the last second, bringing her left hand around and clocking the man solidly on the back of the head. He dropped like an anchor, thudding to the deck beside his still-flickering lantern.

Ryia stuffed a pair of the bejeweled costumes down the front of her shirt, turning to leave. She rolled her eyes, whirling back around as she remembered why Edale's Worst Swordsman had come to check the cargo hold in the first place. Any captain checking rations twice a day might be suspicious enough to notice the missing costumes, even if they were just extras.

She groaned, head lolling back as she knelt beside the senseless man.

"You couldn't make this easy for me, could you?" she asked, grabbing his feet and pressing one ear to the hatch.

Wet boot prints would dry, but bodies had an annoying habit of staying exactly where they were least convenient. At least the dead ones couldn't spout any stories. She sniffed the air. Clear.

Hearing nothing on the other side, Ryia shouldered the hatch open and unceremoniously dumped the man beneath a swaying hammock, setting the lantern down beside him. Now for the finishing touches.

She rooted around in the man's pockets until she found the jingle of coins. She walked a silver half across her fingers. "You're overpaid, my friend."

A half-empty wine bottle lay on the floor a few steps away. She popped the cork free and dribbled a few drops onto his shirt before stuffing the bottle under his arm. He might be telling some tales when he woke up, but who the hell would believe a drunken sailor who'd clearly gambled away his last silver?

With that, Ryia slipped above deck. She kept to the shadows, sneaking past half a dozen crew members who were too distracted by their duties to spare a look over their shoulder. The ship's captain shouted orders from the bow as Ryia leapt over the rail near the stern, barely skimming the gangway as she soared back onto the docks.

What had happened back there? She ran a hand over her hood as her heart rate began to slow. *Monster*. It was something she already knew. Something she had never let bother her before, but honorable Captain Evelyn Linley had gotten into her head.

Her gut leapt into her throat once again as uneven footsteps sounded to her left. She dove for her axes, hoping to Felice she would have the brains to actually use them this time, then sagged with relief as the figure emerged from the shadows.

Evelyn.

"You," Ryia said sourly.

"Is that the thanks I can expect every time I risk my arse to save yours?" Evelyn asked.

"Yep."

Evelyn rolled her eyes. "Did you get the disguises?"

"No, Captain. The dancers got the best of me."

". . . And?" Evelyn asked hesitantly.

Ryia suppressed a smile at the new bruise Evelyn was sporting on her chin. "No feathers." Her amusement died suddenly as she remembered why the captain had had to pick her little fight in the first place. "Still no sign of Tristan?"

Evelyn shook her head, looking troubled.

"Well, shit," Ryia said. That couldn't be good. But there was nothing they could do. Nothing but make their way back to *The Hardship*, wait for Nash and Ivan, and hope he turned up.

The short walk over the docks passed in anxious silence. They reached the ship, and Ryia froze halfway across the gangway when she saw that Nash and Ivan were already aboard.

"Party end early?" she asked hopefully, striding forward onto the deck.

"For us it did," Nash said glumly.

"I take it you have bad news, then?" Evelyn asked, slipping aboard behind Ryia.

Nash nodded. "We were almost made. Had to split. You're going in blind tomorrow."

"Fucking fantastic," said Ryia. "We have bad news too. We lost Tristan."

"We know," said Nash.

Ryia's stomach dropped.

"What do you mean you *know*?" asked Evelyn.

"You saw him," Ryia guessed.

Nash sighed. "We saw him."

"Where?"

But she already knew.

"They were taking him to the manor," Ivan said quietly, confirming her suspicions. No need to ask who "they" were. The Disciples. Who else could it be?

"How did he get caught?" Nash asked.

"I don't know," Ryia said. "The little runt went off to set the distraction and never came back."

"*Schiss*," Ivan swore. "He must have been caught picking pockets. The Guildmaster does not tolerate theft."

"You don't say," Ryia said sarcastically. If torture and death were the penalty for a little pickpocketing, she didn't even want to know what punishment would greet them if they were caught stealing the Quill.

"Not helping, Butcher," Evelyn said. After a pause, the captain said, "So how are we going to get him back?"

The question caught Ryia off guard. "What do you mean 'get him back'?" she asked.

Ivan pulled out the stack of maps she and Evelyn had stolen back in Carrowwick, leafing through them until he found the blueprint of the Guildmaster's manor. Ryia laughed incredulously.

"He's not locked up in some Kestrel Crown back room. He is in the Guildmaster's dungeon," Ryia continued. "There are only four of us. There are at least two hundred Disciples on this goddess-forsaken island. I don't think getting him back is an option."

"So you'd rather leave him here to die?" Evelyn snapped. "Murder, theft, now betrayal? You really are an honorless thug, aren't you?"

"I . . ." Ryia broke off, guilt swirling in the pit of her stomach for the third time tonight. What was the point? She was planning to betray them all anyway, but she had never intended for any of them to get *killed*. She pinched the bridge of her nose. This was why it was dangerous to stay with one crew for too long—she was going soft. "Damn it." She snatched the blueprints from Ivan's hands. "Let's figure out how to rescue the little twerp."

23

EVELYN

Evelyn stood belowdecks, covering her telltale freckles with a suffocating layer of powder and pulling on the worst outfit she had ever had the misfortune to wear: a thin, bejeweled shirt, bracelets that jingled louder than an alarm bell, and a fluttering skirt that skimmed her ankles. At least Ivan had been able to sew in some trousers, but they were so tight Evelyn felt like she was pressing herself into sausage casing.

"You have no idea where the entrance is? Or how it's secured?"

"None," Nash said, slouched on the far side of the hold. "We barely got within spitting distance of the tower before all hell broke loose."

"We were fortunate to spot the guards before they noticed our interest in the tower," Ivan said as he swirled half a dozen different colors onto Nash's face. "With luck, they will not have extra Disciples posted there today."

"With luck?" the Butcher called from the deck. "If you sons of bitches do your jobs right, the Disciples won't have their eyes on the tower at all."

"Yes, yes. If we do our jobs right, the Disciples should lose sight of many things," Ivan said darkly.

He was referring to the dungeon, of course. After last night's lengthy discussion, they had realized stealing the Quill and rescuing Tristan each required a distraction. Why not use the same distraction for both?

That meant that their plans were largely unchanged. Well, aside from the fact that Nash and Ivan were now one man short in their task of creating that critical distraction. And the fact that Evelyn and the Butcher had no idea how to get inside the bell tower to steal the Quill. And the fact that Nash now had the additional suicide mission of breaking into the Guildmaster's prison. And they all had the additional task of finding Nash again before they could get off this ruddy island. And that was assuming the Guildmaster hadn't yet tortured Tristan, forcing him to spill all their plans and ruin the whole bloody mission.

Okay, fine. Their plans had changed quite a lot.

"We'll get the job done," Nash said, ducking away from Ivan as he leaned forward to blend one last smear of paint into her cheek. "And after I risk my ass to get into that dungeon, you lot had better not leave me here."

"Of course, we can't leave without you," Ryia called down from the deck.

Nash touched a hand to her chest. "I'm honored."

"I just meant we can't leave without you because someone's got to sail us out of here."

"There it is," Nash said, pulling on the coat Ivan had sewn her last night. Its pockets were bulging, filled to the brim with their secret weapon. The smuggler prodded one gingerly, looking nervous. Evelyn didn't blame her.

"All right, well, first things first, let's focus on getting into that arena today without getting caught, hmm?" Evelyn said. "Then we can worry about the rest."

"Easy for you to say," Nash said. She took a swig from a nearby wine bottle and grabbed the blueprints of the Guildmaster's manor. "Are we ready?" she asked, folding the parchment into a tiny square and tucking it into her pocket.

"We are waiting on you," said Ivan, shoving a hat into her hands.

Nash stuffed her hair into the hat. By the time she turned around, the smuggler was easily mistakable for a large man. "Don't fuck this up, Red. I'm not dying for nothing."

Ivan's jaw tightened. "No one is going to die."

"Easy for you to say. You're not the bait," Nash said, shaking her pockets gently. They rattled noisily, like they were filled with glass beads.

But Evelyn knew what was really weighing down those pockets was far more valuable and far more dangerous than glass.

Ivan's hand darted out. "Be careful with those!"

"Sounds like a stirring conversation," the Butcher called from the deck, "but if you want the cover of the crowd you might want to get moving."

"All right, everyone," Evelyn said, "try not to die. At least, not before we get the Quill. And Tristan."

"Good speech," Nash said. She pulled herself up the ladder and onto the main deck. Then: "Whoa."

"Not a twice-damned word," Ryia said, leveling a hatchet at Nash's throat.

Evelyn couldn't keep her jaw from dropping at the sight of Ryia, swathed in the same skintight, sky-blue costume she was wearing herself.

"I think you look nice," Nash said, breaking Ryia's "not a word" rule.

"Do you?" Ryia's eyes glittered dangerously. "Because I'm starting to think this is our worst idea to date." She thrust her arms out, and Evelyn turned away, averting her eyes from the stubbornly clinging fabric. "I think it would have been more subtle if I'd just gone naked."

Ivan huffed. "I did what I could. You did not give me much to work with."

Evelyn's eyes jumped to Ryia's wrists as she wrestled with the near-transparent sleeves. A pang of something that felt suspiciously like pity rattled through her nerves as she caught sight of the puckered scars barely obscured by gauzy fabric. How long would someone have to be shackled to get marks like that?

The whole party fell silent as a tinny sound rang out over the docks. The bell clanged from its tower, announcing the approach of the auction.

"I believe that's our funeral dirge," Nash said, clapping Evelyn on the shoulder. "See you all on the other side. Either here or in one of the hells."

With that she hopped over the rail and melted into the crowd on the docks. Evelyn took a deep breath. This was it. No matter what happened, they would all be leaving the island tonight; though, whether they would be leaving on *The Hardship* or bundled in sheets and thrown into the sea remained to be seen. Their fates rested on a loudmouth smuggler, a Borean disguise master, the most reckless mercenary in Dresdell, and a kid who may have already cracked.

Adalina save them.

Evelyn and Ryia covered their ridiculous costumes with long coats and joined the throbbing masses on the docks. With Ivan close behind, they allowed themselves to be pushed along the roaring current of excited merchants.

"What's wrong?" Evelyn asked. The Butcher looked troubled, eyes locked on the Guildmaster's manor in the distance.

"Nothing."

"Right," Evelyn said. The Butcher had been distracted ever since Tristan had been caught. "The last time 'nothing' was wrong, an Edalish sailor turned up dead."

"What, last night?" Ryia asked. "No one turned up dead. Unconscious, maybe . . ."

Evelyn looked back at her. "Losing your touch?" she asked, struggling to inject the usual venom.

"You'd better hope not."

Evelyn stared after her as she stalked a few steps ahead. Could there truly be some mercy left in her after all? She certainly seemed worried about Tristan and the others. Could there still be some *good* lurking there?

What did she bloody care? It didn't matter. Just like it didn't matter what Tolliver Shadowwood meant to do with this mysterious Quill they were after. All that mattered was that as soon as this mission was over, she would deliver the Butcher to the Bobbin Fort dungeons, and then Evelyn would finally have a rich, purple Valier cloak draped around her shoulders. She spun her father's ring around her finger. That was what she needed to focus on. Not the cold that crept up her spine every time she imagined slapping those scarred wrists back into shackles.

"Good luck," Ivan whispered as they reached *The Silver Swan*, a steady stream of dancers slipping from its belly. "Try not to get dismembered." He pulled the cloaks from their shoulders and shoved them forward.

Then he was gone.

"Ladies! Form a line!" shouted a voice as thin as a razor blade. Evelyn flinched as a clawlike hand tightened on her shoulder. "Now is not the time for this kind of nonsense." Without giving them as much as a passing glance, the woman shoved her and Ryia to the back of the line of dancers weaving their way toward the arena.

Nothing looked out of order. The same number of Disciples as yesterday, no one seemed on unduly high alert. Hopefully for Tristan's sake, the chaos of the auction had occupied all the Guildmaster's men.

It was fine. Everything was fine. One foot in front of the other no matter how much she wanted to vomit. She looked anxiously over each shoulder in turn. Unless the Guildmaster knew their plan and he was just trying to lure them all into the arena. Was this a trap?

"If you're trying to look as suspicious as possible, you're doing a great job," Ryia hissed.

"Sorry, I'm not as resigned to my death as you seem to be."

Ryia flashed a distractingly wicked smile, tossing the brown locks of her wig over one bare shoulder. "I've worked hard to get to this level of apathy."

Evelyn couldn't tell if she was kidding or not.

Her heart thrashed against her rib cage like a fresh-caught fish in a net as the arena came into view. Once they were inside, they would be surrounded. Hemmed in by Disciples and nobles, with their only hope of an exit hanging on luck, her own spotty memories, and Ryia's lock-picking skills. None of her Needle Guard training had prepared her for this.

If she survived this job, she was never going to break another law again—and she was ashamed to admit it wasn't even just her sense of honor driving that decision anymore. Crime was too bloody stressful.

"Keep up," Ryia warned as Evelyn started to lag behind. "Once we get into the back room, this job is in the bag."

"Assuming we can get into the tower. And past the guards in the courtyard."

The Butcher snorted. "We'll get past them."

"*Without* killing them?"

Ryia looked at her in mock innocence. "I just told you I didn't kill anyone yesterday!"

"Going one day without committing murder is not exactly a bragging point for most people."

"I'm not most people."

If that wasn't the understatement of the age.

There was something . . . *odd* about Callum Clem's attack dog. Evelyn still hadn't forgotten about the Disciples on the southern dock back in Carrowwick. The way Ryia must have scaled the sixty-foot walls of the Bobbin Fort the night Efrain Althea lost his finger. Her vicious scars.

Evelyn had been so sure she had figured it out. Had been so positive that when Ivan shaved her head they would find a curling *K* already inked there. She'd thought that Ryia was a Kinetic, escaped from her master, but the Butcher's skin had been nothing but brownish and bare.

Maybe there wasn't anything special about her at all. Maybe Evelyn had been listening to the woman's arrogant bluster for so bloody long she'd started to believe it.

Evelyn's breakfast threatened to reappear as they reached the three rooms at the bottom of the bowl, set behind the thrones on the back wall. One door for animals, one for humans, and one for Adept.

"Are we sure about this?"

Ryia grinned. "It's a little late for doubts, Captain."

And it was. There were only a few minutes before the Guild-master would arrive to begin the auction. Then they would have only minutes to slip the net before Nash set the plan in motion. Why had she agreed to go along with this? The door loomed larger with every step, the maw of a ferocious beast about to swallow her whole.

The moment they were inside, the only escape routes were back through the arena or out into the heavily guarded courtyard.

Dressed like chandeliers. She swore she saw her own fear reflected in the Butcher's jet-black eyes as they slipped through the doorway. The door clicked shut behind them.

"Damn it's crowded in here. Maybe we should have tried for the other room," Ryia whispered, eyeing the droves of performers between them and the battered back door of the room. "We'll never make it out without being spotted."

"The Adept are packed in twice as tightly as this."

"I meant the room with the horses. With that face of yours . . ."

"Ha-ha." Evelyn shot her a glare, bending to touch her toes. "Let me know if you have any other brilliant ideas."

"Are you honestly stretching right now?"

"If you don't think of something quickly, we'll be prancing around onstage in a few minutes. I'd rather not pull a bloody muscle."

"*Now* you develop a sense of humor."

Evelyn rolled her eyes. "I—"

"Excuse me."

Evelyn broke off mid-sentence as a new voice cut into their conversation. She raised her eyes, finding herself face-to-face with the talon-handed woman who had shouted at them on the docks.

The Butcher turned to face her. "Can we do something for you?"

"Yes." The woman pursed her lips. "You can tell me who you are."

Evelyn's gut sank like a stone.

She opened her mouth to speak, but the woman held up a hand to stop her. "Someone alert the Disciples," she said, grabbing Evelyn and Ryia by the wrists. "We have a pair of intruders on our hands."

24

NASH

Nash willed her shoulders to relax as she wove through the crowds. Back on board the ship, their plan had seemed daring. Gutsy. The stuff of folk tales and legends. Here and now it seemed laughable to think there was even half a chance she'd end the day with all her limbs intact.

She shook her pockets nervously as she walked, listening to the rustle of the little black beads. She had never heard of Ivan's *Trän vun Yavol* before. He said they were a tool used by the *medev* royal guards up in Boreas. Apparently the name translated to "Tears of the Underworld," so they had to be good.

At least, good enough for a distraction. And if they weren't, well, she would be joining Tristan in his cell one way or another.

Last night everyone had worried about the boy—about how much Tristan might have been *encouraged* to tell the Guildmaster about their plan. Everyone but Ivan, that was. Nash had asked him why, and the disguise master had said, "None of you were there the night he was brought in to Clem."

"So what?" Ryia had said.

Ivan had reminded them. "So why do you think none of us knows where he really came from? The boy can hold his tongue."

Ivan's hunch was good enough for Nash. Besides, if they couldn't trust one another, what were they even doing here? Ivan had to trust Nash to plant the *Trän vun Yavol* so he could do his part. Ryia and Evelyn had to trust that Ivan would do his part to draw the eyes of the arena away from the courtyard. And all of them had to trust that skinny little Tristan Beckett could hold out in the Guildmaster's torture chamber for half a day.

Nash ducked her head as she passed beneath the archway leading into the arena. "Pardon me, excuse me, apologies," she muttered under her breath as she brushed her way through the crowd. Each person she passed received an amiable pat on the side, and each amiable pat slipped a few small black beads from Nash's pocket into theirs. She was a little rusty on the technique—it had been years since she had picked a pocket at all, much less reversed the process.

It should have been Tristan who planted the *Trän vun Yavol*. With those quick fingers of his, he could have filled twice the pockets Nash managed as she bumbled through the crowd, bumping elbows and knocking against the sheathed swords of guards and merchants. Thirty-three was all Nash could hit before she made it to her seat near the servants' entrance to the arena. Would that be enough? She watched her unsuspecting carriers as they picked their way toward their own benches, spread out all around the left-hand side of the bowl. Of all the beads she planted maybe half would work out as planned—and that was a best-case scenario.

A grating quiet rippled over the crowd as the royals started to arrive, flanked by their marching guards and fluttering flags. It would have to be enough. She took her seat, resisting the urge to roll her eyes as the crowd cheered for the smiling, waving royals. As if every last one of them wouldn't sell those crowned bastards out in a heartbeat to take their place. That was the first thing she'd learned after traveling every inch of the Thamorri coastline.

Places like the Lottery had a hard reputation, but everywhere was the same. The lawful types made you peel back a layer or two of gold before you reached the shit, but it was still there. In the Lottery, the shit just sat proudly on top.

The cheers continued as the Adept wards for sale slid dream-like into the arena, filing into one of the three rooms behind the stage. Whatever brainwashing process the mainland Adept went through must have happened sometime between last night and this afternoon. Every last ward crossing that auction block now had a face as vacant and staring as a doll's. They were followed closely by a slew of prancing Gildesh show horses, then the dancers and acrobats. Nash held back a chuckle as she caught sight of Evelyn, looking about as comfortable in the tiny, sparkly outfit as a cat in rain boots.

Her smile fell as the arena suddenly went quiet, leaving nothing but the sound of waves crashing against the cliffs beneath them. A silence like that could mean only one thing. The Guildmaster.

He swept across the center of the arena, sleeves billowing with every step. Unlike the royals onstage, he was accompanied by no armed guards. No Kinetics, no Sensers. He walked alone. A bold move—one Callum Clem was famous for back in the Lottery.

Where Wyatt Asher tended to surround himself with a team of heavies, Cal went solo. Rather than making him seem unim-portant it had made him look confident—and made Asher look like a twice-damned coward. It had the same effect here. The roy-als looked frail, crouching behind their guards' chain-mail skirts. There was no way that message was lost on the crowd. Everyone knew exactly who ruled Thamorr, and it wasn't a single one of the bastards on those velvet-coated thrones.

And Tolliver Shadowwood really thought he could hold this

Quill hostage for some kind of *reward* from this man? If he tried, he was more likely to find his castle razed and his crown handed off to someone the Guildmaster found more agreeable. But that wasn't Nash's problem. It was just like when she was smuggling drugs across the various borders of Thamorr—if she thought too hard about what people meant to do with the things she sold them, she might not want to sell them at all. It was best not to know.

"Welcome, once again, fine visitors from the mainland," said the Guildmaster. "We have gathered this day to celebrate the two hundred and eighty-ninth anniversary of peace among the five kingdoms. To fully recognize . . ."

Nash's heart raced. This was it. The second he started calling wards up onto that stage the wheels would be in motion, and, like a runaway carriage down a cliff side, there would be no stopping it. She clapped distractedly as the rest of the crowd roared with applause.

"As always, we will begin with our strongest wards. First for acquisition is one of our most powerful Kinetics. A practiced tele-kinetic with seventeen summers on the island."

A Kinetic in a plain brown robe was led onstage, swirling *K* marking its head, its face blank, its cheeks unbranded. She winced, imagining the blood-drenched, white-hot iron that would press into the young Kinetic's face, binding it with its new master. She had heard the Adept lacked the fear or pain to flinch when it happened. But to Nash, that sounded like the usual bullshit people used to justify doing shitty things.

"Excuse me, I'm sorry, excuse me," she intoned again, pushing herself up from her seat and edging along toward an aisle. She managed to slip beads into another three merchants' pockets along the way.

She wasn't alone in her jostling. Much of the crowd was shifting and moving around. Servants and employees ran back and forth between nobles and merchants, carrying jingling pouches and little slips of parchment, organizing bids and offers before calling them out. But instead of looking for a merchant or employer, Nash was looking for Ivan.

He wasn't in position yet. When they were ready to go, he would be in the lower middle section of the bowl, directly in front of the stage. That section was reserved for the noblewomen of Briel and their guards, so it would be tricky for him to get inside, but if anyone was capable of that it was Ivan.

She took another few steps forward, jingling her coin pouch (mostly coppers, not that anyone needed to know that). The first Kinetic went to the king of Boreas for seven hundred crescents. *Bully for the king of Boreas*, Nash thought distantly, eyes locked on the place where Ivan should be turning up any second now. The minute he was in place, he would give her the signal. She ran her fingers over the smooth marbles remaining in her pockets. Then it would be time for each and every one of the hells to break loose. They might actually pull this off.

At that moment, sounds of a muffled commotion broke out somewhere to the right of the stage. Nash snapped her eyes toward the noise. Her stomach dropped as the cries of *"Intruders!"* sounded from the room the dancers had disappeared into.

Shit.

More eyes started to shift toward the door as a series of loud bangs sounded out behind it, almost like the sound of a body being slammed against a wall. Ryia was back there—that was probably *exactly* what that noise was. They had about thirty seconds before the Disciples went to see what all the fuss was about. Then Ryia and Evelyn would join Tristan in his cozy cell, and Nash could say goodbye to her dreams of selling the Quill for a ridiculous amount of gold.

They needed the distraction now more than ever. She looked back toward the Brillish nobles, to the spot where Ivan would be sitting when the plan was ready to be set in motion. Still not there. What if he hadn't made it into the arena at all? It wasn't against the rules to bring weapons into the arena. Half the bastards in here were carrying swords and daggers, more for show than anything. Ivan's possession of a weapon wouldn't cause suspicion, but what he intended to *do* with that weapon could set off the Sensers. Ryia had been so sure the crowds would protect him—overwhelm the Sensers and allow him to slip by, at least for a while. She saw the Guildmaster whisper an order to a pair of Disciples at the edge of the stage. They turned, heading for the third door. Shit, shit, shit.

There!

She locked eyes with Ivan, watching as he milled through the increasingly restless crowd, jaw working steadily to chew Ryia's lemon balm into a pulp. He had made it inside, at least. The first part of this cursed plan to go right. He was a little less than halfway up the bowl. Too far away. *Definitely* too far away. And too exposed, standing in the middle of an aisle. Her heart sank as she realized what he meant to do. She shook her head, eyes wide, hoping to convey the message *Don't be a fucking idiot* over the distance between them.

Either the message was lost, or Ivan had become a fucking idiot, because he turned toward the stage, his hand reaching down his leg.

All the blood drained from Nash's face. True, without Ivan's distraction, Evelyn and Ryia were dead. But without Nash's distraction, Ivan was dead. She turned back to the crowd surrounding her, looking for one of the poor souls she had planted her little black marbles on. Not one in sight.

She froze, the pieces clunking together far too slowly in her brain. The Disciples drew another step closer to the door to the dancers' room. Ivan's hand started to move back up his leg, now clutching a glint of steel. She still had some of the *Trän vun Yavol* in her coat pockets. Which meant it was time to do something colossally stupid.

Nash plunged her hands into her pockets, counting the remaining spheres. There were only twelve left. She grabbed as many as she could fit in her palm at once. Hopefully it would be enough.

She cocked her arm back, then released, flinging the tiny black marbles into the air. She threw them hard—would they fall to the ground hard enough, though? For the *Trän vun Yavol* to work their magic they had to break. Easy enough for the spheres she had tucked in the merchants' pockets—they would soon be crushed by the press of the panicking crowd. But for the panic to start, for all those other capsules to break . . . first, these ones had to shatter. Out of the corner of her eye she saw Ivan moving. His arm shot back as the capsules tumbled toward the ground in slow motion. Time shuddered to a stop.

The sound of the first capsule breaking was silent and deafening at the same time. A cloud of noxious-looking smoke billowed up from the ground a few rows ahead, dancing on the wind, spreading, taking over. As people started to panic, she saw another puff of smoke rise a few steps away and another halfway down the next row.

Like cats watching a dangling string, the eyes of the crowd followed as one by one the capsules burst, releasing ever-expanding clouds of hard-packed coal dust into the heavy, humid air.

Nash spun on her heel, turning the opposite direction. She saw it just as it happened. Ivan's hand flicked up, flinging a small throwing axe toward the stage. The speck of silver glinted in the setting sun as it spun forward. Nash blinked and Ivan was gone, melted back into the crowd, probably already wearing a different face.

A gasp rippled through the crowd as the axe darted, seemingly out of nowhere, whirling end over end. The Butcher was a good teacher. Or maybe Ivan had just gotten lucky. Either way, it was a good throw—especially for the distance. A spiral of hard wood and sharpened steel heading straight for the Guildmaster's hollow throat.

How had Tristan put it when he'd proposed this plan? The bigger the prize, the bigger the distraction. If an assassination attempt on the twice-damned Guildmaster of Thamorr wasn't a big enough distraction, Nash didn't know what was. Draw every set of eyes—every guard, every Disciple—to the arena. Keep the eyes off the bell tower long enough for Linley and the Butcher to sneak inside and get the Quill. And now, keep the eyes off the manor long enough for Nash to get Tristan out of that dungeon.

Her neck muscles tightened. It was time for her to get the hells out of here. She ducked backward into the nearest cloud of Borean coal dust. She lifted a hand to her collar and pulled roughly at Ivan's sewing. The thread parted immediately, spilling a layer of dark green fabric over her burgundy coat. She pulled a false mustache from her pocket, leaning over as though in a coughing fit from the smoke, and pressed it to her face with a dab of spit. She was a new person all over again.

Now for the tricky part—getting out of the arena and into the manor dungeon.

Lucky for her, Evelyn and Ryia had secured blueprints to every building on this island. She knew the servants' entrance ten paces behind her led to a path that would take her directly to the manor. Getting inside there was another story entirely, but one step at a time.

Nash edged toward the door. She was only a few steps away when the Guildmaster's voice cut through the chaos.

"Block all the exits. No one leaves the arena until this would-be assassin is caught."

Just as they had hoped. All eyes would be on the arena for sure now. This was a good thing, assuming she could get out in time. And assuming no one had seen Ivan throw that axe.

A foolish thought. No one could have seen. Nash had been *watching* him, and she had hardly seen, for Felice's sake. Sure enough, the crowd in the arena started pointing fingers in different directions.

"I saw him over there! Skinny little man in a bright red coat!"

"No, he went this way! Snuck down toward the Adept entrance."

"This big man shoved me! It was him!"

Nash ignored them all, edging closer and closer to the abandoned servants' entrance, half-hidden behind an alcove in the arena wall. Nash eased the door open, stepping one foot silently inside.

"No." The Guildmaster's voice was soft, but still somehow carrying.

Nash took one last glance toward the stage to see him standing, stock-still, staring at the throwing axe he'd stopped in midair. A knowing smile curled on his puckered lips, a horrible fire burning in his cold, crushing eyes.

"We're looking for a woman."

25

RYIA

Ryia had worn a dozen different masks in her day. The Butcher of Carrowwick. The Poison Blade, terror of the Rena desert. The *Neightgeiver*, in Borean, had been a personal favorite. It would be a twice-damned shame if "jewel-encrusted ballerina" was the alias that finally got her killed.

The dance instructor's grip was surprisingly strong, wrapped around Ryia's wrist as she called out for help.

"Intruders! Someone get the Disciples! We have frauds in our midst!"

Unfortunately for Miss Talon-Hands, Ryia did not take kindly to being snared by the wrist. She lifted a sparkly sandaled foot and kicked the aging woman in the sternum. The woman's piercing cry for someone to get the guards was interrupted as the air whooshed from her lungs. In her surprise, her grip loosened, and Ryia wrenched herself free. She shoved the already reeling instructor into the closed door with a bang, then grabbed Evelyn, yanking her forward.

"Back door," Ryia said, tugging Evelyn behind her as she ran.

Most of the dancers screamed as they came through, jumping out of the way like Ryia and Evelyn were snakes. A few stared at them, frozen in shock. Ryia shoved them as she and Evelyn tore past, toppling them like dominos.

They reached the back door in just a few seconds, but it was still too long. Miss Talon-Hands was already back on her feet, screaming for help twice as loudly now. They needed to get the hell out of this room before the Disciples came in. Ryia tested the door handle. Locked. Damn it.

"Keep them back," Ryia said, pulling out two long, thin sticks of metal from her costume.

Evelyn turned her back to the door, arms out at her sides in apparent challenge, glaring at the restless crowd of increasingly panicked dancers and acrobats as Ryia threaded the picks into the lock, twisting and jiggling, waiting to hear the sweet click that would win them their extremely temporary freedom.

"Who do you two think you are?" said a brusque, commanding voice behind her. Ryia looked over her shoulder to see a tall, blond dancer standing nose to nose with Evelyn. "You cannot assault Miss Eloise."

"Assault? We didn't mean to—" Evelyn started. "You're misunderstanding what's going on here. Just leave us be and no one has to get hurt."

Sweat beaded on Ryia's forehead as she twisted the two sticks in unison. The lock finally gave way, and the door swung open. Ryia turned just in time to see the skinny blonde throw a half-assed slap at Evelyn.

The captain ducked. She wound up and popped the dancer firmly in the nose with a rabbit punch. Ryia grinned as the dancer fell back, clutching her nose.

"Ready to get out of here, or did you want to beat up some more defenseless dancers?" she asked.

"Defenseless? She swung first," Evelyn protested, clearly rattled by what she had just done. She looked guiltily down at her hands. "It was a reflex."

They barreled through the door, slamming it shut and clicking the lock back in place behind them. Ryia grabbed a stone bench from beside the door, grunting as she dragged it to block the entrance. It wouldn't stop a Disciple, but it might slow them down, at least.

"Now what?" Evelyn asked, eyes wide as the door to the dancers' room banged against the makeshift barricade.

Ryia turned toward the tower, then nearly choked as the smell suddenly washed over her. It was horrible. Acidic and familiar, the sensation of a hundred scorpions fleeing up her nostrils. *Danger.* The strongest she had sensed in years.

"Get down," she hissed.

"What is it now?"

"What do you think?" Ryia shoved them both into one of the tangled shrubs lining the circular pathway leading around the courtyard. The door they had barricaded jiggled and thudded against the bench one more time, then stopped as gasps spread through the arena, followed by a hush.

"That's the signal. We need to move."

"Not yet," Ryia said, still nearly gagging on the scent of raw death.

"Now is really not the time for your bullshi—"

"Not. Yet."

Evelyn's mouth snapped shut as the sound of footsteps and flapping robes sounded outside their hiding spot. Disciples. At least half a dozen of the bastards, streaming past them into the arena, taking the stench of danger with them.

Ryia released her grip on Evelyn's shoulder. The captain glared at her, suspicious.

"How did you know they were coming?"

"Not all of us are deaf as turtles," Ryia said.

"Turtles?"

"Yeah, turtles. They don't have any ears, right?" Ryia said distractedly, sniffing the air lightly.

Evelyn quirked one eyebrow.

Ryia held out a hand. "We don't have time to talk about twice-damned turtles." Her heart raced as the sounds of panic swept through the arena behind them. The door to the dancers' room started banging against the bench-barricade again. She waved Evelyn toward the tower. "Go, go, go."

"Are you kidding?" Evelyn gestured down at herself. "We'll be spotted. We're basically human beacons every time the sun hits us."

Ryia gave her a look. "How many times have you been forced to listen to me on this job, Captain?"

Evelyn didn't answer.

Ryia nodded. "And, remind me, how many times have you lost your head?"

Still silence.

The door leading to the dancers' room banged against the bench again; this time the thud of wood on stone was punctuated by a sharp crack. The wood was starting to give way. It wouldn't be long before it broke to splinters.

"Look, you have to trust me to get us into that tower, I have to trust you to watch my back while I'm in there, and Tristan has to trust all of us to save his sorry ass from the Guildmaster. Then we can all go home and collect our prizes from Tolliver Shadowwood, okay?"

She turned toward the tower. Not bothering to see if Evelyn was following, she broke into an all-out sprint. The glass beads on her skirt rattled noisily as she ran, but it hardly mattered. The arena was growing louder and more restless by the second. It only made sense—there were hundreds of people stuck there, squeezed into those stone walls like a plump merchant into his waistcoat.

Good. The more chaotic the arena was, the more chaotic the docks would be later. And the more chaotic the docks were, the easier it would be for her to slip aboard a ship and escape.

Guilt clawed at her stomach. Escape and leave her crew behind. Best-case scenario, they would return to Carrowwick empty-handed—as good as a death sentence whether Callum Clem was alive or not when they returned. Worst-case scenario, they would all be blamed for destroying the Quill and killed in the Guild-master's murderous wrath when he realized he wouldn't be able to hunt down every newborn Adept in Thamorr anymore.

Shut up, she scolded herself. They were a team of professional criminals, for fuck's sake. The rules of the Lottery were clear as *stervod*. A team stuck together . . . until the cards were down. Then it was every man for himself. Or woman, in this case.

Ryia skidded to a stop at the last ring of shrubs, closing her eyes and sniffing one last time. "The Disciples are gone."

"How do you know?" asked Evelyn.

"They just ran past us two minutes ago," Ryia lied. "I'm guessing logic isn't a big part of Needle Guard training?"

The ex-captain shot her a glare, then tugged at the sleeves of her dress, ripping them at the armpits. She stretched out, miming a sword strike with her bare hands.

"What are you doing?" Ryia asked.

"If we're attacked—"

"Attacked?" Ryia looked pointedly at her outfit. "What are you going to fight with? A pirouette?"

"Very funny," Evelyn said. "You don't think we should be ready for a fight?"

"I'm always ready for a fight."

"And what are *you* planning on fighting with?" Evelyn griped, thrusting her dyed hair behind her shoulders.

Ryia slid a single throwing axe from a small fold of fabric just below her bejeweled waist. Ivan was truly a master, managing to hide the weapon in such a revealing costume. "This."

"You didn't think to bring me one?"

Ryia ignored her, sprinting the last few steps to the base of the tower. She pushed through the greenery climbing up its stone walls, feeling her way along, looking for a door.

"Looks like I might have to climb this thing after all," Ryia said, casting an anxious glance back toward the arena.

The door to the dancers' room banged against the makeshift barricade one last time, finally splintering in half. Ryia peered through the foliage as two Edalish guards muscled their way into the courtyard—Shadow Wardens, Tristan had called them. Shit. Ryia pulled back, ducking into the brush before she was spotted. At least their pursuers weren't Adept. If they could just get inside this damned tower.

"Climb it? Good luck." Evelyn looked up at the smooth sides of the tower. "I don't think you're as impressive as you think you are."

Ryia's forced smirk turned into a genuine smile as her hands stumbled upon a flat stretch of wood, covered by vines. She felt along the panel, groping blindly until she found a metal bulb.

"You will continue to find," she started, twisting the knob sharply, "that I am just as impressive as every story you have ever heard." The door popped open, swinging into the tower.

"You are the most arrogant person I have ever met."

"Is it arrogance to recognize my own genius?"

"Yes," Evelyn said flatly.

Ryia shoved Evelyn into the tower, climbing in after her. "Then you're probably right."

The walls of the tower were so thick they nearly drowned out the sounds of panic boiling in the arena. Evelyn eased the door shut, and Ryia was overwhelmed by the unpleasant sensation of being stuck at the bottom of a very deep well.

"So, where is this thing?" Evelyn asked, like they were looking for a lost shoe.

Ryia straightened the stiff bodice of her ridiculous outfit, looking up the narrow staircase. "Up there, I'm guessing."

"You're *guessing*?"

"I'm not a fucking bloodhound," Ryia said.

"You could have fooled me."

Ryia clapped her on the shoulder. "Watch the door." She cleared her throat, pulling away. "I'll be back before you have the chance to miss me."

Her nostrils whistled with every breath, jeweled skirts rattling noisily as she climbed higher and higher up the tower, spiraling around the long rope dangling from the bell high above her head. Her stomach clenched as she rounded the last loop to see . . .

Nothing.

Just a flat platform, some fifteen feet below the bell, holding nothing but dust.

"Shit," she breathed. She had been so sure it would be here. So certain that pompous prick would hide the thing in plain sight.

She narrowed her eyes at the bell above her head. There was still one more place to look. She kicked off the ridiculous sandals and threw herself at the wall, latching on to the crevices and pulling herself up the inside of the tower. The hand- and footholds were clear and worn enough that she knew she wasn't the first person to make this climb. It was almost as easy as a ladder, hand over hand, step by step.

Ryia's skirts tangled around her knees as she hugged the wall, steering clear of the rope. One bump of that rope and the bell would ring out over the whole island. If that wasn't worst-case scenario, she wasn't sure what was.

When she was just a few handholds beneath the bell, she saw it. A tiny cutout in the wall. A hidden chamber leading to a skinny, ragged staircase. Blood thundered past Ryia's eardrums as she swung inside, mounted those last few steps, and pulled herself, blinking, into the sunlight.

The light glinted off the waves outside the weathered walls of the arena in front of her and reflected off the massive bell behind her as she tiptoed, barefoot, along the foot-wide ledge. The view was breathtaking. She could see the whole island. The sails of every ship in the harbor, the stage, the roiling mass struggling to escape the arena. The training barracks, one each for Sensers and Kinetics, positioned on either side of the Guildmaster's manor on the eastern cliffs.

Click, click, click.

The sound pulled Ryia's eyes back to the tower.

Click, click, scratch.

She slipped along the edge of the bell, heart leaping into her throat as she saw it. The relic of Declan Day. It was here. The Quill.

It looked just like the drawing. A long, ornate writing stick made of stone and carven wood. It shuddered, hovering on its point, sloshing, whirring, and hissing.

Beneath it lay the map of Thamorr, covered in tiny pinpricks of deep red ink. Ryia blinked. The dots were *moving*. Shifting slightly. One cruised along the western coastline. Another moved slowly across the border from Gildemar to Dresdell. Hundreds milled around the small island marked *Guildmaster's Stronghold*. It seemed more sinister than she had expected. Its energy felt less like a hunting dog, sniffing out Adept, and more like a fox, cunning and dangerous. Once again, she was struck by the feeling that there was something about this relic that she just didn't understand.

Click, click, scratch.

The Quill darted across the map, floating through the air before placing a fresh dot of ink right in the heart of the Rena desert.

Ryia drifted a step closer. After all this time. After all this running, it was right here. On the desk beside it sat half a dozen thick leather books. She picked one up, leafing through with numb fingers.

Known Adept per city; Oryol, Boreas, the first page read.

The following pages were covered with city names and neat tally markers. A count of the number of Adept that should be there corresponding with each dot on the map.

No wonder it was against the law for anyone other than the Guildmaster to sell Adept. The whole key to his power was knowing where they all were and where they all *should* be. Finding the splotches of ink that didn't belong on the map. Without that power, he couldn't find new Adept babies. Couldn't kidnap them and brainwash them into submission. And then eventually, slowly, the Guilds would fall.

Would it throw Thamorr into complete chaos? Probably. But what did she care? She would just find a nice quiet corner of the world and watch the Guildmaster's hold on Thamorr crumble. Watch with a smile on her face as he faded into irrelevance, powerless and alone. She grabbed a splintered wooden beam from the floor, raising it over her head like a club to smash Declan Day's treasured Quill into a thousand tiny pieces.

But just as she tensed, preparing to strike, she hesitated.

Here it was, her freedom, the only thing she could ever remember wanting, staring her in the face, and she was hesitating.

Ridiculous. There was no other option. If she stuck with the Saints' plan and stole the thing, she would still be in the same situation she was in before, only the Mad King of Edale would be hunting her instead of the Guildmaster. After all she had gone through to get here, she would have to be an idiot to just leave it untouched. No. She was going to crush it to splinters and run like hell.

Thamorr would figure itself out. And the team . . . the bastards were from the Lottery. Betrayal wasn't exactly a novel concept there, right?

Her blood ran cold as she heard the unmistakable scuff of a boot on stone.

Mind full of images of Disciples closing in on her, she turned on her toe, blindly flinging her axe toward the noise. Her stomach clenched as her eyes found her target.

Evelyn Linley stood sideways, edging carefully around the bell. And Ryia's axe was spinning straight toward her ivory throat.

No!

Without thinking, Ryia thrust her power out like a lasso. The weapon froze in midair, inches from Evelyn's skin. The captain's eyes grew wide. She stared at the axe as it hummed softly, frozen for a moment, then dropped at her feet. She turned her gaze to Ryia.

"I knew it."

26

NASH

We're looking for a woman.

What in the hells did that mean? The Guildmaster had sounded so certain, but of course, he was dead wrong. Maybe the bastard wasn't as all-knowing as everyone thought. Her spine crawled as she remembered the familiar way he had studied the axe, *Ryia's* axe. Or maybe he knew even more than she had suspected.

But that was irrelevant for now. Nash pressed herself into a broom closet in the servants' passageway as footsteps clicked down the hall. She held her breath, waiting to be discovered . . . but they thundered right past. Like Ryia had said, Sensers could only detect someone who posed a physical threat, and Nash didn't plan on hurting anyone. Either that or those footsteps had belonged to Kinetics. Either way, it was the first stretch of good luck she'd had this whole damned job. If that luck held until the sun went down, they might actually make it off this rock alive.

Nash eased the door open, peering left and right down the hall and adjusting her fake mustache. Empty again. She extracted herself carefully from the closet, sidestepping the broom and buckets inside before slipping down the hall to the right.

The servants' entrance led to a maze of corridors and rooms. There were kitchens and larders and dressing rooms. Nash peered at her blueprint again in the low light of the lanterns on the walls. She edged past a deserted icebox full of expensive liquors and fruit wines, finally stopping before an elegant oak door.

Blood thundering noisily through her veins, Nash pressed an ear against the door, listening for footsteps or voices, but it was useless. The racket from the arena was deafening, bouncing around the enclosed corridors like a hive of bees trapped in a bottle. She winced, closing her eyes and flinging the door open.

Sunlight flooded the corridor, and Nash opened her eyes slowly, letting out a relieved breath as she saw nothing but a deserted path stretching out in front of her.

"All right, Tristan, you surprisingly resilient son of a bitch," she said under her breath, shutting herself inside the servants' corridor and shuffling to the right. "I'm coming for you."

She had plotted out her path a hundred times last night, but she would only get one shot at this. Tristan had clearly resisted whatever torture he had been subjected to so far. He had kept the Saints' plans to himself and kept them all safe. Once she got him out of that dungeon, she was going to apologize for all the shit she had given him over the past few weeks.

Well, maybe not *all* of it.

Nash ripped the false mustache from her upper lip, tracing a soot-stained finger along her path on the map. The manor was just on the far side of the next hill, positioned along the northern cliffs of the tiny island. There were two proper entrances to the building, according to the drawings.

The front door—no good, there was bound to still be at least *one* Disciple left there, no matter how big a commotion they made in the arena.

The other door was at the top of an outdoor staircase, leading directly into the Guildmaster's private chambers on the third floor. Nash wasn't sure if Disciples would be posted there when the Guildmaster wasn't inside, but it was pretty far out of her way. She wanted to get into the basement, after all. Seemed just plain dumb to risk running into whatever Disciples might be inside on three unnecessary floors on her way there.

Thankfully, the building plan had offered a solution.

Massive, deadly storms were pretty common on the southern seas, especially in autumn. On an exposed island like this, even Kinetic powers couldn't save someone from the destructive force of those winds. A storm-cellar entrance stood twenty paces from the edge of the manor. The cellar itself was just a rough-looking rectangle, some ten feet below the ground, but it was connected to a snaking tunnel that led to the manor's storerooms. Even Adept had to eat, apparently.

The storerooms were just a few corridors away from the steep staircase that led down to the infamous dungeon.

Sure, there were bound to be a few locked doors in the way. Nash stowed the sketches in her coat pocket and slipped up the hill, clinging to the shadows at the edge of the outer arena wall. But she knew the doors would not be her only obstacle. The dungeon was plenty secure from the inside, but there was still no way the Guildmaster would leave a prisoner completely unguarded. She would come face-to-face with a Disciple before the day was through.

Shit.

She patted her pockets, feeling to see if any of Ivan's magical black marbles were still tucked there. She found two lonely *Trän vun Yavol*. If worse came to worst, she hoped they would be enough to cover her tracks—to cloud the Disciples' vision long enough for her and Tristan to escape. It was a long shot, but it was the only one they had. They had started this job as five random members of Clem's crew, but in the past few weeks Nash thought they had become something of a family. At this point, she had the distinct feeling they would be leaving the island together or not at all.

The ground fell away in front of her as she crested the hill, the cliff side manor now clearly visible in the distance. Although "distance" was a strong word for it: it was only a few hundred feet away. Nash dropped to her stomach, peering over the top of the hill toward the building, looking for the telltale sign of blue robes swirling in the wind.

Nothing. No sign of a single Disciple—or a single breathing body—in sight.

Suspicion tugged at the back of her mind, but she shrugged it away. Maybe the Disciples were doing rounds and happened to be on the far side of the building? She couldn't afford to turn down a stroke of good luck.

But she also couldn't expect that luck to hold out forever. She sprinted across the open stretch of grass surrounding the manor. It was only a matter of time before someone turned up, and she didn't want to be caught out in the open when that happened. She tore around the side of the building, bent over in an attempt to diminish her six-foot frame.

The storm cellar doors lay flat against the ground: two slabs of heavy wood that looked like they might just have been tossed onto the grass. To the north, the ground dropped eighty feet into the ocean. Just as she had hoped, the storm doors had no locks—it wouldn't be a very useful emergency shelter if no one could get inside quickly. Nash wrenched one door open and found an old wooden ladder leading to a scraped-earth floor.

Shooting one last look at the deserted manor lawn, Nash lowered herself into the darkness, closing the door behind her.

First hurdle: cleared.

The door leading from the cellar to the storeroom was sealed with a rusting padlock and a heavy chain. Nash picked it easily enough, tiptoeing her way through the empty storeroom and peering into the hallway beyond. The manor was eerily silent. She could hear the sound of her own breathing, echoing in her ears. Where were all the Disciples? They wouldn't really have left the entire manor and dungeon unguarded to run off to the arena, would they?

Nash shivered uncomfortably, thinking of the Adept she had seen before. They could move quieter than jungle cats. She could be completely surrounded and not even know it. She whirled suddenly in a circle at the thought, fists raised . . . but there was no one there.

"Keep moving," she intoned to herself. The lack of guards was suspicious, sure, but she wasn't about to throw away her chance to rescue Tristan because of a little suspicion, right?

But the suspicious voice in her head got louder and louder the deeper she moved into the manor. As she snuck through larders and wine cellars and corridors, all silent and empty. She pulled the *Trän vun Yavol* from her pocket, rolling the capsules between her fingers as she reached the door at the top of the dungeon stairs.

This was it. The place where her luck was bound to run out. She was ready. Or as ready as she possibly could be to face an impossibly strong magical being in single combat.

She pulled her lockpick out again, inserting the sticks into the knob, then frowned. Her stomach swirled uncomfortably as she turned the knob and the door swung open. It was unlocked. Why in Felice's bitterest hell would the door to a *dungeon* be unlocked? It made no sense.

Unless . . .

Was Tristan already dead?

Her heart thudded in her chest, sending pulsing beats down her arms and into the tips of her fingers, still clenched tight around her two precious *Trän vun Yavol*, ready to chuck them at the ground at the first sign of trouble. The stone stairs were coated thickly with dust. Her steps left clear prints behind her as she walked. The only set of prints on the stairs. As though she was the first person to tread this staircase in a very, very long time.

By the time she reached the bottom of the stairs, she already knew what she would find when she turned toward the cells. And she was right.

Nothing. No one. The prison was unguarded because it was empty. Because Tristan wasn't here.

Because he had never been here.

Nash turned in a slow circle, struggling to process the thought. But if Tristan wasn't here, then where the fuck was he?

27

EVELYN

Evelyn barely even heard the clatter of the axe as it fell. She kicked it out of reach.

"I knew it," she breathed. She wasn't mental after all. If the Butcher was Adept, it explained everything. She frowned. Well, almost everything. "But how . . ."

She wasn't quite sure how to finish that sentence. *How are you not a dead-eyed half-wit* seemed rude. But she had never heard of a mother being able to avoid the Disciples when they came for a child. It was why parents never named their children until their first birthdays. Until then, not even a king could be sure his child wouldn't be taken by the Guildmaster.

The Butcher didn't need her to finish the question.

"I might have the skills, but I sure as hell wasn't born with them."

"What do you mean you weren't born with them?"

Ryia studied the ghastly scars on her wrists, still half-hidden by billowing silk sleeves. "Isn't it obvious, Captain? I was made."

Evelyn could almost feel smoke pouring from her ears as her mind tried to wrap around the word. *Made.* Adept couldn't be made.

If they could, then every bloody man and woman in Thamorr would be bursting with unnatural powers.

Her eyes flicked to the device sitting on the ancient-looking table. It looked just like the drawing. A pen, ornate and old beyond measure, hovering over a map of Thamorr. Then she registered the broken timber in Ryia's left hand, poised like a hammer over an anvil, ready to smash the priceless relic into smithereens.

"What about your mate, Clem?"

"This was never about Clem," Ryia said with a hollow laugh.

"You think he'll let you live after you cheat him out of half a million crescents?"

"I wasn't planning on going back to break the news to him, to be honest." A thin line of sweat ran across Ryia's forehead. Evelyn swore she saw her hand tremble.

"You'd just abandon us like that?"

"We don't exactly swear oaths of loyalty in the Lottery." Ryia's throat bobbed. "So what'll it be, Captain? Are you going to climb back down that tower, or were you planning on standing between me and my target?"

Evelyn looked back to the whirring Quill. To the wriggling dots on the map beneath it. It didn't take a genius to figure out what the device did, just like it didn't take a genius to figure out why Ryia would want it destroyed.

"You swing that log, and no one on this island will help you escape," Evelyn said slowly, bare feet shaking as she dared a half step forward. "You'd be trapped. You still need us."

"I've been slipping nets my whole life—I'm something of an expert at this point," Ryia said. "I may have needed you to get this far, but now you're just another obstacle."

Just another obstacle. Evelyn wondered how many "obstacles" the mercenary had overrun. How many other poor sods had she tricked into working with her? How many cities? How many jobs? Was Ryia even her real name?

Not that it mattered. Not that any of it mattered. The "Butcher of Carrowwick" wasn't her *real* name either, but it was the one that would win Evelyn her prize when she turned her in to the Needle Guard. . . . Her father's ring felt like it was made of lead.

She twitched a hand toward her jewel-encrusted hip. A useless gesture, with her sword tucked safely aboard *The Hardship*, but an obvious one nonetheless. A challenge.

Ryia followed the motion with her eyes and tutted derisively, sending Evelyn's pulse skittering through her fingertips. "Bad call."

Evelyn ducked backward, swaying into the cover of a support beam as the Butcher brought the makeshift club down toward her head. She pushed her skirts aside to roll forward, placing herself between Ryia and the Quill. Evelyn fumbled around on the floor for a weapon, coming up with nothing better than a frayed length of rope. She held it, taut, above her head, catching the second swing of the broken beam. The rope pulled and burned her palms, but it held.

She could only imagine how ridiculous they looked, grappling for their lives, armed with makeshift weapons, dressed in silken skirts and clattering glass jewels.

"How does all this end for you?" Evelyn asked, snapping the rope toward Ryia like a whip. Ryia took a step back, away from the Quill on its table.

"What does that matter to you?" Ryia asked, ducking sideways and bringing her right fist toward Evelyn's jaw in a vicious hook.

Evelyn swayed backward, teetering on the ledge, barely catching herself from tumbling headlong into the bell hanging beside them. That was a good question. She jabbed a fist forward, catching Ryia in the stomach.

She shrugged as the mercenary gasped for breath. "Just curious to see what you're willing to sell out your entire team for."

Ryia clenched her jaw. "I have no team. I knew what I was doing from the start of this bullshit job."

"I guess I was asking for a bit much," Evelyn said, forcing Ryia back another pace around the curve of the bell, "looking for loyalty in the dregs of the ruddy Lottery." The Quill was completely out of view now.

Ryia blocked Evelyn's left hook with her steadily deteriorating chunk of wood. "I guess so." She tossed the remains of the beam from hand to hand, eyeing its splintered end. "Now, are you going to let me do what I need to do, or are you really going to make me kill you for it?"

Evelyn hopped as Ryia kicked at her ankles, nearly falling out the window to her left. She regained her balance, then thrust a heel up, kicking toward the broken beam.

The wood beam broke to splinters, and Ryia hesitated just long enough for Evelyn to swing her fist around in a right hook, smacking the merc in the temple.

The Butcher's eyes crossed and she blinked. "Maybe I . . . ," she started, sounding dazed. Then she trailed off, nostrils flaring.

"Maybe you what?" Evelyn asked. Ryia swayed, almost like she was going to topple out the window.

Without thinking, Evelyn leapt forward to catch her, wrapping a hand around her arm. Ryia flinched away, and Evelyn let go immediately, brushing off her skirt. But the mercenary's eyes were still distant.

"What is it?"

Ryia's head snapped toward the arena, like a hunting dog on the trail. She dove forward without warning, heading for the place they had left the Quill sitting on its rickety table. "Someone's coming," she hissed.

"How do you know?" Evelyn asked, suspicious.

"Just listen to me, before you get both of us killed."

"Oh, suddenly it's 'us' again, is it?"

A floorboard creaked around the far side of the bell, and Evelyn froze. Ryia shouldered past her, sprinting around the curve of the bell.

Evelyn chased after her, her legs growing numb as the table holding the Quill came back into view. And the person whose fingers were now wrapped around it.

She had never met the woman before, but she had seen sketches. The round face and sinister eyes were unmistakable. Wyatt Asher's right-hand man. What was her name?

Tana Rafferty.

The woman cackled, brushing her hands against her trousers to clean off the dust from her climb up the tower wall. "Wow, don't you two look nice."

"I thought you said the Crowns turned down this job," Evelyn said to Ryia. "Or was that just another lie?"

Ryia ignored her, lunging for Rafferty. "Drop it. Now. Or I'll shave a few inches off those nice round cheeks of yours."

"Original," Rafferty drawled.

"How did you find it?"

Rafferty gave a childlike laugh. "Your little bird gave you away."

"Little bird?" Evelyn frowned, looking to Ryia, but she looked just as confused.

"What?"

Rafferty laughed again. "So you really didn't know? Felice, no wonder the Saints are the bottom-feeders of the Lottery. You fuckers have been sitting on an absolute gold mine for months, and you had no idea. Well, this has been fun, but . . ." Tucking the Quill into her cloak pocket, she tipped an imaginary hat to them, then sprinted back toward the rickety wooden steps.

"Shit!" Ryia swore, darting after her. Evelyn followed close behind, but by the time she reached the hidden staircase, it was too late.

"Give my old buddy Cal my regards, won't you?" Asher's sidekick called with a wink. Then she leapt from the platform, grabbing on to the rope dangling from the bell.

Evelyn cringed as the first deafening clang rang out over the island. Somehow the second clang was even louder. And the third louder still.

"Dammit," Ryia swore again, grabbing on to the windowsill. "Dammit, dammit, dammit."

The Disciples in the arena stirred, turning toward the tower. No doubt the Guildmaster was already shouting orders. They had seconds at best.

"What did she mean? About a little bird?" Evelyn asked.

"What does it matter? Look out the fucking window, Captain," Ryia said sourly. "We're about to have an army on our ha—" She stopped mid-word, her eyes jumping to the sandstone walls surrounding the courtyard.

There was Tana Rafferty, sprinting over the northern half of the courtyard like a deer, making for a rope dangling from the top of the wall. And perched up top, anchoring the rope in place . . .

Tristan.

That prick. That selfish, traitorous arse.

Ryia clenched the windowsill, threatening to turn the stone to powder as she glared after him. He looked up at the tower then, almost like he could feel her gaze. His face was dripping with shame and guilt and longing . . . but none of these emotions were reflected in the Butcher.

In fact, there was no emotion in her at all, from the looks of it. Just cold detachment. The face Evelyn had expected to find when they first met . . . and a face she had yet to see the unexpectedly jovial—if crass—mercenary actually wear.

The boy turned as Rafferty made it to the top of the wall, nearly tripping over his own gangly feet. Then they were both gone.

"Damn it all," Evelyn whispered, looking back to the arena.

"What?" Ryia asked. Evelyn felt her turn beside her. Then: "Shit."

A group of Kinetics sprinted across the courtyard, and in front, the Guildmaster himself.

"What are we going to do?" Evelyn asked. Her voice was so small and fearful she wanted to smack herself around the head.

"We?" Ryia asked. Her voice was soft and dangerously level. "I thought the *little bird* just made it pretty damned clear, Captain." She dropped from the window, latching on to the sill with practiced fingers. "There has never been a 'we.'"

28

IVAN

The arena was in utter chaos. Louder than the Catacombs, tenser than a cheat in the back room of the Miscreants' Temple. Ivan slipped through the gaps in the crowd, making his way toward the entrance to the courtyard.

Anxiety prickled over his skin. If all went to plan, the Butcher would sidle up beside him for the handoff any minute now. That had been his own addition to the plan. He had told the team it was to reduce risk—if anyone had seen Ryia and Evelyn leaving the tower they could be stopped and searched. But if they handed the Quill off to Ivan first, there would be nothing to find. It was a good argument, one he had won quickly. But that was not his true motivation for the handoff.

Once Ivan had the Quill, he would not make his way back to the dock. He would follow the stream of the crowd as they left the arena, and then he would stow himself away on one of the Borean balingers he had seen lining the western docks. The instant his foot touched that dock he would be crossing Callum Clem. If Clem was alive that was as good as a death sentence in Carrowwick, but there was no guarantee the Snake was still breathing . . . besides, the world was so much bigger than Carrowwick.

But to betray Clem would be to betray the entire crew. He shook his head to clear it. That had been the plan from the start. Of course, the rest of the plan had changed quite a bit. From Callum's arrest to Tristan's capture this entire job had been a *kataström*. Now he was stranded alone in this turmoil-ridden bowl, Ryia and Evelyn were charging blindly into danger, for all they knew, and Nash was likely inches from capture or death. His stomach curled. It was his fault Nash was headed for that prison cell. If he had not insisted on this handoff, he would have been the natural choice to break into the Guildmaster's dungeon. Instead they had sent a clumsy smuggler straight into the belly of the beast, armed with nothing but a lockpick and a pocket full of *Trän vun Yavol*.

His stomach squirmed with guilt. Or perhaps something more. His intuition was spiked like the needle on a seismic reader in an earthquake. Something was wrong.

A sound burst through the still-rising chaos like a rock shattering a glass pane. The melodic gong of metal on metal. The bell tower. Ivan's head whipped around in unison with a thousand others. Sunlight glinted off the bell's burnished surface as it clanged noisily in its perch.

On stage, the Guildmaster froze, still holding Ryia's axe. By now he had surely inspected the blade, discovered the heavy dosage of dormire's blood. Ivan had hoped to nick his flesh, to knock him senseless, but the man was quicker than expected.

The Guildmaster pressed his lips together until they turned the color of chalk, like he was dying of the Gildesh Whisper. Then blood rushed into his face all at once, dyeing the skin a vivid, wrathful crimson. Ivan watched carefully, reading his lips as he turned to one of his Disciples.

"She is not here," he said. Then: "I know the axe is hers, but she is no longer here. She is at the tower, you idiots."

The Guildmaster flicked his wrist, and a wave of Kinetic power parted the crowd as easily as a pair of scissors cuts through parchment. Ivan's jaw nearly hit the ground at his feet. He had never seen a display of Adept power so strong. They had been fools to think they could succeed in this task.

Ivan rolled his lower lip between his teeth. His plans were unraveling more rapidly than a poorly knit sweater. If the Guildmaster knew someone was in the bell tower—the place where his precious Quill was kept—it was unlikely that anyone would be permitted to leave without being searched. And somehow the Guildmaster knew the axe was Ryia's. . . .

He pushed the thought aside and ran a few rapid calculations, then set his jaw, turning away from the courtyard, making his way toward the hidden servants' entrance Nash had escaped through. Would it be difficult to free Kasimir without the Quill to use as a bargaining chip? Absolutely. But he would certainly not be able to free him if he were dead.

Perhaps there would come a time when he would regret abandoning his schemes, but now was not the time for doubts. Now was the time for action. He ducked around a knot of Brillish merchants, darting up the last few steps to the top of the bowl. Adaptability was the second lesson Kasimir taught his *Fvene*. If a mission turns bad, do not fight it. Turn with it.

The Guildmaster's eyes were on the tower. That meant they were almost certainly not on the manor. It seemed less likely by the instant that all of them would escape this island alive, but if Ivan could get to Nash . . . He narrowed his eyes, darting into the alcove and through the door into the servants' corridor beyond. It was utterly deserted.

Heart racing in his chest, Ivan broke into a sprint, charging through the darkened halls until he reached the door leading to the manor path. Throwing all sense of caution aside, he charged into the door shoulder-first. His stomach surged into his throat as he crashed into a tall, broad body.

"*Whoof*," said a familiar voice. Nash.

Ivan scrambled gracefully to his feet.

"The Guildmaster knows Ryia is here," he said.

At the same time Nash said, "Tristan wasn't there."

Then they both said, "What?"

Ivan shut the door behind him, dusting himself off. "What do you mean Tristan was not there?"

"In the dungeon," Nash said. "No sign of him. No sign of anyone."

"Then where is he?" Ivan asked, stomach prickling again.

"No clue," Nash said hopelessly. "Now, what in the hells were you saying about the Guildmaster?"

"He knows Ryia. Knows she is here."

"What? How?"

"He recognized her axe."

Nash shook her head. "That reckless bitch is going to get us all killed. . . ."

"Not if I can help it," Ivan said slowly.

He and Nash were alive and out of the crowd. They could make for the ship now, leave this terrible mess behind . . . but before he even finished the thought, he knew he could not live with himself if he fled now. He was not one for sentiment, but he did not want to abandon a crew who trusted him—not here, in this terrible place. It was not what Kasimir would have done. He chewed the inside of one cheek, thinking. If Tristan was not in the dungeons, Ivan had no way of knowing where he could be. In all likelihood, he was already dead. They would mourn the boy later, but Ryia and Evelyn could still be saved. They would need an escape route.

The courtyard was surrounded by high stone walls. The Butcher could climb them, and, with any luck, Evelyn could follow. But then came the matter of the cliffs and miles of open ocean below.

Ivan locked Nash with a penetrating stare. "We need to get to the ship."

Nash gaped at him. "I'm not leaving them behind."

"Who said I was planning to leave them behind?"

"You did. Just now."

Ivan sighed, frustrated, and shot an anxious glance back toward the arena. Already a few parties had escaped the Disciples' barricade, heading for the docks. It would not be long before the mayhem spread across the entire island. He broke into a fast walk, making his way down the hill.

"Evelyn and the Butcher will never make it through this *schiss* to the harbor. We need to get them off the island another way."

"And what exactly do you plan to do, Ivan?" Nash protested, long legs somehow struggling to keep up. "Recruit some friendly seagulls?"

"No," Ivan said, "I suggest we use *The Hardship's* rowboat like sane people."

Nash chewed her lip. "How will they know where to find us? It's already getting dark. It's not like they're just going to know to leap into the ocean and trust we'll be there to catch them."

Ivan fell silent, stitching the threads of an idea together. "Do you still have those fireworks?"

Nash's face split into a cautious smile. "To the ship."

They melted into the growing crowd, pushing their way toward their stolen ship. Ivan only hoped they were not too late.

29

EVELYN

Ryia had left her. Jumped out the window, climbed down the side of the tower like a spider on its ruddy string, and left her. True, they had been trying to kill each other just a few minutes ago, but it still stung.

A beatdown from the Guildmaster himself would sting worse, though.

Shite. He was already past the first ring of shrubberies. Evelyn knew panicking wouldn't do her a speck of good, but her training hadn't exactly covered this. Fingers tapping an anxious rhythm on her kneecap, she knelt down, grabbing the axe Ryia had thrown.

Thrown and then frozen in thin air. She brushed a hand over her throat, remembering how the blade had hovered just a hairsbreadth away. She had no doubt the throw had been perfect . . . which meant the Butcher of Carrowwick had saved her life.

She shook her head, tucking the axe into her glittering belt. It didn't really count as saving her life when she was the one who had endangered it in the first place. She needed to get out of this cursed tower, and there was really only one option.

Evelyn jumped off the platform, grabbing on to the rope dangling from the bell. It let out another deafening gong, rattling her skull as she slid eighty feet to the floor below.

Blood dripped from her rope-burned hands as her feet hit the ground. She would have to have a chat with Ivan about incorporating leather gloves and greaves into each disguise. But first she needed to survive the next ten minutes.

She wiped her bleeding palms on her skirts and sprinted for the hidden back door, only to freeze at the sound of boots striking the stone courtyard just outside.

"Secure the tower," said the Guildmaster's unmistakable voice. "If she discovers the Quill's purpose, we are finished."

"Why would she take it if she did not know its purpose?" asked a second voice. A Disciple.

There was a grim pause, then: "She knows only a part of it. We will just have to hope she does not discover *everything* it does."

Evelyn edged backward as the voices drew closer and closer to the front door to the tower. She pressed herself against the wall, fingers fumbling with the latch behind her.

"But without the Quill—"

"You do not need to lecture me on its importance," the Guildmaster interrupted. "Sort out the tower. I will deal with the Grayson girl."

Grayson girl?

The opposite door finally creaked open, flooding the tower with the light of the setting sun.

Evelyn had always thought she would like to test her mettle against a Kinetic, but now she wholeheartedly disagreed with her past self. Heart hammering, she dove through the back door and sprinted across the courtyard, burying herself in the maze of shrubs beyond before they could catch sight of her.

She squeezed her eyes shut. She needed to think. Hiding here wouldn't save her for long. A lap dog would be able to find her here, never mind the strongest bloody Sensers in Thamorr. She needed to keep moving . . . but to where?

The most obvious choice would be to head for the harbor, but that wasn't really an option. Even a fool would know to block everyone from departing the island, and the Guildmaster was no fool. If no one could leave, his prize couldn't either.

Her heart skipped as she saw the sails on the horizon. It was too late for that. People were already leaving. If she could lose herself in the crowd, scrub off this blasted face paint . . .

She froze as a familiar, raspy voice caught her ear.

"You're too late, you massive sack of horse shit. It's already gone."

Evelyn looked through the foliage to see Ryia flat on her back in the courtyard, surrounded on all sides by the high stone walls hemming them in. The Guildmaster towered over her, silhouetted against the darkening sky. His fingers held no ropes, but Ryia struggled like a rabbit in a snare, her limbs pressed firmly against her sides, held in place by magic. Blood poured thickly from her nose, and both eyes were ringed in deepening purple.

"Gone?" he asked, his voice the whisper of a funeral shroud on stone. "Gone where?"

"Hell if I know." Ryia's grunt of laughter was gutted by a gasp of pain. Evelyn's eyes widened as the skin on Ryia's shaven head peeled away, seemingly of its own accord. The fresh wound watered the grass with heavy drops of blood.

"Whoever you are working with, Miss Grayson, do they know what you are?" He smiled coldly, showing off tiny, brown-rimmed teeth. "Think of all the proper Adept that had to die to create this poor imitation," he said. He tightened his right hand into a fist, and Ryia's breaths reduced to whining gasps. "What would they do to you if they did? If your little secret got out, do you really think I would be the only one hunting you?" He tightened his fist even more. On the ground, Ryia's face began to purple. "This is mercy, Miss Grayson. A quick death at my hand is far kinder than what someone more curious might do."

Fear and amazement and a dozen other emotions swirled through Evelyn's mind as she watched from the cover of the immaculately trimmed shrub. Ryia, the infamous Butcher of Carrowwick, the woman who had tossed two Disciples aside like rag dolls back in Dresdell, was completely powerless here.

The Guildmaster raised his other hand, and Ryia rose, stiff, from the ground. The Butcher's neck muscles spasmed frantically, eyes wild. She was about to die, and she knew it.

"Goodbye, Miss Grayson," the Guildmaster said. He drew one hand back, as though preparing to stab forward with an invisible sword.

"Stop!" Without thinking, Evelyn sprang out into the courtyard. Ryia's bulging eyes clouded with confusion as they met hers. Shit. Now they were just *both* going to die. Well, she wasn't going to go down without a fight, at least. She pulled Ryia's axe from her belt and flung it toward the Guildmaster.

The axe flipped end over end, heading straight for her target. But in the end, it betrayed her. The weapon skidded to a halt inches from the Guildmaster's pallid flesh, then sped away, straight toward Ryia's throat.

Evelyn tried to lunge forward—to do what, she wasn't sure— but her legs were suddenly frozen in place, anchored to the ground by the Guildmaster's power. Unexpected emotion clawed up her throat as she prepared to watch the Butcher die.

Ryia gritted her teeth. The muscles in her arms flexed and convulsed until she finally tore one free of the Guildmaster's invisible grasp with a feral growl. She threw her newly free hand in front of her, glaring at the axe. The weapon wobbled on its trajectory, then fell to the dirt beside her.

The Guildmaster smiled. "Who might this be?" He beckoned forward with one finger, and Evelyn began to slide across the ground against her will, dragged toward him on an invisible string.

Evelyn watched as he shifted his weight. There was a glint of silver at the waist of the Guildmaster's robes, tucked beneath the fluid silk. He held his left hand back out toward Ryia, squeezing his fist tight. Ryia gasped again, but Evelyn caught another glimpse of the thing tucked in the Guildmaster's belt. It was another one of Ryia's axes. The one she had given Ivan this morning. The Guildmaster must have picked it up in the arena.

"Ryia!" Evelyn shouted.

"Ryia?" the Guildmaster asked. "Is that your name, or Miss Grayson's newest title?"

Evelyn thrashed against the Guildmaster's invisible bonds, but nothing happened. She met Ryia's eye, then stared meaningfully at the Guildmaster's waist. The Butcher had a strong connection to those axes of hers . . . but what ruddy good did that do anyone when both of them were frozen? They were nothing more than a pair of puppets on the Guildmaster's magical strings. He could probably kill them both with a snap of his fingers if he wanted to.

"No matter. Soon it will—" The Guildmaster broke off mid-sentence, confused as a low crack rumbled through the air. His eyes flicked toward the deep purple sky as multicolored sparks rained down toward the sea to the east.

It only broke his focus for an instant, but an instant was all Ryia needed. The tendons in her neck looked tight enough to snap as she wrenched her arms forward, crooking her hands into rigid talons. Still suspended a few inches above the ground, she yanked back with one hand. The axe flew from the Guildmaster's belt, flinging itself up toward his thick neck.

Evelyn swore she saw fear in the Guildmaster's eyes as he looked down from the sky. He pushed back with his own power, redirecting the axe, but he was too late. The blade slashed him across the face, releasing a gout of deep red blood. He staggered backward, and Ryia ground her teeth, reeling the axe into her waiting palm.

In shock, the Guildmaster raised a hand to his face. Then he deflated, collapsing to the grass. Evelyn sagged forward, and Ryia fell to the ground as the invisible ties holding them in place evaporated.

Evelyn doubted the wound had been fatal, but that axe blade had been absolutely drenched in dormire's blood. The sleeping drug was highly effective, even against poison-immune Kinetics.

Evelyn shook out her newly freed arms, running the last few steps to where Ryia lay, collapsed on the ground.

"Are you okay?"

The Butcher's chest heaved as Evelyn rolled her over. Ryia was in bad shape. Her eyes were puffy and swollen. Blood dripped from both nostrils and down the side of her shaven head. She looked so fragile, lying there. So vulnerable. The illusion didn't last long. Evelyn ducked back as Ryia bolted upright, aiming an exhausted punch at her shoulder.

"Attacking the Guildmaster? Are you insane? What the fuck did you do that for?"

Evelyn opened her mouth, then shut it again. She didn't have an answer. It would have been easier to run—smarter to run. But in that moment she had known she couldn't leave the Butcher behind. Even now she felt it, the pull toward the mercenary. A mix of fascination, sympathy, and something stronger.

Ryia pushed herself to her feet, walking to stand over the Guildmaster's prone, unconscious form. She hefted her axe. "Do you know how long I have been waiting for this?" she asked no one in particular, holding the bit to his throat.

The bushes to Evelyn's right rustled. Before she even had the chance to look, her hands were snared again, this time by thick, robed arms. *Shit*. The Guildmaster might be out cold, but this courtyard was still crawling with Disciples. Hundreds of the strongest Kinetics and Sensers in Thamorr. Evelyn grunted, her skirts tearing as she wrenched herself around to meet her captor's steady gaze.

"To me!" he called, summoning his fellow Kinetics. "I've got one of them!" He pulled his scimitar free of its scabbard, preparing to whip it across Evelyn's throat.

"Duck left!" Ryia rasped.

Evelyn didn't question the order, diving immediately to the left. Something small and silver whistled over her shoulder as she crashed to the ground.

An instant later, the Disciple fell to the grass beside her, blood pooling around the axe bit embedded in his neck.

"Run, you idiot!" Ryia shouted, darting past her. She grabbed the second axe from where Evelyn had thrown it and took off running again, heading straight for the courtyard wall. "They'll be all over us in seconds."

"But the Guildmaster—" Evelyn said.

"No time. Let's go."

Evelyn pulled the axe from the Disciple at her feet, tucking it into her skirt. Her dyed hair flew free of its braid, frizzing into chaotic ringlets as she sprinted to catch up with the Butcher.

"Go where?" she asked.

"Still working on that."

"Brilliant," Evelyn griped.

"I've been waiting to kill that son of a bitch for a long time. Don't make me regret saving your ass instead."

Evelyn opened her mouth to retort, but nothing came out.

"Shit," Ryia muttered, dragging them behind a half wall as another set of Kinetics marched past. "They're everywhere. We need a—" Her eyes glimmered as another flash split the dusk, another crackling boom ringing out over the island. Evelyn's stomach flipped as a grin spread across Ryia's face. "That brilliant Borean son of a bitch."

"What?" Evelyn asked, struggling to keep up with her unnatural pace.

"We're getting off this island."

"How?" The docks were no doubt locked down by now, crawling with nearly as many Disciples as the courtyard, and the only other way off the island was a steep drop off the towering cliff on the far side of the courtyard walls surrounding them. If the fall didn't kill them, the drowning certainly would.

"This way," Ryia said, pelting toward the eastern wall of the courtyard. "Can you climb these?" she asked, pointing at the skinny vines snaking up the wall.

Great. So the Butcher had chosen the cliff, then.

"Are you mental?"

"Generally speaking."

"The only thing on the far side of that wall is a hundred-foot drop-off into the—" Ryia streaked past her, scuttling up the wall. "—ocean," she finished lamely.

Letting out an exasperated breath, she grabbed hold of the vines, pulling herself up as quickly as her rope-burned hands would allow.

She panted as she reached the top of the wall, looking out at the place where the seemingly endless ocean met the darkened sky. The Butcher just stood there, staring down at the Luminous Sea. Then she said, "Do you trust me, Captain?"

"Do I *trust* you?" Evelyn asked. Her cheeks heated, and she averted her eyes. "Absolutely not."

Ryia nodded, rivulets of blood still coursing down the side of her head. "Probably for the best."

The Butcher latched on to Evelyn's wrists without warning. Then she leapt off the edge of the cliff, dragging them both down into the crashing waves below.

30

RYIA

The fall lasted only a few seconds. Short, sure, but long enough to be painfully aware that they might be her *last* few seconds. Especially if that firework hadn't meant what she thought it meant.

Her breath was squeezed from her lungs as she slammed into the unforgiving surface of the sea. She treaded water, fighting to keep her head up.

"You all right there, Captain?" she called out. No response. "Evelyn?" Still nothing.

Shit. The salt water burned and stung her wounds as she thrashed and spun. *There.* A pale shape lay faceup in the water some fifteen feet away, surrounded by rent silk and seeping black hair dye like blood.

"Honestly, you'd think she'd never jumped off a cliff before," Ryia grumbled, kicking toward her.

She looped one arm around Evelyn's middle. Ivan's powder had washed off, leaving her face as scarred and freckled as it had been the first time she had seen her in the Bobbin Fort courtyard.

"Captain . . ." Ryia shook her, but she just lay there, limp as a worm. Maybe that dark cloud spreading out from her wasn't all dye.

She tucked her left arm underneath Evelyn's armpits, swimming with her right and struggling to keep both their heads above water. "If I lost my chance to slit that fucker's throat just so you could die five minutes later, I'm going to be so pissed."

Ryia panted, tossing her head to keep the blood from dripping into her swollen eyes as she searched the darkening waters. "Any second now, Ivan." If the waves didn't get them, the sharks would. They probably looked like a feast at the moment.

But then she heard it: the hollow slap of waves against wood.

She wheeled around to see a tiny rowboat. And sitting on the bench, his blond hair plastered to his perfect fucking face, was Ivan Rezkoye.

"Either I am brilliant, or you are a *verdammte* fool," Ivan said, grabbing on to Evelyn's shoulders and hauling her into the boat.

"How do you figure?" Ryia asked, pushing Evelyn's legs over the side one by one.

"Either you caught my signal, or you were fool enough to jump off a cliff without knowing anyone would catch you at the bottom." Ivan gestured toward Evelyn. "What is wrong with her?"

"Not sure." Ryia pulled herself aboard, kneeling by Evelyn's still form and pressing an ear to her chest. There was still a heartbeat there, and her chest rose and fell with ragged breaths. "She's still alive, though. Did Nash make it?"

Ivan pointed south. There were already a number of ships dotting the horizon, but one mast stood several yards shorter than the rest. *The Hardship.* A grin started to creep up Ryia's cheeks, but she stopped it in its tracks. What the hell did she have to be happy about?

If your little secret got out, do you really think I would be the only one hunting you?

The Guildmaster's taunt echoed in her skull. She hated him. Even more than that, she hated that he was right. If the kingdoms of Thamorr discovered Adept could be made? That anyone could be given those powers if they were willing to pay the price?

If that secret got out, a quick death would be merciful compared to the inevitable studies and experiments. The *curious men* who would cut her open just to see how she worked. Steal her blood, like the blood of all the Adept her father had killed in order to create her.

She snuck a peek down at Evelyn, still unconscious at her feet. Now there was one more person who knew that damning secret—and Ryia hadn't silenced her. In fact, she had saved Evelyn's life instead.

Why the hell had she done that?

"Have you seen Tristan?" Ivan asked, looking up at the cliff top as the last threads of sunlight were swallowed by the night. "Nash said he was not in the dungeon."

"You'd have to ask Wyatt Asher—little bastard answers to him now."

Ivan's lips tightened. "And the Quill?"

"Gone."

The word stung like venom. She'd been so close, had her freedom at her fingertips, and somehow she'd let it slip right through.

Ryia grabbed a second oar, dipping it into the water. "More on that later; for now let's get the hell out of here, shall we?"

She didn't spare a single glance for the island as they wove their way south through the waves.

IT DIDN'T take them long to reach the cog, anchored in the shallows off the coast of a small Brillish island. Ivan caught the tow line as Nash threw it toward them.

"What's wrong with the captain?" she asked, eyeing Evelyn's limp form on the bottom of the boat.

"Knocked out," Ryia said. "She'll bounce back." She hoped that was true. *Why* did she hope that was true? A living, conscious Evelyn could spill her darkest secret. . . . What was wrong with her?

Nash nodded, then peered back at the boat again. "No sign of Tristan?"

"Oh, we had more than a sign of him." Ryia pointed back toward the Guildmaster's island with her chin. "You can thank him and Tana Rafferty for that bullshit."

"He's with Asher now?" Nash grimaced, helping Ivan onto the deck. "I was afraid of that."

"You saw this coming . . . how, exactly?" Ryia said, rolling her eyes.

"Never really trusted the son of a bitch."

"And you are normally very trusting of con men?" Ivan asked, grabbing Evelyn's still-unconscious form as Ryia hefted her up.

"That's just it, though," Nash said, laying Evelyn out on the deck and reaching back to help Ryia aboard. "He never really felt like a real con man, did he? Something was always a little off."

The *Saint of Soaps*, they'd called him. He had washed up in Carrowwick surrounded by filthy freebooters, but he had looked like he had just stepped out of a Gildesh bathhouse.

A frail cough interrupted Ryia's line of thought. Her stomach flipped as she turned to see Evelyn stirring, a callused hand reaching up to cradle her sopping head.

"Good to see I didn't drag a corpse all this way," Ryia said.

"I'm not dead yet." Evelyn touched her forehead, examining the blood on her fingers. "Not for your lack of trying, obviously." She blinked blankly for a few seconds, then suddenly pushed herself up to her elbows. Panic rose in Ryia's chest, but all Evelyn said was, "Tristan! He—"

"Is a traitor, yes, we know this already," Ivan interrupted. Evelyn tried to start talking again, but Ivan held up a hand. "What we do not know is how a *vretch* like Tana Rafferty managed to get the best of both of you." He looked between them, arms folded. "Well?"

Ryia avoided Evelyn's eye in the silence that followed. Why hadn't she just let her die? She'd had so many chances.

"You said it yourself. Tristan was a bloody traitor," Evelyn finally said.

"Rafferty got the jump on you?" Nash asked. "Both of you?"

Ryia narrowed her eyes at Evelyn. Why was she covering for her?

"Rub it in all you want, Nash. Rafferty's a quick little gutter rat. Nimble," Ryia said, forcing a wink at Ivan and belting on her axes. "Almost makes you wonder what she's like at certain other activities. . . ."

Ivan looked exasperated, and Nash thrust a hand out.

"You're not getting off that easy here."

"What's your problem?"

"What's my problem?" Nash asked. "My problem is that Ivan and I almost got killed. Everyone on this job almost got killed, and I think you knew that was going to happen."

Ryia let out a bark of laughter, stomach sinking at the accusation. "You think I'm with Wyatt Asher? I thought you knew me better than that."

Nash reached out, grabbing Ryia's chin as she moved to turn away. "Wyatt Asher? No, I think you're in much deeper shit than that. Would you care to explain yourself?"

Ryia cast a pointed glare at Nash's hand, still pinning her chin in place. "Would you care to calm the hell down?" This was a far cry from the *we're all a team—we have to save Tristan* bullshit from last night. How quickly things turned.

"Explanation. Now."

Ryia ducked out of the smuggler's grasp, pulling one of the large hatchets from her back and leveling it at Nash's throat. "I usually only explain myself one way. I don't think you'd enjoy it."

"Quit fucking around," Nash said without flinching. "Why does the Guildmaster know who you are?"

Ryia's weapon dropped to her side. She felt like she'd been clubbed across the temples. How would Nash know about her history with the Guildmaster? "What?"

Ivan pursed his lips. "He recognized your axe." He shared a look with Nash that told Ryia the pair had already discussed this. Stupidly, that felt like a betrayal. "You know what this Quill does. You know why it is worth a *verdammte* fortune."

It wasn't a question.

Fear climbed up Ryia's cheeks as she felt Evelyn's gaze on the back of her head. *Shit.* She hadn't been backed into a corner like this since the assassin's guild in Doreur. That time her escape route had been simple: racing on a stolen mare over the border to Briel. This time things were a bit more complicated.

Ryia sighed. "I know what it does."

"And how long have you known?" Nash asked.

"Since before we even shoved off from the damned southern dock, all right?"

Nash's face went purple. "And you decided not to say anything. Did you even tell Cal?"

"Oh please, what does that even matter anymore? Callum Clem is probably still rotting in the Bobbin Fort cells."

"You don't know th—"

"What does it do?" Ivan interrupted.

Ryia closed her eyes, taking a breath.

"What does it do?" Ivan repeated, firmer this time, taking a step toward her on the deck.

"It knows the location of every Adept in Thamorr," she said, squinting one eye open like she was expecting to be smacked across the face.

"It *knows*?" Nash asked, looking even more agitated, stepping back to allow a few members of her crew to pass by to tug the rowboat out of the water. They released the sails, and *The Hardship* nosed out into open waters. "What do you mean it *knows*? How does it know?"

"Do I look like Declan fucking Day to you? I didn't build the damned thing."

Nash stopped for a moment. Then: "So you're saying whoever has that Quill . . ."

Ryia nodded wearily. "Whoever has it could track down every Adept in all five kingdoms." *Including her.* She left that bit out. Nash and Ivan had already started to turn against her.

There was another pause. Then Ivan said, "You still have not answered our question. How in *Yavol's* realm does the Guildmaster know who you are?"

Damn it all twice to the hells. Trust Ivan Rezkoye to keep a conversation on track. How could she answer that question without spilling the secret she had kept for almost a decade? She looked at Evelyn's pale face, almost glowing in the light of the moon. How long would Captain Honor keep this quiet?

"I used to trade them," Ryia lied. "Adepts, I mean. Used to traffic them through Gildemar." She shrugged. "The man wants me dead, what can I say? He's not the only one, but he's probably the most powerful."

"Probably," Ivan echoed dimly.

"If you knew he wanted you dead, why the hell would you bring all of us waltzing right into his twice-damned arms?" Nash roared.

"Nash, Nash, Nash," she crooned, sinking back into her usual swagger. "You know the answer to that question. How do I usually deal with people who want me dead? But I didn't succeed this time. Captain Helpless saw to that."

Provoking Evelyn was probably not the best idea right now, but old habits died hard.

"All right, but how—"

"Look," Ryia interrupted, brushing crusted blood from her upper lip. "We can sit here and bicker back and forth about who lied about what—"

"You, about everything," Nash said.

"Or," Ryia continued, talking over her, "we can figure out how to get our prize back."

"Excuse me?" said Ivan. "Do you have Tana Rafferty tucked inside your *trüsen?*" He gestured toward Ryia's soaking-wet pants.

"No, but I think we all know where she's heading."

"You don't seriously think they'll go back to Carrowwick?" Evelyn asked.

"Wyatt Asher has the biggest ego I have ever seen," Ryia said, looking out over the waves. "There's no way he'll miss the opportunity to bring Tolliver Shadowwood groveling to the Lottery."

Evelyn looked unconvinced.

"No, she is right," said Ivan.

"Of course I am," said Ryia, turning away. "We still have one more chance at this thing. Let's not let precious Callum down this time, all right?" She clapped a still-seething Nash on the shoulder, stalking to the bow.

She didn't look back, but she could feel Evelyn's shrewd eyes on the back of her head. Her skin prickled, and with every hollow thud of her bare feet on the deck the same two questions needled her brain.

Why had the captain kept her secret? And what would she expect in return?

31

NASH

The sound of groaning timbers filled the hold while the swift southern winds rattled the sails on the deck above. Nash knew she should be sleeping, but her legs wouldn't lie still and her mind wouldn't shut up. At any moment they might see blue sails crowding the horizon, Disciples gliding across the water to stick the lot of them like squealing pigs.

She cleared her throat, hammock swaying as she adjusted herself for the thousandth time. Sure, they had pissed off the most dangerous man in Thamorr, but he wasn't the one keeping her awake. Her eyes popped open, blind in the darkness. First, half her crew had decided to slip themselves into the Harpies' back pockets; then the Beckett boy sold them to Wyatt Asher. Who would drive a knife into her back next?

The easy bet would be the Butcher. Then again, Nash generally was a smart gambler, and she hadn't bet right yet. It could be any one of them. What about the ex–Needle Guard and her mysterious pact with Cal Clem? Or Ivan . . .

She shook her head, pulling herself to her feet and lighting the candle beside her hammock. She was just being paranoid. She stopped at the stack of crates forming a makeshift desk just beneath the stern. It was littered with charts and the maps of the Guildmaster's island. She hunched over them, looking at them without really reading them. Just being paranoid. After all, they were now all fucked to the same degree, weren't they? Fugitives of the seventh Guildmaster of Thamorr, heading back to Carrowwick empty-handed, outsmarted by a sixteen-year-old boy so green he could be mistaken for pipeweed.

Best-case scenario, they would be laughed out of every tavern south of the Bobbin Fort. Worst case, Cal had managed to escape captivity while they were away. If he was back on the streets, she doubted he'd take kindly to the fact that they had abandoned him . . . not if they came back without the Quill.

Nash shuffled the charts around, grabbing one and holding it up to catch the light of her flickering candle. She'd sailed this exact coastline a thousand times at least, but she needed something to do with her hands. Maybe if she forced her eyes to study these well-known patterns, they would finally grow tired enough to stay closed.

"Planning to whisk us all away somewhere?"

Nash jumped, smacking her left kneecap on the crates. "Don't try to tell me you're not a little tempted."

"Perhaps a little." Ivan cleared his throat, turning so his sharp features were drowned in shadows. "But no, I do not think there is anywhere to run. Not from this. You heard what the Butcher said." He lowered his voice, leaning closer. "What it does."

Nash snorted, shooting a mistrustful glance toward the deck above. Ryia would be perched there somewhere, hanging from the rigging like a damned bat, no doubt. "If she's even telling the truth."

"I think she is. What cause does she have to lie?"

"The same reason she lied to us in the first place."

"Did it really matter that she lied, though?"

"Did it— What?" Nash asked. "Of course it mattered. How else do you explain that?" She gestured vaguely south.

Ivan scratched his chin. "Would it have changed anything? If she had told us what the Quill was for . . . would you have cared?"

Nash stared blankly at a chart outlining Gildemar's trade routes for a long moment, then sighed. She hadn't really cared what Shadowwood meant to do with the Quill. She had barely even wondered. She had just seen the promise of a massive payout and run in headfirst without thinking—caught up in the excitement and the adventure.

"No. And I don't care now." The second part was a lie. She leaned back on her palms. "As long as I get paid, I don't care what the damned thing does or where it ends up."

Ivan's lips tightened. "You would still sell it to Edale?"

"For four hundred thousand crescents? Absolutely. Unless you know someone who would pay more."

"And when Tolliver Shadowwood uses the Quill's power to build an army and carve a giant *slicht* through the heart of Thamorr, will your gold protect you?"

"The things I can buy with my gold will."

Ivan shook his head, his perfect face wrinkling sourly. "Do you not understand? Declan Day stopped the Seven Decades' War with this device. It has kept the Guilds in power for nearly three *zenturren*. Three hundred years, Nash." He pressed a hand to his forehead. "Whoever has the Quill will be the greatest power in Thamorr."

"So, what, you want to gift it to some peace-loving lord?" Nash chuckled mirthlessly. "Didn't know you were the noble type."

The smell of chamomile teased her nostrils as Ivan leaned forward, eyes like the southern seas pulling her in. "I would not call myself noble. But I believe we must be careful about who we let lay hands on this Quill of Declan Day." He paused. "This will have larger consequences than gold, Nash."

"Like what?"

"Think of this—Tolliver Shadowwood will have no use for us once he has the Quill."

"And?" Nash asked, unconcerned.

"If you were truly that foolish, you would not have survived with Clem so long," Ivan chided.

Nash knew he was right. If Shadowwood was ambitious enough to steal from the twice-damned Guildmaster, he wouldn't stop there. He would be ruthless enough to dispose of anyone who outlived their usefulness.

"So what do you want to do if we manage to get our hands on it, then?"

"Make sure it finds its way into the hands of someone who *will* have a use for us, of course." Ivan's eyes crackled like fireworks in the darkness as he extended a hand toward her. "What do you say?"

Nash's eyes darted toward the hatch. She didn't trust her crew, or the Butcher, or the ex-captain. Hell, she hardly trusted herself anymore for that matter, but, for some reason, she trusted Ivan. He might just be the only one left in this world who she trusted. She grabbed his hand, giving it a firm shake.

"I say lead on, Mr. Rezkoye."

32

RYIA

Ryia looped one arm over the top of the mast, body silhouetted against the sails. She ran her tongue over her teeth,
watching the world bend away, curving down past the horizon. As
ridiculous as it sounded, she had been lucky so far. Lucky she had
lasted this long with the Saints without being discovered. Lucky
Evelyn had not decided to share her deadly secret with Nash and
Ivan. Lucky to still be breathing at all, honestly.

But Felice was a wily bitch. No luck ever held for long.

Ryia weighed her options. She could stick it out with the Saints,
cling to the hope of getting one more shot at the Quill, or she
could bolt for the North Road the second her feet hit dry land.
But if she ran, she would lose track of the Quill. Once Shadowwood had the thing, who knew how long it would take to resurface
somewhere she could find it?

But there were too many variables now. Too many cheats at the
table, not enough marks.

She jumped, sliding silently down the rigging toward the deck.
She had to run. That was it. She had stayed with this crew too long

as it was. The clench in her gut at the thought of leaving them only strengthened her resolve. Friendships and trust were things normal people could count on, but Ryia wasn't normal.

Running the second they made port would solve all her problems . . . except one. She dropped onto the deck, glancing toward the bow, where Evelyn Linley stood, rigid as a statue in the near blackness.

"If you're trying to sneak up on me, you're losing your touch, Butcher."

Ryia leaned against the rail beside her. "Oh sure, *now* you have ears like a damned bat."

"What's that supposed to mean?"

"In the tower. I can only assume you went deaf, since you failed to hear Rafferty barreling in like a bear on *vitalité*."

"Sorry, I was a little distracted by the fact that you were trying to kill me."

"Was not," Ryia protested. "I could have killed you at *least* four times. I showed some serious restraint."

"I think you need a new definition of the word 'restraint.'"

They stood in silence for a long while, the salt breeze tangling Evelyn's hair into a messy red cloud.

"Why?" Ryia finally asked.

"Why what?"

She pursed her lips as if to say, *What the hell else could I possibly be asking about?*

"What do I possibly have to gain from spilling a secret like that?" Evelyn asked.

"What do you have to gain from *keeping* a secret like that?" Ryia countered.

Evelyn paused, then: "I don't know. But that's kind of the point, isn't it?" She cleared her throat. "You've got some serious bloody firepower, Butcher. Could be useful."

"Looking to put me on a leash?" Ryia asked flatly.

"Sure would beat being leashed by Callum Clem, wouldn't it?"

"Clem only *thought* he had me leashed. There's a difference."

Another long silence. Then she said, "Why do you work with gits like that anyways? With your skills—"

"I'm guessing you'd rather I pledge myself to some honorable, royal shit?" Ryia shook her head bitterly. "I'll let you in on a secret. Honor's a myth. Loyalty, love: all bullshit. Callum Clem might be a rotten son of a bitch, but so is Tolliver Shadowwood. And Duncan Baelbrandt. And your father, from the sounds of it." She shrugged. "Good people never end up in power, Captain. They don't have the stomach for it."

She expected Evelyn to refuse, to list the many honors of one Duncan Baelbrandt. But instead she said, "I'm starting to think you might be right about that."

"You've known for a while, whether you'll admit it or not," Ryia corrected. "About three weeks, by my count."

"How do you figure?"

"I'm not the only one leaning on this rail who signed on to work for Callum Clem," she reminded her.

Evelyn looked over the water like she was searching for something in the distance. Finally she sighed. "Aren't you curious about what Clem promised me?"

"Not really." That had been irrelevant since the second Clem was arrested.

"You might be." Evelyn locked Ryia with a severe stare. "Since he promised me you."

Ryia blinked. "Excuse me?"

Evelyn's hand twitched nervously toward the sword at her hip, but she didn't elaborate.

"Promised you what? My head? My hand in marriage? You're going to have to be a little more specific."

"Not your head, exactly. Your . . . capture." Evelyn winced on the word.

It made sense. Clem had never been her biggest fan. By promising her to Evelyn, he could get his maps and be rid of Ryia in one calculated move. The bastard was brilliant. A little too brilliant. "Why the hell are you telling me this?"

"I couldn't really expect you to trust me if I didn't, could I?"

"Trust you?" Ryia almost choked on the words. "Rule number one of being hunted by the most dangerous man in Thamorr: I don't trust anyone."

"I guess I'll have to remember that one now."

"Why's that?"

Evelyn looked at her like she had lost her mind. "The bloody Guildmaster saw my face. I *attacked* him. You really think he's going to forget that?"

"The Guildmaster might have seen your face, Captain, but by the time this ship docks in Carrowwick there will be a new 'most dangerous man in Thamorr,' and he's only going to be looking for one person. Here's a hint—it's not you."

Evelyn glanced around nervously as a few of Nash's crew burst into raucous laughter over a game of dice across the deck. "And if no one ended up being the most powerful man in Thamorr? If the Quill were destroyed?"

"Well, that was plan A, but it's pretty clear we're past that now."

"Are we?"

Ryia raised an eyebrow. "You're not the brightest one, are you?"

"I'm serious."

"All the bloody time, I know," Ryia said, mimicking her accent.

"I mean it, Ryia. So what if you didn't smash it to smithereens in that tower? So what if Tristan lied and gave it to that gutter rat? You said it yourself back there—the Quill is still in play for the rest of them," Evelyn said, waving a hand to indicate Ivan and Nash, belowdecks. "That means it's still in play for you, if you have the stones for it. I didn't take you for a coward."

"And I didn't know the opposite of 'coward' was 'idiot.'" Ryia moved to adjust the sheet as the sails started flapping in the changing wind.

Evelyn yanked the line from her hands. "How is stealing from Wyatt Asher any more idiotic than stealing from the ruddy Guildmaster?"

"Because I had you assholes to use last time around. Asher's going to have that thing under lock and key tighter than that damn bird of his. I'm good, but I'm not a miracle maker."

"What if you still had one of these assholes?"

Ryia turned sharply. "What game are you running?" First keeping her secrets, then giving away Clem's plans, now offering to help. No one would do that for her. Not without expecting something in return.

"Game?"

"Scheme. Plot. Use whatever word you like. How the hell does helping me get you what you want?"

"What makes you think you know what I want?"

"You're not as difficult to read as you seem to think you are, Linley."

"Am I not?" Evelyn reached up, resting her hand on the line now stretched tight above their heads.

Out of habit, Ryia's eyes flicked to the captain's middle finger. The Linley family ring was gone. She frowned, squinting at Evelyn's freckle-dusted face.

"Look, you can either run for the desert the second we hit Carrowwick, or we can try one last time to destroy that damned thing."

"And why in the hells would you want to do that?"

"Now that I know what that Quill can do, I can't exactly let Clem sell it to the craziest son of a bitch in the world, can I?"

Of course the captain would have an honorable reason for helping her.

"So you want to team up with the most wanted criminal in Thamorr? A risky plan." Ryia gave a hollow laugh, walking her fingers absently over the axes lining her belt. "What if it fails?"

"Then we run," Evelyn said. "If you really are the most wanted criminal in Thamorr, I figure you should be pretty good at that."

"We?" The word fell oddly on her ears. Would the captain really want to come with her? "You sure you're ready for life on the run? Not as glamorous as those stupid Edalish poems make it seem."

Evelyn studied her own bare middle finger. "No, you're right. I've got so much waiting for me back in Carrowwick."

Ryia stared at her blankly. Sarcasm was a new color on the captain. She had to admit, she didn't hate it. Surprising even herself, she held out a hand. A shiver spanned her shoulder blades as Evelyn grabbed it, giving a firm shake. "Welcome to the team."

33

TRISTAN

The two weeks Tristan spent in the smugglers' compartment of Lord Niall Wilson's ship were the most unpleasant of his life. The stuffy heat and constant odor of feces wasn't even the worst of it. No, the worst was the guilt pummeling his brain like a battering ram every second of the night and day. He hadn't had a choice; he knew that. Wyatt Asher and the Kestrel Crowns had backed him up against the wall.

The instant he was alone, Rafferty had dragged him halfway across the island and reminded him of what the Crowns knew. Reminded him that he needed to cooperate, and if he didn't . . . well, then she would alert the Shadow Wardens that the boy they had been chasing for months was sitting right under their noses. Tristan would have been shipped back to Edale that very night, so he had agreed to the Crowns' terms. Agreed to sell out the Saints. To sell out Ryia.

He kneaded his temples, balancing the stolen relic of Declan Day on one kneecap as a fresh wave of anguish washed over him. If she had just looked angry when he had looked back at that tower he might have been able to stomach it. But instead her expression had been . . . hollow. She would never forgive him.

Thwack.

The dull thud of metal biting into wood shook him from his torpor. He turned, irritated, toward his companion.

Tana Rafferty.

She sat crouched in the shadows, round face wide in an oddly childlike smile, dark hair piled on top of her head. She pulled a small, silver object from her belt. Circular, lined with blades. A Gildesh throwing star. It snapped through the fetid darkness, embedding itself in the rotting wood. She threw another. Then another. And another.

Tristan finally snapped as she reached for her belt yet again. "Can you cut that out?"

"Look who's found his voice again." She threw a sixth star.

"At least one of us is keeping quiet," Tristan griped.

The deckhands on this ship might be friendly with Wyatt Asher, but Tristan doubted Lord Niall Wilson had any idea that two highly sought-after criminals were stowed away beneath his feet. Rafferty would surely give them away if she kept chucking those cursed throwing stars around. . . .

Of course, it wasn't just the threat of discovery that was annoying him. If he was being honest with himself, Rafferty's bored habit of engaging in target practice reminded him a little too much of Ryia. Another wave of guilt crashed down.

You didn't have a choice, he intoned silently. *Even Ryia would understand that, right?*

Tana Rafferty laughed, the sound of fingernails scraping down a chalkboard. "Settle down, *Mr. Beckett.* We're almost there. If the bastard tried to throw us overboard, we could probably swim for it at this point."

Tristan flipped the Quill around in his fingers. It was heavy.

Much heavier than it ought to be. "If I have to swim with this thing in my pocket, I think I'll drown," he said, fiddling with the engraved edges.

"How terrible that would be," Rafferty said drily.

"Ha-ha," Tristan said. "Don't forget you owe me a cut. You would never have gotten within a bowshot of this without me." He shook the Quill. It sloshed way too loudly for such a little thing, the ink moving in a strangely sluggish way as it flowed around inside the chamber.

Asher had promised him a thousand crescents for his cooperation. Though "cooperation" was a strong word, seeing as the alternative had been for Asher to collect the bounty on his head. He picked at the edge of the Quill, frowning as a piece of carved wood pulled free, revealing a small panel dotted with smudges. Fingerprints? He counted them. One, two, three . . . seven. Seven distinct prints, most old and faded, one still prominent and clear, all reddish brown in color. Blood? Odd.

He snapped the panel on the Quill shut again as Rafferty cackled. "Don't you worry, you'll get your cut," she said, bowing sarcastically. "We'll meet up with Wyatt in the harbor, then you can run off to Boreas or wherever in the hells you're trying to go."

He had no idea where he planned to go, in truth. Anywhere several hundred miles away from Duskhaven would work just fine. He turned back to Rafferty.

"Fine by me."

Rafferty grinned, cracking her knuckles absently. "I'm so glad you agree." She threw another star across the compartment with a wink. "Otherwise this whole operation would fall apart."

"Any plans on how to get us past the docks without getting picked off by the Saints, by the way?" Tristan griped. "Maybe you should work on that instead of your snarky comments."

"The Saints? Last I heard Callum Clem was chained to the

walls of the Bobbin Fort dungeons. The Saints are deader than the rest of the crew you brought with you to that island." She drew a finger across her throat.

"They're not my crew," Tristan said, stomach flipping. Was she right? Were they all dead? "And the Saints can burn for all I care."

She shrugged, indifferent. "Either way, if they got off that island, I'm Declan Day."

Tristan rested his head against the inside of the hull, peering through the inch-wide knothole that had been slowly flooding their compartment with frigid sea water since they'd set sail. The sun glinted off the surface of the Yawning Sea, and above he could feel the quickening pulse of footsteps, hear the call of gulls circling. He smelled the familiar reek of stale beer, urine, and salt water. And there it was. Carrowwick Harbor.

It looked just as it had the day he left: the steep roofs of the houses, the rows of ships lining the docks, the busied people bustling through the streets and alleys. A pang built inside him as he realized he'd soon be leaving, never to return. Strange that the city that had taken him hostage had somehow come to feel so much like home.

But no. If the Lottery had somehow felt like home, it was only because of the people he had doomed back on the Guildmaster's island.

It was the only way, he reminded himself again. If the others had made it back alive . . . well, the Saints had no shortage of punishments for traitors. No punishment for Tristan would end with him walking free of Carrowwick. In fact, none of them would end in him walking again at all.

Or breathing.

Tristan nervously ran his fingers over the swirling markings carved into the Quill as the ship slipped into its cozy slot on the northern dock. The noises above slowly subsided into silence. Finally, he could escape this horrible box. When the hidden slat of wood above them shifted, he breathed a sigh of relief.

But it caught in his throat when he saw the face that greeted them.

Wyatt Asher.

The Kestrel Crowns' leader was as tall as a winding willow, his long face haunted by deep shadows beneath sharp, copper eyes. Eyes matched almost exactly by the set inside the head of the tawny-feathered bird perched on his shoulder. It cocked its head, snapping its beak as Asher's face split into a reptilian smile.

"Sybaris wants to know if you've brought him anything," he said.

Rafferty leapt to her feet, letting Asher pull her from the dank compartment with one spidery hand. "Sorry, Syb. I only brought one rat with me," she said, looking at Tristan. "He's not for eating."

Very clever.

Asher's eyes flicked to him for the first time. He looked him up and down. "So you have." He tipped his head mockingly. "Honored."

Tristan scowled at him, dropping the Quill unceremoniously into Asher's waiting palm. The Crown's hand bobbed downward under its surprising weight. The bird shrieked and snapped its beak at him.

"There," Tristan said. "You have your prize. Now if you'll hand over my crescents, I'd like to get out of this cursed city."

Asher didn't respond, just stared at the Quill, running a finger along its carven edges and studying the deep reddish ink covering the nib. Rafferty pulled the scroll of parchment from her pocket and handed it over as well.

"Do you know what this is?" Asher asked, unrolling the top few inches of the scroll with shaking fingers.

"No clue," Tristan said. "But you get paid either way, right?"

Asher smiled, examining the scroll. "At least that double-crossing snake managed to teach you the value of a crescent," he said, clearly referring to Clem.

Tristan craned his neck, sneaking a peek as Asher unrolled the scroll another inch. Was that a map of Thamorr? They had gone all that way for a fancy writing stick and an ordinary map? That made no sense.

Then he saw the dots.

Tiny smudges of reddish brown, the same color as the finger-prints on that hidden side panel, moving across the landscape of the map. There was some magic at work here. Some very old magic that showed the location of something. The Adept in Thamorr? Yes, that must be it. Coming from the Guildmaster, what else could it be?

Tristan straightened, looking away as Asher rolled the map back up, tucking it beneath one arm. The Crowns' leader then inspected the Quill again, inky hair shadowing his face. He extended a single finger, pulling it away as it marked him with a tiny crimson dot. "Red ink? I had no idea the Guildmaster had such a flair for drama."

Tristan stared at the vivid red dot on Asher's finger, thinking of the slow way the ink had sloshed inside the Quill. Of the way the marks on the map had faded to brown. No ink he had ever seen faded like that.

"I don't think it's ink," he said, unable to stop himself as his curiosity welled up inside him.

"Oh?" Asher asked, looking amused. "And what, pray tell, do you think it is?"

"Blood."

Rafferty sniffed Asher's finger, then looked up. "He's right. It's blood."

"Blood . . ." Asher's eyes lit curiously as he spun his finger to one side, allowing the red droplet to catch a ray of sunlight filtering through the uneven slats of the ship. "Interesting."

Tristan frowned, staring at the Quill. He thought back to the Adept he had seen growing up in his father's house. Each bore a near-identical scar in the crook of their arms, hidden in the folds of the elbow. The scars were deep and twisted, like the kind he had seen on patients in the infirmary after bloodletting. Was the Quill filled with the blood of Adept servants? But why? The Guildmaster was rich beyond measure—surely he could afford to purchase ink. There had to be a reason for it. Perhaps the blood powered the Quill? Gave it the magic it needed to find the Adept? Too many questions, not enough answers.

Then again, what did he care? With any luck he would never see this Quill or any of the men interested in buying or selling it ever again.

"Fascinating," Tristan said drily, forcing his mind to stop racing. "Now, my cut. I'd like to get my hands on it while I still have enough fingers left to spend it."

Asher looked up, rubbing his own fingers together to dilute the blood. He stared at Tristan a moment, then snapped his fingers. A group of filthy, broad-shouldered men crowded into the lower deck. Tristan's heart pounded a steady path up his trachea as he backed up, nearly falling back into the smuggler's compartment.

"What in the hells is this?" he asked. But he was pretty sure he already knew.

Asher smiled as two of the men grabbed Tristan. A third approached with a clanking set of manacles, a fourth with a canvas sack for his head. Tristan thrashed, yanking one arm free. He plunged a shaking hand into his pocket and pulled out a tattered square of parchment, waving it in Asher's face.

"We had a deal."

Wyatt Asher plucked the letter from his fingers, holding it up to the light for a minute. Then he tore it into four neat pieces, letting them flutter to the deck. Tristan's head was forced down just in time to see the last piece waft to the damp wood. The piece bearing that horrible name. His name. The one he had tried so hard to leave behind.

Dennison Shadowwood.

"Nothing personal, my dear prince. Just business."

Tristan flailed against his captors as the manacles clicked into place around his wrists.

"No need to cause a scene," Asher said, his voice half-muffled by the thick sack as it was thrust over Tristan's head.

Tristan's voice faltered as the men surrounding him began to walk him forward, step by step. "Where are you taking me?"

Another question he knew the answer to already. His stomach sank lower than the bottom of the ocean. He had betrayed his crew and left them for dead for nothing.

Tristan thought he could feel the smile creeping up Asher's face, even though he couldn't see it.

"To see your father, *Your Highness.*"

34

NASH

I t had been years since Nash had spent enough time on dry land for anywhere to really feel like "home." Believing she didn't call anywhere home was easy enough, and it made setting sail much simpler. After all, it was awfully hard to miss something she didn't have. But now, standing in front of the burnt-out shell that used to be the Saints' row house, Nash had to admit she was homesick.

"What in *Yavol's* realm happened here?" Ivan asked, prodding a charred scrap of wood with the toe of his boot.

"Needle Guard?" Nash guessed. She should have expected this; the last time she had been here, the place had been crawling with guards. But still, she felt numb.

"Clem?" Evelyn asked, her voice oddly small.

Nash didn't respond. Last they had heard, Cal had been arrested, and they had been gone over a month. In all likelihood, Callum Clem had been hanged for his crimes by the king of Dresdell. The row house was already a pile of used kindling, and when they had shoved off from the southern dock it had been crawling with Harpies. The rest of the Saints were probably gone.

Then again, "in all likelihood" never seemed to apply to Cal. Nash put even odds on him being dead or alive, at the moment. They would find out soon enough.

"Well. What now?" Ryia asked.

There was a long pause, then: "The Miscreants' Temple would seem to be a natural choice," Ivan said, naming the Saints' infamous gambling hall.

Ryia tapped a finger along the axes lining her belt. "If it's still standing, I'll meet you there."

Evelyn started. "Where in the hells are you going in the meantime?"

"To see if I can catch any sign of our good friend Mr. Beckett." With that, the Butcher scaled the abandoned shop across the street and was gone.

"Nash, Evelyn," Ivan said, turning down the alley that would lead them to the Temple. Nash took one last look at what was left of the Saints' beloved row house, then followed.

DESPITE RYIA'S dark implication, the Temple looked just the way they had left it some five weeks ago. Dingy, rotting, and lopsided, but still standing. Nash hesitated. It looked the same as always from here, but if Cal really was gone, they could fling that door open to find it full to the brim with Kestrel Crowns or worse.

"Oh, for Adalina's sake. Do I have to do everything?" Evelyn marched forward, rapping on the door with one hand, the other hovering over her sword.

They shared several long, silent breaths. Then the door creaked open.

Nash's face broke into a wide smile as Roland, the Saints' slowest card man, answered the door.

"Nash, Ivan! How the hell are ya?" he asked. Unnaturally friendly son of a bitch.

"Confused, Roland," said Nash. "What in Felice's darkest hell is going on?"

Roland scratched his cheek with the three fingers left on his right hand. "Tonight? Nobleman's Luck tourney, I think—"

Nash rolled her eyes. "Not the schedule, you ass." She laughed incredulously. "The row house?"

Roland's smile faltered. "Ah, you've been gone that long, eh? Yeah, we lost the house. Terrible. Clem was in a mood for weeks."

Nash shared a look with Ivan, then with Evelyn.

"Callum is . . . here? In the Lottery?" Ivan asked carefully.

Roland nodded slowly, as though worried Ivan had lost his mind. "Where else would he be?"

So, Cal hadn't just escaped, he had done it so quickly the rest of the Saints didn't even know anything had happened to him. Nash knew they shouldn't have been worried.

Her burgeoning smile fell as her eyes met Ivan's.

"He will not be happy," he said, pushing past Roland and into the bustling interior of the Temple.

"Which is different from usual how, exactly?" Evelyn asked, looking somehow both relieved and horrified.

"You haven't seen the man angry yet." Nash shot her a look. "What you're about to see will probably make the Callum Clem you met last month look like a cuddly little kitten."

"Where is he?" Ivan asked, looking back at Roland.

The rotund man gestured toward the back room of the Temple, the place where the scheme for this whole bullshit adventure had been hatched in the first place. "You sure you wanna go in there?"

"No," Evelyn said.

"Why would we not?" Ivan asked.

"He's been locked in there for weeks," Roland said. "All serious-like."

Nash exchanged a look with Ivan. "Doing what?"

Roland treated Nash to a look like she was crazy too. Cal didn't generally make his business common knowledge. But when the Snake of the Southern Dock locked himself away, it usually meant he was plotting something. And that was rarely a good thing for anyone but him.

Nash took a deep breath and opened the door.

The infamous back room of the Temple looked almost exactly the same as it had the last time Nash had been here, except for the addition of Cal's writing desk in the corner, and . . . Ryia would have a fit. Cal's precious chandelier hung from the ceiling, bathing the hideous, blood-spattered room in the soft, golden glow of candle-light. In the chair beside the desk, manicured fingers running along the edge of a crisp ledger, was Callum Clem. Alive and well.

"So you're still alive, then," he said. He scanned them each in turn. "Some of you, at any rate."

"As are you," said Ivan.

"Of course. Did you expect to find me otherwise?"

"I don't know—last we heard, you were up to your bloody eye-balls in Needle Guard," Evelyn said brusquely.

Cal's lips twitched. "I have been back on these streets since the day you left."

"The day we— How?" Evelyn asked.

"Gold, Captain," said the Snake. "It's a magical thing."

"I see," Evelyn said coldly.

"I doubt that you do." Cal leaned back in his chair, resting the ledger in his lap. "The streets have been buzzing with the news ever since the birds brought it in last week. *Chaos at the auction.*" He ran his pale blue eyes over them, sending a shiver down Nash's spine. "And yet I see no signs of my prize. I am sure this will be a most interesting story."

Evelyn shook her head. "No it won't. You already know every blasted detail somehow, don't you?"

Cal took a sip from a ridiculously tiny tea cup. "Such a strong plan you must have had, to make it so far without me. Where did it go awry, I wonder?"

Nash couldn't tell if he was being sarcastic or not. Evelyn took the bait.

"We were betrayed."

At that moment, the door burst open, and for the first time since the beginning of this conversation—perhaps for the first time since Nash had met him—Callum Clem looked surprised.

"No sign of the little shit," Ryia said, pulling off her hood. Her hair was starting to regrow, sticking out of her head like the needles on Ma's old pincushion. "But I did learn a few things."

"What?" asked Evelyn.

"First of all, the Harpies are gone."

"Gone?" Nash asked. "What do you mean gone?" A whole syndicate couldn't just disappear. "Double-crossed by the Crowns?"

"No," said the Butcher, looking pointedly at Cal.

Nash followed her gaze. "Cal, did you . . . ?"

"Harlow Finn stole my ship," Cal said matter-of-factly.

"Your—" Nash started. She stopped quickly when she saw the look in his eyes. That slight glow of insanity that had been growing steadily stronger for months now. Even with the Saints in their weakened state, he had managed to dismantle an entire rival syndicate in a month. How? Nash's stomach squirmed. She didn't think she wanted to know.

"What else did you learn?" Evelyn asked in the silence that followed. "You said 'a few things.'"

The Butcher grinned. "I saw a Shadowwood ship. Hiding behind some bullshit merchant sails, but I know a royal ship when I see one." She turned to Cal again. "It's got to be in the city. We still have a shot at those crescents."

Cal rose, placed his ledger on the table, and walked to the kettle beside the fire. He poured a fresh mouthful of steaming water into his cup. "Of course it's in the city. My dear friend Wyatt is a proud man, and he has a king on the hook."

"You already knew we had failed, then," Ivan said.

"Knew? No. But I planned for that possibility." Cal cocked his head, stalking back across the room to his waiting chair. "And it's lucky for you that I did." His eyes lingered on Ryia as they combed over the group again.

"Why is that?" she retorted.

"Careful there, Butcher," Cal said softly. He leaned back in his chair again, the picture of easy relaxation . . . if the string of a bow was considered "easy and relaxed" just before it was released. "It's lucky because it means I already have a plan. I always have a plan." His voice grew hard. "Even *think* about leaving me to rot again and you will find out quickly what *plans* I can devise for all of you."

He picked his ledger back up again, holding it close to his face and peering at it through the ringlets of smoke swirling down from the sputtering candles on his chandelier. "You are all dismissed. I will call for you again when I'm ready."

Ryia left first, Evelyn hugging her shadow. As Nash made to follow, she heard Cal's voice again.

"Not you, Ivan. I have a project for you."

Nash froze, one hand on the open door. She felt the weight of Ivan's gaze on her back and turned, raising a brow in silent question. Was *this* the force Ivan had wanted to ally himself with? The person he wanted to end up with Declan Day's relic? The Snake of the Southern Dock, the most infamous criminal in all of Carrowwick, skilled deceiver, murderer, and schemer? He couldn't be serious. Of all the hands to go all in on.

Ivan gave a tiny nod. Damn it all.

Evelyn's and Ryia's footsteps faded into silence. Nash eased the door shut again.

"Can I help you?"

Nash steeled herself, standing tall against the Snake's paralyzing stare. "I know you well enough to know the game has changed again, Cal."

"Has it?" Cal asked, carefully unrolling an ancient-looking scroll.

"Yeah, it has. I know the two of you are cooking up some side scheme. One you're not clueing the others in on." She looked between him and Ivan, gritting her teeth. She wasn't waiting for someone to double-cross her again. Ivan was the only person left in Thamorr whom she trusted, and if sticking by his side meant joining Cal in this new betrayal, then so be it. "Whatever this new game is, I'm in."

35

EVELYN

Even in the middle of the day there was something sinister about the Lottery. A creeping rot so foul that not even seagulls and sunlight could take the edge off. Evelyn scrunched her nose, ducking into her shabby merchant's coat as she waded through the scourge of the city.

A month ago Evelyn wouldn't have dared venture into this part of the city without a whole squad for backup, but something had changed on that stolen ship. Everything seemed lighter now. Maybe it was the missing weight of her father's ring, now at the bottom of the Luminous Sea. Or maybe she was finally just cracking up.

Option B seemed more likely, at this point. After all, she had volunteered for this jaunt into the Kestrel Crowns' territory. Clem's plot just required *someone* to venture into the Catacombs today. Ryia's plot required it to be her.

Evelyn ran a finger over her scarred jawline. No face paint today. No need for it, since none of the Crowns had seen her bare face before. She was glad to be free of the sticky creams and clinging powders, but wearing her real face opened other challenges.

She ducked behind her collar as she passed a company of Needle Guard. They were nearly a full block away, at the end of the next alley. Robert was there with Crane, the latter unmistakable with his lopsided gait. Old friends of hers from her days in the training barracks. Two of the few cohorts who hadn't scoffed at the idea of fighting alongside a woman. Those old friends would arrest her without a second thought, if they discovered what she had become.

Her head spun at the thought. She paused, leaning against a salt-encrusted door. That lightness that had felt so freeing a minute ago just seemed irresponsible now. Stupid.

She reached unconsciously for her left middle finger. *Stupid, stupid, stupid.*

Evelyn stood, breathing like she had forgotten what air tasted like, resting her head on the back of her hand. It wasn't too late. There was still time to turn her coat again, to help Clem collect his prize, then trust that he would help her collect hers.

But that wasn't an option anymore. Now that she knew what that Quill did, she couldn't let it be sold off to the most power-hungry king in Thamorr.

She thrust herself into the western streets of the Lottery. Ivan had tried to give her directions to the Catacombs, but Evelyn had waved him off. The Needle Guard was indifferent to the Crowns, not ignorant of them. She turned left down another alley.

The Butcher might be in it for her own reasons, but she had it right—the Quill of Declan Day had to be destroyed. Because even if Tolliver Shadowwood never got a hand on the thing, it was only a matter of time before someone else discovered what it did and decided to use it for their own selfish gain.

There might not be much glory in saving the world in secret, but it was a good bit better than watching war take the five kingdoms, all the while knowing she could have stopped it.

And if an incredibly fascinating mercenary with a sharp tongue and sharper wit also happened to avoid capture in the process? Well, maybe that was just an extra bit of good fortune.

"Hey, you there."

Evelyn's eyes snapped up as she realized she had reached the Catacombs already. She faced the two men at the door, one tall, one short. Neither had opted for the subtlety of Asher's standard knuckle tattoo, instead going for a much more practical swath of ink across their throats. She bit back a laugh. Imagine going through that many needle pricks just to look like a complete git.

"You simple?" asked the tall man.

Evelyn remembered Ivan's coaching. "You must act as though you are better than them or they will see right through you," he had said. "Pretend they are rodents beneath your boots."

"That shouldn't be too much of a challenge, eh, Cap?" Ryia had stopped in the middle of juggling axes to point excitedly at Evelyn's withering scowl. "Just like that."

This was critical. If she didn't manage to get Ryia added to the list of fighters, their chances of getting that relic back were gone along with Clem's. If she didn't play her part just right and get inside right now, Clem was probably going to have her murdered before she even made it back to the Temple to tell him she'd failed. She shook the nerves from her shoulders, hitching her best look of irritation onto her face.

"Should I take my fighter and my crescents somewhere else, then?" she drawled.

The taller man looked her up and down. "I don't see no fighter." He craned his neck, peering around like he thought she might be hiding her Kinetic in her shadow.

She shot them a look. "Are the pits open now?"

"No."

"There's your answer."

The shorter, bearded man cracked his neck. "You'd think you'd want it with ya. Skinny little thing like you needs protection in a place like this." The wink that followed sent a writhing mass of imaginary earthworms slithering down her back.

"You think I'm going to risk losing my prize Kinetic to some Carrowwick dock scum?" Evelyn said derisively. "I know how to handle these streets. I'm my own protection."

The tall one squinted. "Do you now? I don't remember seein' you around here before."

"Haven't seen you before either," Evelyn said, shrugging. "Now are you going to let me in to make my wager, or should I take my coin to the Undertow?"

The fighting pits in the back of the Harpies' dice hall had nothing on the Catacombs, everyone knew that, but after a moment the Crowns waved her forward.

"Arms out."

She complied lazily, as though bored, and gave two loud coughs. The sound was followed by the slight scrape of leather on wood, coming from the roof above them. The taller man's eyes wandered toward the roofline, and Evelyn stamped a foot, pulling back a pace to draw his eyes back down.

"Get any ideas and I'll show you I don't need my Kinetic to win a fight," she said, glowering as the shorter man patted her down.

"Don't flatter yourself, Freckles."

She glanced back up just in time to see a flash of black fabric melting into an upstairs window. Ryia was inside. "Are we done here?"

"Get down to the pit. Matthieu'll sort you out," said the tall man.

Evelyn squeezed between the two of them, allowing herself a miniature breath of relief as she sank into the dank misery of the Catacombs.

It took several blinks to adjust to the lighting in the Kestrel Crowns' fabled fighting club, so her first impression of the place came from her nose. Over the past month she had grown accustomed to the scent of the sea: the fresh sting of icy water, the tang of salt. The Catacombs smelled just the opposite.

The air was heavy, a vat of molasses hanging over her like a sticky cloak. She caught whiffs of blood and urine, mildew and old ale. She wanted nothing more than to escape back into the sunlight, but she set her jaw as she caught Ryia's shadow creeping along the ceiling beams. They only had one shot at this.

She walked toward the reedy little man lounging alone at a table beside the fighting pit.

"You Matthieu?"

He took a sip of deep red wine, looking her up and down. "Why?"

She pulled her coin purse from her pocket and dropped it on the table. "I'm looking to put down some coin on my Kinetic, that's why."

He prodded the purse with the stem of his glass. "You're a confident one, aren't you?"

"Once you see my fighter you'll understand."

Her eyes flicked to the ceiling where Ryia was perched, just over the pit. The mercenary looked furiously toward Matthieu. Evelyn could almost read her mind: *Stop fucking around and get that asshole away from the pit.*

Patience: not a trait the Butcher had.

Evelyn snatched the purse off the table just as the Crown reached for it.

"Not so fast. I need to know my Kinetic's got a good spot in the fight before you see a single copper." She walked back toward the bar, letting the pouch jingle.

Follow . . . follow . . . come on . . .

There.

Matthieu rolled his eyes, extracting himself from the booth. "A good spot? Tonight?" He scrubbed a hand over his face, snagging a clipboard from the bar. "I've already got top fighters coming from everywhere from Sandport to Volkfier, Sticks," he said. "I can give you a spot in the first round. That's all I've got for you. You win tonight, you can come back later in the week for a better slot."

First round? No deal. Asher wouldn't bring the Quill anywhere near this place until everyone inside was piss-drunk. Best-case scenario, Ryia won the fight and was escorted out to the holding room before the Quill ever made it inside. Worst case? She would have to watch Ryia get her throat ripped out by another Adept. She swallowed. She didn't want Ryia to have to enter that bloodstained pit at all, but the later the better.

Across the room, Ryia crept along the edge of the fighting pit. She yanked on a seat cushion just beside the ring. Matthieu frowned, moving to turn toward the noise. Unsure of what else to do, Evelyn grabbed his pimpled chin.

"Bottom seed?" she seethed. "Horse shit. Who else is bringing this much coin?"

He sighed, flipping the pages on the board back and forth. "I could move you up to the third round?"

Third round. Would that be late enough?

Evelyn saw a flash of silver across the room as Ryia tucked her hatchets and axe belt underneath one of the wide, cushy seats. Only Crowns were allowed to carry steel in the Catacombs. Ivan said everyone would be checked at the door, the same way Evelyn had just been patted down. If they wanted their weapons tonight, the steel would need to already be inside when they arrived. The scrape of metal made Matthieu's head turn again, and Evelyn jingled her coin pouch violently in his face. "Top coin for the top fight. My Kinetic fights your champion tonight." The words were out before she could stop them.

Evelyn winced. But, at least, Matthieu's eyes were now fixed on her. Ryia slid another gigantic cushion loose. Another flash of steel caught the candlelight as she slipped Evelyn's sword under the seat. Then the Butcher was gone, up the wall like an insect and out the second-story window.

"Fine," Matthieu said, leaning close. His breath smelled like rot and sour grapes. "You're so determined to get your Kinetic killed, I won't stop you." He pulled a pencil from his pocket and licked the tip with a swollen tongue. "What's your name?"

"Roisin McGillvery." She dropped the coins onto the board. "And I'm bringing the fastest damned Kinetic in Golden Port."

"Golden Port," Matthieu chuckled, shaking his head. "All right. You and your fighter'll need to be checked in by last toll."

Last toll. Eleven o'clock. The last time the temple bells rang out for the day. She turned, heart beating a steady track up her throat as she pulled herself back out into the day.

She held her head high, kept a smirk frozen on her face, but her mind was racing in circles like a dog tied to a stake. *Breathe.* Just a few hours and this ruddy nightmare would be over. The champion of the pit fought last. There was no way Asher would wait that long to close his deal with Shadowwood. But, if she was wrong, Ryia would have to face the toughest pit fighter in all of Carrowwick.

Felice help them.

36

IVAN

Ivan tucked his hair behind his ears as he tilted the candlestick, watching the droplets of clear wax drip onto the desk in Clem's chamber in the back room of the Temple. He leaned forward, blowing softly on the wax until it started to whiten. Prying it up carefully with one fingernail, he prodded it into shape.

Perfect. He added it to the row of wax blobs already lining the edge of the table. As strange as it was to be back in Carrowwick, he was glad to be off that *verdammte* ship. The waves would have been a nightmare for this project.

He set about making another. Ivan had used wax to make fake scars many times before, but this was a unique challenge. The Butcher's face would be half wax by the time he was done.

As the last wax scar lay drying on the tabletop, Ivan reached for his ink pots. A dab of crimson, two of yellow. A pinch of blue for bruising. The door creaked open. He pushed the hair out of his eyes with his wrists, looking up. Callum Clem.

"Are the disguises complete?"

Ivan lay a particularly gruesome-looking bit of wax on the desk "Nearly."

He was struck by a sudden coldness as Clem leaned over his shoulder. It was almost like leaping into the waters of the *Höllefluss* back in Boreas. A gentle, creeping freeze spread from the tips of his toes to the tips of his ears, nearly unnoticeable until it was already too late. Clem's coldness intensified as the man took a step closer. It was the exact opposite of the warmth he had felt aboard that stolen cog, working a job with that team. And he was about to throw half of them to the *wölfen* all on the bet that Callum Clem would be a trustworthy ally. . . .

He shook himself. Ridiculous. He did not have time for *warmth*. Clem may not be the friendliest man in Thamorr, but Ivan needed him to rescue Kasimir. And if that meant Ryia and Evelyn drew the short straw here, well . . . that was something Ivan would have to live with.

Clem nodded slowly. "Good. Very good." He crossed the room and grabbed a decanter from the end table, pouring a mouthful of rich red wine into a goblet. Clem examined the glass, holding it up to the dancing light of his chandelier before tilting it back and swallowing the wine in a single gulp.

Ivan watched him carefully. Clem did not generally drink alcohol. He was in a good mood. A very good mood. He could see it, glinting in his cobalt eyes. That hidden sparkle that might be considered attractive in another man. In Clem, it stirred dread.

Perhaps that is because what is good for Callum Clem is usually bad for everyone else, said a little voice inside his head.

Foolish. Ivan pushed the voice away. He had chosen his side. Not only that, but he had convinced Nash to come with him. If they could not trust Clem, then there had been no point in coming back to Carrowwick at all. No, if Clem's plan was going well, it meant he was one step closer to the Quill—one step closer to taking control of Thamorr, if what the Butcher said was true.

Once he had learned of the Quill's power, Ivan knew he could not trade it to the Borean king. With Declan Day's creation in their grasp, the Tovolkovs would never be dethroned. Even if he did manage to free Kasimir, his brother would skin him alive for what he had done. Kasimir's resistance was hanging on by a thread as it was, but if the Tovolkovs could find all the future Adept born in Thamorr? There was no chance Kasimir's movement could ever succeed. His brother would rather die in a cell than live in that world. But if Ivan had his way, his brother would still breathe free air again. He could not trade the Quill, but he could guide it into the hands of an ally. One who could help him free Kasimir another way.

The Guildmaster had a reputation for being power hungry, but he had chosen to share the power the Quill gave him. He could have kept all the Adept for himself, but instead he sold them to the people of the kingdoms, allowing the mainland kings and nobles and merchants to go about their business—within reason. And so under the Guildmaster's reign the kings and queens of Thamorr still held some true power.

It had never been Clem's way to have a second-in-command, let alone to allow others to rise as his equals. If Clem had the Quill he would rule Thamorr, and if Clem ruled Thamorr, it was a sure bet that no one else would rule anything inside it. The king of Boreas would fall, certain as the sun fell from the sky each night. Ivan was confident that Clem would have no interest in Kasimir's crimes. Once the Borean king was dethroned, Kasimir could be freed.

He painted in silence for several long moments, pausing only when Clem cleared his throat, feeling the hem of the garment hanging over the back of Ivan's chair.

"Is there a problem?" Ivan asked, setting his brush aside.

Clem rolled the hem between his fingers. The ripples sewn into the sleeves clattered together quietly. "I just hope she will be able to draw the eye. . . ."

"You are wondering if the Butcher will be able to draw attention?" Ivan picked up his brush again. He dabbed a dot of brown coloring onto the last piece of wax, matching the Butcher's skin tone. "Has she ever been able to stop herself in the past?"

Clem's lips hardened into a thin line. "My dear smuggler has taught you how to joke, I see."

Ivan painted in silence for a moment, then paused. "I know the Butcher is strong, but . . . a pit fight? Against a real Kinetic?" The plan was risky at best. Of course, infiltrating the most secure building in the Lottery to steal the prize of a lifetime from Wyatt Asher was risky in itself. More than risky, perhaps. *Seicherende*. Certain death.

"Yes?" Clem asked. "You are concerned. No need to worry."

"There is more to the plan, then?" Ivan asked, feeling more relieved than he cared to admit. "An escape route for the others?"

"No," Clem said quietly. "But you, Nash, and I will be long gone before you ever have to see if she is alive or dead. Does that soothe you?"

Ivan gave one curt nod, though he felt far from soothed.

"Good," said Clem. The Snake tilted his head to one side. "Have you completed the other project I set you?"

Ivan's stomach twisted. He pointed toward the corner of the room with his chin. To the sheet draped over the small tea table set there. Clem stalked across the chamber, the orange glow of the chandelier throwing his shadow long against the wall. It was some of the fastest work Ivan had ever done, requiring every skill in his arsenal. Clem lifted the sheet gingerly, peering at the object that lay beneath.

He turned back toward Ivan wearing his most reptilian smile.

"Any adjustments?" Ivan asked, reaching for the tattered black robe Clem had just been inspecting.

"No, it should do nicely. For a fool like Wyatt Asher, at the very least."

"Good." He stitched in silence for a few moments, adding a patch here, tugging a few threads loose there, adding a slick of reddish brown ink to the hem, blurring it to make it look like blood.

With every motion he worked to silence the guilty voice buzzing in the back of his head, fighting for attention.

The Butcher and captain risked their lives for this job, it said. *How does this make you any better than Tristan?*

But that was ridiculous. The Butcher had nearly gotten all of them killed with her secrets on that island. Who could say what secrets she still kept? Now that the ex-captain was so clearly mooning after her, she was lost as well. Lottery alliances were not made to last. The only tie that mattered any longer was that of blood, and his only surviving blood was trapped beneath the Reclaimed Castle in Oryol, drowning in darkness. Ivan would save his brother if he could, no matter the cost to these Carrowwick gutter rats.

Ivan jumped as the door banged open again. The Butcher of Carrowwick strode in. She looked distinctly naked without hatchets dangling from every inch of her torso. Her face lit in an ambitious smile, but Ivan could tell she felt it. The insistent pull of fear that threatened to take them all this night. Her hands were nervous, tapping along her legs, subconsciously searching for a weapon to grasp.

"All right, Ivan, darling, you have two hours to make me gorgeous," she said, running her fingers over the wax wounds dotting the desktop. She held up the most gruesome with a smirk. "Try not to fall in love with me."

Ivan glanced at Clem, unease still curdling in the pit of his stomach. But it was too late for doubts. The wheels were already in motion.

37

RYIA

"Would you relax?" Ryia muttered, pulling her baggy hood farther over her face as she and Evelyn cut through the alleys, making their way toward the Catacombs.

"Relax?" Evelyn asked, looking around for the thousandth time. "Seems like a bloody stupid thing to do in a place like this. Bound to be a knife up every sleeve."

She wasn't wrong. The Shanty. That was what the locals called it. The only part of the Lottery so shitty none of the syndicates had bothered to claim it. The type of place where you would find your purse cut if you were lucky, your throat cut if you weren't.

"Every sleeve but ours," Ryia corrected.

That was probably a first.

Then again, she did have *something* tucked up her sleeves. She fiddled with the tiny spheres sewn into the hem of her robe. *Trän vun Yavol.* Tears of the underworld. *A coward's weapon,* Evelyn had called them. Maybe, but Ryia would rather be a coward with a head than a hero without one. Honorable types never survived long enough to hear the songs sung about them.

Clem had called them "more expensive than your life is worth," so she would have to tread carefully. For now, at least. By the end of the night she would be dead or leaving Carrowwick for good. Either way, she wouldn't have to care what Clem thought of anything anymore.

"All right," Evelyn said, stopping at the corner of Keel Alley and Flaxen Row. She peered around the boarded-up shop beside them toward the Catacombs. "Just a few minutes until last toll. Let's see what our Borean friend has given us to work with."

Ryia lifted a hand to her hood, pulling it off. Evelyn's face paled, thin lips parting into a comical O as she looked her up and down. Ryia didn't blame her. She had seen Ivan's work back in the Temple. There was no other word for it—she looked gruesome.

When she had posed as an Adept on the island the costume had been relatively simple. A black robe, shaven head, and a fake tattoo. For a true, lawfully acquired Kinetic that had been enough. But if she was going to be believable as a pit-fought Kinetic, things needed to be taken a few steps further.

In addition to shaving her head bald again, Ivan had worked her face into a tangled mess of scars. Several layers of brands marred her left cheek, and deep fingernail scratches cut down the length of her right. Her throat was scored with scratches that looked as though they should have been deep enough to spill every drop of blood in her. But that wasn't the worst of it.

Ivan had forced her left eye shut, gluing it in place with a mangled chunk of wax that made it look like the eyeball had been gouged from her skull. It really was a masterpiece, if a little inconvenient. She had hardly recognized herself in the mirror.

"You look bloody terrible."

"Does that mean I don't usually?" Ryia asked wryly. "I'll take that as a compliment."

"No, I—" A blush crept up Evelyn's long, thin neck. She looked around as the bells began to ring out over the city. "Come on, we need to go. Unless you're interested in having Clem rip out our entrails and eat them."

Ryia fell in step beside her. "He's a man, not a street dog."

"Right. And you're as gentle as a daisy." Evelyn shook out her shoulders, falling into a confident swagger as she stepped onto Flaxen Row.

They stopped at the side entrance to the Catacombs. Evelyn looked up at the heavy, late-summer clouds as she banged on the knotted wooden door. The mournful notes of the day's last toll began to peal out from the temple as the door popped open, revealing a stout woman with stringy yellow hair. Selwyn. A little slow in the head, but brutal as a cave bear when it came to a fight. Ryia should know—she had caught Selwyn spying in the Foxhole last winter. Her gaze stumbled over the gaping hole where the woman's right ear had once been.

That may have been her hatchet's doing.

"What're you here for?"

Evelyn pursed her lips. "What the hell does it look like I'm here for?"

Selwyn cackled, looking Ryia up and down. She resisted the urge to hold her breath. That cranky bitch had lost an ear because of her. That wasn't the kind of thing a person forgot. Shit. Their whole elaborate scheme was going to be brought down by the Crowns' chief guttersnipe.

Selwyn's eyes flicked over her face, gaze lingering on the wax-covered eye.

". . . Ugly fucker."

Relief rumbled through Ryia's chest like a crack of thunder. Ivan's disguise had saved the day—they were inside. Of course, that was less than half the battle. The real challenge would be getting *out*.

Ryia had never been to the Catacombs for a fight before, but she could tell this wasn't an average night. The club was bursting at the seams. There were dozens of sailors and dockhands, seedy merchants and whores, but the place was crammed mostly with Kestrel Crowns. Two of every three people wore the kestrel-skull tattoo somewhere on their body.

"Looks like Clem was right," Evelyn breathed, taking in the Crowns' show of force with obvious discomfort. It would make getting out alive nearly impossible, but it did mean one thing.

The Quill was here.

Every inch of the scheme had been plotted to death, from Ivan's disguises to Nash's spot by the back door, to the *Trän vun Yavol* stuffed into the seams of Ryia's robes. But at its heart, the whole plan had been built on a guess. The guess that Wyatt Asher would be bold enough to insist that the king of Edale come to him.

"If it isn't my most demanding customer," droned a voice as they approached the pit. Matthieu. He lounged on a padded chair, looking bored. Ryia stood still as a painting as he looked her over. "This your fighter? For fuck's sake, it looks like you ran it through a damned mill."

It. Ryia resisted the urge to grind her teeth.

"Take a good look at those scars," Evelyn said, raising her voice so the other owners could hear. "Every fighter to lay a hand on this one is breathing soil now."

"Yeah, yeah," Matthieu said, clearly unimpressed. "Prizefighters to the left box. You take your seat up there." He waved a hand toward the row of cushioned seats just beside the pit.

Evelyn snapped her fingers, pointing toward the enclosure to the left of the pit. Ryia turned, loping inside like a horse into its pen. Her eyes locked on an Adept in the opposite box, his hollow stare pouring into her core.

His neck was pulled back, an axe blade buried in his throat, the blood caught in a small silver cup.

"Drink," her father hissed. "Adept from birth . . . must be in the blood."

She blinked, and the vision faded.

Matthieu bounced into the center of the pit. Either he had just injected a near-lethal dose of *vitalité*, or he was as good an actor as Ivan was. He beamed out at the crowd, a different man from the one who had pointed Evelyn to her cushion.

"Ladies and gentlemen!"

The crowd snickered appreciatively at the titles.

"Our first fight is about to begin. Prepare your bets!" He bowed in a flourish as the room settled into a dull roar.

"First up, all the way from the snowy peaks outside Oryol, the dirtiest fur trader in all of Boreas, Deniskov Illarion!"

Deniskov Illarion stood, his boyish face locked in a grimace as his Kinetic shuffled into the pit. A massive woman, a few inches taller than Nash and twice as broad. Ryia wondered where she'd been born. With that bald head and branded face it was hard to tell. Briel? Maybe Gildemar, with those blue-green eyes. Not that it mattered anymore.

"Yes, yes. Strong-looking brute, isn't it?" Matthieu chortled. "Which means the only fitting opponent would be . . . Mehri *fija di* Vaseli!" he boomed. "From the heart of the Rena desert."

The boy beside Ryia stirred, moving into the pit like a sleep-walker. He was as skinny as a damned alley cat. Ryia's stomach turned. He was about to be pummeled into jelly.

But at the sound of the whistle the boy sprang to life. Or at least, his body did. He bent back like a stalk of wheat in a prairie wind as the other Kinetic swung a fist forward. He dove sideways, barely avoiding her second fist as it hurtled toward him like a crossbow bolt.

Ryia had been a part of her fair share of fights—all right, more than her fair share—but this? This bothered her. There was a difference between choosing to fight and being pushed into a ring with an invisible collar around your neck. Watching the fights on the Guildmaster's island had been difficult enough . . . this was pure savagery.

She allowed her gaze to flit up to Evelyn. Something erupted in Ryia's chest as she studied her, lounging on her padded seat. Her posture was relaxed, her face a careful mask, but her eyes radiated emotion like heat from Clem's damned fireplace.

Disgust. Disgust that morphed into raw sorrow as her eyes locked on Ryia's.

Three more pairs of fighters were unleashed upon one another after the reedy boy finally fell to Deniskov Illarion's massive Kinetic. Three more corpses bled out on the ground, staining the pit's floor with thick crimson. But still, no sign of Ivan's signal. Was something wrong? Where was Shadowwood?

Ryia had no doubt she had the skills to unseat whatever champion this hellhole had given birth to. She stared at her hands, resisting the urge to clench her fists. The real question was whether or not she would be able to bring herself to do it.

Ivan had to give the signal before she was called.

"Next up, from the shit-stained slums of Golden Port, the fighter of Roisin McGillvery!"

Shit.

She forced herself to stand, struggling to keep her left eye shut beneath its wax covering as she walked numbly into the pit.

"Nasty-looking one, eh?" the announcer said gleefully. "I wouldn't bet against it if I were you . . . or would I?" He grinned, throwing his arm out wide.

Ryia's eyes flicked over the crowd again. Where in the hells was the signal?

"Because the opponent might just be twice as nasty!" the announcer hollered. "Belonging to Aedin *fija di* Sarwell of Briel, the reigning champion of this pit for over one month's time! It's a record, it's true!"

Ryia's face went numb as she looked at her challenger. Small, slight. Bronze skin, slender fingers, long, bruised neck. Aside from the hollow, hazel eyes she could be looking in a damned mirror.

Come on, come on, she thought, half listening as the announcer called out the odds. She was dimly aware that they were not in her favor. He gave a sweeping bow, false smile dripping from his cheeks as he exited the pit.

Any time now, Ivan. She took one last anxious look around the crowd. Unless they were wrong. Could Asher have outsmarted Clem for once? All of them had been outwitted by Tristan fucking Beckett—anything was possible.

The announcer lifted the whistle to his lips. The *Trän vun Yavol* seemed to vibrate in her sleeves, screaming, *Screw the signal, just go!* But if Shadowwood wasn't here yet, the Quill wasn't out in the open. If the relic wasn't here yet, the distraction was worthless.

The Catacombs snapped into horrible focus as the whistle shrieked. She could see every scar, every sun wrinkle, every drop of sweat on her opponent's face as she sprinted toward her. Ryia ducked sideways, rolling on the ground as the Kinetic dove forward. Her nails passed a hairsbreadth from Ryia's throat. They were sharpened to jagged points, coated in dark brown blood. Perfect. One touch of those and she would be riddled with disease at best. *Come on, Ivan.*

She snuck a peek at Evelyn. The captain's knuckles were white against her cushion, her eyes wide. Was she *worried* about her? Emotion surged through her at the thought, but she pushed it down as Evelyn shook her head, less than an inch from side to side. The meaning was clear. Still no signal. No sign of the Quill.

Were they wrong?

The thought—and wind—was knocked out of her as the Kinetic charged forward again, slamming her shaved head into Ryia's sternum. Ryia fell back, not even attempting to keep the pain from her face as she landed heavily on her tailbone.

"There is that infamous head-butt!" the announcer shouted. "The regulars in the crowd know what's next, don't you?"

The Kinetic stalked toward her from her left, but the reek of danger seeped into her from the right. Trusting her senses, Ryia rolled left toward her opponent. The Kinetic turned so fast she almost became a blur, then leapt at least ten feet into the air, crashing down in the exact spot Ryia had been a moment ago. Her filthy nails embedded themselves three inches in the hard-packed dirt. That inhumanly strong strike would have flattened her throat like it was made of parchment. Instinct took over, and Ryia leapt across the pit, tackling her.

"There's a move we haven't seen before!" yelled the announcer. Ryia wished he would shut the fuck up.

Hollowness stole through her as she looked down at the Kinetic pinned beneath her. She knew the ungifted saw the Adept as inhuman. Monsters. And she could see why. The Kinetic's face was slack, her too-strong limbs flailing as they struggled to get a grip on her, the scars and brands covering her standing out sharply against sweat-slick skin, but her eyes ruined the illusion. They were as clear as a damned summer's day. Blank. Innocent.

Ryia hesitated. The Kinetic did not.

The Kinetic lunged up, sending Ryia flying several feet into the air. The breath whooshed from her lungs again as she landed flat on her back in the center of the pit. Before she could react, the Kinetic was on top of her. One knee pressed into her windpipe. The other pinned her chest. Ryia rolled from side to side, trying to shake her attacker, but the Kinetic was just as nimble as she was strong. A single second of hesitation had robbed Ryia of any advantage she might have had. Now she was completely at the mercy of this pit fighter. Time slowed to a crawl.

"No!" yelled a familiar voice she couldn't quite place.

Other voices cheered, excited. A glass broke somewhere.

There was the sound of a struggle near the back of the Catacombs. Shouting. The sharp scrape of swords leaving sheaths.

Ryia watched dimly as the Kinetic reared back, her knees still driving into Ryia's chest, pinning her to the floor. Out of the corner of her eye she saw Ivan's yellow pocket square flutter through the air. She wriggled again, thrashing around on the floor, trying to free herself. The signal. Ivan had eyes on the Quill. But it was too late now. She was unarmed. She was trapped. Ryia sagged back, giving up the fight. She was going to die.

She squeezed her eyes shut as the Kinetic's sharpened nails screamed toward her unprotected throat.

38

TRISTAN

The door to Tristan's makeshift prison banged open. He stared at his knuckles as Tana Rafferty swaggered toward him across the back room of the Catacombs.

"Why the long face, princeling?" she cooed as she clinked shackles onto his wrists.

He turned his face to the light. His lip was split in two places, one from the time he'd tried to steal the keys to his cuffs, and the other from when he'd decided it was a good idea to ask Wyatt Asher where his other two fingers were.

Then there was the gash across his cheek. He'd earned that trying to run for it on the docks. Blindfolded, bound, in a part of the city where his captor was king. Not his brightest idea to date. But still, he'd had to try.

He went limp as Rafferty tried to lug him to his feet. "Stop being so difficult—you're going home. You should be happy."

He directed a pulsing glare at her. She knew just as well as he did that the odds were approximately a million to one that his head would still be on his shoulders by the time they reached

Duskhaven. There were gold mines to seize, borders to expand, kings to overthrow, and empires to build.

He will be so much more than just another prince this way. He will be the spark that lights the fires of the new world.

He had overheard his father's words and made a run for the harbor that very night. After all, he was smart enough to put the pieces together. The world had been dividing itself for decades now, the two powers of Thamorr, Edale and Gildemar, inches from tearing each other apart. Boreas never concerned itself with the kingdoms to the south, and Dresdell was too small to be of much use to anyone. The key was Briel: a foot in each kingdom, with Queen Calandra Althea's king-consort hailing from Gildemar, and her youngest daughter sitting in the Edalish throne room.

It wasn't like his father could just march off to war—the Guild-master hadn't allowed something like that to occur in three hundred years. But if Gildemar assassinated the Edalish crown prince? Well, then the rest of Thamorr could hardly fault his father for retaliating.

The reality of royalty was much more sinister than balls and crowns and tournaments. It was a game where every single player was working to stack the deck in his own favor. As long as he had been alive, Tristan had just been another card for his father to play.

"I should have stayed with the Saints," he said.

"The Saints? You really are lucky you have that handsome face of yours, princeling," Rafferty laughed. "Pity there's nothing behind it."

"What?"

Rafferty's cherubic face leered at him in the darkness. "You honestly think Callum Clem didn't know who you are? If he planned on you making it off that island, then I'm the king of Boreas."

The blood drained from Tristan's cheeks. He knew immediately that she was right. Why else would he have been dragged along on that job? Just a little insurance for the Snake of the Southern Dock.

He supposed he should be used to it by now—he wasn't the biggest, strongest, or smartest, but he seemed to make one hell of a bargaining chip.

The inside of the Catacombs passed in a blur of foul smells and filthy faces as Rafferty carted him toward a decrepit table beside the moldy curtain shrouding the back door. The pits were behind him, the bar rail on the far side of the room. Half-hidden in shadows, it was a perfect place to see and remain unseen. She looped his chains around the arm of a chair so stained he wasn't sure what color it might have been to begin with.

"Stay here," she said, smirking.

As though he had a choice.

She tossed her long hair over one shoulder, turning away as the announcer's jolly voice echoed through the chamber, followed by the telltale jingle of coins. Tristan craned his neck to look back over his shoulder, peering toward the fighting pit. His stomach fell into his knees as he caught sight of a familiar figure perched on a cushioned seat across the room.

She was dressed in a garish sailor's outfit, but her hair was unmistakable. Evelyn.

If Evelyn had made it back in one piece . . . His heart hiccupped. Did they all make it back? He remembered Ryia's parting glance—the coldness in her eyes. Well, that settled it: he was going to die tonight. If his father didn't kill him, he could be damn near certain she would.

The fights wore on as he sat in his corner, anxiously scanning the crowd. No sign of Ivan, not that he would look anything like himself. Or Clem. Or Ryia, as far as he could tell. He turned toward the back door again just in time to see Wyatt Asher sweep into the Catacombs. And just behind him . . . Tristan went deaf, slumping in his chair to hide himself from view. It was Tolliver Shadowwood.

It was obvious his father had tried to blend in with the crowd, dressed in a plain, dove-gray coat, but the glint in his eyes gave him away. Well, that and his entourage. He was flanked by four Shadow Wardens and two of his most terrifying Kinetics. Tristan held his breath, ducking his head as his father swept past. The king seated himself opposite Wyatt Asher, distaste for the venue written clearly on his pale face.

"Nasty-looking one, eh? I wouldn't bet against it if I were you . . . ," the announcer shouted across the room. Every pair of eyes was locked on the pit, where the champion's fight was about to begin. The perfect time for the exchange, when every soul inside the Catacombs was looking the other way.

"I trust you did not drag me into this filthy ditch of a town for nothing?"

Tristan's spine crawled as his father's voice wound a serpentine path through the bodies separating them. Wyatt Asher smiled a madman's smile. His bird blinked as he pulled a sack from his shoulder and placed the Quill on the table between them. His father's eyes flooded with white-hot greed and triumph.

It was an expression Tristan had seen only a few times before. His stomach curled. It didn't tend to be followed by peaceful, sensible actions. Tristan knew in an instant that his father had no intention of paying Asher for the Quill. But how could he ever hope to escape this city alive if he stole it? Asher had twenty times the men his father did. His father had his Kinetics, but against all the pit fighters in the room? They wouldn't have a prayer.

And he still didn't know why his father would want this relic in the first place. From the looks of the map he'd seen, it would tell him the location of all the newborn Adept. His father could collect them, train them, keep them for himself, build himself an army. Tristan shivered at the thought of a massive army of those mindless beasts . . . but that would take decades. Tolliver Shadowwood had been called many things in his time, but patient was not one of them. His father wanted control of Thamorr, and he wanted it now. What game was he playing?

"There's a move we haven't seen before!" the announcer boomed.

Tristan peered over his shoulder at the champion's match as the crowd roared. His heart froze into a solid block of ice as his eyes found a familiar figure pinned to the dirt. She was in heavy disguise—or at least he hoped the scars were only a disguise—but he would know that midnight black eye anywhere. Ryia.

"No!" The word was out of his mouth before he could stop it.

He surged forward, tugging against his chains.

"No you don't, you royal prick," Rafferty growled, turning back toward him and aiming a backhanded slap at him.

Tristan ducked, then tugged again. The chains held fast. Swallowing his fear, he bucked backward, kicking his legs up. He slammed his heel into Rafferty's right kneecap, lip curling in disgust as the bone gave way. His practiced fingers flicked into the pocket of her coat as she slumped forward in pain, lifting the key to his manacles.

"Don't mind if I do," he muttered. He worked the key toward the shackles, twisting until the lock popped free. *Go, go, go.* His pulse pounded the word throughout his entire being. If he was going to save Ryia it had to be now.

But how could he save her? It wasn't as though he could just march up to the Kinetic and nicely ask the beast not to kill her. And fighting the Kinetic himself? That was a joke. If Ryia couldn't best an enemy, there was no way he could, even if he could summon the courage to try.

Back at Asher's corner table, his father pried at the edge of the Quill. The same panel Tristan had accidentally discovered aboard the ship back to Carrowwick popped open, revealing the collection of smudged, reddish-brown fingerprints. Seven fingerprints, he recalled. His father pulled a dagger from his pocket, pressing its tip to his thumb.

Tristan frowned, mind racing as he watched the blood well around the blade. In his mind's eye he could see the blank faces of the Adept servants. The near-identical scars on every single Adept in his father's castle. The Quill was filled with blood. Adept blood.

And there were seven fingerprints.

Seven.

Like the seven Guildmasters of Thamorr.

A dozen puzzle pieces thunked into place at once. The Quill didn't just *find* the Adept. It did so much more than that.

In the name of Adalina and Felice and all that was holy. That was why his father wanted it so badly.

Blood roared past his eardrums as he tore across the Catacombs. Fully aware that it was most likely suicide, he charged toward the back table.

The sound of metal on metal was deafening as the Shadow Wardens wrenched their swords from their sheaths. His father paused, thumb an inch away from the plate.

"My son, is that you?" he asked.

A month ago—maybe even a minute ago—the sound of his father's voice would have stopped Tristan in his tracks. But now he didn't hesitate.

Tristan leapt forward. He reached out in midair, snagging his thumb on one of the Shadow Warden's blades. Blood gushed from the cut, dripping over the back of his hand and down his forearm as he landed with a crash on the table.

"I am not your son," he said, staring his father in the eye. "Not anymore."

Then he smashed his bleeding thumb down on the exposed plate on the side of Declan Day's Quill.

For a second, nothing happened. Then his head exploded. Metaphorically speaking only, fortunately. But he imagined the pain had to be about the same as if his skull had truly burst. His vision blurred white, then red, then black as tremors snaked through his body. He could see nothing. Then, suddenly, he could see everything.

A thousand viewpoints flooded through him. He saw the throne room in Gildemar, a merchant's dining room in what looked like a city in Briel, the deck of a ship . . . Ryia's face, bloodied and torn.

The eyes of the Adept servants of Thamorr. They had to be. Tristan let out a scream. It was too much for him to bear. The power rushing through him felt like a river, swollen after a hundred nights of rain, but he needed to hold on, just for one more second. His face contorted with effort as he tried to bring the entire world to a grinding halt. The Adept Senser in Gildemar stopped its throne-room rounds. He grunted, and the one on the ship froze mid-step. He could feel the Quill sapping his energy, but he couldn't let go. Not yet.

A scream erupted from him as he focused on the Kinetic crouched over Ryia in the fighting pit. The Kinetic halted, its filthy nails freezing in midair, a hairsbreadth from the Butcher's throat. Tristan thrust one arm out in front of him, then pulled it back. Amazingly, the Kinetic mirrored his motion, slowly withdrawing its own daggerlike fingers, its fist coming to rest at its side.

This was the power of the Quill—the secret to the Guildmaster's reign. Declan Day had figured out a way to sap the independence and personality of any Adept, erasing their entire being and placing control of their physical form and their magic inside this device. This was why the Adept servants of the mainland were so obedient—it had to be. The magic of this ancient relic had been used to break them.

Over the centuries, the Guildmasters had allowed the lords and kings of the mainland to purchase these mind-wiped Adept. They had found a way to give control to the merchants and nobles who purchased the brainwashed wards . . . by branding them with blood and flame. It all came back to blood, didn't it? But clearly the Quill could override the power of the brand. Whoever possessed the Quill could seize control of any Adept whose blood lurked inside—any Adept in all of Thamorr except for the Guildmaster and his Disciples. Tristan was more sure of that than he had been sure of anything else in his life. It was an insane amount of power— a power that now belonged to him.

Or perhaps not.

The weight of his new power had not even settled on his narrow shoulders before his vision flashed again. Black, then red, then white. When he opened his eyes again, the only view he had was his own. What had happened? Had he lost the Quill's power somehow? He sagged forward, exhausted from the effort as the power and his own energy seeped from him in equal measure. His eyes fell on the Quill, still half-clasped in his bleeding fist. Even as he watched, his own bloody thumbprint faded from sight, leaving only seven staining the panel. The Quill had rejected him as its master.

Head lolling to the side, he let the Quill fall from his grasp. It rolled off the table, landing with a too-deep thud on the floorboards below. He turned his gaze to the pit, and Ryia's uncovered eye found his. Confusion flashed in the starry black depths. Relief flooded through him. She was alive. Though maybe not for long. His throat clenched as the Kinetic she had been fighting rounded on the Butcher once again. Now that Tristan's fingerprint no longer marked the Quill, control of the beast seemed to have returned to its master. It had returned to its original task. He opened his mouth to shout a warning, but already the edges of his vision were blurring, unconsciousness threatening to take over.

Thankfully, Ryia didn't need to be warned. She rolled away from the Kinetic, then thrust both arms down in a single, jarring motion. Tiny black spheres tumbled from her sleeves. *Trän vun Yavol.*

Thin tendrils of smoke the color of a nightmare uncoiled into the air as, one by one, the capsules burst. Shouts of *"Fire!"* rang out in every direction, and everyone in the Catacombs scrambled for the exits. Asher's guards immediately fell into a panic, climbing over the booths, over the table, over one another, desperate to escape. Tristan's vision blurred again, barely registering a Crown with a massive throat tattoo bent double beside the table. Wyatt Asher dove toward the table, but one of the Shadow Wardens drew his sword, pushing him away from the place where the Quill lay, just out of sight, on the floor.

"Get that Quill," Tristan's father snapped at his guards. "I'll get this fool." The voice lowered, sounding directly into his ear. "I trust you remember what patience I have for fools, my son?"

None. Tristan meant to say the word aloud, but it was too late. Consciousness left him. The last thing he felt before sinking into senselessness was his father's iron grasp on his wrist.

39

RYIA

Ryia plunged through the smoke, charging toward the cushioned seats. What in Felice's bitterest hell had happened back there? The Kinetic had been about half a second from punching a hole through her throat when she had just . . . stopped. Blinked. Then pulled her arm back, exactly mimicking the motions of one Tristan fucking Beckett. He'd had the Quill in one hand and had clearly saved her ass with the other. Just when she was ready to cut his throat, he had to go and be the twice-damned hero of the day? Unfair.

Even more unfair was the fact that, somehow, he had puzzled out the secret she had never quite managed to—that Declan Day's relic did more than just *find* the Adept, marking their positions on a map with magical, moving ink spots. She had felt like there was a piece of the puzzle missing all this time, and Tristan had just shown her the answer. Tolliver Shadowwood had never meant to grow his army from newborn Adept . . . he had meant to build it by taking full-grown Adept from their masters.

Somehow Declan Day had figured out how to sap the humanity from his own fucking people, placing control inside that oversized writing stick. It must have been part of the training on that island—some sort of cleansing or something—that wiped those poor island-raised Adept blank before their mainland masters sauntered over to the auction block to buy them. The thought made her sick. If there had been any doubt before, there was none now. That Quill needed to be destroyed. The sooner the better.

Evelyn's seat had been ripped apart, her sword missing from beneath the cushion. No doubt she was already in the thick of it, shouting about everyone's lack of honor and clashing steel with anyone who came too close. Ryia suppressed a smile at the image and ripped the cushion from the other wide, overstuffed seat, sending sheep's-wool padding flying everywhere.

Her weapons still lay inside, just where she had tucked them earlier. She peered around the room as she cinched the belt on tight. No sign of Clem. Good. She needed to get to that back booth before he did.

She skirted the edge of the chaos, fingers caressing the handles of her hatchets on her back.

"Sorry about that, loves," she muttered to them as she ducked out of the way of a drunken man screaming about a *medev* attack. "I won't be leaving you again, I promise."

The smoke from the *Trän vun Yavol* filled her nostrils. Felice, it was thick in the center of the pit. If she could just push her way out to the edge of the room, it would be thinner . . . then she wouldn't have to stumble around like a newborn kitten. She felt her way forward, pausing at the sound of a menacing voice.

"I trust you remember what patience I have for fools, my son?"

Ryia pushed forward another step. The smoke was already starting to thin. Her eyes screwed up in confusion as she caught sight of the speaker. Tolliver Shadowwood . . . talking to Tristan Beckett.

Son?

No fucking way.

Without thinking, she pulled a hatchet from her back, moving toward them. Tristan was unconscious now, limp in the Mad King's grasp.

"Hands off," she said to Shadowwood, summoning every ounce of the energy that made the Butcher of Carrowwick so infamous. "He belongs to the Saints of the Wharf. You're going to want to stay out of this."

"Ryia, no! The Quill!"

The voice was Evelyn's. She was fighting her way through a knot of Crowns some ten feet away, her slender sword whirling through the thinning smoke. She pointed at the corner booth, just a few steps from where Ryia was standing. One of Shadowwood's guards held Wyatt Asher at sword point. Three more Shadow Wardens closed in on the Quill.

Her breath caught. There it was. So close. And Shadowwood's men were going to steal it away.

She shook her head, looking back at Tristan, but he and the king were already gone. Shadowwood might have wanted the Quill, but he was clearly too chickenshit to fight for it himself.

Forget Tristan. The Quill was all that mattered.

Throwing axe in hand, she turned back to the knot of Edalish soldiers crowding the Quill. "Hate to break up the party here," she said, flinging the axe at no one in particular.

The closest Shadow Warden turned on the spot, lifting his sword in the span of a hummingbird's wingbeat. He would have been fast enough if anyone else had thrown that axe, but Ryia had an unfair advantage. She pushed out with her Kinetic power, flinging the blade wide and bringing it back to impale the poor warden right in the groin. A cheap shot, but effective. He went down hard. She reeled the axe back in with her power, returning it to her belt. That left two Shadow Wardens between her and the Quill.

She pulled out both long-handled hatchets, swinging them around her wrists to dispel the last few tendrils of smoke. "Who's first?" she asked.

The warden on the left looked over her shoulder. "Them," he said with a smirk.

A whiff of danger suddenly pressed against her nostrils, but it was too late. Two Kinetics with Shadowwood brands on their cheeks sprang from the churning crowd. She flung her right arm out, catching the first in the forehead with the butt of her hatchet, but the second was too strong. He didn't even use his body to restrain her, just his power, tying her in place with intangible ropes, like the Guildmaster had.

He was old. Old enough that he should have smile lines around his eyes, but, of course, there were none. This man hadn't smiled since he was a child. When she looked at his face, she saw nothing but cold, unfeeling strength. Not a person. Just a weapon.

Fuck that.

This wasn't just about her and her freedom anymore, was it? This was about the freedom of everyone unfortunate enough to be born with a touch of magic. She had always had pity for the mainland Adept, but now she was what, their freedom fighter? Damn Evelyn for poisoning her brain with these stupid noble thoughts.

She thrashed against her invisible chains, letting her hatchets fall to the floor. "Don't you see what I'm trying to do here?" she yelled at him, fully aware that it was pointless.

The Kinetic didn't budge, just stared at her blankly. Over his shoulder, Ryia saw one Shadow Warden scoop the Quill from the floor, then snag the rolled-up map from the tabletop. It would take only seconds for him to follow his king out the back door, and the Quill would be gone, lost in the night.

Hopelessness was just starting to sink its teeth into her. Then a freckled hand darted into view, stabbing a slender sword point into the Kinetic's sandaled foot.

His aged face didn't show the pain, but he obviously felt it somewhere deep inside that brainwashed shell, because his concentration broke. That instant was all Ryia needed. She jerked sideways, diving out of his line of sight.

"Get that ruddy Quill so we can end this already!" Evelyn shouted. Ryia hesitated. Evelyn gave a shadow of a smile. "I'm right behind you."

Ryia grabbed her axes, somersaulting into the Shadow Wardens' midst. The one she had taken out with the groin shot was still down, but Wyatt Asher appeared to have fled the scene, leaving her facing three of the bastards again. Callum Clem was suspiciously nowhere to be found.

"Hello again," she said slyly. "You're going to want to give me that Quill. Unless you're interested in meeting Adalina face-to-face tonight."

The Shadow Warden holding the Quill drew himself to his full height. "Keep your threats, street rat. This belongs to King Tolliver Shadowwood."

Ryia shrugged. "Just remember, I tried to be reasonable."

She transformed into a whirling blur of steel as the other two Shadow Wardens charged. She thrust her hatchets overhead. The bits blocked both swords easily, knocking them aside as though they were feathers. She grabbed the shoulders of the closest warden, pulling him in front of her. His eyes grew wide as his comrade's sword glanced off the chest plate of his armor, nearly impaling him.

Ryia vaulted over the warden's shoulders, catching a glimpse of the last Shadow Warden—the one who had taken the Quill and map—through the still-frantic crowd. She latched on to the rafters, swinging back and forth like a Gildesh acrobat. She released her grip, barreling into the man's back.

He had at least fifty pounds on her, but she had surprise on her side. He crashed to the ground. His fingers lost their grip as she slammed his wrists against the floorboards. They struggled, kicking and scratching like animals. The warden's arms flailed, scoring a line of the Quill's dark red ink down the side of Ryia's arm. Ryia jammed an elbow into his face. He fell back as his nose shattered. Ryia tucked one hatchet away, clenching the Quill protectively, her pulse beating throughout her entire body.

"Give your boss my regards," she said, reaching down to grab the map as well. "And let him know I'm coming for him."

"Time to go, Butcher." Evelyn streaked past her, the Kinetic not far behind. The captain hopped onto the table and clumsily scaled the wall, pulling herself up into the rafters. "I see a way out—do you trust me?"

Do you trust me? She didn't trust anyone—had she not made that clear? But Ryia's certainty weakened as her eyes jumped to Evelyn's left hand. To the bare middle finger where her father's ring had once sat.

Ryia wrapped the map tightly around the Quill, then clamped the whole bundle between her teeth. She cast one last glance at the Shadow Wardens and Kinetics. Still no sign of Clem, but there was no way that luck would hold for much longer. She sprang from the floor to the rafters in a single bound. The chaos of the crowd covered their tracks as she followed Evelyn out the second-story window and onto the rooftop beyond.

Adrenaline carried them over crumbling shingles and moldering gables. They finally skidded to a stop on top of the wall along the southern dock, the Saints' territory to their left, the rushing current of the Arden to their right. Ryia pulled the Quill from between her teeth, slid it free of the rolled map, and set it down on the wall between them. It was still, lying on its side rather than hovering over the map the way it had back in the bell tower.

Evelyn pulled a matchbook from her cloak pocket and held it out to Ryia.

Ryia looked from the tightly rolled map to the matches, then back again. "You sure you're in? Once this thing is gone, there's no turning back. Declan Day built it for a reason." Anarchy and chaos, that was what they would sow. Was that really something the captain was ready for?

Evelyn's freckles almost seemed to dance in the moonlight as she set her jaw in her familiar, stubborn way. "A shite reason. Let the bastard's legacy burn."

Ryia stared at her for a second, then let out a snort of amazed laughter.

"What?"

"Nothing," Ryia said, eyes flashing mischievously at her as she struck the match. "I just think I'm finally starting to rub off on you."

"About damned time."

"Care to do the honors?" Ryia held the burning match out.

Evelyn took a deep breath, then thrust the ancient parchment into the match's tiny flame. Ryia's heart stuttered as the flames licked over it, slowly chewing through every last one of the secrets the map had held. They sat in silence as its ashes floated away on the wind, listening to the sounds of chaos still raging from the direction of the Catacombs.

Next came the Quill itself. Ryia hefted her right-hand hatchet. She blinked back tears of relief as she brought it down, swinging it with every last ounce of strength inside her. Two swift chops was all it took. Red ink spilled from the Quill like blood from a beast. And just like that, Declan Day's foul relic was defeated. Ryia kicked the remaining splinters into the Arden, watching the churning waters claim them, sucking them down to the depths. Lost forever.

It was over.

"Now what?" Evelyn asked after an impossibly long silence.

Now what. Their alliance was over, wasn't it? Ryia swallowed the emotion leaping up her throat. "What do you mean?" she said gruffly. "Now nothing. It's done."

Another long silence. Then: "You know I'm still coming with you, right?"

Ryia kept her face immobile as something crackled in the pit of her belly. Was this what hope felt like? She stifled the emotion with a chuckle. "You might not be so sure about that once I tell you where I'm going."

"Where . . ." Evelyn broke off, studying her with what looked like satisfaction. Or maybe pride. "You're going after him, aren't you? Tristan. Dennison. Whatever we're supposed to call him now."

"Yep," Ryia said, looking out over the coastline to avoid Evelyn's eye. A few months ago, she would never have considered anything like the rescue mission she was currently planning, but the captain had rubbed off on her, too. Slowly, Evelyn was chipping away at the thick protective layers she had coated herself with for years, clearing the way for feelings like trust, guilt, and forgiveness. It was inconvenient to say the least. But she had to admit, she didn't hate it. "What can I say? The little bastard grew on me. And I'm pretty sure he saved my life back there." She paused. Then: "They're heading for the Shadow Keep."

The fortress of Edale had never been breached. Not by thieves, assassins, armies. Probably not even by a damned cockroach. It was impregnable. Evelyn had risked a lot to help her destroy the Quill, but that had been to save the twice-damned world. Ryia doubted the captain would risk her life—not to mention her honor—again just to help her save one man.

"In that case, I'm definitely coming."

Ryia's head snapped back around. "What?"

"If you're going to break into the Shadow Keep, you're going to need help. Anyone with half a brain can see that."

The fledgling hope in Ryia's gut exploded with the fiery sparks of some other emotion. She tried to put her finger on it. Joy?

"Half a brain?" she asked, cocking her head playfully. "Don't you think you're being a bit generous to yourself there, Captain?"

Evelyn's face split into a slow grin. "Fuck off."

The scents of danger washed away with the rhythmic breaths of the Yawning Sea as they turned and sprinted along the narrow rooflines. Together they disappeared into the velvet night, a pair of shadows on the wind.

EPILOGUE

CALLUM CLEM

The shadows sucked the world into their gaping maw as the sky outside the hatch faded from orange to purple to black. Callum Clem rose from his pitted wooden chair, loping across the hold of Nash's newest ship as waves churned beneath his feet. Boots stomped across the deck overhead. Not many; there were only four bodies on board other than Clem himself. Ivan and Nash, of course, and Clem's two Adept servants, hard-won in his negotiations with Hackle Holdings just over a month before. Clem grabbed a ragged scrap of cloth from the table, dipping it into a waiting bucket of water.

Watching himself in the mirror, he ran the scratchy fabric over his neck. Rivulets of black ink ran down his bare chest as the tattoo Ivan had drawn there washed away. The kestrel's left eye went first, then its right. He had cut away the real tattoo from his knuckle when he had left Asher's floundering syndicate all those years ago, but he still recalled the exact lines. Something Asher was clearly too careless to consider.

He drew a match across the tabletop, lighting the candle beside him. It was nearly expired, a dripping puddle of wax surrounding a wisp of guttering flame. Nowhere near as magnificent as his chandelier back on the southern dock. He wouldn't be going back there. Not now, for certain. Perhaps not ever. But there would be other chandeliers.

He looked out the hatch again, watching the rounded spires of the Bobbin Fort fade into the distance. There was no more Callum Clem. No more Snake of the Southern Dock. He had instructed Nash to leave a surrogate corpse in the Catacombs. Some old drunk they'd found in the gutter, one about his own size and weight. Once the face had been disfigured beyond recognition and the body marked with his trademark scars and tattoos it had been convincing enough. By morning everyone in the city would think him dead. Good. If there was one thing he knew for certain, it was that dead men were far freer than live ones.

No one would be surprised to hear of his demise, and he couldn't imagine Wyatt Asher would deny that the Kestrel Crowns had killed him. After all, it had been his dearest wish for near two decades now.

After a time, Asher might even start to believe the rumors himself. He knew the Saints had infiltrated the Catacombs. How could any of them have made it out with the Crowns watching every door? But there were things about the city that Wyatt Asher did not know. An unforgivable weakness for the man who would claim to be her true king.

He knew that Carrowwick was built into a valley, or at least Clem assumed he knew that much, but he had probably never stopped to consider how foolish that had been. A city built on the coastline at the lowest spot in the hillside, in a place where it rained nearly half the year. Asher hadn't bothered to learn how, in the years before the Seven Decades' War, drains had been built beneath the city, to keep the rains from washing Dresdell's capital into the Yawning Sea.

If Asher had known that, he would never have placed his flagship tavern in one of the new buildings. Many of the new buildings in the city were built directly over those old drains, which created a network of tunnels. Of course, it was good for Clem that Asher had known none of these things, otherwise his path to the sea wouldn't have been so clear. Just a few pried-up floorboards behind the Catacomb's bar rail and half a mile of sloshing through ancient filth. Then, freedom.

A faint smile pulled at his lips as a scratching sound whispered across the cargo port. A common man might mistake it for a mouse skittering over the planks, but a scribe would recognize it immediately: the delicate scrape of a quill on parchment.

Blistering flames sparked in his blue eyes as he examined the object on the half-rotted desk. He watched hungrily as it whirred to life, springing upward and hovering over the parchment, spinning and twirling like a tiny Gildesh dancer. The Quill dipped down, leaving a tiny, precise dot on the magical map beneath it.

The delicate whorls of stone and hardened wood shuddered to a stop and the Quill tipped sideways, falling dormant. He did nothing to stop his anxious hands from shaking as they fell on the diagrams laid beside it on the table. The ones the Butcher had been absentminded enough to leave him with when those fools had fled for the auction.

One look at the drawings and he had known he would never sell the thing to that beast Shadowwood or anyone else. It was better the original job had failed. He smirked as he recalled the copy Ivan had created. His forger had filled the thing with ink rather than blood—a mistake anyone could make, and one he had not bothered to correct. After all, there were only a handful of souls in this world who knew of the Quill's existence, and of those, even fewer knew it was powered by Adept blood. By the time any of them discovered that what they held was no more useful than a paperweight, he would be long gone from this place.

With his plans laid, all that had been left was to sneak it into the Catacombs, wait for his old friend to arrive, then make the switch when the Butcher threw the *Trän vun Yavol*, distracting all the other simple fools seated around that corner table. A painted-on tattoo and a smidgen of patience were all it had taken. Easy. Too easy.

He had known he would need Ivan's help, and had trusted he would have Nash's as well once Ivan was on board. His lips curved upward as he thought of his faithful smuggler. No doubt she thought herself subtle. Thought the secret glances she stole at Ivan went unnoticed.

But there was nothing that escaped his notice. Poor, lovesick Nash would follow Ivan to the ends of this earth and back. He just had to be sure Ivan stayed by his side, and there would be no trouble. And Ivan would—he was the only hope the fool had left. All he had to do was say one name, and Ivan would fall to his knees. The name he had thought hidden, tucked beneath the floorboards of the row house.

Kasimir.

The Quill sprang to life again, whirring and shaking, racing across the parchment to place a new dot on the outskirts of Safrona. Another Adept. A Kinetic or a Senser? He didn't know. But it didn't matter; now he and only he could find them all.

Of course, that was only the barest sprout of his new power. The roots of it were far vaster, lurking out of sight, beneath the surface.

His hand drifted to the side of the Quill. To the tiny slit carved there, no wider than his immaculate fingernail. He popped the side compartment open, revealing the blood-coated panel. There it was, the secret the Guildmasters of Thamorr had kept for centuries. It had been exposed for everyone in the Catacombs to see just a few hours ago, not that anyone had been paying attention.

The Quill had rejected Dennison Shadowwood's thumbprint almost the moment he placed it there. Even now, Clem counted only seven faded prints on the panel. Yes, poor Dennison was too weak to master this device, and the Quill clearly knew it. But Callum Clem was not weak. He breathed in the ocean as the ship cut south through the Yawning Sea. He was strong enough to wield the Quill as it had not been done since the time of Declan Day himself. He could feel it in his bones.

Yes, yes. There was a new ruler of Thamorr. A new master of kings and men. The kingdoms just didn't know it yet.

He leaned over the Quill, stroking it lovingly with one slender finger. No, they didn't know it yet. But they would. And soon.

ACKNOWLEDGMENTS

Among Thieves's journey from fledgling idea to fully realized, published novel has been a long one, filled with doubts and struggles at every turn. In short, it's a journey I never would have been able to make alone.

First of all, I would like to thank the RF Literary team, specifically Abby Schulman, also known as the World's Best Agent. Thank you, Abby, for your insightful notes, your publishing world savvy, and for always listening to my anxious ramblings. Without your help, this book would truly never have made it into the world, and I cannot thank you enough for being at my side for every step of my publishing journey.

To Ed Schlesinger and Madison Penico, for your edits and guidance through the publication process, and for understanding the vision I had for *Thieves* from the beginning, and helping me make that vision shine through all the clearer.

To Lauren Jackson, for kicking off the publicity and marketing plan for this book, and giving *Among Thieves* a great platform from which to pick up steam. Also, to the rest of the Saga Press team, including Joe Monti and Jennifer Long. Thank you so much for your guidance, notes, and unwavering support on my debut journey!

Next, I'd like to thank Rachel Brenner for stepping in as interim publicist. Thank you so much for your hard work and for always keeping me in the loop and answering my millions of questions. I would also like to thank Kayleigh Webb for jumping in and seeing our publicity for *Among Thieves* through to its release! Thank you, Kayleigh, for your open lines of communication and for all of your efforts to create buzz and excitement for this book!

I also want to thank Brian Luster, Alexandre Su, and the rest of the production team for going through this manuscript with the finest-toothed of combs, and for preventing me from sounding like a total fool when I try to talk about sailing.

To my supremely talented cover artist, Christian McGrath, for creating cover art that captures the energy of *Thieves* better than I could ever have hoped or imagined.

A special thanks as well to Navah Wolfe, for seeing the potential in *Among Thieves* and kicking off the process to acquire the project at Saga to begin with. May our paths cross again someday soon.

To my parents, I want to thank you for supporting me in all my creative endeavors from childhood on. From driving me to (and paying for) creative writing camps and developing fun writing exercises to do during summers off from school, to taking me seriously when I first vocalized my desire to pursue writing as a career. Your support from literally day one has been invaluable.

To Haley and Mike, my eternal early-stage beta readers and hype squad. You were the only people I ever asked to read my first serious attempt at writing, and you slogged through the terrible early projects all the way to the present. Without your kind but honest notes I would never have learned how to receive feedback gracefully, which is a vital skill for any writer.

ACKNOWLEDGMENTS

To my husband, Ryan, for being my sounding board and alpha reader. Thank you for always believing in me. You have always been a shoulder to cry on when the rejections pile up, and a drinking buddy to celebrate with when I get a win. There are no words strong enough to articulate how much I appreciate you taking my dreams seriously from the beginning, when there was no concrete reason to believe I would ever succeed.

To my niece Kaylin, future reader and current cutest toddler on the planet.

To all the members of my wonderfully massive extended family who have taken an interest in my writing over the years, and to my childhood best friend Lee, who was the last person to read this story before the folks at Saga Press did.

To my writing buddies, Hannah, Genevieve, Mica, and the entire 2021 debut group. Thanks for helping this long and lonely process feel a lot less lonely.

To Brian Jacques and Diana Wynne Jones, for sparking my enduring love of fantasy.

And, last but not least, I would like to thank my cat, Thorin Oakenshield, for napping at my side as I worked, night or day, and for always protecting me from the evil printer.